PURELY
ACADEMIC

◄ a novel by ►

STRINGFELLOW BARR

SIMON AND SCHUSTER
NEW YORK • 1958

To the memory of
JACK GOODMAN
who possessed both the
warmth and the irony that teaching requires

Tu le connais, lecteur, ce monstre délicat,
Hypocrite lecteur,—mon semblable,—mon frère!

—Baudelaire, *"Au Lecteur"*

∽(I)∾

EVERYBODY walked with a springier step, but the social scientists fairly danced. It was not only the crisp October day. They had promised to meet the President at the Triangle Club at four sharp; the departmental heads were there by three. They met casually, but they were carefully dressed.

"If the Winthrop Foundation really wants to do something," said Schneider, "the surface is barely scratched. Our department is strong in political and economic history; however, the library could spend five or ten thousand on diplomatic history and still be behind."

"Diplomatic history of what?" inquired Nast. There was skepticism in his voice.

"Origins of the First World War," said Schneider. He laughed, almost apologetically. "That's about what the term *diplomatic history* has come to mean with us historians. It's been one of the most remarkable developments in my professional lifetime. And the foundations like it. It requires good linguists, of course. Fortunately, the department is rather strong there."

"Unless I miss my guess," said Nast—and it was obvious he was not guessing—"the Winthrop people would a good deal rather see their money go to finding out how we achieved People's Capitalism than how we got into the First World War."

"That's an economist's guess, Nast," said Weed. "As a political scientist of sorts, I think Schneider's correct in wanting to develop diplomatic history. Though I think there would be even more point in studying the spread of totalitarian government between the wars. It's almost a virgin field in this country. And it would tie in beautifully with graduate work in my own shop."

Kendall, the psychologist, smiled knowingly.

"I think Weed's got something," he said. "And it may not be wholly irrelevant to our meeting, gentlemen, that the larger foundations in this country think totalitarianism—that's a polite term for communism, of course—is the real problem. I rather think that if this chap Denby gathered from today's conference that the departmental heads in the social-science division were really concerned with the problem of totalitarianism—well, manna would fall, that's all. And it would fall without any personal commitments, too. It's a broad enough subject to allow each of us to follow his own research interest. But we've got to talk his language, or he'll help a faculty that can."

There was a general nod of assent from all but Nast. Nast stated that, unless he missed his guess, back of contemporary history lay totalitarianism, but back of totalitarianism lay the failure of most countries to achieve People's Capitalism. People's Capitalism was one of the few deep realities of modern times. And Denby would know it. You couldn't run the Winthrop Foundation without knowing it.

"I wouldn't perhaps realize it myself," he added, "if it weren't for my wretched extracurricular activities. You chaps are forgetting that I run a weekly newspaper column, do a monthly telecast, and lecture around a good bit to boot. You chaps live in the ivory tower of pure intellect. Schneider doesn't care what happens, provided it yields historical documents for his research work. Weed thinks governments are things to write books about. Kendall believes group psychology is the proper study of mankind. Well, I'm just a humble economist with an income tax to meet. To meet it, I took to off-campus activities. And I think I know what John Doe wants to know about. And what he wants to know, the foundations want to know. So I still vote for People's Capitalism as the project that will nail Denby."

At that moment Schneider loathed Nast more than usual. Schneider would have been delighted to go on television: nobody had asked him to. He would have reveled in a weekly column, but he had been told that his historical research was too scholarly to interest the readers that lapped up Nast. Failing everything else, he would have been satisfied to enjoy Nast's reputation as a lecturer to undergraduates—and the salary it had brought him. What if Nast's lectures were considered "popular"? What if his off-color stories in class had caused his students to call him "Nasty Nast"? They did it admiringly. As for Nast's income tax, Schneider was sick of having it flung in his face. He turned to Nast.

"Well," he said pleasantly, "why don't you frankly tell Denby that your interest is People's Capitalism, and the rest of us will steer the talk toward totalitarianism? That is, if the President agrees."

For at this moment President Pomton entered, and everyone rose.

President Pomton was a remarkable man. He was perhaps less remarkable than his wife supposed, but he was remarkable just the same. Education was only one of his many concerns, and he gave the impression not so much of ornamenting the University as of ornamenting himself with the University. He was the sort of man who would be essentially too big for any job. Neither did he ornament scholarship: scholarship ornamented him. He had published a little, in the days when he was still a professor of education; but the dubious status which schools of education enjoy in educational circles early turned his interests toward administration, and his most valuable books had been statistical studies of the academic credit system. Every college registrar in the country knew his work and admired him.

But Pomton was not primarily a writer; he was a speaker. He was widely known as being willing to speak, not merely on education, but on any subject. He could make any subject important, for the simple reason that he was important himself. He was a great favorite with women's clubs, and even the Rotary clubs and other men's organizations were glad to fall back on him. In fact, "Get Pomton" came to be their favorite solution to a difficult or boring program mess. Years of platform success had given him a smile and a manner, a personal charm not based on anything in particular except long practice.

His reputation as an orator rested, more than he realized, on the discreet assistance of his personable young secretary, Miss Thelma Stilton, who had a kind of genius for ghosting extempore speeches. These Pomton could memorize in three readings; his mind was a *tabula rasa* in many important respects; this was one of them. That same capacity for seizing his highest thoughts even before he himself had formulated them enabled Miss Stilton to create in the President's office an atmosphere in which Pomton's self-esteem, so essential a trait in a popular orator, could flourish.

Meanwhile, Miss Stilton deftly and silently saw that his paper work was done almost while he talked. And she made his environment subtly stimulating, as only a woman could. Young—she admitted to twenty-nine—slender, reasonably shapely, with dark hair and eyes, and a good olive complexion, she struck her employer as most agreeable to look at. It is true that the faculty found her cold, toplofty, sallow, and physically angular; but what faculty has ever judged its president's personal secretary with a charitable eye? Miss Stilton was aware of a good deal of criticism of herself but merely considered the source and went on writing speeches, tactfully steering Pomton through his administrative chores and subtly bolstering his self-confidence. Not many secretaries can have achieved more.

The only man on the campus with whom Pomton felt really at ease was his young treasurer, Bill Sanders. Bill was concise, energetic, and efficient, with an unbridled love of memoranda and of I.B.M. machines. To Pomton he brought the loyalty, admiration, and devo-

tion which executives dream of obtaining from their staffs. For Bill
Sanders, Pomton was The Boss, the personification of the University,
rightful monarch of all he surveyed; Bill came from the business
world and was a convinced monarchist. As the king's man, he felt
lonely in this Republic of Learning, where The Boss was regarded
by his faculty as a necessary evil, the only means of obtaining funds
for salaries. Conscious as Bill was of the scorn the true scholar feels
for the administrative officials of the academy, he secretly returned
their scorn fourfold: he looked on professors as a special class of
kept women, eager for their monthly allowances but unwilling to
contemplate the sordid operations of the butter-and-eggs man who
supports them. Bill Sanders faced facts about which the faculty still
remained at least publicly coy: that the students were customers, that
the University must therefore give them whatever courses they demanded, that education was the only business in the country in
which the customer regularly got what he ordered at less than cost,
that you could not cure this hideous defect by raising fees without
losing all your customers to tax-supported institutions. Although a
college graduate of sorts himself, Bill had never discovered what the
faculty was actually doing other than competing fiercely with each
other, clamoring for more pay, boring or insulting the customers,
and snubbing the nonteaching personnel.

He was a fine type of young American, tall, well built, good looking in a vulgar way, healthy, alert, with a deep respect for money.
He loved the American way of life and would as soon have betrayed
his country as vote Democratic. The studiedly sloppy dress of the
faculty had led him to choose his own clothes with great care: he
wore pin-stripe suits, expensive and emphatic ties, and looked as if
he had just stepped out of a bandbox. Only at meetings of local
service clubs like Rotary and Kiwanis did he affect the academic
manner. On campus, he defiantly represented the great world of affairs, the world which grudgingly supported these segregated eggheads, covering with ivy in lieu of fig leaves their ghetto buildings,
their insolence to The Boss, and their shameless waste of market-
able man hours.

The business office housed the one operation on the campus in which Pomton felt genuine confidence. As a matter of fact, it was the only operation that was in any real sense audited. There were many days when Pomton wondered secretly whether the University had any real function in this world from which he was compelled to wring money to support it. On those days it was only the sanity and the feudal loyalty of Bill Sanders that gave him the strength to make another trip and to solicit another gift, with or without strings.

Whenever Pomton returned from a speaking tour to the University, which appeared to the faculty to occur rarely, it was a sign that some financial problem was in process of solution. Despite his scholarly achievements in terms of publication as well as teaching (he had done college teaching for four years before his unusual political talents turned him toward administration), his real forte was finance, and he knew it. Because he avoided the appearance of personal vanity, and because it was both impossible and unwise to ignore or deprecate his own talent for finance, he tried to put his faculty at their ease by laughing at himself as a scholar. "After fifteen years of administering a growing university," he used to say laughingly, "I am less fitted to teach than to head U.S. Steel." One of his critics had observed behind his back that the University, unlike U.S. Steel, did not have to show profits. But, as the remark never reached the President's ears, he had not had to rebut it, and he continued to think of himself as primarily a successful financier who, out of devotion to the higher values of human life, had turned from big business to academic affairs.

He had not gone unrewarded for this sacrifice. His salary was a good one and he had invested it prudently. He had avoided the stock market because he did not want his attention diverted from his official responsibilities. But, observing that the University was growing rapidly—indeed, he recognized the president's obligation to make it grow—he had bought up a good deal of real estate near the campus and had made a handsome profit. A development on the side of the campus opposite his own holdings had for a while threatened to damage his reputation for practical wisdom; but his official responsibilities had providentially intervened to save him from ruin. The real-estate development that rivaled his own could be reached conveniently only by driving through the University grounds and directly past the University infirmary. It became obvious that through traffic disturbed the patients, and President Pomton had acted promptly. He had closed one entrance of the University grounds with a heavy chain, and the real-estate development beyond it withered and died.

One action of his on this occasion deserves mention. He knew that in any large community there are men and women eager to trace any administrative decision to base motives, and he realized he would be accused of ruining a development that threatened to lower property values where his own holdings lay. Pomton had in him none of the moral coward, eager to justify his own acts. He was, however, jealous of the reputation of the University and he did not want its official head criticized, for fear the institution might suffer. He had therefore taken care, just before putting up the chain, to buy a few lots just beyond the driveway it would block. He got them cheap, because the realtor who was developing the tract had noted the possibilities of a chain and was glad to have President Pomton personally interested in keeping the drive open. When the chain clanked into place, no property holder was prompter than President Pomton to lament its presence, but he did so good-humoredly.

"I suppose," he would remark to his friends with ironical melancholy, "our patients come before my wretched little lots."

The realtor who had sold them to him was full of the most malicious accusations, but the scoundrel received poetic justice: fate forced him shortly into bankruptcy.

This afternoon, at the Triangle Club, where the social scientists awaited the advent of Mr. Denby, Director of the Winthrop Foundation, President Pomton was obviously in good form. Why shouldn't he be? The Winthrop Foundation had been set up with a capitalization of forty millions for the sole purpose of promoting the study of the social sciences; and although the salaries of its staff were high and consumed a major portion of the foundation's income, there was plenty left to affect profoundly the trend of American research in the field of the social sciences. Every alert social scientist from Maine to California studied the annual report of the foundation to keep abreast of the trend; and, as the interests of the trustees shifted rapidly from year to year, research workers were kept on the *qui vive* if they hoped to get the financial support necessary to their work. The wholesome result had been that new acreage had been, so to speak, plowed up each year; and that submarginal land, once it had been proved sterile, had been allowed to revert to weeds. Some of the slower research workers had naturally charged the foundation with following fads; but the trustees, who rarely heard these charges anyhow, knew that fad-following is an accusation that arises wherever there is lively intellectual ferment. And it was precisely ferment that they were after.

President Pomton had had several long conferences with Mr. Denby in Mr. Denby's New York offices, one of those plushy, *moderne* foundation offices on the twenty-fifth floor where basic academic policy is hammered out and the trend of American scholarship is planned—made casually and colloquially, as it should be, by men who control big money and who are far enough removed from the petty grind of academic life not to be blinded to the main issues. President Pomton had reason to remember those conferences with pleasure. He had certainly concealed all personal anxiety; he had remained quite as casual and colloquial as the best of them; he had at the same time, through the vaguest hints, given the impression of a man back from the intellectual firing line, taking a proper interest in the problem of supplies and munitions. Even had he had any ideas on social research, he would not have been so naïve as to voice them to Denby for fear Denby might consider him pedantic. The talk had been chiefly about personalities—other college executives and some of the foundation big-bugs, their foibles and their contacts. He had let Denby do most of the talking, because Denby liked talking. Finally, he had more or less definitely assumed that Denby intended subsidizing Pomton's social scientists—"a rather remarkable group," as Pomton casually called them—and hoped Denby would come out soon and see what they were doing. Denby replied warily that he would enjoy doing so. Now he was in town.

Pomton listened judiciously to Schneider and Weed and Nast as they presented the cases for diplomatic history, the rise of totalitarianism and People's Capitalism respectively; and skillfully harmonized their opposing views. As a matter of fact, he was less interested in the trend of social-science research—he could trust Denby's volubility to give the group the right cues on that—than in the personal appearance of his little flock. He glanced approvingly at Nast, who was always well and even expensively groomed. He felt a little resentment that none of the others could earn money outside, over and beyond their University salaries. It would take away that hungry look and it would perhaps keep their wives from discussing their household budgets in front of Pomton, which seemed to Pomton extraordinarily bad taste anyhow. None of them, in his judgment, was worth a cent more than he got, although it might prove difficult to replace them at their present salaries. He particularly observed that Schneider's shirt cuffs were slightly frayed, although he had tried, in summoning the group, to make it playfully clear that the occasion perhaps called for more formal dress than usual. Denby dressed extremely well, and Denby would see no point in the pose of the "poor scholar." Good scholars needn't remain poor.

Others joined the group. They were younger members of the departments and had been invited because they showed promise in research and looked socially presentable. Milton, the sociologist, began to count noses. Milton had been told by Pomton that, in the event of a handsome grant, Pomton would appoint him chairman of a research council to deal out the funds where they could do the University most good, although he made it clear that in the last analysis Milton could not be expected to know as well as the President would just where this would be. The thing would be decided in conference; decisions would be rubber-stamped by the council, if that body were wisely selected. Even so, Milton had concluded that as future chairman of the council he might well be in line for a more important administrative post: Pomton could not be expected to last forever, and his mantle must fall somewhere when it finally fell. Milton jotted names on a slip of paper. At last, he turned deferentially to Pomton.

When Milton spoke, he always spoke with gravity. He was more conscious of the responsibilities of the intellectual life than his colleagues were, partly because he was a sociologist, partly because he had done his doctorate at Chicago, and partly because his temperament was naturally a grave one.

"I think," he remarked now to Pomton, "that all those who expect to be president are here, Mr. Pres— I think that all those who expect to be *present* are here, Mr. President."

Nast guffawed. The others joined in, but with less noise. Milton was surprised, and showed no awareness that his *lapsus linguae* had implications. But Pomton scored.

"Then," he said carefully, "many of them will be disappointed."

The whole group laughed now, with genuine appreciation. All of them had long been aware of Milton's hopes. All except President Pomton, who, once he had savored the success of his repartee, began suddenly to feel old and jostled and wondered if the chairmanship would make Milton too self-important. Some men could not wear prominence gracefully: perhaps Milton was one of them.

Pomton was saved from these disagreeable thoughts by the arrival of Denby. Everybody rose quickly, and Pomton grasped Denby's hand cordially. Hasty introductions followed—introductions which Denby acknowledged without much enthusiasm. For Denby had concluded long ago that professors bored him. He was willing to grant them other people's money, but he would be hanged if he would listen to them talk. Let the undergraduates do that: they got degrees for doing it. Denby already had a degree, and he could see no valid reason for suffering further. Denby had already made up his mind to recommend a grant. Not that he was impressed with the research this group was doing. As a matter of fact, he had barely turned the leaves of the monographs which President Pomton had sent him. His only impression of the stuff was that it was even duller than most social-science research. But Denby had concluded that the whole purpose of the Winthrop Foundation was bogus, and that probably its only useful expenditure was his own salary. On the other hand, the money had to be spent. Why not spend some here? This conference at the Triangle Club would be the last hard pull: the thing was, to make it entertaining.

Talk began. There was no indecent haste. It was assumed that when scholars talk, a good deal can be said by indirection, by implication, and, where personalities are concerned, by insinuation. Each conferee was engaged in trying to follow and in trying to recognize the titles of scholarly works cited from his own field. One of Nast's little studies of People's Capitalism won a word of praise from Denby, and a wave of smothered anger ruffled the urbanity of the group for a few moments. But it soon passed.

Professor Schneider, head of the department of history, discreetly watched the head of the Winthrop Foundation. What he saw was a huge, hearty man, not fat but bulky. Through Denby's present boredom Schneider thought he discerned a most enviable gusto for life. Expensive clothes, worn a bit carelessly; a kind of rough civility; quick intelligence; and an occasional wicked twinkle in the eye.

Denby suddenly grew grave. "I think we ought to be clear on one matter," he said. "Suppose the foundation were to find it possible to make at least a small grant to foster social-science research here. I don't know that they will: the claims on us are numerous and heavy. But suppose they did."

President Pomton leaned forward heavily. This was the first time Denby had expressed definite doubts as to the possibility of a grant. Pomton had felt so sure of his ultimate success that he had told at least two prospective donors that the Winthrop people were determined to develop the social sciences here. Both donors had reacted unfortunately. Instead of "coming in on the ground floor," as President Pomton had half jokingly invited them to do, they had both promised to consider carefully a small gift the moment the University had won the imprimatur of the Winthrop Foundation. They had pointed out modestly that they themselves were mere businessmen

{11}

and could certainly not hope to make as good a judgment on scholarly matters as specialists hired to make just such judgments. President Pomton had suggested that since the Winthrop people were certain to act favorably, a private donor would get more pleasure out of forestalling them than in following along. He reminded them that they had been pioneers in industry and he expressed himself as confident that they would want to be pioneers in giving to education. Looking back on these two conversations, President Pomton still thought he had taken the best line; but he had lost. Well, if these two men learned now that the Winthrop people, after an investigation by specialists, had turned thumbs down, what, pray, would they do with their own thumbs?

Denby was looking even graver than President Pomton.

"Suppose," he repeated, "the foundation did make a grant. And suppose Dr. Nast here, or one of his colleagues in economics, published a book that leaned a little to the left. What would happen?"

President Pomton almost lurched forward in his chair to answer that one.

"Nothing," he declared simply. "Absolutely nothing. I mean, of course, as far as criticism is concerned. Either from the state legislature or from what I may call our own public. There is a powerful tradition of academic freedom here. There would not be a murmur of criticism. Am I right, Dr. Nast?"

"Absolutely," replied Nast. "There wouldn't be a murmur."

"Then," answered Denby, very deliberately, "it scarcely seems worth while making the grant. You see, we are interested in ferment. In discussion. Even in a good fight now and then. What you say of your peculiar situation here troubles me."

There was a sudden loud explosion that sounded at first like laughter but turned out to be a violent fit of coughing. Professor Schneider was holding his handkerchief to his mouth and trying to master himself. Denby looked keenly at him. Could it be that the division of social sciences contained a man with a sense of humor? If so, was there any means of subsidizing it without destroying it?

Opportunities for service like this one, he thought, do not often present themselves to educational foundations. He decided to keep Schneider under observation.

The other faculty members present looked more than grave and either lacked the desire or the energy to cough. As for President Pomton, his face had suddenly sagged, had gone a little gray. A wave of nausea swept through him. Always troubled by nervous indigestion, he suddenly felt dreadful things happening in the pit of his stomach, and even lower down. He started speaking rapidly.

"I don't think I made myself clear. I don't think even Dr. Nast made himself wholly clear. What I meant was that there was no chance of research being stifled. No chance at all. There would of course be ferment. A great deal of ferment. It may be worth observing that some of Dr. Nast's previous works have caused immense ferment. There would be extremely wide discussion, and over a long period. I don't doubt there would be a fight, if Dr. Nast leaned far enough to the left. A good fight. And we would be all the stronger for having won it."

Mr. Denby nodded gravely, pondering how best to give the screw another turn. The tension that had shot through the whole group—except for Schneider—when his reply had staggered Pomton had eased. Even those members of this respectfully silent group who felt least admiration for Dr. Pomton were reflecting that there was some point in having a man of his stamp at the head of an educational institution. Precisely because the academic mind is unworldly and unselfish, there was point in having a practical and, if you like, a worldly man to stand between the academic mind and a skeptical world. Denby detected a sort of wave of good will and loyalty sweeping from this silent cheering section toward President Pomton. It was as if, to use Pomton's last remark, he had indeed won a fight and was all the stronger for winning it. Something had to be done, if Denby's day was not to fizzle out in defeat and boredom.

"I'm afraid," he resumed evenly, "I haven't made myself clear either. The foundation would be considerably less interested in having you win your fight than in your starting the sort of fight one doesn't win easily or quickly. We are not interested in political victories. We are not even interested in intellectual victories, in the sense of definite authoritarian conclusions. We are interested in the clash of ideas."

Again, with great suddenness, explosive noises came from Schneider, and again he seemed to be gagging himself with his handkerchief. But his colleagues were so horrified by the tenor of Denby's reply that none of them paid Schneider any genuine attention except an immediate neighbor who thumped him absent-mindedly on the back a couple of times. President Pomton, in his agony, appeared not even to have heard him. Denby glanced again at Schneider. I want to meet that guy, he said to himself. Then he heard Pomton, almost moaning, "But that's just what I mean. I don't mean by winning that Dr. Nast's ideas would win. I only mean the University would win the right for Dr. Nast to publish his ideas, no matter how unpopular they might be. We would win the right to continue the intellectual game, if you like."

"There again," said Denby, and his voice was smooth and cool, "I wonder if our purposes are sufficiently the same to justify collaboration between the University and the foundation."

Collaboration! Pomton felt a surge of bitterness. How was it collaboration when they had all the money and the University nothing but the ideas—if that? But he controlled himself.

"You see," Denby was continuing, "we don't think of it as a game so much as a fight. I admit that, in educational institutions, it tends to become a game."

"I'm afraid," said Pomton, "that I'm choosing my words very badly. Certainly 'intellectual game' is a cliché. Frankly, I mean precisely the same thing by the term as a good stiff fight."

"Well," said Denby, "I'm glad we've had this frank discussion. It's clarified a good deal for me." And with this ambiguous statement the conference closed. Denby excused himself by saying he must dress; he had promised to dine with Professor Nast. He shook hands perfunctorily with several of the distinguished scholars present, and then found Schneider.

"Aren't you Professor Schneider?"

"Yes. And you must excuse me for my fits of coughing. I—"

"Don't mention it. This kind of situation always gives me fits too. It's not often I meet a fellow sufferer. Look, I expect to be out again before long. What about my seeing you when I return? Maybe you wouldn't mind breakfasting with me if I let you know the date a week or so in advance."

"I'd love to," said Schneider, with a candid grin.

Denby went out with Nast, while those other members of the group who felt they had most to gain, personally and intellectually, from a foundation grant, crowded around President Pomton to congratulate him on his conduct of the meeting. Milton, the future chairman of the research council, asked him knowingly for an appointment in his office. Milton felt jubilantly sure of his future.

But Pomton, when he had acknowledged the compliments paid his presidential skill, excused himself and went home alone, wondering precisely what Denby had felt was clarified now and recalling almost with pain the stolid expectancy of the two prospective donors. This conference represented the flowering which had followed months of careful cultivation. What man could tell if fruit would ever ripen?

Milton went home too. Once the conference had gotten under way, Milton had seen no earthly way to insinuate himself into it. For that matter, nobody but Nast had been able to. Yet surely, thought Milton, since it was himself, not Nast, who would head the institute that they were all busy hatching, some deference should have been shown him. First, Denby had commented on Nast's published work, and on nobody else's. Then Denby had imagined a crisis in which Nast's research, not Milton's, would draw fire. Then President Pomton, engaged in single combat while his henchmen stood silently by and, knowing him too well to hazard an interruption, had called on Nast to support him. And at the end it was Nast and not Milton, the future director, who had borne Denby off in triumph to a dinner Milton would never taste.

Schneider also went home. Unlike Milton, he had no reason to regret not having spoken during the Pomton-Denby duel. But he was glad he was to see more of Denby. Denby's skillful torture of Pomton had delighted him.

II

THERE WERE heavy buckwheat cakes and it was gray outside. The three stocky little girls had plowed their way through innumerable cakes and had gone to school, each one slamming the front door behind her. How did they study with those knots of dough inside them, glued together with maple sirup? Schneider knew the answer: they didn't study. So why not enjoy the cakes? Perhaps they were right.

This November morning would have been less grim had there been two electric globes burning. Henrietta's customary economy had forestalled that. He wondered she could see her newspaper. He imagined three lights, and bacon, sliced thin. If he had had three lights and bacon, he could have gone to his office cheerfully. Suppose he had a study of his own, book lined, here at home. His father had had one. Schneider himself had had a study; but now Henrietta did dressmaking in it—not often, once a month perhaps. But Henrietta had said it was a sewing room, and she would not have books and papers strewn about. He had suggested timidly that a study was a professor's workshop and books were his tools, and Henrietta had said that when his work produced a good enough living for the family so that no sewing woman was needed there would be time to talk about a workshop.

He heaved his weight, plus some restless buckwheat cakes, out of his chair and wondered if he should interrupt her reading to say good-by. But she read on, tight-lipped; so he got his rubbers and raincoat and briefcase and slipped out. He had no lecture until noon, and then one that required no preparation. He could use last year's notes and give it a little rock 'n' roll. He smiled to himself at the words. That was slang. He was good at slang. It was his use of slang that held his undergraduate lectures together. You needed more than facts when you faced fifty of those young barbarians.

He usually had a pipe with young Ripley, his student assistant, before going to work in his own office, but not this morning. He didn't want to see anybody. He was puzzled over something and he wanted, if possible, to find out what it was that puzzled him. So he sat in his dingy office sucking his pipe and trying to think. There were the cakes and the one light and those doors slamming and that grim face over the newspaper and the grime of his office here and the awful class he would meet at noon, and for the first time in his life he realized that he was thoroughly wretched; that he disliked his job; that he hated his home.

There was a melancholy pleasure in feeling quite clear about things he had sensed blindly for so long. But the feeling of having thrown away his life tempered the pleasure of discovery. He had chosen the wrong wife and the wrong job or, anyhow, the wrong wife for this job. Or maybe he had just chosen the wife too early. Why was it, anyhow, that so many men in academic life married before they got their doctorate, and why did half of those marry the daughter of their landlady? A lonely Harvard graduate student, living across the hall from his landlady and her daughter. And then, by prearrangement, the daughter had crossed the hall. That, except for a few words in an ugly church, was really all, and yet the Rubicon had been crossed. And it was not Caesar who had crossed it. Rome had crossed it, coming Caesar's way. Oh, what a fall was there. Then I and you and half our graduate-student friends appeared to fall, in the same fatal manner. They must have all been mad. And yet it seemed courageous at the time.

Three children. All slammed doors. All dull with buckwheat. No money, except a professor's salary. What was it he used to hope for? Oh, yes: books and travel. Well, there were no books and travel. There was a car, not yet paid for. And a radio, paid for. No television: he agreed with Henrietta on that. You got your books from the University library, and you traveled in the car. Not very far. You would have needed a vacation to travel far. And, what with the three children and all the buckwheat to buy, you taught summer school instead.

The job? The job wasn't a bad job. He had a full professorship. He was head of the department of history. If he could wangle a call from somewhere, he would probably get a raise: Pomton obviously wanted to keep him. He enjoyed his teaching, sometimes. He had published two books and was on a third. They were not very interesting books, but they had been well reviewed in the *American Historical Review*. As head of the history department, he had enough administrative work to keep him from being a pure intellectual.

The job wasn't the real catch. Henrietta was the catch. Henrietta, who came of good New England stock and knew that successful people are not in want. She knew it at first hand. Her father had made a fortune in doughnuts: "The Doughnut That Is Different." Her father had ridden to wealth on those different doughnuts. And he was hardly as cold as one of his own doughnuts when his widow lost everything and opened lodgings for "paying guests" three blocks off Harvard Square. But Henrietta could remember the doughnut period. She had meant to marry money. In a moment of madness poor Henrietta had crossed the Rubicon and found herself living across the hall from herself. By the skin of his teeth he had got his first job, and after all too few years the door-slammers started arriving.

If he had had private means, who could say? Certainly, his domestic life appeared to be one long well-thought-out punishment for not earning more money. Not that Henrietta was a spender. She was a budgeter. And practically nothing Schneider really liked was in the budget.

But it wasn't really money. It was Dorothy Nast. Dorothy was a Southerner; and where Henrietta had brought to the University all the reservations New Englanders bring to the Middle West, Dorothy had just loved it, or told it she had, from the first day. Love conquered all, and the social principality Henrietta had set up came clattering to the ground. Henrietta had ruled her subjects through terror. Dorothy lulled them into not caring for freedom. The angularities of life gave way to curves, some of them fairly intricate, most of them banal. An unfocused cordiality suffused the whole community. Man's goal became, not ideas, but gentleness of manner, and Henrietta became that most ridiculous of feminine types, a queen without subjects. Or, anyhow, without many of them. The smell of fried chicken and hot bread hung in the air, as heavy as honeysuckle or magnolia. Seven faculty wives learned to say you-all in as many days. In fact, they outdid the South itself: they used it in the second person singular. R's fell off the ends of words. There was charm. Faculty feuds died down. Everybody ate more, slept more, worked less. The community stretched, yawned, sprawled, and relapsed permanently into good humor.

Dorothy had come on a Tuesday; had discovered on a Wednesday that Henrietta owned the place; had challenged her the following week end. But worst of all, and least sporting, she had named her weapons: charm, gentleness, fried chicken, hot bread, cordiality, compliments to your face. She had even flattered Henrietta to her face; and Henrietta, who could have won the war hands down on the basis of books read, houses well kept, housekeeping budgets balanced, and community morals guarded, met bitter defeat. Not a drop of her blood did she spill: she was drowned in molasses. Before she went down for the third time, with her Massachusetts accent unscathed, she recognized the thing for what it was. It was Evil, the thing the Grand Army of the Republic had fought against for four long years, the thing the Republican party had tried decade after decade to cleanse America of. It was lotus. It was fun.

Looking back on Dorothy's first week, and trying to play the detached historian, Schneider knew he had witnessed a recurrent struggle in American history. It was the old struggle over who should get the Western lands. And it had all seemed settled at Appomattox. The North had won them in fair fight, opened them up with its treasure, peopled them with good Republicans, and lo! the Confederates had sneaked in from the rear and now owned the place. As for the Middle West, they never knew what was happening. When Dorothy arrived, unpacked her clothes, made up her pretty face, and turned on the charm, they recognized it instantly, resented it deeply, still distrusted it, inhaled it just once to see how it really tasted, and sank back into pleasant unconsciousness.

Schneider reviewed all this in his mind and then, being a historian, made one deft correction. It was not true that no blood had been spilled. He had wondered how such momentous conflicts could be settled without bloodshed. Now he remembered one brilliant skirmish, brief enough but, viewed in its setting, one of the decisive battles of the renewed Civil War. Faced with the problem of selling charm to a community that had sworn fidelity to culture, Dorothy had instinctively and blindly appealed to tradition. In speaking of personalities, she identified their county seats if they were Southern and connected them with their collaterals; if they were Northern, she identified them tentatively with a trade-mark. She had learned about the Different Doughnuts on the second day of the campaign, from a deserter. But Henrietta knew what lay back of doughnuts, back of wooden nutmegs, textiles, shoes, clocks. It lay in a harbor, in sweet New England sunshine, with trim white sails and curving prow: it was the *Mayflower*. And she merely mentioned the fact in front of Dorothy, congratulating the South on its traditions and pointing out that the *Mayflower* had in 1620 brought the first permanent English colony to our shores. Dorothy said she had always loved the *Mayflower*, its passengers were such simple, unpretentious people; that she loved all those early ships; that she couldn't help feeling sentimental about the Dutch sloop that brought the first Negroes to Jamestown in 1619. She supposed it was because of her Mammy she felt that way; her Mammy, and indeed many of her family's slaves before-the-war, were descended from one of those same Negroes who had landed in Virginia a year before the *Mayflower* arrived. She didn't know how we Southerners ever got along without them for twelve long years. Henrietta was outraged by this fib; had denied it flatly; and had rushed home to report the slur to her historian husband. And poor Schneider, bearer of evil tidings but fearless in his love of historical truth, had had to break the news that Dorothy was right about those annoyingly prompt Negro arrivals. From that instant dated Henrietta's suspicion that Schneider himself liked charm. He was always careful never to mention Dorothy in her presence.

It was a decisive defeat and it turned the tide of social history in at least one community. *Mayflower* ancestors who had been dug up or even bought and paid for were hastily heaved over the side, as it were, and there was an epidemic of great-grandmothers from Virginia who had crossed the Alleghenies in their private coaches because pioneering frankly bored them, or perhaps merely because they liked nice things. The thing was not a defeat; it was a rout, and Henrietta's acidity had increased a hundredfold, beginning with the day the *Mayflower* was lost, all hands on board.

Henrietta's acidity had, if anything, made her more wiry and robust; but it had wrecked Schneider's health. He had developed a series of minor, but nagging, disorders; and they were peculiarly nagging because they were almost invariably unmentionable. He had caught mumps—at his age!—from the door-slammers, and it had settled in various portions of his anatomy for several painful weeks. Then, for three wretched months that culminated in a painful operation, he had had to secrete a pneumatic pillow in his office or else work standing. When he had barely turned forty, he developed prostatitis, which would have made perfect sense fifteen years later or even ten, and which involved the most disagreeable treatments. Every summer he had bouts of dysentery that made him socially undependable. Athlete's foot oppressed him.

He was, in short, prematurely middle-aged, sickly, unhappily married, in debt, and terrified by the prospect of twenty or thirty years more of the same paltry guerrilla warfare with life. He believed that if Henrietta would relent, he could probably recover his health and even his zest for his work, and he might even find a way to increase his income. Or if he could, merely by wishing, feel really well, he might develop a tolerance for Henrietta and throw himself into his teaching and writing. Or if he were younger, he might handle all his problems simultaneously. But he was not young, and he could find no leverage. He sucked his pipe and turned his problem over and over, trying to find in it a beginning and an end. Actually, granted all the difficulties, it might be easier to do something about his finances than about anything else. They were of course the least essential aspect of the problem: Schneider was no economic determinist. But an increased income might, by lightening his worries, give him strength to recover his health, to do more work and better work, and to silence or dodge Henrietta. But how could he increase his income?

Schneider was not so naïve as to be ignorant of the professor's favorite method, but he had always had conscientious scruples against using it. You simply wangled a "call" from another university and waved a telegram at the President. Pomton didn't mind: he joked about telegram-waving. Pomton felt that the surest way to discover who were the best men in your faculty was to see which ones other university presidents wanted. He recognized, of course, that to make this system work well in the interests of pure scholarship and a decently balanced budget, there had to be a gentleman's agreement between university presidents not to bid against each other more than was absolutely necessary and certainly not to connive at imitation calls. Schneider knew about the gentleman's agreement too, but he knew that it could be circumvented because he had witnessed circumventions.

There were two alternatives: wait for presidential recognition of scholarly merit, which certainly wouldn't work with Pomton; or go to Pomton and frankly tell him your needs, which Schneider balked at doing and which wouldn't work anyhow. If finance was the only available leverage to escape from a ruined life, hadn't one better be ruthless and appeal to Western Union? As a matter of fact, Schneider knew he was worth more than he was paid and he knew that Pomton knew it. At worst, he would be merely furnishing Pomton with a budgetary pretext, and Pomton couldn't think without budgetary pretexts. And, once he had the salary he needed and had earned, his usefulness to the University would be correspondingly increased. Surely that was the correct statement of the morals of the case. It did not make Schneider happy, but it did free him from a sort of moral paralysis. He felt ready to act.

Still sucking hard at his pipe, he began naming over in his mind the really close friends he had who were teaching in other institutions. Obviously, Keye was the man. They had known each other since Harvard days. Keye understood his problem already, Henrietta included, which would save embarrassing explanations. Keye taught at Barker University in Buffalo. Keye was an intimate of President Camp of Barker. Best of all, Camp disliked Pomton and would enjoy breaking the gentleman's agreement if not asked to admit he was breaking it. Schneider would write Keye.

He explained briefly but with plenty of innuendo that he was writing because he had reached one of those dead ends one does reach in academic life, and not because there was anything fundamentally wrong with the place he had. In fact, in the event that Keye could induce President Camp to act, and in the event that Pomton parried with an increase, he might decide not to move. He was aware that moving involved expense and bother. He would like, of course, to work at the same place as Keye himself. But he would have to consider many things. Finally, if Keye thought there was literally no place for him at Buffalo, or Camp thought so, it would suffice to have lively explorations without a firm offer. He believed negotiations would suffice to redefine his contractual relationship with President Pomton.

On reading over the letter, he was rather struck with the phrase "to redefine his contractual relationship with President Pomton." It seemed to him both more accurate and less offensive than other phrases that had sprung to his mind in the first moment of revulsion from telegram-waving. After all, a scholar should be free to redefine his contractual relationship with the institution to which he is giving his life.

He said nothing to Henrietta. In the first place, he did not want to leave the University, not at least until he had tried out this new leverage on middle age and ailing health and domestic tyranny. And Henrietta would want to go to Buffalo, if she thought there was a chance. She would want to get there, partly because it represented a step back toward New England and civilization and partly because she had lost her principality here in the West, where principalities are so quickly won and lost. It was essential to the perilous negotiations of the next few days or weeks that there be no back-seat driving.

Keye's response was so prompt that Schneider experienced a sudden surge of self-confidence. Keye questioned whether Schneider's general depression had not led him to underestimate his scholarly reputation. Keye wired that Camp definitely wanted Schneider to come and that the only reason for delaying an offer was to check up on his budget. But he felt sure Schneider would get a letter in a day or two.

He didn't. He didn't get one in a week or two. And he dragged miserably into December, almost regretting that he had broken his code and succumbed to the subtle temptation to redefine his relationship. Then, just when he was suspecting that Keye's wire signified nothing more than Keye's desire to exhibit his influence with President Camp, the letter came.

The letter frankly stated that no money was available, so far as Camp could see, that would enable him to call Schneider. But you could never tell. Just in case, what salary would Schneider consider? Cordially yours.

Schneider wanted to wire, but refrained and wrote a dignified letter saying that he would consider seven thousand. He implied, though he could not truthfully state, that he was already getting practically that where he was, that he was head of his department and very well treated. Still, he greatly admired Barker University and the research program President Camp was so ably fostering. And he repeated that seven thousand would give him pause. He suggested that, since there were other alternative solutions open (God knew what they were, except beating or strangling Henrietta) it might save time if President Camp could wire collect, stating in the wire, in order to be businesslike, the precise conditions of his offer. Schneider assured him that he would understand without restatement the tentative nature of the offer. Camp flashed back: TENTATIVELY OFFER YOU FULL PROFESSORSHIP SIXTY-SIX HUNDRED HURRIED DECISION UNNECESSARY.

This telegram, thought Schneider, makes good reading but bad waving. And the whole point of the negotiations, when you came right down to it, was to get something worth waving. But he could scarcely attempt to get another wire out of Camp. TENTATIVELY made the whole bomb a dud. And as if TENTATIVELY weren't bad enough, the salary named was so little more than the one he received that it was no real lever at all. You couldn't bluff with a thing like that.

Nevertheless, the telegram was a gift horse, and a moment's reflection on the so-called alternative solutions open determined Schneider to mount the gift horse and ride him straight into Pomton's office. Nothing attempted, nothing gained. He was facing the crisis of his negotiations and he must keep his eye and hand steady.

Pomton could not have received him more charmingly. Pomton's rather simple origins frequently showed through the veneer, and it was these worn spots that had led a not too original critic to observe that Pomton was every other inch a gentleman. But today the veneer was all polish. There was courtesy, almost deference.

"I am somewhat troubled, Mr. President," said Schneider, "by a decision I must make. And I need your advice." Without more ado, he drew Camp's telegram from his pocket and passed it to Pomton. "Please read it," he said simply.

Pomton read it, but once he had read the first word, TENTATIVELY, his mind refused to focus on the rest of the wire, except of course on the sum SIXTY-SIX HUNDRED.

"But there's nothing to be troubled about, my dear chap," he said. "I congratulate you. I heartily congratulate you. I take this sort of comment on your work as a very genuine endorsement of my own judgment in placing you at the head of a department. Camp is no hero of mine, but Barker is Barker and I'm glad they agree with me. I think you ought to take the whole thing as a compliment and make it clear in your reply that you take it so."

"But," began Schneider, trying to get things back on the track, "but ought I—ought I to accept? This is a grave decision I face. And I felt, in view of the confidence you have shown in my work here, I ought to tell you I was facing it."

"Nonsense, old chap," said Pomton heartily. "Camp says himself you don't have to hurry in making up your mind. And frankly, while it's none of my business, I don't see how the slight difference between your salary here and what Camp offers justifies you in upsetting yourself."

"Still," said Schneider, "I ought to do him the courtesy of as prompt a reply as possible. He may want to fill the post."

"I don't agree. I don't agree. You take your time. I don't think we are reading the same thing between the lines. I suspect," Pomton added, with a grin, "I suspect I've had more practice than you in reading wires of this sort. In fact, I may have written a few myself! And the operative word in this wire is TENTATIVELY.

"I think, Schneider, that with all my too obvious weaknesses, I do know how the executive mind works. Well, mark my word, Camp merely means by this wire that he would like to know whether you can be had for sixty-six hundred in case there is ever a place open in history at Barker."

It struck Schneider that every other inch of the veneer was wearing pretty thin. He hadn't thought of himself as "being had" by anybody, unless it was by Pomton in this interview. The sixty-six hundred might be a modest figure, but it was better than what he was getting. And to talk as if a place in history might open in a growing university or might never open was merely to be perverse. Professors don't live forever. And professors do sometimes move, even though not as often as they threaten to. Schneider's resentment at Pomton was rising so fast that he hardly trusted himself to speak. But if brutality was to be the medium of communication, then let's be brutal.

"What I need to know," he said evenly and a little coldly, "is not whether I am being called to Buffalo. This telegram is not President Camp's first communication. What I need to know is whether you have any plans for developing history at the University that might make it unwise for me to accept this offer."

"Lots of them," said Pomton calmly. "But, unlike Camp, I don't discuss my plans when they are tentative. I discuss them when they are definite." That was that.

"In that case," Schneider continued in the same even tone, "I shall not bother you again with this matter."

"But it's no bother!" cried Pomton, with something of the old gaiety coming back into his voice. "No bother at all. If Camp ever makes you a firm offer, either this year or at some date in the future, I count on you to let me know. And I think I ought to know. Meanwhile, I consider it a feather in the cap of my administration that you are being thought of, even tentatively, at other institutions."

The veneer was hanging in loose strips, and Schneider almost stumbled over them in getting to the door.

~III~

WELL, what'll you have?" asked Denby, studying his menu with obvious gusto.

Schneider studied his own, glancing furtively and automatically at the prices listed on the right, all of which seemed to him shockingly high. The hotel dining room was quiet. The traveling salesmen had all breakfasted early and had descended on their local victims, bundled tight against the November wind, a case of samples in one hand and a briefcase in the other. A pretty waitress, dressed in immaculate white, stood beside Schneider, pencil poised. Even though her white shoes were as clean as her uniform, Schneider nevertheless recognized her as a student from the University.

Through the haze of shocking prices, Schneider caught a quick vision of his girl students in class; of their vacant faces; their sweaters stretched tight over their young, pointed breasts; their soiled blue denim trousers rolled at unequal heights from their appalling, dirty-white saddle shoes, badly run down at the heels; their jaws working on their eternal gum—and their pencils poised, just as the pencil of this immaculately uniformed child was now. He reflected bitterly how much more appropriately occupied they would all be if they were clean waitresses instead of dirty, grade-chasing pseudo-scholars. The men students could wash the dishes.

He started from his daydream and smiled at Denby.

"What about you?" he asked. "What are you having?"

"Corn cakes with honey," replied Denby greedily. "But first I'm having scrambled eggs with plenty of thin sliced bacon. Plenty of coffee with heavy cream. And of course I'll start with orange juice."

"I'll take the same," said Schneider. Automatically, he did a lightning calculation. But what did it matter? Denby had insisted on playing host.

"Okay," said Denby to the pretty waitress. "That's the order. Now double it."

"Double it?" she repeated vaguely. "Shall I set two more places, then?"

"Good God, no, child! We don't want to move between courses. You're thinking of the Mad Tea Party. This is merely a Mad Breakfast: Dr. Schneider and I are going to discuss education. We've got to have food to do a thing like that on. So just double the order."

The waitress still looked bothered.

"Look," said Denby. "Are you a Republican?"

"Yes, sir," she said proudly.

"Well," he replied, "then you naturally believe in an economy of scarcity. I don't. I should think you people here in the Corn Belt would want to encourage heavy eaters like me. So, instead of bringing us each an orange juice, bring us each a double orange juice."

"Yes, sir," she said.

"How many eggs in the menu order? Two?"

"Yes, sir," she said.

"Then double it. Twice two makes four. And there are two of us, so that makes eight eggs. As for the bacon, slaughter a hog if necessary. But if the bacon gives out, I shall complain to the manager. And

Dr. Schneider looks to me like a man who would enjoy a great deal of bacon. Are the eggs fresh?"

"They were laid yesterday," she answered.

"That's fresh enough," said Denby. "We don't insist on them hot from the hen. But mind you bring 'em hot from the stove. And, for God's sake, whatever you do, don't let us run short of butter."

This cry so obviously came from the heart, or the belly, or somewhere deep down in Denby, that it confirmed Schneider's judgment that he was not playing smart aleck with the waitress but that his enthusiasm for eating had carried him away. It was an enthusiasm that had proved infectious. Otherwise, Schneider would never have ordered hot cakes, not even corn cakes, although he liked corn cakes better than Henrietta's eternal buckwheat. In any case, it was the bacon he was looking forward to.

The waitress was walking swiftly toward the kitchen, shaking her head. Denby glanced after her casually, then turned his vast bulk in his chair to make a more judicious appraisal.

"Pretty girl," he muttered with real appreciation. "Not too bright. And pretty. Very appealing combination."

"Yes, she is," said Schneider. "Off campus."

"I know precisely what you mean. I used to teach myself. All female undergraduates should withdraw from college and become pretty waitresses—Hebes, bearing great platters of newly laid, hot, soft-scrambled eggs. With a hell of a lot of bacon, of course. The men students should stop pretending they want an education and wash the dishes."

Schneider was startled. Was this huge, roaring, lusty skeptic his own alter ego?

When the eggs finally came, Denby was still denouncing the academic world. Between Gargantuan mouthfuls, he rumbled on: "Campus life! My God! I couldn't take it. The place awash with perfectly decent boys and girls, sweating through the most ghastly textbooks, copying down in their notebooks the appalling stupidities and ineptitudes that tired, underpaid, repetitious, frustrated professors droned at them, trying to get a grade that would add up with other grades to get them a diploma, printed on imitation sheepskin for real sheep. Faculty wives, worn out with trying to make two ends meet, or gone hard and bitter and spiteful, carrying on social vendettas with each other. And, over all, an uneducated ex-general or ex-banker blandishing tax-evading donors into perpetuating their own egos. It's a truly hideous picture of perfectly nice people caught up in an absolute web of pretense. Why, I even began to develop obscure illnesses, due partly to frustration and partly to the low diet I was on, thanks to my ridiculous salary. I couldn't take it, so I became a philanthropoid. This way I dish out other people's money to people still in the racket. I don't accomplish much, I guess. But the pay is excellent, and I imagine it helps guys that are up against a promotion policy of print-or-perish. Now and then I meet a guy that I can talk to. Or a university president to tease."

"You tease well," replied Schneider, wondering which diseases Denby had developed in the days before he had escaped from the academic . . . racket. "You tease awfully well. You know, the reason I looked forward to seeing you again was the unutterable joy I experienced watching you play Pomton on the grant. I imagine deep-sea fishing has the same charm, though I've never done any. You know: play him along, reel him in a little, give him his head, let him wear himself out, reel him in, and so on. There was real art in it. Then, I think I was feeling at the end of my rope, with all these waitresses and dishwashers taking down notes in order to stay in college long enough to be crowned May Queen or make a football team or at least please their parents—who wouldn't want them to get a real education anyhow—by getting a worthless degree and making useful contacts. I felt if another colleague undertook another piece of phony research, written in gobbledygook about the obvious; or wangled another promotion; or even cited another authority—well, I'd go mad. And since you get around to so many campuses, I thought maybe you'd know if there was any hope anywhere of this thing rising above the level of farce."

"Not a chance!" said Denby conclusively. "You know what they're all talking about now? 'Creative.' They all want to be creative about something. The word is sweeping our campuses like wildfire: it threatens to replace 'semantic.' It's like the New Look in Washington—more of the same, but more confused. Look," he said joyfully, interrupting his jeremiad and gesturing toward the waitress, who was approaching with another mountain of hot corn cakes. "Isn't that a beautiful sight?"

The waitress misunderstood him, and blushed pleasurably.

"I mean the corn cakes," murmured Denby softly to Schneider. "They're superb. Should we tell her to go grind more corn?"

"Not for me," said Schneider. "Or I won't be able to get out of my chair. And I've got two lectures to give before lunch."

"Forget 'em. We're discussing education."

"Oh, all right," said Schneider, surprised by his own words. "I was only going to give them two bits' worth, anyhow. I was going to spray them lightly with facts about the sixteenth century."

"They can read those," said Denby. "Bring some more hot coffee, will you, my dear?" said Denby to the blond waitress. "By the way, where did this cream come from? It's superb."

"Skimmed from last night's milk," she answered, beginning to catch the spirit of joy from Denby. "And the milk came from a cow the hotel owns."

"Is she for sale?" demanded Denby. "I could take her around with me the way Gandhi did his goat."

"No," said the waitress, growing more and more relaxed. "We'll keep her here to make you come back to the hotel."

"If I do, will you be here?" said Denby eagerly.

The blond waitress blushed furiously, and rushed off. Denby murmured approvingly, "Pretty girl. Not too bright. Appealing combination. Have a cigar," he urged.

Schneider adored cigars, more even than bacon; but he hated cheap ones. He could not afford expensive ones, so he had not smoked a cigar in years. They lit up, and leaned back luxuriously. He was in paradise. Through the haze of bluish smoke he thought he could see again the dirty, slouching, ill-dressed members of the classes he was skipping, their filthy shoes, the denim trousers of the girls, the lumbering, rolling gait of the boys, and, above all, the empty faces, smooth, banal, unscarred by a single thought or even the beginnings of intellectual wonder. What was it those utterly unmarked faces kept reminding him of? Something that haunted the back of his mind, something he had never brought to full consciousness. Suddenly, wreathed in expensive smoke, stuffed with expensive bacon, he knew: the faces of the students he ought to be lecturing to right now reminded him of nothing so much as row upon row of babies' bottoms—just soft, smooth, pink, healthy flesh—faces quite unscarred by thought. Damn it, he thought, you ought not to have to lecture to a person unless you could tell one end of him from the other. There were, of course, exceptions—exciting, noble exceptions. Else he would not be teaching. But, decade by decade, the exceptions got fewer.

"I'm glad I'm cutting those lectures," he said happily. "I don't believe I like the young. Anyhow, the kind of lecture we give around here will never teach them anything."

"Imitation pearls before real swine, as the saying goes?"

"That's about it," said Schneider, still wreathed in this exquisite smoke.

"Is anything exciting happening in this place?"

"Nothing whatever. At least, nothing relevant to liberal education. The professional schools aren't too bad, except for being a bit trade-schoolish. What would make anything happen educationally? There's no common purpose. The trustees want to prevent subversion and stay solvent. President Pomton wants to get publicity and, eventually, if it isn't too late, a bigger job somewhere else. The department heads want to raid each other for students, especially for majors, and thereby enlarge their departments. The professors want to publish, get promoted, get famous, and meanwhile stave off their creditors. Weed—you met Weed—tries every three or four years to get a decent undergraduate curriculum started, but he always fails and takes to drink again. Anyhow, Weed is an exception. The wives of the professors—including mine—are socially ambitious and go in for cutthroat competition. The men students try to make fraternities, make athletic teams, avoid study, and then graduate somehow or other. The girls try to make sororities and find a husband. The parents of the students hope their offspring won't 'get ideas.' The dean of women hopes the girls won't conceive anything more dangerous than a concept before they find husbands. And the alumni hope the teams will win, and hunt promising high-school athletes to send us. As for me, I no longer know what I want, but it's not this. Maybe, somewhere else, undergraduate education is possible. Maybe, at Harvard or Yale or Princeton, something goes on."

"Don't be silly," said Denby severely. "What you've just described is a coast-to-coast operation. And there's a certain naïveté, a certain innocence, about it out here that you won't find in the Ivy League. The thing to do is not to take it too seriously. Your troubles are, if I may say so, purely academic. I detect a certain intellectual honesty in you. I like it. But you mustn't let it confuse you. If you do, you'll never get ahead. Take it lightly. When in Rome, show the Romans a trick or two. Or quit Rome, get a decent salary, and get some reading done. That's what I did. But, whatever you do, take it lightly."

They rose. Schneider wondered if he had betrayed Pomton, or the University, or something. But sitting here talking pleasantly with an adult, it seemed so silly to lie, to make sage, weighty remarks, to indulge in professional platitudes. Anyhow, if it was a coast-to-coast operation, as Denby claimed—and Denby was well placed to know—there was no reason for Denby to penalize this outfit. It was not as if it were Denby's own money, after all.

"I hope to see you again," said Denby cordially. "I'm glad you suggested we get together. Let's keep in touch. I always try to keep in touch with people who have seen through this shell game."

They shook hands. Denby was due in twenty minutes at Pomton's office. Schneider started walking meditatively toward the campus. The waitress began joyfully to clear the table, where Denby had left a huge tip, courtesy of the Winthrop Foundation.

Schneider strolled, and pondered Denby's advice. He decided he didn't want to go to the campus, because for the moment he didn't want to meet his colleagues. He didn't want to go home, because he didn't want to meet Henrietta. What he wanted was to think. So he struck toward the open countryside, under the gray November sky, somehow strengthened and sustained by having cut his lectures.

It was all very well for Denby. Schneider was prepared to trust Denby's judgment that this farce was a coast-to-coast operation. A bona fide call to Barker wouldn't really help. When in Rome, show the Romans a trick or two. But he could think of no trick, or none the Romans didn't already know. Or quit Rome? But Schneider loved and respected the teaching art.

Take it lightly. That might be good advice at that. Hadn't he, as a matter of fact, turned into a conscientious bore? And if he had, why on earth should Henrietta respect him? Or Pomton? Or, for that matter, his colleagues and his own students? He must take a stronger line with the department he headed.

~IV~

THE HISTORY DEPARTMENT had finished its indifferent luncheon and was sipping its coffee. An air of well-fed gentility temporarily united what was traditionally a quarrelsome department. Each member was basking in the atmosphere of important leisure that the Triangle Club always managed to afford. The weak December sunshine filtered through the mullioned windows and brought out the false lines of the paneled private dining room. It also sharpened the contrasts in the familiar faces of Schneider's colleagues.

Cardwell, the only full professor in the department except Schneider, had by reason of that fact no further promotion to seek and no reason to pull his punches. Although he was no Republican, a streak of sheer cussedness in Cardwell had led him to write two books, one whitewashing the Harding Administration in so far as anybody could achieve such a feat, and one that acrimoniously discredited Woodrow Wilson. In both cases he had uncovered materials not hitherto used, chiefly because they had always seemed to be of questionable relevance. Since staking out these two preserves he had had his hands too full defending them against late-comers to write a third book. His defense took the form of devastating book reviews in learned journals, and he had by this means wrecked more than one budding career. His long hatchet face was deeply furrowed by these scholarly battles and his tongue dripped venom. Schneider had always disliked him.

Quimby had specialized in English history. Still an associate professor, he had almost completed a social history of England in the fifteenth century. For this magnum opus he had ransacked the British Museum, picking up any odds and ends that might discredit his predecessors in the field. He counted confidently on his forthcoming book to prize loose a full professorship here or elsewhere. Meanwhile, he bored his undergraduate students with minute and laborious accounts of his travels in England. He was a chunky fellow, with vulgar, blunt hands and a stubborn, undershot jaw.

Linton was nondescript. He had been driven into the Middle Ages, Schneider had concluded, by his dislike of his own age and by the fact that he saw no place else to hide. He would have gone clear back to Rome had not his sharp eyes detected there the same cultural cheapness that he saw in America today. He hated his students, primarily because they had been born since the thirteenth century. His cadaverous, yellow face showed a fine scorn for the generation among whom he had been condemned to live. He was working on a book that would defend serfdom against both absolute monarchy and the democracy that had overthrown it. In rank he was an associate professor.

Pratt, although only an assistant professor, was the best-known authority on ancient Sicilian coins to be found between the Mississippi and the Rockies—except for Texas, where a retired oil magnate had bought up huge quantities of Sicilian coins and would not let Pratt examine them. On the oil magnate's death, his collection would go to the University of Texas. When that happy event should occur, Pratt was confident, he could quickly extend his empire of knowledge to the Rio Grande and even make inroads on academic reputations in the East. He had never published a book, but monographs in learned journals fairly poured from his office. He had no other interest in money but Sicilian coins and, of course, his own salary check. Even so, Schneider found in him a vein of practicality that always surprised him.

Greer, also an assistant professor, was primarily a bibliographer, in the field of modern European history, Schneider's field. He secretly regarded Schneider as a merely amateur scholar and was critical of the sources Schneider had used in his published works. He sat opposite Schneider now, young but stoop-shouldered, peering intently at him through the thick lenses of his steel-rimmed spectacles.

For some years Schneider had hoped to make these departmental luncheons regular monthly affairs, and the distraught home life of most of the historians had been a powerful argument on his side. But unless he came armed with a carefully thought-out agenda for discussion, the luncheon had invariably degenerated into a dogfight, and it was not always easy to think of subjects interesting enough to make discussion genuine yet sufficiently neutral to arouse no slumbering jealousies. Schneider, who had planned this luncheon before his enlightening talk with Denby, had felt he had compelling reason for risking even a dogfight. His recent interview with the President had convinced him that he could not hope to resuscitate his dead life by an injection of salary increase. On the other hand, he had not the courage to desert his wife. In the circumstances he had decided to throw himself with renewed vigor into his work. He knew that the recognized method for renewing one's vigor in academic life was to reorganize the departmental course offerings. It was a way one could never count on, but certainly one could count on no other. His only remaining problem was whether to warn the other eight members of his department that course offerings would be discussed, thereby risking the formation of blocs and cabals ahead of time, or whether to spring it on them after lunch, thereby risking the charge of tyranny. He decided to risk the charge of tyranny and count on what he felt was a natural skill in diplomacy to meet revolt and sidetrack it. Now that the coffee was here, the moment had come.

"My reason for suggesting that we hold one of our periodic luncheons," he began, "was not merely that we enjoy lunching together. I think we ought to consider from time to time the course offerings of the department. Is our work so arranged as to guarantee maximum departmental efficiency? That is a question which I know interests the President and which largely decides how he will react to my recommendations for appointments and promotions."

The last phrase, he noted with satisfaction, had been well chosen. It had completely eliminated the slight stir of limbs and feet which is normal to men who turn from eating to ideas. At the same time it served as a reminder, and a very modestly put reminder, that in the last analysis Schneider held the whip hand in matters of promotion. That fact, he hoped, would help maintain the kind of discipline this afternoon without which he scarcely dared appeal to the common good.

"I am not speaking of our graduate work. I regret, as doubtless you do, that there are several duplications among the graduate courses which the department offers. We all know the reason. It has been our policy to let members of the department offer pretty much what they chose in the way of graduate courses. And while we tried through the years to recruit men who would fill gaps in our graduate offerings, at times we deliberately sacrificed balance in order to get the man we wanted.

"I am talking today about our undergraduate courses. There some confusion reigns and it is a confusion that we can eliminate if we pool our best wisdom. Our catalogue shows the following undergraduate offerings—" and he put on his glasses—"History 5: General American History. A survey of our national history from its colonial origins to the present, with particular emphasis upon the social and cultural. Mr. Cardwell

"History 15: General English History. English history from the period of Roman Britain to the Atomic Age. Mr. Quimby

"History 25: Modern Europe. 1453 to the present, with emphasis on diplomatic history. Mr. Schneider

"History 35: The Middle Ages. Primarily cultural in scope and economic in emphasis. Mr. Linton

"History 45: Ancient Times. The Egyptians, the Babylonians, the Hebrews, the Assyrians, the Persians, the Greeks and Romans. Mr. Pratt

"Those are our courses. And the fact is, gentlemen, that every one of those courses shows lower registration than last year. That means cutting off the potential supply of graduate students at the source. And it is precisely the field of graduate studies that the administration is committed to develop. If we can't create the conditions that will make it possible to expand graduate history, then the expansion will take place in the other social sciences. Nast reports that every single undergraduate course in economics is growing. So must ours. Gentlemen, I have several suggestions to make. But I should like to hear from other members of the department first."

"Let's not model ourselves on Nast and his economists," said Linton dryly. "I am only a humble historian, not a television star or a journalist. The courses in economics in this University have been jazzed up to where they compete with the movies. My History 35 gives an undergraduate a picture of the Middle Ages according to the latest historical scholarship. But it doesn't profess to amuse him. The Middle Ages were not amusing."

"I don't agree," cut in Greer. Greer had no undergraduate course of his own and was exceedingly anxious to be assigned one. "I don't agree at all. The Middle Ages could be made damned amusing. Undergraduates would lap it up. And not by debauching it the way the economists do either. Simply by presenting the right kind of materials for the undergraduate mind."

"When the undergraduate deigns to study medieval history," said Linton coldly, "I suspect that the 'right kind of material' for him is medieval history. Not incidents chosen from it for their entertainment value."

"Gentlemen," said Schneider, "I don't think there is a genuine disagreement here. Obviously, we have got to teach the truth, whatever the economists do. But equally obviously, all of us charged with teaching undergraduate courses are aware that the truth must be entertainingly presented. The undergraduate has a right to be interested. Every human mind has that right, I take it."

"I suspect," drawled Pratt, "that you are overlooking one important difference between undergraduate history and undergraduate economics. The average undergraduate doesn't want to know what happened, even if you tell it entertainingly. He wants to know what's going to happen. To him. Economically. Nast's course in People's Capitalism makes him feel he is getting hot dope. The Babylonians can't compete with hot dope, and in History 45 I don't try to make 'em do it."

"But they can," cried Greer excitedly, with a sudden vision of the popular course he could make out of the Babylonians. "And the Egyptians—my God!"

Pratt flushed, started to speak, kept quiet. His friend Quimby came to the rescue. Quimby taught General English History and had suffered a smaller drop in registration this year than any man in the department.

"Your real problem, gentlemen, appears to me not to be that of making truth entertaining but of keeping truth from being superficial, if I may say so. Cardwell, here, has a whole academic year in which to trace the development of one country and a young one at that." Cardwell taught General American History. "But I have to cover English history from Roman Britain to the present in precisely the same number of lectures. The result is necessarily superficial, and nobody knows it better than I."

From Schneider's point of view this last contribution was the most unfortunate yet. For his own private plan had been to wring from this meeting permission to split his Modern Europe into two undergraduate courses, 1453 to 1815 and 1815 to the present respectively. But if Cardwell started claiming that a year was too little for one country, Britain, he would merely caricature in advance Schneider's natural desire to have more than a year for twenty countries. Should he come in at this point? Too late.

"The country I spend a year on," Caldwell was saying, narrow-eyed and flushed, "is the student's own country. He has already studied its history in high school: a second superficial survey of it would be preposterous. Moreover, as a citizen and a voter he needs to know its history as he knows the history of no other country. The fact that History 5 is the largest of our undergraduate courses suggests that the students don't feel it is inflated."

Schneider made a rapid estimate of the psychological strains that had developed and concluded desperately that he had as good a chance today as he would have at any other time. They always quarreled like this. And Quimby's point about superficiality was out now. It had not only spoiled Schneider's approach today: it had spoiled it for good. Once Quimby made a point of his own, he never forgot it. While Schneider was deciding, Linton stated the case again for teaching the truth even though the truth was generally dull. Cardwell spoke of the disadvantage of teaching foreign histories to students who had not mastered the history of their own country. His point was that an undeveloped historical imagination found it easiest to begin at home, and the moral he drew was that his own undergraduate course, History 5, might well be prerequisite for all the other undergraduate courses in history. It was a bad tactical blunder, since it necessarily stacked everybody against him from then on. Greer made another privateer effort to seize an undergraduate course from somewhere. And that gave Schneider an idea, a very good idea.

"I think Greer might profitably have a go at undergraduate teaching," he announced out of a blue sky. "And since I daresay none of you people would care just now to surrender your undergraduate work, what about my splitting 25 into two courses? Greer could give 1453 to 1815, and I could do 1815 to the present."

It really was a clever move. By an act of self-sacrifice, he had placed himself in a strong position. Greer would naturally prefer to have had the nineteenth century—it was his field. But it was Schneider's field too, and he was determined to keep it. And beggars could not be choosers. Meanwhile he had not committed himself as to how long he would let Greer have 1453 to 1815, and in a year or two he would take it back. That would allow him to give the two periods in alternate years, and that in turn would give him the time to go into detail, detail which he wanted and the student needed.

Only Quimby was obstinate, as one might have predicted. He thought that Greer would do a splendid job on 1453 to 1815. He only wished there were another man on the staff whose field was English history. Then he could divide England at 1689 and really give the students what they needed. Since he was the only member of the department equipped to do English history, perhaps it would be wise to split it at 1689 and let him teach both parts in alternate years. Certainly, if a period as brief as 1453 to the present needed dividing—and he gladly conceded it did—then England, from Roman Britain on, needed it more. In order to have a bargaining point he tentatively added that, since the background of our civilization was British, his double-barreled revamped course might be made prerequisite to American.

Cardwell coiled to spring. But before he could speak, Schneider observed acidly that it was a good deal simpler to tell the story of one nation, even for two thousand years, than to weave together the story of a score of nations for nearly five crowded centuries. Cardwell did not let him finish.

"Precisely why a student should have to study English history under Quimby for two years before he can safely be told about the United States, I don't profess to know. Precisely why Quimby should be allowed to spend two years telling young men and women about his travels in England—"

"Dr. Cardwell!" Schneider's voice was sharp. "Please. No personalities. The issues we are dealing with this afternoon are scholarly interests: they are not personal interests."

"Is that so!" cried Cardwell recklessly. "Well, they sound pretty damned personal to me." The allusion was to the tardiness of his next promotion, and everybody, those who hoped he would get it sooner and those who hoped he would never get it, understood perfectly. "You personally want students to spend two years instead of one studying European history under you with emphasis on diplomatic history. You won't deny the diplomatic emphasis is personal, I hope? Poor Greer here personally wants to teach a few undergraduates, so he can steer them into his own graduate courses instead of yours. But he's too naïve to realize you won't let him keep the course when he gets it. Europe from 1453! Why don't you let the poor devil teach it from 1450? Why 1453?"

"Only because Constantinople fell in 1453," answered Schneider dryly.

"I rather thought it did. Even so, I'm told its prospects were gloomy by 1450, and what's three years to men like us, accustomed to centuries? But while you are busy driving a hard bargain with Greer, Quimby tries to slip in and spread his General English over two years without even bribing Greer to back him up. Do you think Linton and Pratt and I are going to lend ourselves to such petty machinations? In a pig's eye!"

"Dr. Cardwell," thundered Schneider, "I must ask you to stop ascribing motives to other people!"

"After all, he's a historian: he's paid to do it," remarked Linton nastily.

Pratt waved all these angry remarks aside with an air of getting down to business.

"I doubt," he said, determined to try understatement, "that there can be any common agreement in the department on redistributing our undergraduate courses. That leaves us with a very real problem still in our laps, the problem our chairman brought up. The economists, and to some extent the other social scientists, are draining off students from our undergraduate courses. That means ultimately drying up our graduate courses and wrecking our whole program of expansion.

"What can we do? Reshuffling undergraduate courses, even if we could agree, is no answer. The courses have got to be made more attractive. Ideally, of course, the Curriculum Committee would require one undergraduate history course of every candidate for the bachelor's degree. You know and I know that this should be done, quite aside from the problem of finding students to go into graduate history. It's an outrage that a man can get a B.A. from this university without studying a line of history. But you know also, as well as I do, that the Curriculum Committee we have now would never consent. So that's out.

"Our courses have got to win, then, in an open market. I agree with Linton in declining to jazz up our subject as the economists do. I personally decline. I would rather see history dropped from the curriculum."

He settled back to take in the full effect of this last courageous statement. There was general nodding. It was as if a band of lonely men had made a last stand for truth in a world that no longer cared for truth. Only one member of the group showed a moment of weakness. It was Greer.

"And for God's sake, what would we teach, then?" he inquired.

"We would either find positions in other institutions or we would sell used cars," declared Pratt, undaunted. "But it needn't come to that. The place to make courses attractive is not in the classroom, where intellectual integrity is at stake. The place to make them attractive is in the catalogue, where some good sales talk can be used with complete propriety. And I think our course announcements are appallingly dull. Under each listing of an undergraduate course we ought to have a snappy blurb that would awaken the student's interest. I don't even see any necessity for pedantic accuracy in the description of a course, any more than in the title of a book. Once they elect one of our courses and get the rest of their schedule made out, they won't drop, no matter how disappointed they are. It's too much red tape. Besides, they won't be disappointed. This staff can be counted on not to disappoint them. What is disappointing them now, and boring them, is not our teaching but our horrible, dry course announcements.

"I should like to say a word, even so, about our teaching. I see no reason why an undergraduate lecture can't start with a jest or a colloquialism, without going economist on the problem. Something that arrests the attention and that allows the instructor to get in a half hour's good teaching before the student awakes to the fact that he is learning.

"Finally, there is the matter of grades. A college student chooses his course for one of three reasons: either he likes the professor, or he likes the hour the course comes at, or he thinks the course is not unreasonably difficult. There is no use kidding ourselves about this. No undergraduate gives a damn about what subject he is studying if only these three claims are satisfactorily met. Well, we meet two of them. Fortunately, no history courses come at unpopular hours. The earliest is ten o'clock. This staff enjoys reasonable student popularity—all the student popularity a staff can enjoy without stooping to the means employed by men like Nast. And a good joke at the beginning of a lecture will clinch that popularity. But, gentlemen, if you want to know the real reason history is evaporating at this university, it is because the failures in our department are higher than in almost any other department in arts and sciences. Translated into terms which I hope our economists will understand, we are selling a better article than our competitors and at a lower price. We have reduced our margin of profit to the point where we are being forced out of business. This commercial statement of the problem, gentlemen, is as distasteful to me as it must be to you; but the time has come when this department has got to be realistic or wither away. So long as the student is allowed to elect what he likes, he occupies the privileged position of a customer, and the customer is always right. My final word, then, is that we should reluctantly ease up on our grading."

"But," said Schneider, "I don't see how I can ease any further than I've eased already. I'm passing people now who can't write, can't spell, can't punctuate, can't think. It's shocking."

"That's the affair of the English department," said Pratt firmly. "They have a required freshman course. Let them use it. It's not our function to grade on English. You may be sure the economists are assuming no responsibility in the matter. All we can hope to give undergraduates is a few historical facts, and not many of those. Our first responsibility is to save the department, not to save American education."

"It's shocking," repeated Schneider with genuine horror.

"Of course it's shocking," said Pratt. "But it's quite possible that undergraduate education is past helping. Unless," he finished sarcastically, "you think the Curriculum Committee will do something constructive."

"But you are saying," said Schneider, "that in the long run student opinion decides how much work and what kind of work students need do to get a degree."

"That's precisely what I'm saying. And I'm hoping we will recognize it. University policy is made by the President because the President has all the gravy to distribute. And the President depends on the good will of the students. It's like the government of the United States under Roosevelt. Labor controlled the President, and the President controlled business."

"But the students don't elect the President. The trustees elect the President."

"Only if he is good at getting more and more students."

The inexorable logic of Pratt's argument won. Linton, who was not the man to hold out against odds, recognized that the game was up.

"Pratt's right, and we all know it. I therefore suggest that the chairman appoint a committee to draw up new catalogue statements of our undergraduate courses. And I heartily endorse Pratt's suggestion that those courses not only be made as attractive as they can be without sacrificing their intellectual integrity, but that they be made definitely easier."

There was general agreement on this program and, as the hour was late and several of those present had afternoon seminars, Schneider made it clear, by rising, that the meeting was over. The matter of whether his Modern Europe should be divided with Greer had not been definitely decided upon, but he suspected that sending around a memorandum to be penciled would get everybody's approval except Cardwell's. Even Cardwell might by now be so ashamed of his behavior at luncheon that he would sign. And Schneider's main objective in reorganizing the course offerings of the department had in a sense been achieved: Schneider considered it essential in academic work to get together occasionally and exchange ideas. It gave everybody something to think about, and universities ought to do just that.

And yet, he could hardly believe that Denby, for example, would be much impressed by this luncheon, quite aside from the fact that the food was bad. Could any one of these undergraduate courses, or all of them taken together, hope to touch the central problem? A mob of largely illiterate graduates streamed annually from these halls to furnish leadership—the word was a must in every Commencement oration—to a confused and bewildered society. If the University could revive the kind of teaching that could cure the higher illiteracy, would any of its graduates find it unreasonably difficult, over some long week end, to learn everything of consequence that any one of these courses contained?

The coast-to-coast operation, the squirrel cage from which Denby himself had now happily escaped, was still a squirrel cage, and Schneider was inside it. Worse than that, nobody had forced him to enter it twenty years ago—nobody, that is, but himself. And worse even than that, he had helped build it, or rebuild it, or refurbish it, or rebait it. He had just held a departmental luncheon, and what had come out of it but fresh bait? Something to think about? Something to shudder at.

V

Nast prepared to take on another man in economics, and to take him on for the second semester. This would make an even dozen. Since Nast had been head of the department, he had increased the professorial staff from five to eleven; the graduate students from fifteen to thirty-seven. True, most of these graduate students held generous fellowships and in that sense were ringers. But so are most graduate students, as Nast well knew. Moreover, it was to his credit that he had wrested a plurality—indeed almost a majority—of the graduate fellowships from the other departments in social science. Finally, he was getting jobs for his doctoral candidates and slowly building up an academic empire, not of course in the sense of the Chicago empire or the Columbia empire, but an empire just the same. He had placed graduates as far south as New Orleans and as far west as Denver. He had too good judgment to invade the East: he had no intention—yet—of bucking Columbia, any more than Hitler would have started out by attacking the British Empire.

But he inwardly believed that the Columbia empire was rotten at the core; he had his own dreams at Berchtesgaden. At meetings of the American Economics Association no other single delegate was more in demand for private conferences. And wherever he appeared publicly, knots of other delegates glanced toward him enviously.

His domestic policies, so to speak, derived powerful support from his foreign policies. The fact that his desk was a clearing house for teaching posts and even for posts with swank research organizations and private business corporations gave him absolute control of his graduate students. They knew that they would be taken care of if they won his favor. They knew likewise that, if they failed to win it, they would not even get a degree, no matter how strong a dissertation they wrote. For Nast had convinced his colleagues that the common good of the department required that all graduates be well placed. One single graduate wandering about the country advertising his joblessness could break down the morale acquired by years of brilliant work. The moral was clear: never grant the Ph.D. to a man until you were sure he could get a job, no matter how well he satisfied the so-called requirements.

Three years before, a couple of the department's least personable graduate students were apparently heading straight for Ph.D.'s and unemployment. Nast had promptly finessed a postponement of their degrees until he could get them placed. The two students had insisted: they had met all stated requirements for the doctorate and they intended to get it—now. In one of his rare false steps, Nast had admitted that the department's only reason for holding up the doctorates was the absence of suitable jobs for them to go to. Whereupon, the two students in effect told Nast where to go with his jobs; declared that they had a right to their doctorates even if famine should later drive them to eat their own diplomas; and threatened to take their case to the Committee on Graduate Studies, several of whose members were violently jealous of Nast and in ambush to throw him on a technicality. Nast judged it wise to retreat; but he covered his retreat by a desperate, and successful, search for the needed jobs. So, in a sense, his principle and his power remained intact.

This power that Nast held over his graduate students automatically assured him power over his colleagues in the department. Besides, Nast had proven himself the ablest departmental chairman on the campus when it came to securing promotions and salary increases for his staff; and this quite properly guaranteed the loyalty of his staff. For Nast held a whip hand over the President. Nast's off-campus activities included cultivating tycoons, and so far as endowment for the University was concerned, Nast had cultivated fruitfully. That was the true basis of his department's strength in research. That was why what they wrote printers printed and postmen distributed throughout the land. And, although every man in the department knew who got these gifts, Nast had never tried to rob Pomton of the credit with his trustees—yet. All he wanted for the moment was a whip hand, plus his prospects when Pomton retired.

Meanwhile Nast's television talks on investments, his newspaper column on economic trends, his frequent appearances on the lecture platform, all conspired to make him the best-known scholar on the faculty. Nast touched the public on its pocketbook nerve and the public realized, as it never had, the justification for research and the thrill that comes to any society which dedicates itself to the disinterested search for truth. Nast knew his public. He had revised the Aristotelian statement that man is a rational animal, to read: Man is an acquisitive animal. And the success he had achieved on that hypothesis proved to his own satisfaction how much more profound his statement was than Aristotle's.

Now he was ready to take on his twelfth man. There are ways and ways of taking on a twelfth man, but Nast knew the right way. First he called a meeting of the department. There was no question with the economists of monthly luncheons or empty speculation over coffee in the private dining room of the Triangle Club. Their meetings, whatever the occasion, were business meetings. They always met in Nast's office, and while Nast presided, Nast's secretary took brief minutes. Since most of the economists had been chosen in the first instance by Nast, and since all of them had sat at his feet, they were by heredity and environment, so to speak, his intellectual children. Which meant that they were brief to speak, quick to act. A meeting of the department was like the practice of a well-drilled football team. Young, clean-cut, square-jawed, they offered a pretty contrast to Schneider and his stooped historians, and they knew it. Under no illusions as to the democratic process, they now expressed their general will incisively and handed over their powers of action to a committee to be appointed by the chairman, a committee which would work, at least nominally, with the President.

The committee met next day. (Here again, had the historians faced a similar problem, their committee would have met the next week. For all their preoccupation with dates, the historians had no sense of time.) In five minutes Nast had secured from his fellow committee-men their adhesion to his statement of policy. What they were after was a young man who had published at least one successful book and who had drive. His doctorate must be from a reputable university, strong in graduate economics. No questions would be asked about his previous general education. They were after a specialist, not a cultivated dilettante. A little business experience outside the academic pasture would work in a candidate's favor. As to salary, that could be negotiated. Nast had no foolish prejudices against academic haggling. He could not have respected a man who did not know how to bargain. He would not have trusted him to teach young men who must some day make their way in a world not too well understood by the scholar. Finally, while Nast classified himself as a liberal, he did not propose to burden his department with a Democrat or even a leftish Republican. It seemed to Nast only fair that those who paid the piper—and Nast knew personally the names and addresses of those who paid in his neck of the woods—should call the tune. Nast did not, of course, propose to sacrifice academic freedom. Neither did he propose to have the issue arise. The economist's job, as he saw it, was to tell the layman how money is made, or at least how our economic system produces wealth, not to reform the world. Nast left that job, with a smile, to the philosophers. He thought it germane to the problem that the department of philosophy at most of the better institutions was drying up. It would never be

{53}

missed. Its eternal speculation had given way to speculation of a very different sort, a sort considerably more relevant to the needs of modern man, and a sort that Nast had one or two interesting opinions about, based on hard statistical study.

Running true to form, the economists, now in committee, had no need to write letters. One of the regular "services" which Nast had set up for the department years ago was a card-index Who's Who with relevant data on everybody in it from the point of view of hiring. For the purpose of the present meeting Nast had digested this down to a single folder of annotated names. He now began to comment on them; and the oral style he used on such occasions had been formed by assiduous reading of Worldgram, in *U.S. News and World Report,* the staccato style of the big executive, or at least the style ascribed to big executives by readers of *U.S. News.*

"Frederick Landon," he began crisply. "Warm letter from the only decent school of economics in the South. No need to name the institution. Teaches there. But no room to advance him. I think you can assume in this case they are not trying to palm off shoddy. Excellent man. I've met him. Only thing I know against him is a letter here from a Southern friend of his saying he comes of a good family. I wrote back that if we ever got him it would be for research work and teaching, not for breeding purposes. Here's his academic vita—" and he handed over a sheet. "Plenty of experience. No sign of wildcat panaceas. Lively style. Might be a sort of Stuart Chase some day, plus a brain.

"Henry Grant Thompson. Knows his stuff. Personally, I'd be interested if he didn't have a mouthful of gold teeth and a slouch. This isn't a beauty contest, but there is such a thing as minimal personality. But he's written a damned well reviewed book. Said to be a brilliant undergraduate teacher, which is neither here nor there. I'll return to him as soon as I've run quickly through the list.

"William Ridgley Kern. Harvard. Did a turn at Brookings. A little inclined to take sides. At least I judge so from a couple of men I queried. Probably quarrelsome temperament. Not necessarily fatal, if he's as good as they say. Wife's pretty painful, I'm told. And Pomton knows it. Told me she was one of the most troublesome faculty wives in the Mississippi Valley. Sharp tongue. I suspect that would determine Pomton. He has enough of those problems now. I don't blame him. Might as well be realistic. When a president engages a married man, he's taking on two faculty members, not one. One for a job and one that will be out of a job.

"Well, here's Wilkinson. You two know his story. If he didn't drink, I'd say he was a good bet. But there are limits. We don't want another Weed around this campus. Fact remains, Wilkinson does more good work on his sober days than anybody else I know does by abstaining.

"Here's a man that's going straight to the top and that would grow with this department: Charles P. Inman. You both know his stuff. But you don't know him, and I happen to know he's an awfully poor mixer. God knows, we don't demand a Rotarian; but this department has a good reputation for getting about and making contacts. No use to take on a recluse when there are good mixers available like Frederick Landon."

Nast continued crisply with a few more names, adding always the telling comment, viewing each case practically as well as intellectually. But when he finished, Bird and Turner, his fellow committeemen, were of one mind. Frederick Landon was strongly indicated. He had had unusual professional preparation, was a socially attractive bachelor, a man of the world, a witty lecturer, and, despite his youth, had written two books that even the lay public read with appreciation. It looked as if he were that rare bird in academic life, a chap you would really enjoy spending Sunday afternoon with. Bird liked Landon's reputation for hard work, and Turner liked him because he wasn't stuffy. He sounded made for the job. His special research interests—which were broader than most scholars' anyhow—fitted in nicely with the graduate program.

Nast was pleased. Like poor Schneider, he had known before he called his department together precisely what he wanted. He had wanted Frederick Landon. But, unlike Schneider, he had a well-disciplined department back of him and heavy patronage to back up the discipline. Unlike Schneider, he did not go in for friendly lunch-eons or the democratic process. He had got his committee in record time and he had appointed committeemen he could trust, since both Bird and Turner were definitely in the running for promotion, and sweetly reasonable.

But his reason for wanting Frederick Landon was a new one in his experience and one which, precisely because it was quixotic, the practical chairman hugely relished. He wanted Landon because Dor-othy wanted him. Ever since the scuttling of the *Mayflower,* Doro-thy had been working fast. She had been busy salvaging pilgrims; and her terms were generous. Whoever publicly snubbed Henrietta Schneider could be sure of immediate and solicitous rescue. In that chaotic social world where faculty wives are made or broken, Doro-thy was building an empire quite as formidable as the one her hus-band had constructed through the department of economics. Nast watched her admiringly and realized what had drawn him to her. It is true, their weapons were different. Nast was a male, an econo-mist, and an acquisitive animal. He worked through jobs landed, books printed, gifts bagged, and swift reprisals. Dorothy preferred flattery. Within a month she had said something nice to every mem-ber of the faculty and to the more deserving of the faculty wives, and they loved it. Most of them denounced her flattery publicly as being a dangerous thing and even cited instances of its corrupting influence. But they denounced it just as they sank beneath its spell, like a drunk-ard who denounces the demon drink as he slithers beneath the table.

Even Nast would have disapproved of her methods, had she been a man. But she was a soft, helpless, adorable little woman from Georgia; and if she avenged Sherman thirty times over, it was be-cause the hardy descendants of Sherman's men would rather sur-render to her than remain free. In addition, she was the prettiest woman in the community and dressed well. She dressed expensively—Nast saw to that. And she dressed smartly—Dorothy saw to that. Nast had watched the battle across teacups, at tennis matches, among bridge tables. It was ghastly, but it was lovely. Where Nast decimated, Dorothy exterminated. He who had known the bloodlust that comes from bayoneting the enemy in their own trenches, now beheld the advantages in terms of tidiness of deluging them with a sweet gas that made them lie down, smiling and helpless, like little children at bedtime.

'Way down in Georgia Dorothy had been born knowing one thing. Nothing adds greater luster to a salon than a young, handsome bachelor. He is what Nast would doubtless have called capital, for you can use him at six per cent, nay, in this case sixty, without diminishing his total value: you have him as a sort of second husband but without the monotonous intimacy of the first. And in a crisis you can spend him outright by a crucial marriage alliance.

As soon as Dorothy learned that Nast was looking into Frederick Landon, now teaching at a Southern university, she had written several important letters. The answers she got convinced her, long before the department of economics had appointed a committee, that they badly needed Freddie Landon. So she told Nast she wanted him. Nast had the strong man's dislike of meddling women. His first reaction was negative. But Dorothy made it clear that she would judge his strength by whether he could impose Freddie Landon on his department. In fact she implied that she would judge his strength by how quickly he could impose Freddie on them. And Nast had for the first time tasted the illicit joy of tyranny, the joy of guiding the state to suit a mistress's whim. It seemed to him suddenly that the power he had previously exercised had been so pale, so virtuous, so adolescent that it cloyed. Perhaps he had increased and conserved it precisely because he had never subjected it to any real strain. It was delicious to risk it all as loveplay with his bride. And, most delicious of all, he won without arousing so much as a suggestion of revolt. He delivered Freddie to her, with a tremendous flourish and at no real cost. It was a triumph, and it was the sort of triumph that only an economist could savor: a triumph at bargain rates.

It would perhaps have been unnatural if Nast had not felt some misgivings later. The habits of a lifetime are hard to break, and Nast's habits had been those of prudence and providence. The department of economics had not been constructed on whims, even on whims that came from Georgia, dressed well, and appealed to one's personal pride. Moreover, just as Nast was beginning to feel he might have been less precipitate, Henrietta Schneider began to play Cassandra. Henrietta, despite the poor judgment she had recently displayed in picking an antagonist, was nobody's fool. Although certainly not from the South herself, she knew two upright New England women whose husbands had accepted jobs at Southern universities until jobs opened that would take them back to civilization. And by strange good fortune one of them was at the university which Freddie Landon now graced. Henrietta shortly issued a communiqué to her dwindling field forces that Freddie was a drunkard and a Lothario. And one of her lieutenants, the female McCarthy of the Mayflower party, added that he was a Communist. It was Dorothy herself who first relayed the story to Nast, and Nast joined her in laughing at it. Really, Henrietta had overshot her mark: if she had used either one of her epithets without the other!

But, although Nast could see perfectly the foolish malice in this libelous name-calling, the libel served to remind him how little he had checked on Freddie Landon in his desire to give Dorothy what she wanted and to give it quickly. True, negotiations were not formally complete and would not be complete until Freddie had come to the University and conferred with the President. And even then, his visit might be simple telegram-waving for a better salary where he was. But, granted that Freddie's visit was in good faith, it would be difficult for Nast to retract without infuriating Dorothy and losing prestige with his department. He had been so positive in his praise of Freddie. On mature reflection, he saw the folly of allowing Henrietta's wicked gossip to shake his nerve; he could, after all, withdraw if Freddie's visit in any way confirmed her gossip.

Freddie's visit took place late in December and was made a pivotal move in Dorothy's campaign. There was a very formal tea to which everybody was invited who was not a convicted Schneiderite and which finally swung a handful of neutrals into line. Then there was a small, cozy dinner for members of the grand party council. Freddie had caught the spirit of both and had shown that he understood the problems of sponsorship as only a man of the world can. The gallant deference he showed Dorothy and the delicate touch of more masculine deference he showed Nast were precisely, Nast felt, what neither drunkards nor Lotharios nor Communists show anybody. He deferred to her wit and to Nast's learning. He had, in short, an exquisite social sense.

Henrietta's gossip promptly boomeranged and her stock reached an all-time low. It was not merely mothers with marriageable daughters who were impressed with Freddie as an addition to the faculty. Every faculty wife within flattering distance experienced that pleasant elation which married women feel when the arrival of a virile bachelor in the community seems to threaten the sanctity of every home. It was a thrill unspoiled by any genuine threat of rape or adultery. And they reacted to it exactly as men react to a not quite real threat of war. Nobody wants such things to happen except harlots and generals. Yet the knowledge that they may happen makes life just a little more worth living. The delicious sense of anticipation which made that Christmas the perfect Christmastide confirmed Dorothy in her judgment that Freddie was the man the University needed. And a day's careful observation made Nast laugh at his recent fears. When it was finally announced that Freddie's acceptance was definite, and even that he would join the faculty in February, in time for the second semester, some people said Pomton had an extraordinary flair for building up his faculty. But the day's round of teas, bridge, and dinners would have convinced a visitor that it was not really Pomton who got the most credit for the confidence with which the faculty wives faced the challenge of a new semester. It was Dorothy Nast. In addition to her personal charm, they said, Dorothy Nast had accepted the duties of the wife of a departmental head more gracefully and efficiently than one would have thought possible in a girl so young and so apparently irresponsible.

Henrietta had too much iron in her to admit permanent defeat; but though the iron kept her going, it somehow managed to enter Schneider's soul. And since it was her iron, not his, it entered his soul as an extraneous body, always an uncomfortable sort of thing.

In short, he had to pay for his wife's leonine courage with increased acidity and taciturnity. The pain was all the greater because he found Dorothy Nast pleasantly disturbing, as indeed did most of his colleagues. And he found Freddie Landon a charming, civilized fellow. No doubt Landon was impressionable so far as pretty women were concerned; and like more than one Charlestonian, he showed no recalcitrance before a drink. But Schneider liked him.

The fact remained that Landon, by joining the faculty and strengthening Dorothy's forces immeasurably, had unwittingly dealt Schneider a frightful blow. A henpecked professor of history, depressed by bad health and harassed by debt, suddenly found domestic discipline tightened by his tyrant's increased moral tension. To escape martial law, he almost longed for Henrietta's victory over these two charming young people.

~VI~

HENRIETTA was washing the dishes after Sunday dinner when Schneider entered the kitchen. He looked thoroughly embarrassed.

"That was Mrs. Nast on the phone," said Henry. "She wanted to speak with you. I asked if I might take a message. So now she wants to know if you and I can attend a cocktail party Saturday which she and Nast are giving for Frederick Landon. She said they were anxious to have all the department heads in the division of social science. And of course their wives. I'm to phone back."

"I won't go," said Henrietta. Deftly, and more rapidly than ever, she polished a glass. "I won't go."

Her back, which she always held as straight as a soldier's, was now stiffer than usual. Her long, finely shaped head, with the severe hairdo, was tilted proudly back. Her pale-blue, sea-captain's eyes looked at and through her husband.

"It's insolent of her to ask me."

Here we go again, thought Henry.

"Wouldn't it have been rather insulting of her not to?" he asked mildly.

"I don't see that."

"Well, if she had invited me without you, she would have been uncouth. If she had failed to invite the head of the history department, Nast—who loathes me—would have objected, and I think rightly. The whole party is purely official, isn't it?"

Henrietta was a hard infighter; but she was not irrational. On the contrary, she had what men call, for understandable reasons, a masculine intelligence. And she was usually just.

"Very well," she said coldly. Then she suddenly started. "Good heavens! What am I thinking of? I promised Linda Pratt faithfully that I'd come to her birthday party then."

"Then let me tell Mrs. Nast that. You've a perfect alibi. If she's obligated to invite the department heads in her husband's division, you certainly have obligations to the wives of the men in my department. I'll go alone."

"Are you sure I oughtn't to excuse myself early and join you?"

"There's no earthly reason to," said Schneider. "All you need is an alibi."

"Maybe you'd rather go alone anyhow," she said, her face bent over the dishes again, her fine, strong hands plying their work expertly.

"Nonsense! But I'll go for a while."

"She's very pretty," said Henrietta.

"That has nothing to do with it. I'll phone her back."

When he had phoned, he returned.

"Let me help," he said.

But she pushed him firmly away.

"When the children eat out, it's nothing," she said, her head still well lowered.

"Where'd you say they'd gone?"

"To a schoolmate's birthday party. They'll be back soon."

In the unnatural calm, Schneider read a while in a book he had to review. And soon enough, with a great chatter, in came his three small daughters, Elsie, Charity, and Jane. With a whoop they fell on him and started, all three speaking at once, to tell him about their party.

"They had b'loons, and we busted 'em!" shouted little Jane, bringing her fat, dimpled hands sharply together to show him how you break a balloon at a party.

He listened with one ear, while they climbed over him and prattled. We have little, he thought, to do with our own lives. When I was a boy, I adored blond hair on girls, and violet-blue eyes. So I married Henrietta, who has dark hair and pale blue eyes. When we were married, I hoped for a son. So I have gotten myself no son, but three boisterous little daughters. As for Henrietta, the little rich girl, she was to study music. So she lost her father, her mother lost his fortune, and now she washes dishes, scrubs floors, makes clothes for herself and three children, goes a bit rigid, holds her head high, and wars on Dorothy Nast.

Moreover, he thought, she magically finds time to cultivate her mind, maybe a little self-consciously, but still she does it. She was taught that you do that till you die. Dorothy Nast was never taught such things. She was taught to look pretty and mind your manners, chile. Now, he thought, while the three fat little daughters clambered over him like bear cubs, Henrietta is hurt and a shade sulky because I am going to the Nasts' cocktail party. But, then, everything hurts Henrietta these days—as, indeed, everything hurts me.

So from Sunday to the following Saturday the coming cocktail party stood between them, unmentioned. Then Saturday came; and Schneider set off, with a light heart, for Dorothy's.

In this collection of gray academic people, his hostess looked blindingly beautiful, and the interior she had created in this bleak frame house, which Nast had proudly bought for his bride, was charming. True, Schneider loathed parties of this sort. But his imagination now came to his aid: it swept his fellow guests away, even Freddie Landon, the very personable and pleasant guest of honor, whom Schneider liked; even his host, Nast, whom he had always heartily disliked. Schneider's imagination simply shoved open the double storm door that had shut out a near blizzard raging outside. Still clutching their drinks and screaming to each other to make themselves heard, as people do at cocktail parties, his fellow guests were blown down the street like unwanted, withered and dry autumn leaves, until they had disappeared; and Dorothy Nast and Schneider were left alone, sitting by this open fire, chatting pleasantly. Then, to his amazement, the February snow one now saw through the French windows was whisked away by this same powerful imagination of his, the fire on the hearth died down, a brilliant sun shone on the terrace outside, and he and Dorothy, still chatting but more intimately now, strolled out to inspect the spring flowers.

Schneider's imagination broke under the strain; he came down to earth with a thud, or rather down to the floor of this crowded sitting room, in a meaningless babel of academic gossip. Dorothy had only fifteen minutes ago achieved the impossible, the unheard of: men were talking to women and vice versa; a millennial academic tradition had been ignored and thus temporarily vitiated. Now it reasserted itself: by some sociological law which Milton here could doubtless formulate in the correct professional jargon, these two antipathetic elements were now, despite his hostess's deftness, separating themselves out. The men were gathering at one end of the room to talk shop, and the women were gathering at the other to talk personalities. Old Manley, of course, was as usual the exception—Old Manley, who had been invited to a social-science party precisely because he found professors intolerably dull and who could always find something attractive about almost any female. Over the din Schneider could hear Mrs. Weed, blissfully unaware of Schneider's presence nearby, dissecting Henrietta for Old Manley.

"I understand that all this talk about the *Mayflower*," she was saying torrentially, "is sheer fabrication. It seems her father was an uncouth businessman, a *nouveau riche*. She herself never even went to college. They say she was man crazy but had no luck and even had a hard time landing Professor Schneider. She neglects her housekeeping and gives all her time to tormenting Mrs. Nast. But to hear her talk, you'd think she was the most skillful housekeeper in this community. She has a truly vicious temper and never hesitates to strike those poor little daughters of hers in the face. She pretends to be a good Methodist, but I hear she is really a Christian Scientist and afraid to admit it. They say she is part Boston Irish and that she has twice been confined to an institution."

Out of the corner of his eye he could see Old Manley, his head bent respectfully toward the mouth that spewed this venom, his expression suave. Mrs. Weed stopped for breath, and Schneider heard Manley's gentle, ironical voice saying "Dear me, dear me."

"Of course," spat out Mrs. Weed hastily, "I don't know whether all these things are true. I merely repeat what her friends say."

"And what do her enemies say?" asked Old Manley.

Schneider chortled to himself and moved quietly away; neither would know he had heard. Mrs. Pomton, having tasted a drink and having carefully greeted all hands, was making her excuses to Dorothy and preparing to lead the President out into the blizzard and home to blessed quiet. Then they left. No sooner had the door closed than Schneider heard the thin voice of Mrs. Kendall directed at two other faculty wives.

"Wasn't it extraordinary that Mrs. Pomton should have allowed her dreadful friend, Mrs. Salton, to pour first at her last tea, while the wives of two deans stood there, helpless?"

"She is an extraordinary woman," replied one of her listeners bitterly. "A most unfortunate choice for a university president."

Ah, thought Schneider, by the time this party is over, there won't be a shred of Mrs. Pomton's flesh untorn, and even her bones will be crunched to splinters. No wonder she always goes early. She's afraid they may not be able to control their appetites for raw meat until her back is turned. And he felt better somehow about Mrs. Weed's malicious attack on poor Henrietta. After all, he thought, if you enter a bearpit, you get hurt, and there's no use taking it personally.

He was surprised to find himself listening respectfully to Kendall.

"Your generation of historians," Kendall was saying ponderously, "will be the first to make full use of the findings of group psychology. It will revolutionize—" His voice was lost in the general din.

Bird and Turner were smoking cigarettes. "No cigars, you economists, at my party! Remember," Dorothy had said playfully to her husband's crew. Thank God, they had heeded her warning. Bird and Turner were consoled by the spotlight that now played on them. Everybody present knew that they and Nast were the committee that had chosen Landon; and Freddie Landon, the guest of honor, was a terrific success. Except for Old Manley, he was the only academician present who found himself talking to women guests, known to his colleagues as "the girls," without seeming somehow to betray "the boys." The girls, prematurely old and tired, were overcome by his unpatronizing flirtatiousness. The boys liked his unmalicious wit, his lack of pretentiousness. Bird and Turner, subtly reassured by the manners of their hostess and of her guest of honor, were discussing interesting openings in various departments of economics and venturing predictions on who would seize them. Coached for several years by Nast, each of these scholars carried in his head a map of the academic employment world; each could see in his imagination colored pinheads marking the openings, and pinheads of other colors marking the ivy-covered headquarters of suitable sponsors for candidates. Each could predict at which December meeting of the American Economics Association the deals would be finally closed, the compromises worked out, and the reciprocal favors exchanged. Each knew in advance who would review whose latest books and whether the review would be sycophantic or murderous. And each was quietly sure of his own career, because that career had been arranged by Nast.

"Show me a single monograph that Bailey has written that amounts to a damn," said Turner defiantly, gesturing with one stubby hand and clutching his cocktail with the other.

"Two hundred and seventy bluebooks!" exclaimed Kendall, in another corner of the living room. "And they might as well have been written by high-school sophomores. If I hadn't made out a true-and-false section, I never would have gotten through. But the essay portion! My God! You'd think a university could make more fruitful use of a scholar's time than asking him to read that junk. We need more student assistants, I tell you—"

"Where on earth did you find that hat?" Old Manley demanded ingratiatingly of Mrs. Turner, a pitifully dumpy little woman, with a sad, yellow face. "In Paris? It reminds me of Paris—in the spring."

The tired, yellow face beamed happily for a moment under the muddy-brown hat, and Schneider would have hugged Old Manley if he could have reached him.

"I made it," said Mrs. Turner, trying to keep her voice free of the pride she felt.

Schneider was growing dizzy. The room, like most rooms in which people drink cocktails and shout competitively, was awfully warm; and one was more conscious of the warmth precisely because the blizzard outside looked so terrifyingly cold. What, he asked himself, made faculty parties so perfectly horrible? This one was far better than most, if only because Dorothy Nast illumined the room with her beauty, and Freddie Landon moved so gracefully among his fellow guests, and Old Manley had made a small, tired, yellow-faced faculty wife imagine for a moment that she wore a Paris creation. Yet even this party was pretty bad.

It was, he thought, because almost none of the guests had any technique for coping with a purely social occasion. They had come from homes where there was no speculative exchange of unnecessary ideas; no sweet rustling of the pages of a book one read simply because it contained ideas, or wit, and not because it *had* to be read if one was to "keep up with the literature" in one's field. The way the guests stood, what they did with their hands, their overemphasis when they decided to be humorous, their forced guffaws when they tardily recognized the elephantine jocosity of a neighbor, all bore tragic witness to the fact that not even Dorothy could put them wholly at ease. They would have been happy, and very much at ease, running little stores or selling harmless household gadgets from door to door. The brothers and sisters of many of them had done just such things; several had become prosperous suburbanites, able to speak casually of "my brother, who is a university professor" and to gain a little kudos from the allusion. Schneider's colleagues reminded him of the peasant families of Ireland who manage to push one boy through school and through holy orders, and to shine thereafter by reflected light.

He himself, he recalled, came of sturdy South German peasant stock. He would never adorn a drawing room. But then, he had no desire to. These people apparently had, even though the effort was torture. To get there, they had done nothing more awful than to turn a noble profession, the profession of teaching and learning, into a retail business. And yet, thought Schneider, granted that the same thing was happening to the other professions, what an appalling thing to do!

Now he became aware that this party was unlike other local faculty parties, partly because of Dorothy's charm, partly because she was making her guests forget their intellectual pretensions, if only for a moment, and be merely human, but partly, too, because the drinks were better. It was that simple. At most of the cocktail parties given here, Coca-Cola and ginger ale were available for those who could not shake off the early Methodist background of the university. The daring drank cheap California sherry, a little guiltily, and were rewarded with a headache. But Dorothy was unabashedly serving Manhattans and Old Fashioneds, and they had relaxed her guests. And although she had been able, even so, to make no silk purse out of any sow's ear present, she had given a certain gay tilt to the sows' ears.

Still, why was it faculty parties were so deeply disappointing? Was it because Schneider, deep down inside himself, always assumed that some day, spang in the middle of a tart California sherry, a conversation would suddenly occur, some sort of communion would suddenly take place? But surely, the whole point of T. S. Eliot's play was that a cocktail party in all its blaring emptiness was the nearest thing to human communion that we could now achieve. This is our sacrament, such as it is. The problem must be, mustn't it, how to stop expecting more, how to remain or become a sow's ear? When Harvard-Yale-or-Princeton threw a faculty cocktail party, did they ever achieve a Conversation? Or were the whisky and gin merely more expensive? Denby, he suspected, would report that expense was the only essential difference. Denby might add, thought Schneider, remembering their breakfast together, that the sousing was more sophisticated and hence the betrayal more terrifying.

But surely, reasoned Schneider, no matter what zenith of social gaucherie a faculty might attain to, might they not still want, however haltingly, to exchange a few ideas? Old Manley, who loathed the exaggerated Germanic specialization, with its rewards of prestige and salary, that had turned American professors into persons hired to be interested in something—Old Manley claimed the trouble with his colleagues was that they had lost their amateur standing in the world of ideas. When Old Manley thought about something, whether a woman or a poem or a philosophic concept, it was because she or it interested him: he would be thinking about it whether he received a university salary or not. But most of his colleagues, he had noticed, thought only about things that paid off, just as their students studied only to get grades. Should one expect people in that frame of mind to converse, whether elegantly or vulgarly? As for their research, Old Manley used merely to snort, Paris-fashion: *"Mystificateurs!"*

The fact is, thought Schneider, my profession is uniquely organized for the destruction of conversation and the production of bores. In what other profession does a man expect a large audience of adolescents to write down whatever he says? After one's captive audiences have done that for four or five years, can one be expected to converse? Can one listen long enough to another to make any relevant answer to what he says? And if another expresses a judgment, can one refrain from automatically grading it rather than considering it?

Of course, ministers and priests have captive audiences too, and heaven knows they show it. In addition, they are stupefied by the belief that, when they speak, they are speaking God's truth, a belief calculated to strangle a conversation at birth and even to exercise a contraceptive influence on all human thought. At their worst, indeed, they start explaining things to God, as witness their invocations at Commencement exercises. Still, no congregation Schneider had heard of was expected to take notes on the sermons it endured.

Lawyers? It is certainly true that court stenographers take down every word a lawyer says in a trial, including even the numerous unnecessary words. But so does the court stenographer take down every word that your illiterate witness stammers out, every word your hardened criminal utters, every sententious remark uttered by your publicity-hungry judge.

As for the politician, he knows while he is talking that nobody present will either write down what he says or even believe it. Not even if he declares war on a foreign country without the assistance either of the President or of the Congress. Not even if he passionately defends the interests of the scores of millions of widows and orphans who monopolize the ownership of our largest corporations. True, he often gives himself airs, but only as a protection against the general contempt of his constituents.

No, thought Schneider, professors are uniquely unfitted for conversation, and monologuing is their inevitable occupational disease. Theoretically, their wives could laugh them out of it by taking notes at table on what their learned husbands said. Practically, these husbands, their shoulders bent under the burden of the knowledge they carry, their eyes half blinded by the checking of irrelevant footnotes, their ears deafened by a steady roar also detectable in certain sea shells, a roar caused by countless wandering lectures from their own mouths—these husbands would never even notice that the woman taking notes was not a student at all but rather a forgotten bedmate. Or if, like Schneider himself, they happened to be henpecked, they would treat their wives, not as they treated an undergraduate, but as they treated President Pomton, with silent deference and secret rebellious hate. A professor can lecture or he can clam up. He can even take turns lecturing with a colleague, thereby at a distance creating the illusion that they are conversing. But he cannot converse. He, even more than the rest of the adult population, must settle for a cocktail party in lieu of conversation. And for a kind of half-drunken, fuzzy, raucous loneliness.

As for cocktail parties in general, he thought as he stared about him, he personally inclined toward the prescription of his smallest, fattest daughter: their so-called conversations are b'loons that one should bust. It could add very little to the noise that already deafened him.

Schneider suddenly decided that he was being pompous, so he got another Manhattan. He was already pleasantly giddy. If he got just a wee bit more giddy, he would soon forget that almost every remark he had heard this afternoon was malicious, or boring, or both.

"Dr. Schneider!" The musical voice came from just behind his left shoulder and he recognized it for the voice of his charming hostess. "Dr. Schneider, I want you to tell Cousin Freddie about the University."

He turned and saw them standing beside each other, radiant.

"Cousin?" he repeated in a dazed voice. "I didn't know you were cousins. My congratulations."

These Southerners, he thought. They are always cousins. Now they can use each other's first names. They will be close enough cousins so Landon can be always standing, radiant, at her side and yet not look like a gigolo. But they will be distant enough cousins so he can be gallant without being the least incestuous. Schneider had never made a professional study of Southern mores, of the sort that would have commanded Milton's respect; but he knew about cousins.

"Well," he said, "if it weren't for our hostess, it would be a dreadful place."

"Now, Dr. Schneider," said Dorothy archly. "You know it's a wonderful place."

"Dr. Landon will find it good enough, I imagine, to write his eighth book in," said Schneider slyly, but his smile was cordial.

"My eighth book?" asked Landon, bewildered. "But I've written only two."

"I sincerely congratulate you," said Schneider. "Everybody here believes you've written seven. I hope you won't disabuse them."

"You don't approve of research?" demanded Cousin Freddie, thoroughly entertained.

"I consider it an occupational disease," said Schneider. "Like silicosis, which is also caused by digging where there is already too much dust. But two's all right. I've written two myself, both very dull."

"I hear they're both excellent," said Dorothy, "and I'm going to read them, too."

"Don't do that," Schneider said. "I do so want you to like me."

"I do like you. But if Cousin Freddie isn't to write a third book, should he do committee work or what?"

"That I cannot permit—although I have no authority here. That, my dear lady, would require him to dictate letters, issue memorandas, and go into conference, the way little businessmen do. In fact, committee work is the professor's way of proving that he is just as important to society as businessmen are. No, I'd rather he risked a third book."

I am being sententious, thought Schneider, very sententious. Why should Landon do anything at all, with a cousin like this exquisite creature at hand?

"Pay no attention to me," he said, "and I hope you like the place and stay here with us. We aren't as bad as we look. We couldn't be. We're just frustrated. And the elms on the campus are really lovely. And spring will come someday, not as soon as in Charleston or Georgia, but it will come. I may have sounded cynical, but I have the completest confidence in spring. I hope you're going to be very happy here."

"Thank you," said Cousin Freddie, and he and Cousin Dorothy drifted off together.

"Is that the Mayflower's henpecked husband you told me about?" asked Cousin Freddie. "I like him."

"So do I."

Schneider dutifully sought out his host.

"Charming party," he said.

"Glad you're enjoying it." Nast's voice was correct, noncommittal.

"Curious," said Schneider. "This is the precise group that met Denby on his first visit—plus, naturally, your two fellow committeemen and Old Manley. How's that business going anyhow?"

"Oh, we'll get something."

"You ought to know," said Schneider. "I gather you saw more of Denby than any of us."

"He's interested in some of the things our department is doing." Then, with a touch of triumph, "Notably in People's Capitalism."

"You've made your department hum. In the process you've gained experience in raising money. In fact, I keep hearing you've helped Pomton raise money for a good many things besides economics. Watch out you don't become a university president!"

Nast ignored the ironical warning: he despised and feared irony.

"I help when I can," he said. "Universities can't be run on compressed air, even though some of my colleagues haven't heard."

Luckily, Kendall, the head of the department of psychology, bustled up importantly just then; and Schneider, having done his pretties, escaped.

He almost collided with Old Manley, who was fetching drinks for some of the girls. Hale at sixty-four, his bright eyes dancing with pleasure in his florid face, an audaciously gay waistcoat adorning his still slim figure, he greeted Schneider.

"What an exquisite creature!" he said, glancing toward their hostess. "What a figure! There you have Woman. I gather our guest of honor thinks so too. He's discreet; but he's in a state of suppressed excitement—as well he may be. Charming fellow. Instructive contrast with our host. Oh, well, Beauty and the Beast, you know. But a Prince Charming is breathing down the Beast's neck."

He dashed happily off with his tray of drinks. Schneider was interested. He respected Old Manley's insights in such matters. This, after all, was Old Manley's field. Even the book or two that Old Manley had published, though technically in French literature, had more specifically dealt with the non-Platonic relations between men and women who were neither boys nor girls, and who had no intention of segregating themselves by sex in opposite corners of the room. The problem, if there was one, had been rather to keep them apart.

He watched Freddie Landon. He really was an interesting young man. Dorothy Nast was introducing him to his new colleagues, one after another. He was tall, slender, dark, and he would have risked being a matinee idol had he not possessed so much race. He had the faintly effeminate chiseled features Schneider had observed in a number of upper-class Southerners, ease without familiarity, a dignity that was utterly free of pomposity. Fom time to time, through the din, Schneider could hear Landon's amusing and fascinating Charleston speech, as different from the flabby accent of the stock Southerner as it was from the prairie twang that now all but drowned it out.

A few days before, Schneider had glanced at a book of Landon's in the library. It missed brilliance, but it was an extraordinarily civilized book for a young professor to have written, and Schneider was genuinely impressed. He watched Landon now with his new colleagues: deft, considerate, attentive, modest. He was obviously making a hit, and there was no slightest sign of effort to please. For all Schneider knew, if Nast died suddenly of heartstrain in some television studio, and if Dorothy, after a barely decent interval, married Landon, then this little closed-in university world would fall at their feet, and there would be nothing Henrietta could do about it. As for Landon's being a drunkard, Schneider profoundly suspected that this merely meant he could hold his liquor and more of it than his detractors. As for his being a Lothario, Schneider could detect no reason either to doubt it or to regret it.

Dorothy and Landon passed close to him again. Schneider gently touched her arm.

"It's been a lovely party," he said. "But I've got to go on. Besides, if I do it ostentatiously, I may be able to unfreeze some of your guests who have never learned the difficult art of departure. Eventually, you may need to go to bed. Thanks ever so much."

He put on his galoshes, his overcoat and muffler, his ear muffs, and his old felt hat, and stumbled out into the blinding snow. Very few guests followed suit: most of them stayed, drank, shrieked, and tried to decipher the shrieks of their fellow revelers. Schneider decided not to go straight home. The fact of the matter was, he was slightly tipsy, something he had not been in years. He did not propose to face Henrietta until he had walked off some of his giddiness and had recaptured the full use of his tongue.

He and the other guests, jostling and babbling in that hot and crowded room, had merely dreaded the snow that swirled outside; but meanwhile the snow had worked its kindly magic. The wind that had come howling out of the west had dropped now, and the snow fell silently, without swirling, without commotion, but with a kind of quiet obstinacy. The ugly little university town had been completely transformed. Under the street lamps it lay glistening, its most hideous landmarks hidden, its angular houses graciously curved, its blackest objects a pure and chaste white, its raucous noises now made quiet. Ah, thought Schneider, how discreet a thing is snow.

Maybe, he thought charitably, this academic research I have been bitterly and stupidly decrying to Cousin Freddie and Cousin Dorothy is, in the long run of mankind's intellectual history, a benison. It is hard to wade through; it makes one's eyeballs sting; but in the end perhaps it covers all until another spring can come, and I believe in spring. Now in the winter of our cultural discontent, the pages of thousands of doctoral dissertations sift silently down onto the library shelves—the separate pages, since nothing ever held these dissertations together anyhow except the binder's glue. Down waft the pages of the thousands of master's theses; the final papers that led to the myriad bachelor's degrees; the white pages of all the final term papers and of all the examination bluebooks. Even the pages of books, like those that he and Freddie Landon had guiltily perpetrated. Perhaps academic research was a vast cultural snowstorm. All these commentaries on the great landmarks of human striving, these commentaries on the really great books that men have written, and the commentaries on these commentaries, and all the footnotes and appendices—all had to sift slowly into place, had to come to rest at last; for now is winter when genuine human thought freezes up to await the passionate spring, the rebirth of learning.

What is so immoral about snow? True, these paper snowflakes of ours have been sadly smirched with printer's ink or undergraduate scrawl. These flakes are less dazzlingly white than those that fall about me in the street tonight, less crystalline in their inner structure; but they too fall, and lie, and cover all. Can snow be immoral? Fortified by a few Manhattans, a good man can struggle through. And, surely, it has a kind of beauty.

His head was quite clear, at least of alcohol, when he reached the front door of the house. He stamped the snow from his galoshes and entered the brave dry fortress of warmth in the midst of hundreds of miles of silently falling snow. Henrietta and the girls had already begun supper.

"You are late," she said in her accusing voice.

"It is snowing," he said. "But spring is bound to come some day."

~VII~

THE REPORT of the Curriculum Committee lay on Pomton's desk, with the imprimatur of the Committee on Academic Legislation of the Faculty of Arts and Sciences. Even Pomton found it pretty futile reading. He shed no tears. Some twenty years of university administration had completely convinced him that undergraduate instruction was a burden to be borne in order to operate good professional schools and carry on graduate research. That the College of Arts and Sciences should be dominated by athletics and fraternities seemed to him fairly just. Certainly they offered the student more than the undergraduate courses did.

Pomton had dreamed once of working out an educational policy with the college faculty, a policy designed to give the student a sound liberal education. But his efforts brought him no thanks, and Pomton was a man who had to be thanked if you would get the best out of him. The college faculty, torn by departmental jealousies, could agree on nothing and ended by complaining to the trustees that Pomton was trying to dictate educational policy, when the real duty of a college president was to get more money. So Pomton turned his attention to developing research. Meanwhile one new department after another was added to the undergraduate curriculum, as one donor after another discerned some new and pressing need of American youth. The alphabetized list of courses an undergraduate might elect began to look like a Sears, Roebuck catalogue. Pomton made a virtue of necessity and talked to the public about satisfying every student need and thereby developing personality and preparing a young man or woman to make a better livelihood. For Pomton was sensitive to opinion, and he discovered quickly that personality and pay were what parents wanted for their children.

But for one man, that would have been the end of it. That one man was Weed, chairman of the department of political science. Weed was an intellectual phoenix, preserved, between risings, not in fire but in alcohol. Educated in France, Weed had ever since been trying to figure out why French schools educate and American schools don't. He distinctly recalled that French schools did, but he could never remember why. So every third year Weed started a reform of the curriculum, gathering around him the idealists, the troublemakers, the frustrated research workers, and the ex-Rhodes Scholars. There would be a tremendous drive to introduce the Dartmouth Great Issues course or the Sarah Lawrence plan or the Harvard plan of General Education. In each instance Pomton would appoint a special curriculum committee, on which Schneider usually served. The committee would render a report. By the time the report was ready, the necessities of adaptation would have rendered the new scheme unrecognizable; or else on close examination the new scheme disclosed terrible flaws even at the institution that had invented it. And the faculty had never accepted more than a few unrelated details of each successive scheme. Pomton was weary of it all, but he supposed it gave people something to think about.

Weed took each defeat hard and relapsed into drink. He never drank publicly, of course—at least not to excess. No, Weed drank in private, steadily, trying to remember what made the French educational system work. The number of educational defeats he had suffered, as one uprising after another fizzled out in a committee report, was registered in his finely chiseled nose, which from a pale ivory would turn to pink, then red, and finally a blotched purple. This transformation was always a gradual one and signified nothing to the casual observer; but to the older faculty members it represented a chromatic history of educational discussion at the University. Thus, it was generally agreed that it was Weed's failure to adapt the Harvard plan of General Education to local conditions that ultimately changed his nose from a permanent pink to provisional red. Similarly, when the Dartmouth Great Issues had slithered through committee in emasculated form and were torn to ribbons in faculty meeting, Weed's nose darkened toward its purple destiny.

The year that Freddie Landon came was one of Weed's regular third years. He laid his bottle by and demanded a consolidation of the curriculum with preferably a required course for the first two years, the right of election to be deferred to the junior year. Pomton obligingly appointed him chairman of a special curriculum committee, which would report through the Committee on Academic Legislation to him personally; and he promised that, if he approved the report, he would recommend it strongly to the faculty. Not that Pomton expected the faculty to do anything intelligent about it, but he liked Weed for hoping on.

Now, faced with the Curriculum Committee's report, Pomton kept his word. He dictated a circular letter of approval and transmitted mimeographed copies of the report to the faculty, requesting the Dean of the College of Arts and Sciences to call a faculty meeting for its discussion and, if possible, its adoption.

If Weed's committee had stuck together, they might have done something in the faculty meeting, if not by persuasion, then at least by logrolling. But the first meeting of the committee made it clear that not much could be hoped for. Weed, as chairman, had instructed his committee and had suggested that they first formulate, in a preamble to their report, the general objectives of undergraduate education. Nast, who was a member of the committee—indeed its most powerful member—objected. He pointed out that no two professors could agree on such a statement, since each would be bound to consider the problem from the point of view of his own field and since few were so arrogant as to suppose they knew anything appreciable about the fields of their colleagues. Even if the committee could agree on a statement of general educational policy, it would be pretty doctrinaire of them to lay such a statement before their peers. Their peers might have some ideas of their own. Weed replied tartly that he had talked with his peers and that they had no ideas —at least not on this subject. One or two other committeemen felt sure they would certainly get ideas, if such a challenge as Weed's proposed preamble were flung at them, and then there would be the devil to pay. But Nast's most crushing argument was a practical one. He professed to see no point in a theoretical statement of educational objectives, when you knew in advance that the faculty for devious reasons would not go so far. What was wanted was a compromise between such objectives and the brutal political facts to be faced. He disclaimed any knowledge of political science, he was a mere economist, but he knew a little about faculty politics, and he reminded Weed of their existence.

Weed knew only too well that Nast knew faculty politics, this being the very period when Nast and Dorothy between them had achieved imperial honors. But he pointed out, with a flash of the French logic he had perhaps imbibed in his *Wanderjahren,* that you couldn't compromise between theoretical objectives and the facts of life unless you knew what the objectives were. Nast waved the argument aside as being purely theoretical, and the majority of the committee agreed with him.

Despite this inauspicious beginning, they got out a report, with only one dissenting voice. Their quixotic chairman appended a minority report, admitting that the new scheme was better than what they already had but pointing out why it needed stiffening. The new scheme demanded for the first two years of college one year of mathematics, one year of English composition "with emphasis on spelling and punctuation," two years of a foreign language, one year of history, one year of a laboratory science, and three free electives. Weed argued for a year of philosophy, preferably logic. But Nast went to the mat on that: no scholasticism. The mathematics seemed to him pure sadism, but he grumblingly accepted it. Weed also wanted to stipulate that the foreign language should be either Greek, Latin, French, or German. But Nast again objected. He thought it would be outrageous to give a shot in the arm to the classics, which were dying and deserved only a decent funeral. And he thought it just a little ridiculous that, with a student's country committed to a good-neighbor policy and with its South American trade destined to grow, he should be deprived of Spanish. Weed argued that a student could specialize in trade and neighborliness and Spanish when he did his major in his junior and senior year, and insisted his required language should be one of the great languages of scholarship. Everybody present knew there would be a student revolution if Weed won his point. Spanish was enormously popular with undergraduates: it was considered the easiest of all foreign languages. But, in a moment of desperate courage, they rallied to Weed and to the great languages of scholarship.

Another knotty problem remained. Which undergraduate course in history should be required? Nast thought, Obviously American. This was a modern world. Weed, his heart in Paris with Napoleon's, argued for Modern European. A member of the English department pointed out the wisdom of requiring a knowledge of English history of students who must—quite properly—study the English language. Then somebody tardily hit on the happy notion of leaving the decision to Schneider. The question frightened Schneider out of his wits. As head of the history department, he should theoretically have been in a position to decide. But when he remembered the recent history luncheon at the Triangle Club, he shuddered to think what this apple of discord would do to his department. He confidentially suggested, to the amazement of the committee, not making history a required subject at all. Then, realizing what his department would say if they heard he had lightly thrown away a God-given chance to develop the department, he requested time to consult his staff. The staff meeting that resulted exceeded Schneider's wildest fears, and when the smoke had blown away, the verdict was "Any history." Cardwell, knowing he had Nast's powerful support for his course in American history, amended the verdict bitterly to "Any history and be damned." His remark got out. And when the undergraduate daily listed the required courses under the proposed program, which it bitterly assailed, the listing included "Any history and be damned." For history was increasingly unpopular with students.

The faculty met. The faculty habitually met with that cynical disregard of parliamentary order that is one of the charms of academic life. Great scholars would sit hunched and smoking, listening to the futile speechmaking of their colleagues. Spruce young assistant professors would sit in the rear seats betting on the success of this or that motion. Important decisions would be reached with that air of banter that the intellectual assumes when he knows his full intellectual powers are not being utilized. There would be a great deal of good-natured grumbling about spending time on undergraduate problems that should be going to important research now in progress. One or two of the more powerful members of the faculty would ostentatiously nod.

Today, when Schneider entered the auditorium where the faculty was about to meet, his emotions were mixed. On the one hand, it was always possible the faculty might surprise him and do something intelligent. On the other hand, he dreaded the bad temper, the rabid personal jealousies, the interdepartmental guerrilla forays that he was about to witness. Spotting Old Manley, the professor of French, in the very last row, he walked clear back and joined him there.

"Why do you always pick the back row for these battles?" he asked playfully.

"So that none of my colleagues can put a knife in my back," said Old Manley grimly. "When the Dean calls this bunch to order, all hell is going to break loose. They call it parliamentary procedure. For the life of me, I can't see why the Dean cherishes Robert's Rules of Order."

"Oh, come," said Schneider. "Even this crowd has to follow parliamentary procedure."

"But could anything be less appropriate to the occasion? Parliamentary procedure was evolved to guide the deliberations of a body with power to make decisions. They had the power to make decisions because they had the power of the purse. We have no such power. Pomton has it. The only power this gang has is to block Pomton. And they will, too. He knows it. You notice that although it's an open secret that he likes Weed's proposed reforms, he isn't here to fight for them. He knows better. Pomton has never loved lost causes."

"The Dean does, though," said Schneider, and for one, fleeting, sentimental moment he liked the Dean. He never used his name. A proper name would specify too much, whereas this particular dean was mere deanliness.

"That will help a lot. If the Dean is back of Weed, we might as well adjourn the meeting. This crowd loathes the Dean."

"The college faculty will please come to order," piped the Dean, tapping timidly with his gavel a couple of times.

"Now for pandemonium," muttered Old Manley. The assembled scholars milled around, choosing their seats, most of them pulling on briar pipes, others armed only with cigarettes. Only the economists ostentatiously smoked cigars. Schneider sniffed inquisitively: they were not as good cigars as those he had smoked when he had breakfasted with Denby. But they were cigars. And they were symbols. They meant that not even the physicists, backed by juicy government contracts and shopped for by private business, enjoyed so high an average standard of living as Nast's well-chosen team. Schneider noted that, among the economists, only Freddie Landon smoked a cigarette. He wondered what, precisely, this symbol of dissent could mean.

"As the faculty doubtless knows," began the Dean in his mild voice, "this meeting has been specially called—"

"Point of order!" snarled a faculty member. It was Nast.

"The Professor of Economics has the floor," announced the Dean wearily.

"If the Chair feels no profound objection," said Nast, "would it be too much to ask that the minutes of the previous meeting be read?"

"Oh!" said the Dean, and even his surprise at his own forgetfulness was mild. "I am sorry. Forgive me, gentlemen. Mr. Secretary—"

"Point of order!"

It was the dry, brittle voice of the Professor of German. The voice electrified the entire faculty, for they knew that the first thrust and counterthrust had now been given. German had already rallied, to a man, to the new reform proposed by Weed's Committee on the Curriculum, partly because they honestly thought the proposed new plan less absurd than the existing course requirements, and partly because some of the students now taking "snap" courses in Commercial Spanish would have to face up either to German or to French, since obviously nothing would induce them to learn either the Greek alphabet or Latin conjugations. The fact that Nast was trying to delay the discussion by insisting that the minutes be read infuriated the Professor of German. Nast did not feel strongly about any foreign language, since an American could under People's Capitalism always hire an interpreter; but if students were to be dragooned into learning to talk something other than Corn Belt English, he still preferred them to study Commercial Spanish. Besides being useful in South America, it would certainly leave more time for real subjects like economics. What looked, therefore, like two points of order were read immediately by the knowing as one point of combat. The troops were engaged, and the whole College Faculty swayed slightly with excitement and gave off a rustling noise, like a field of corn stirred by a breeze from the west or, for that matter, like the plumed Achaeans straining at their leashes before the walls of Troy. Even Helen, looking down from the walls, was fairly represented, as the Dean looked down, over his heavy-rimmed spectacles and with a nearly neutral eye, at the two armies on the plain below. Beside him sat the Secretary to the Faculty, eager to read the minutes.

"The Professor of German has the floor," declared the Dean, mildly regretting the blood that so many doomed warriors must shed before this day was done.

"May I remind the faculty that the minutes of the previous meeting have been duly circulated by your office, sir?" said the Professor of German in his dry, brittle voice, glancing scornfully at Nast and his platoon of cigar-smoking brigands. "May I move their adoption as circulated?" And he sat down triumphantly.

"Second the motion!" cut in a colleague of Old Manley's in the department of French, anxious that French should share with German in the booty when and if the Spanish Empire fell.

"As a matter of fact," observed the Dean in his mild voice, "it was because I subconsciously remembered that my office had circulated the minutes that I assumed we could excuse our secretary." And he glanced smilingly at the frustrated Secretary to the Faculty. The secretary always loved the reading of the minutes. He felt, with some justice, that it was rather an intellectual triumph to furnish a coherent account of one of this faculty's meetings. He had already seized the minutes of the college faculty and had found the right page. Now he regretfully put down his minutes book and awaited the vote.

"You have heard the motion, gentlemen. Any discussion?"

Nast saw no good opening now, and impatient cries of "Question!" arose from both embattled groups.

"Are you ready for the vote?" demanded the Dean, glancing knowledgeably from side to side of the room. "All those in favor will please say Aye."

A spattering of Ayes arose, among them Schneider's.

"Those opposed?"

"No!" cried the economists, puffing furiously on their cigars, and the Spanish people, dragging hard on their pipes.

"No!" cried Old Manley, tardily but firmly.

"Why did you vote No?" whispered Schneider. "Don't you want Weed's plan?"

"I suddenly reflected," said Old Manley, also whispering, "how awful it would be to have to teach French literature to some of those lazy athletes that are taking Commercial Spanish."

"The Ayes have it," announced the Dean mildly but with the obvious satisfaction of a partially exonerated man. "We can now pass to the real business of the meeting. As the faculty doubtless knows, this meeting has been called especially—"

"Point of order!" interpolated Nast acidly.

"The Professor of Economics has the floor," declared the Dean wearily.

"Under Robert's Rules of Order," began Nast coldly, wondering as he spoke why on earth Pomton had ever appointed this old ass a dean, "it is customary to hear reports from standing committees before passing to reports from special committees."

"Hear, hear," murmured a former Rhodes Scholar approvingly.

"I move that reports from standing committees be postponed till our next meeting," cut in the Professor of German quickly, "and that the faculty should hear the report of the Curriculum Committee."

"Second the motion," droned the department of French as one man, minus Old Manley. It was the first meeting Schneider had ever attended at which the French and Germans had stood together and he could not help feeling that it marked a certain progress, granted that the issue was not too clear a one. And it was exciting to watch this new Falange of Spaniards and People's Capitalists bite the dust. For that is what they would certainly do: the faculty was almost unanimously prepared to postpone reports from standing committees.

But at this point the movement of battle suddenly swirled.

"Mr. Chairman!"

The voice was Milton's.

"The Chair recognizes the Professor of Sociology," announced the Dean with unaccustomed alacrity, obviously sharing Schneider's curiosity.

"Mr. Chairman," began Milton, in his curiously ponderous manner, "I arise to offer an amendment to the motion now before the

{86}

faculty, the motion to postpone all reports of standing committees. I propose as my amendment the clause 'except the Committee on Committees.'"

"Second the motion to amend," Nast cut in sharply. He knew, as did indeed every full professor present, most of the associate professors, and even many of the assistant professors, that the Committee on Committees was dynamite and with proper maneuvering could become TNT, or fission, or even fusion. The real issue before the faculty, therefore, was whether to vote down Milton's amendment and proceed to a free-for-all over Weed's proposed curricular revision or whether, on the other hand, to support him and enjoy the acrimony which a report from the Committee on Committees was pretty certain to produce. Both prospects were interesting to hardened parliamentarians, and in both cases there was the spice of danger: somebody was sure, in either event, to get hurt. They understood each other's motives perfectly. Milton wanted to attack the Committee on Committees, which had circulated in mimeograph form its usual slate of committees for the coming academic session. Milton had been given not a single chairmanship, and Milton felt as strongly as any Southern Senator about chairmanships and seniority. In case something slipped and President Pomton failed to get from Denby enough Winthrop Foundation money to set up the projected Institute for Research in the Social Sciences, with its promised directorship for Milton, a brilliant committee chairmanship was just about the only chance Milton had for demonstrating the executive capacity of an inactive candidate, and not too inactive at that, for the presidency of the University. Yet before long Pomton must in common decency either die, or resign, or get called to a bigger job.

Milton was so intent on securing his chairmanship that he was still standing. His face was flushed and displayed a variety of minor habit tics, all familiar to his colleagues, those little grimaces which many women, and nearly all university professors, acquire over the years because of the real or imagined effects they have produced on long-forgotten swains or students. He pursed his mouth; he half closed his eyes; he tossed his head slightly, like F.D.R. The chairman of the Committee on Committees watched him narrowly: they might shortly be locked in battle, and the more he understood of Milton's present mood, the more likely Milton could be thrown, or really get his throat cut in debate.

Nast, for his part, though more in control of his features than Milton, was no less eager for the gong. If Milton and the chairman of the Committee on Committees could be really set on each other, the discussion of Weed's reforms would simply have to be postponed till the next meeting. Nast and the staff of the Spanish department could do much better then.

At this tense moment, the Dean confused the original motion and the proposed amendment, and had to be extricated. Nast undertook the task, with heavy sarcasm, suggesting that the secretary read both the motion and the amendment. The secretary did so with obvious gusto, his eyes shining at the prospect of a memorable debate. It was likely to prove the kind of debate worthy of his skill as historian, a debate that would be both confused and important. He believed he was equal to the challenge.

The motion was carried, as amended, and the faculty braced themselves for the hell they had now let loose. By unleashing Milton against the Committee on Committees they were perfectly aware that they had thrown themselves, not into a committee of the whole or anything else so decorous, but into what Thomas Hobbes would call a State of Nature, where every man's hand is against every man. Their banners bore the proud device, so dear to the Irish and perhaps to all mankind, "If you see a head, hit it." Goaded by love of parliamentary glory, by the bile and spleen that prey on sedentary men, by the malice that afflicts the intellectual; half maddened by presidential oppression, financial worry, domestic infelicity or boredom, and by the incredulity and scorn of their students, they went into battle—against each other.

In the heat of battle the warriors lost their grip on the original issue. This issue was whether to accept or reject the recommendations of Weed's Committee on Reform of the Curriculum. Once the real issue had been lost, orators began to appeal to principle.

Indeed, just as our national statesmen do, they appealed to numerous and apparently quite irreconcilable principles.

"Gentlemen of the faculty," piped the Dean in his reediest voice, "may I beg you to rise superior to principle? May I beg you to compromise?"

His plea fell on ears that principle rendered deaf to reason. Schneider would have liked to smash Nast's filibuster by urging, not the acceptance of poor Weed's recommendations, which were a patchwork of compromises between jealous departments competing for students, but a motion that the committee reconsider the whole problem. It clearly ought to be reconsidered, not in terms of existing courses but in terms of what an undergraduate might do for his first two years to repair the damage the high school had done him, and of what might render him halfway literate, so that he might major in his chosen field with some chance of knowing what he was doing. But Schneider was sure that Weed would construe such a motion as a rebuke to himself, and Weed had borne enough. He was also sure the faculty would consider nothing so rational as a fresh start, now their blood was up. Finally, it would have taken a more expert parliamentary maneuver than Schneider could invent to get such a motion on the floor in the midst of this disgraceful bedlam. Schneider did not envy the secretary his task of reporting a discussion that had simply not been a discussion.

When the smoke cleared away, and it was obviously time to adjourn, personal remarks had been made that it would take years to forget, alliances were in ruins, old friendships shattered—and the Committee on Committees had promised to circulate a new slate before the next faculty meeting. With luck, thought Nast, we can use up the entire next meeting arguing over the new list; and it is already March. With luck, thought Milton, I will get my chairmanship. With luck, thought Schneider, I shall be sick in bed when the next meeting occurs. The secretary hurried off importantly, to write up the minutes before time could blur the intricacies of the argument and before his notes got cold. Small groups of faculty members wandered off, gesticulating, to hold post-mortems or to caucus on the next meeting. Weed went home, kissed his wife absent-mindedly, got out a bottle of brandy—in his case it had to be cheap brandy—and, muttering that he had a headache and begged to excuse himself from supper, took the bottle to his room.

Schneider guessed there would be brandy. He was sorry for Weed. And yet he wondered about the curricular reform.

"What a frightful meeting," said Old Manley. "Year by year, their manners get worse. Even a back seat is no real protection. I was writhing."

"Oh," said Schneider, "I can stand the explosion. It's the delayed fall-out that I dread. The atmosphere has been poisoned, and nobody knows how long the debilitating fall-out will last."

He and Old Manley wandered off in opposite directions, Old Manley once more outraged, Schneider thoughtful. Ever since that breakfast with Denby, Schneider had been wondering what he wanted here or whether, indeed, he wanted anything. The solution to his problems, he was now convinced, lay elsewhere. For Weed's sake, he wished he could have spoken today, but only for Weed's sake.

Schneider strolled home under the bare campus elms. You can't, he reflected, get out of this squirrel cage by waving telegrams. Pomton is too clever. And, anyhow, Denby says it's coast to coast. You can't persuade your department to do anything intelligent. Nor the faculty, either. They will die before they let Weed persuade them to do anything except precisely the thing they are doing—and grumbling about doing. The fact is, the members of this faculty can't exchange ideas—either in a formal meeting or at a cocktail party. So around and around we little squirrels must go.

This is an unusually cold March, he thought, and raised his coat collar against the wind that came tearing off the prairies. But, being a professor, I feel braced, braced against the wind by confirming an hypothesis. This university, like others I could name, is intellectually bankrupt: therefore it should immediately raise a lot of money. We have lost our common purpose and we should instantly redouble our efforts. May God have mercy on us.

~VIII~

SCHNEIDER wandered into Milton's dingy little office. He didn't
know why. True, it was between classes, he felt sick and exhausted, and the weather was too foul for a stroll. But those were
not the reasons. There were other offices where he would have been
welcomed for a pipeful and a chat. And, in a faculty not distinguished either for wit or social sense, this sociologist was easily the
least witty and the most desperately lacking in social sense. Presumably, it was precisely this defect that had drawn him inexorably into
sociology, where he could hide his blindness behind the discreet dark
glasses of a vague and voluminous terminology. Or, alternatively,
thought Schneider, Milton might have been driven in by that powerful law of psychological compensation which Schneider had watched
operate in so many of his colleagues. If you could not learn to add,
you became a professor of mathematics. If you could not find your
way to the business section of a college town, you became a professor
of commercial geography. If you had trouble expressing even simple ideas in clear English, you took up semantics. If, he reflected bit-

terly, you could not remember dates, as indeed he himself could not, you became a professor of history. As a matter of fact, as an undergraduate Schneider had flunked but one course—history. As to why he had specialized in diplomatic history, that, he thought, his bitterness and self-hatred increasing, was easy: witness his recent pourparler with President Pomton, in connection with the "call" from Barker University. Nast could have handled that telegram-waving act, and successfully too, between two morning lectures on People's Capitalism.

He awoke from this train of painful thought to find that, somnambulistically, he was still approaching Milton's office. And he suddenly knew why. Yes, it was quite clear: Milton was the village idiot of this faculty. Schneider needed to consult a village idiot, or at least listen to an idiot tell a tale. Schneider had come to where three ways meet, and each of the three was a dead end: his unpaid, unpayable bills; his grim home life; the collapse into utter futility of both his teaching and his research. Only an idiot could know which way to turn.

"Hullo, Milton," he said.

Milton looked up from his cluttered desk and gave Schneider one of those sightless smiles that idiots wear. Sightless and fleeting: Milton was a serious scholar who found scholarship a pretty heavy responsibility. What a worm the fellow is, thought Schneider with sudden petulance. He moves blindly through the soil, hoping to find an old leaf or a withered blade of grass or even a document that he can feed on before he goes his secret, slimy way again; tirelessly, ambitiously thrusting himself forward; crawling, obsequious, nearer to where he thinks the presidency of the university is. And Schneider lost his image of the village idiot and forgot his hope of reading something prophetic in poor Milton's maunderings. Instead, he was intent on teasing this worm, on poking him, on watching his absurd and irrelevant writhings.

"That was quite a remark you dropped last fall the day Denby paid us his first visit," he said admiringly. "Worthy of a member of the Eisenhower cabinet."

"What remark was that?"

"Why, you know: 'I think that all those who expect to be president.' When did Charlie Wilson or Foster Dulles beat that one?"

"Oh," answered Milton, not quite following—or, rather, following but at a distance, "that was nothing. Just a slip of the tongue. That was all."

"Ever read Freud?" Schneider asked gently. "On *lapsus linguae?*"

Milton flushed slightly, but not because he understood the question. He flushed because he had always intended to read Freud; he felt like an undergraduate caught out in a written quiz. He was silent, waiting hopefully for the intellectual weather to change, or for Schneider to offer him an optional question. Schneider suddenly obliged, not to rescue Milton from his embarrassment but because his own glance had fallen on the papers piled high on a table in the corner.

"What's all that?" he asked, putting into his voice a proper awe.

Some of the larger sheets of paper reminded Schneider of an infamous undergraduate course he had taken a thousand years ago in co-ordinate geometry, full of conic sections—ellipses, parabolas, hyperboles and the like. And, indeed, mysterious curves meandered across the wide sheets in different colored inks.

"Sure you aren't muscling in on the department of mathematics?" he said. "They're a jealous crowd, you know."

"That," said Milton, unable to conceal his pride, "is a rather exciting piece of research I am doing. At the request of the President," he added, trying to make the postscript casual. Then, with every effort to be light and gay, he said, "If I'm muscling in on anybody, it isn't mathematics that needs to worry; it's the department of economics."

Schneider whistled, ominously.

"Then you're in for trouble with Nast."

"I'm only doing this research because the President asked me to," objected Milton, secretly glad that the conversation had forced him to make this statement a second time.

"That may not save you. It depends on the project. If it places

{93}

you in the position of joining Pomton's brain trust, then the succession to the crown is at stake. And Nast, as you well know, has his eye on the presidency. I suppose you know that, although the University has no official vice-president, Nast is the Nixon of this outfit. My wife tells me that Mrs. Nast has even bought a dog and named him Backgammon."

Here was a conversational thread that Milton could follow, and his face was even graver than usual.

"Mind you," added Schneider mischievously, "I don't think 'My Boy' is the man for the job. Frankly, I think you are. You've got practically all the traits of the American university president." He was secretly a little proud of the last sentence he had spoken: unlike most such judgments, it was both factually true and polite. Perhaps, he reflected humorously, he was a less inept diplomat than he had thought.

"Thank you," said Milton. "But I'm not after the job."

It was a lie, of course, but it was the decent thing to say.

"Spoken like an inactive candidate!" said Schneider. "I'm going to keep my eye on you. You're going places."

"If, when President Pomton retires, the trustees feel I am needed, I would not dodge the responsibility."

"Spoken again in the best candidate tradition!"

Milton longed to discuss the problem further, but Schneider repeated his question.

"But what are the graphs about?" He nodded again toward the colored lines wandering across the large checkered sheets. "Just what is your project?" His voice vibrated with the respect due from a colleague for work courageously embarked on.

"I'm making a study of the academic salary scale in this section of the country, as compared with the salary scale of comparable institutions in the East. Then I'm comparing the cost of family living in the two sections. The President gave me a small research grant to help me get this work done. If Nast thinks the grant should have gone to the economics people, I can only say there are some sociological problems involved in this thing that only an experienced sociologist is prepared to evaluate, if you know what I mean."

"Of course I know. And I can see how this thing might attract the kind of attention the Kinsey Report has received. Faculty salaries are very much before the public, and faculty families ought to be."

"Oh," said Milton modestly, and quickly for him, "I don't expect that kind of success. There's no sex in this, you see."

"What do you mean—no sex?" Schneider feigned indignation. "Where did the faculty families come from? From storks? And when you begin to look into family mores for this project, you may uncover any amount of stuff, Milton. Stuff nobody ever dreamed of. I know you: you're an absolute ferret, once you get to nosing around! I haven't forgotten that survey you did of that backwoods county and the way you counted flush toilets versus outside privies. When you got through, those farm people had very few secrets you didn't know—and publish! I tell you, I shudder when I think you're starting in on us academicos. I really shudder!"

"I shan't spare any pains," Milton promised loyally.

"And you won't spare us either! As far as you're concerned, we're already on the operating table, and you're sharpening your scalpel on your shoe. Oh, I know you! But seriously, Milton. What've you found out about us so far? All that colored ink must mean something done already."

"Well," said Milton happily, "it's commonly asserted that here in the Middle West, although salaries are lower, so are living costs. Well," and his voice was confidential now, "that's not so certain."

"I'll bet it's not. If you select your data properly, I'll bet the reverse is true. And I know you'll select it properly: you're no mere collator. But this time, Milton, do be extra careful. A lot's at stake."

"Of course," said Milton, "I can't try to prove a case. This is disinterested research I'm engaged in. I'm only after the facts. I'm not sure the President will like what I've found so far. From the way he talked, I think—" and he lowered his voice slightly—"I think he rather hoped my data would show that, proportionately, Midwestern faculties are paid better than Eastern ones."

"Rubbish!" said Schneider in passionate tones. "Midwestern faculties are starving and he knows it. Old Manley says we've got to starve quietly and philosophically. But Old Manley's a bachelor. He says that five centuries ago, all of us would have had to take the triple vow of poverty, chastity, and obedience, whereas now we only take the vows of poverty and obedience. He says if hungry slaves insist on breeding large, voracious families, what can they expect? Cadillacs? But Old Manley lives a pleasant life and goes to Paris every summer and eats his way down the Champs Élysées, sampling every restaurant he has heard somebody praise and scraping acquaintances with midinettes. The old *roué!*"

"Of course, my research can only follow the facts. It's got to be scientific."

"Of course," said Schneider.

"I think the facts will show that, although rents are higher in the East, fuel is higher here. And believe it or not, right here in the Corn Belt food is also higher."

"And yet," said Schneider, as if determined to be fair, "even if food is higher here, doesn't it probably cost more to keep up a front in the East? I imagine in most Eastern colleges now a full professor would have to have at least a decent-looking Chevrolet, where we can run around in a third-hand jalopy and make a joke of it. And the same with clothes and entertainment. So our higher food costs might not tell the story, since even a growing child can't eat but just so much."

"Of course," admitted Milton. "As a matter of fact, it has to be that way. That's Engel's Law."

Schneider was startled. Had Friedrich Engels discovered that the human belly is limited and then declared it a law? Surely, the old man wasn't that stupid? And how was the law formulated, anyhow? He, Schneider, had never even heard of it. Probably, he thought, sinking back into his self-abasement, he was the only member of this large faculty who had never heard of Engels' Law. He was constantly coming across appalling gaps in his knowledge, gaps that made him wonder whether he really rated a decent salary. Maybe he was lucky not to be teaching grade school.

"Well," he said, with forced cheerfulness, "I'd better let you get back to your research, or I never will get a decent salary. Good luck, Milton, and don't be too darned disinterested and scientific." He was making a last effort at banter, but it didn't really come off. He was haunted by his ignorance of Engels.

He had no sooner left Milton's office than he started rapidly for the library, still in his somnambulistic state, but he realized with a start that he was due to meet his graduate seminar in five minutes. So he found his way blindly to the seminar and listened to a student drone out a paper he had written on an obscure point in European diplomatic history, all scissors and paste but nicely garbled in spots, and such bad writing that it was not wholly free of unconscious humor. Then there was discussion; but, since not a soul in the room but this budding author and Schneider had the slightest acquaintance with the data on which the paper had been based, the conversation tended to be languid. Within three or four years this intellectual progeny of his would be teaching history in some other intellectual wilderness and mentioning casually having "studied under Professor Schneider." The idea was so utterly appalling that Schneider hastily adjourned the seminar. Then he started again for the library.

He went straight to the reference works and seized Volume V of the Encyclopedia of the Social Sciences—"Danton, Georges-Jacques" to "Exile"—and looked for Engels, Friedrich. But there was no sign of any law of the sort Milton had invoked. Then his glance fell on the sketch of one Ernst Engel, a nineteenth-century German statistician, and there stood Engel's Law, as declaratory and as final as the second law of thermodynamics. Herr Engel had studied thousands of working-class families and had been driven to conclude that "the smaller the family income, the greater the proportion of the income spent on food."

When in Rome, thought Schneider, remembering a certain breakfast with Denby, show the Romans a trick or two. The libraries of Harvard, Yale, and Princeton also bulged with things like Engel's Law, little, obvious things and massive platitudes, but most of them solemn, documented proclamations of the completely obvious. What a thing scholarship is, especially in the social sciences. And just then he met young Ripley, his most loyal admirer, his most favored apprentice.

"Excuse me, Dr. Schneider," said Ripley, in a whisper adjusted to library rules. "Excuse me, but are you very busy?"

"As a matter of fact," and Schneider's words seemed queerly beyond his own control, "I am, a bit. As a matter of fact, I'm engaged on a rather pressing piece of research."

"Really?" asked Ripley. "Do tell me what it is, if you can, sir."

"That's just the trouble," said Schneider, still speaking as if a hypnotist drew the words out of him. "I can't. Or at least, not very much. There's the problem of security."

"Security!" Young Ripley's eyes shone with professional excitement and with admiration for his master. "Security! Sounds exciting. No wonder you can't talk. Well, I won't detain you, sir."

He walked rapidly to where the offices of the history department were. Pride in his adored Schneider's newest honor and the normal pride of anybody who has been first to share professional news of general campus interest combined now to quicken his pace.

Schneider climbed to his cubicle in the stacks, filled his briefcase to bulging with the most nondescript collection of books and papers, and started for his office. He still moved in a sort of trance, vaguely troubled by the absurd lie he had told young Ripley but elated too by his fantasy. His conscience hurt him, but not intolerably. His gait reflected his ambivalent mood. As he reached the front steps of the library, two students stood smoking in the vestibule, sheltered from a gusty April shower, before returning to their collateral reading inside. One of them glanced quizzically at Schneider, at his sleepwalker's movements, and murmured to the other.

"Look, Ma, no hands!" he said. And they watched this absentminded professor, strangely treading on cement as if he walked on air—hesitantly walked on air.

IX

A. & M. wants you to deliver a special Convocation address on very short notice—May fifteenth," said Miss Stilton the moment Pomton entered the President's office. "It is already May second." Her tone was vibrant with suppressed excitement.

Pomton tried to appear casual. But he noted that Miss Stilton had, as usual, correctly interpreted the invitation. The State A. & M., with a budget six times that of Pomton's, had been looking for a new president, and Pomton had been waiting patiently for developments. He noted also that Miss Stilton, who was always attractive and always well dressed, was slightly flushed and looked even prettier than usual. Jumping slightly to conclusions, he determined to ask that he might bring her along as secretary. He was sensitive to the personal compliment involved in her flush. Although his relations with Miss Stilton had always been absolutely correct, they had been far from impersonal. Miss Stilton had always been aware that, had he been free of his heavy official responsibilities and perhaps of Mrs.

Pomton, he would long ago have made love to her. Pomton had long been aware of Miss Stilton's awareness. This double awareness between them produced a kind of tension in the President's office that greatly increased his effectiveness. For Pomton was primarily an orator, and orators thrive on esteem.

"Mr. John Francis Edwards has asked if he could have the honor of driving you over," continued Miss Stilton. Her voice was studiedly even but the suppressed excitement was mounting. "As chairman of the board of trustees of A. & M., he has insisted on the privilege of introducing you."

The plot was thicker than he had thought, and a wave of satisfaction swept over him. But he preserved his composure. Part of the delight of receiving such invitations lay in assuming one had the right to receive them. He went calmly through his mail, therefore, and then dictated to Miss Stilton for an hour or two. Then he sat back and gazed at her thoughtfully.

"What is your advice on the Convocation address?" he asked deferentially.

"Your Cold War speech," she answered promptly. "Although, theoretically, you will be addressing the faculty and students, it seems to me essential that you speak primarily to the board of trustees. They will all be there, of course. A defense of free enterprise and a ringing denunciation of Russia would offer certain guarantees that they have the right to insist on."

"You don't think the New Look in Washington and Stalin's death and all that sort of thing make some of my line out of date?"

"The trustees of A. & M.," she said, "loathe the New Look. They loathe Eisenhower. They call him a New Dealer. The second most powerful man on the board says we have no proof Stalin is dead. Most of them believe he is dead but consider Bulganin and Khrushchev far more dangerous to free enterprise. Nothing in your Cold War speech will seem old-fashioned. Naturally, you will allude to contemporary developments behind the Iron Curtain, but you will brush them aside as fundamentally irrelevant. You will prove that, when they talk tough, they mean it; and when they are polite, they are trying to trick Mr. Dulles."

"As usual, your judgment is correct," he said; and she blushed charmingly. "You might put the manuscript of my speech on my desk, so I can be thinking about it.

"Something has happened to Schneider. I don't mean the work he is doing for the government. That's a security matter, which I don't think even you and I should discuss. Something else has happened. He has undergone a profound personality change. He dresses better —thank God. But it's more than that: he has a kind of assurance. You don't think he has received a call from another university that he hasn't told me about?"

"I do not. I think his domestic affairs may have cleared up. One of his colleagues in history reports that he is asserting his authority strongly as head of the department. And that his colleagues are taking it. I think the basis of the whole thing is his claim that he is doing high-level research for the State Department, and the faculty is dazzled by his claim."

"His claim? Do you mean to imply he is lying?"

"You have already suggested," said Miss Stilton primly, "that, because of security, we not discuss his research."

"Yes, yes," said Pomton a little impatiently, like a Czar faced with one of his old ukases that threatens to hobble him. "But suppose he isn't under security?"

"That's precisely what I do suppose." Miss Stilton's voice was as near to dry as she ever let it become unless she was talking to an underling. "Why has the State Department never consulted this office on clearance? Look at all we go through with our physicists. Half my time goes to consultations with the FBI. Nobody wants to know if Dr. Schneider is safe. Perhaps because nobody in the government cares. Perhaps because nobody in Washington ever heard of Schneider."

"But I can't ask the State Department whether one of my own professors is working for them! They would wonder why I didn't ask the professor in question myself." He thrummed on his desk a moment. "I will ask Schneider," he said resolutely. "Then, if he says yes, I'll write State and ask if there is any way I can facilitate the project. If Schneider is lying, I'll soon find out. Ask Dr. Schneider to stop by for twenty minutes."

"Yes, sir," said Miss Stilton, and withdrew. It would not have been her way. Her way would have been for Pomton to query the FBI, very vaguely suggesting that he had doubts about Schneider's loyalty. For Miss Stilton meant business. She knew enough about the political life of postwar America to choose the infallible starting point for doing in any possible opponent of her candidate, Nast.

Schneider came by at noon and was shown in. Miss Stilton could hear through her door what was said and regarded it as her duty to listen if she was to assist the President further with her advice. Pomton was very urbane.

"By the way," he said finally, "I was delighted to hear that you are working on a project for the State Department."

Schneider, whose knowledge of diplomacy had increased during the past delightful weeks in proportion to his increased neglect of historical works on that subject, smiled charmingly.

"You are working for State, aren't you?" Pomton tried to be casual.

"I'm afraid I'm not at liberty to answer that question," said Schneider apologetically. Pomton lowered his voice.

"You mean it's really for CIA?" he asked, so low that Miss Stilton could not hear his words, even with her ear pressed against the door that separated their offices.

"I'm afraid I'm equally unable to answer that one," said Schneider, with a little apologetic laugh.

"Then forgive my asking," said Pomton courteously. "You had been quoted to me as saying you were working for State."

"No," said Schneider frankly, "I have been careful never to say which department I was working for."

He never had. He had never had to. He had let the myth-making capacity that characterizes any healthy American faculty do its work.

Since the idea that one of their number was doing super-secret research for the government had flattered his colleagues, some very good myths had emerged. The love of any normal American for security, for cloaks and daggers, cops and robbers, force and fraud, had reinforced faculty habit. Except for his statement to young Ripley, Schneider had never moved a muscle.

President Pomton suddenly felt drawn to Schneider. He had always liked Schneider's transparent honesty, his earnestness, his professional devotion. But a certain weakness in the man had always repelled him. He had sized him up as a failure; and Pomton loathed, and in a way feared, failures. They could so easily pull others in after them, so to speak. Schneider had until recently been a drowning man, and Pomton had always detested the piteous, accusing shrieks of the drowning. But if the drowning made it to shore, they always found Pomton on the bank ready to help them over the edge. For several years Schneider had struck Pomton as an ineffectual department head. His local business friends had reported that Schneider was even more deeply in debt than is normal to a scholar. He was celebrated in the campus community as its most henpecked member. He had had so many physical disorders that Pomton had begun to find him as repulsive as a leper. Now he found him apparently well; Miss Stilton reported that he had his department, if not his wife, now well in hand, or anyhow at bay; and there was even gossip among local merchants that he was becoming a fair credit risk. Finally, his cuffs were less frayed and therefore reflected greater credit on the institution he served.

Above all, this accolade the government had given him in choosing him to do whatever important thing it was that he was doing impressed Pomton; and for once he rejected Miss Stilton's judgment.

"By the way," he found himself saying, "Mrs. Pomton is out of town and I face a lonely lunch at home. You wouldn't share it with me, would you?"

"I'd be delighted to."

"Excellent! Drop back here about twelve-thirty, and we'll go over together."

When Schneider was gone, Pomton felt vaguely puzzled by his own invitation but he still looked forward to lunching with the new Schneider. Miss Stilton, who had listened as usual through the office door, remained stubbornly convinced that a semi-denunciation to the FBI was the only means of showing up Schneider's audacious hoax. She had conferred with Nast on the subject, and Nast had agreed with her.

She now reminded Pomton that he had asked to see Nast and phoned Nast that the President would see him.

President Pomton had merely wanted to check with Nast before Nast left for New York and for a conference with Denby on the social-science grant, which really should be ripe now, after all these months. Denby had first come out in October. It was now May. Even a foundation can kill only so much time. Miss Stilton was not in a position to explain that Nast needed no briefing. She had in the strictest confidence allowed Nast to study the Denby correspond- ence, merely on Nast's assurance that he needed to know whatever had been said to date on behalf of the University to which they were all loyal. But she had not consulted Pomton and she thought it bet- ter to ignore what had happened. She had felt even surer than Nast that, in showing him the correspondence, she was serving the Uni- versity's best interests. She felt morally certain that if Pomton did get called to A. & M., he would take her along, and only today his at- titude had confirmed her in this judgment. But she felt equally cer- tain that, if Pomton was called but she herself somehow got stuck here, the trustees would elect Nast as the new President. In the cir- cumstances, both for personal and institutional reasons, she felt Nast should see the documents. Now she wanted to see Nast, and she wanted to tell him about A. & M.

Nast came and took great care to consult her before he went in to Pomton. She rapidly briefed him.

Pomton greeted him warmly. This man, he thought, has served me as loyally, as energetically, as if he had worn the title of Vice- President. Pomton had, in fact, made up his mind to recommend him to the trustees as his successor the minute he could get a call to a bigger institution, and in this decision Miss Stilton warmly concurred. He therefore told Nast now, in carefully casual tones, that he was making the Convocation address at A. & M. and riding over with the chairman of their board of trustees.

"That can mean but one thing," said Nast in a quiet, deferential tone.

"It can probably mean only one thing for you too," replied Pomton, and his voice was affectionate, if enigmatic. "But to speak of more imminent problems." And he told Nast some of the things Nast had already studied in the Pomton-Denby dossier. But not all of them. "After all," Pomton reflected smugly, "he's not President yet. I am." He prided himself on his nice judgment of which details could be passed on to subordinates and which could not. Behind the door, Miss Stilton smiled, a little proud of his judgment, a little amused by its present irrelevance.

The interview was soon over. Pomton wished him good luck with Denby, reminding Nast that success would reflect credit on him as well as on the person "who happened to be President." The modesty in the phrase made Miss Stilton proud again of her employer, and she was back at her desk reflecting on this modesty when her possible future employer emerged.

"Good luck in New York," she said with a significant smile.

"If I succeed, it will be your doing." And he was gone, off to serve his University, his President, and if opportunity arose, himself.

Pomton picked up the worn typescript of his favorite Cold War speech. It was a speech that wasted no words on education. Education, he had felt when writing, he could safely leave to creatures like Schneider—but what could one trust to the new Schneider, he now wondered as he thumbed the pages.

"At this crucial turning point in human affairs, I know that the American people will stand firm and tight-lipped, like those who fought at Valley Forge," he read. "We are surrounded by scheming enemies, some of whom until just the other day infested our own government by the thousands. Our Allies, regrettably, who should have been our first line of defense in Europe, have too often shown themselves weak-kneed and vacillating and gullible. We have had to get tough. We have had to make it clear that if the Reds want a showdown they can have one; and we have had to make sure through free enterprise and the profit incentive that the weapons for that showdown would be ready, burnished, decisive. We will fight with no holds barred. We will give tit for tat. Our Allies will have to put up or shut up. For the present we will work through total diplomacy to achieve situations of strength. We will not tolerate appeasement. We will be realistic and will act only from enlightened self-interest.

"Fellow travelers will tell you that we cannot depend on our Allies in Europe, that England has gone socialistic, that France and Italy are controlled by Communists, that Europe considers us too belligerent. But, my friends, the Europeans are not our only Allies. When the chips are down, we shall find that Syngman Rhee is with us; Chiang Kai-shek is with us; Thailand—Freeland, the Land of the Free—will stand firm; Pakistan and Iraq will prove loyal, regardless of the folly of Nehru's India. And Franco will not fail us. Let the Godless atheists of Russia beware: God Himself is with us."

Pomton paused. Shouldn't he have placed God first in the list of our Allies, or else have kept the list purely secular? On the other hand, he especially liked the phrase "Godless atheists." Miss Stilton's mild suggestion that it was redundant overlooked the rhetorical necessities of good oratory—of oratorical license, so to speak. And God Our Ally led directly into Godless atheists. The Russians, like Hitler, when they told the Big Lie, never hesitated to repeat themselves. Well, we should learn to do likewise. We would be fully justified rhetorically if not grammatically if we called them the Godless, atheistic, irreligious opponents of divinity: that's what they were. Why not say so?

"It is for moral principles that we are fighting," he read on, "for freedom and liberty." What the devil was the difference between freedom and liberty anyhow? Every orator nowadays always mentioned both. Was this another case of justifiably piling it on? He pursed his lips and decided that it was. "Above all, it is for free enterprise, the very basis of our Bill of Rights. To preserve these liberties—" or should he have said "these freedoms"? No, "to preserve these liberties"—"we will, if necessary, and in General Mac-Arthur's immortal phrase, go it alone. We will take the wraps off our fantastic weapons. Since force is all the Russians understand, we must give them the works. And if the Reds then try to seize Formosa, we must enter their privileged sanctuary, which a Democrat administration for mysterious reasons—" Anderson stopped. That was risky talk. In this Republican area, he had learned to call the Democratic party the Democrat party, thereby vaguely bracketing them with bureaucrats, autocrats, technocrats, and such. But suppose there was a Democrat on the board of A. & M. who announced he had doubts about Repubs who willfully shortened their opponents' names? He added an "ic" to "Democrat," confident that the Republicans on the board would be at least numerous enough to defend "mysterious reasons," with its desirable smell of twenty years of treason.

"For," he continued, "we must defend Formosa, or California may well be invaded." He paused again. Did that sentence seem to concede Hawaii to the Reds? Oh, well, he was not a candidate for the presidency of the University of Hawaii, at least not an active candidate. Let it pass. "We will not submit," he read on, "to Communism and to the famine and suffering it inevitably produces. If Communism is the marvelous system the Reds picture it as being, then why do we constantly see in our free press statements that their factories are breaking down and that they lack industrial know-how? Faced with the vastest industrial war machine of modern times, we—" Oh-oh! Something wrong. If their factories are breaking down all the time, how can their industrial war machine be so vast? Some captious left-winger in the A. & M. faculty would be sure to spot that one. But did it really matter? In the first place, he would be speaking rapidly, nay, tumultuously. And in the second place, Miss Stilton was right: he was not addressing A. & M.'s faculty; he was addressing their board of trustees. Who ever heard of a captious left-winger on a board of trustees? He let the apparent contradiction stand. "But," he continued reading, "it is not our matchless know-how, nor even our equally valuable show-how, that will win victory in the end. To win that victory, we must fight relentlessly for the minds and hearts of men, and that, my friends and fellow citizens, is where great institutions of learning like ours must enter the picture. Our colleges and universities owe it to our fair country not only to design lethal weapons but lethal ideas as well."

He broke off in disgust. The last sentence convinced him the speech must be drastically up-dated. By "lethal ideas" he had, of course, meant ideas that would prove lethal to the enemy, ideas like freedom and liberty and free enterprise and the American way of life and People's Capitalism and so on. But the phrase might easily be misunderstood. The whole speech now struck him as curiously bellicose and emptily threatening. It had a stale sound, like unleashing Chiang Kai-shek, or a roll-back in eastern Europe, or suggesting that the French might force us to an agonizing reappraisal. What so stale, indeed, as last year's slogans? For once, Miss Stilton was quite simply wrong. Her infatuation for her boss had allowed her to encourage him to make a stale speech. And this at the precise moment, if there ever was one, that freshness and originality were called for. Certainly, there were many telling phrases in the speech, or at least many phrases that would tell with the board of trustees. These he could of course salvage. But, to judge by the press, the softness and New-Dealism of the Eisenhower Administration had so weakened our position against left-wingers at home and enemies and neutralists abroad, that a good Cold War speech was no longer an easy thing to write. If Miss Stilton thought it was, let her try her hand at drafting one. She would soon find out. As for threatening a showdown after the things Eisenhower had said about hydrogen warfare, the trustees would think him ill informed and the faculty would think him merely mad. Even the billingsgate against Russia— good billingsgate, he still thought—had lost half its force since Stalin died and Russia had started a New Look of her own. Indeed, it looked as if there might be no war, and Russia might grab all our foreign markets instead. Pomton felt a bitter resentment that Stalin's death or Eisenhower's golf or some other historical factor he could not put his finger on had relegated his best speech to the ash-can. It was work writing these things. Even when Miss Stilton wrote them, it was work learning them by heart—for Pomton always spoke extempore: it was half his appeal.

President Pomton felt old and tired. He had reached his professional apogee in the era of the Cold War and had even declined a little when Senator McCarthy was framed by the Senate. If there was to be peace, then let younger and more vigorous men face its awful problems. God grant, at least, that he be not required to pass through another economic depression when the University had scarcely recovered from the last one. And yet, if there was to be peace, and a slackening of the defense program, what in the name of common sense was going to keep peace and prosperity going? "Peace and prosperity," he murmured. "Pee-Pee: all the American people really want. Well, why not? Wee-Wee the People seem determined to govern. The whole thing should be run by trustees, good Republican trustees."

He heard Schneider entering Miss Stilton's office, glanced at his watch, pushed from him with relief his cold speech on the Cold War, assumed again his air of the experienced executive, and cried out cordially, "Ah, there you are, my dear fellow! Let's be getting along. Miss Stilton, I don't want to speed the parting guest. Dr. Schneider and I may want a good talk. So leave my afternoon free. I'll be back in any case in time to sign mail."

The charlatan, said Miss Stilton to herself. He's completely taken him in. But he hasn't taken in Dr. Nast.

I'VE NEVER CONGRATULATED you on that little safari you made to Chicago," said Schneider.

The cook had given them an excellent luncheon and they were smoking two of Pomton's second-string cigars.

"Oh, that!" said Pomton. The tone was modest, but it was clear that he liked Schneider for bringing the matter up.

"Well," said Schneider, "I don't want to prove an argumentative guest, but I shouldn't think many university presidents this year had raised six million, one hundred and fifty-five thousand in a day."

"Of course, it sounds pretty good when you put it that way. But, confidentially, the six million from Mrs. Riley was something I'd been working on for two years. There are leads like that that a university president is always working on if he's on the job—and most of them don't lead anywhere either. Now and then the fruit ripens and falls."

"I'd love to hear how you managed it, if it's not top secret."

"Not at all," said Pomton, only too eager to give the details of his safari, or at least the more creditable details. "There's really not too much to tell. I took Bill Sanders with me. As treasurer of the University, he can answer more quickly and accurately any budgetary questions a prospective donor may raise. And of course he always has a briefcase full of balance sheets and things with him anyhow. Some donors love balance sheets. You see, as a race they are horribly afraid of being suckers. I got twenty thousand once from a woman in St. Louis who wouldn't budge until Bill had shown her our balance sheet. She had misplaced her spectacles, so she held it upside down when she studied it, but she came up satisfied. She wanted to feel that she had not merely inherited money but that she understood it. But I'm getting off the point, aren't I?"

"Not at all. I'm deeply interested in the behavior of donors. After all, I live on that behavior. My only regular source of income is donors."

Schneider accentuated the word *regular* ever so little as a tactful reminder to Pomton that he also received funds from an unidentified government agency. With gratification he noted that Pomton had correctly read this almost surreptitious signal. It was a pleasure to talk with a man, vain or not, who could handle overtones.

"To return to Chicago," Pomton was saying a little eagerly, "I briefed Bill on the plane on the three prospects we had hopes of activating: Mrs. Riley, who owns a vast chunk of Chicago's stockyards; Milton Marshall, who—as his first name suggests—is Jewish and a successful clothing manufacturer; and Lanny MacDonald, who owns a baseball club and has the reputation, I fear, of being a bit of a racketeer."

"What an assortment," said Schneider. "You certainly have to meet all kinds."

"Oh," said Pomton, with the satisfied air of a hypochondriac boasting of his physical afflictions, "you meet the most dreadful people when you're a university president. I briefed Bill first on the small fry. Milton Marshall was born in Poland, and I was confident that as

{111}

a Jew he would be accustomed to giving and wouldn't panic the way a Christian would; also, that he was more likely to be interested in ideas than Christians are; and, thirdly, that he would know how to count better and might need to be shown the treasurer's books. I already knew he was chiefly interested in the library. Milton had to quit high school to help his father in ready-to-wear. He's since grown rich in the business, but he's a voracious reader, with a European respect for books. Since he never got to college, he thinks the kids that do are as crazy about books as he is, and I didn't feel I ought to disabuse him."

This analysis of Milton Marshall, the immigrant Polish Jew, moved Schneider, but he was surprised by Pomton's portrait of him, which was as close to analysis as Schneider had ever seen Pomton come. But then, he reflected, the President's mind always functioned most impressively when his perceptions had been sharpened by the scent of money.

"I knew," he was saying with quiet authority, "that Milton Marshall wouldn't be interested in paying off the University mortgage or any part of it. He would just say he never bought dead horses. But I felt certain he would help toward the library; and that, in turn, would release funds for the mortgage. In my line of business, Schneider, you have to keep the company's funds in more than one cigar box."

"Does that kind of shift present no legal problems?" As to moral problems, Schneider gladly waived them, at least for the duration of this tale.

"Given our high purposes here, outsiders would be very slow to question our methods," said Pomton. "And I think they should be.

"Well, to proceed with my recent safari, I briefed Bill next on Lanny MacDonald. Lanny is not interested in education; in fact, he thinks it rather dangerous. But he does approve of colleges as feeders to professional baseball, and he'd like to see us shift our emphasis from football to baseball. That's silly, of course: in the first place, it's an educational decision and none of his business; and in the second place, it's a decision our alumni wouldn't tolerate for a second. But,

in the interests of the University, I had intimated to Lanny in a previous interview that we were considering abolishing football on the
grounds of danger to life and limb and on the grounds that baseball
is our official national sport anyhow and in times like these we ought
to support every institution that typifies American culture if we're
going to get anywhere in the Cold War. I told him several neighboring colleges might follow suit."

"What ingenious arguments!" Schneider's voice expressed real admiration, an admiration in which the President allowed himself to
bask for a few moments before returning to his Chicago exploits.
Then he said, "Very generous of you; but, ingenious or not, I didn't
have to lie. I really did consider the abolition of football for a few
minutes and ended by considering it undesirable. I am prepared to
consider it again from time to time. Like our State Department, I am
constantly considering all courses of action that may lead to survival.
I don't know whether any other colleges would follow suit if we
dropped football, so I truthfully told him they might. You have to
give human beings, including donors, hope—hope that their dreams
will come true. Besides, it seems clear that we are not going to drop
football, so whether the other colleges 'might follow' is purely academic."

"It certainly ought to be," said Schneider, and the comment appeared to satisfy his host.

"Well, I warned Bill that some kind friend had warned Lanny
MacDonald that we are out to buy a winning football team for next
year, or at least that our alumni are. Men like Lanny can't make the
moral distinction between what my administration does and what
our alumni may choose to do for us. So I suggested to Bill that
Lanny was more likely to shower down if Bill gave him the impression that football here is on the way out and that next season's
Thanksgiving game is pretty sure to be our last. I didn't of course
order Bill to give that impression, much less to make a flat statement: I didn't feel I morally could, even for the sake of the
University."

"Yet I imagine," said Schneider, "there are times when you must feel that what's good for the University is good in the long run for morals."

"Frankly," said Pomton, grateful for Schneider's subtle understanding of the problems he daily faced and often solved, "there are times when I do feel just that. You have put it admirably.

"Well, after I had briefed Bill carefully on Milton Marshall and Lanny MacDonald, I described the rather peculiar and challenging problem presented by Mrs. Riley and her millions. 'Old Stockyards,' as her critics call her, has had four husbands and they all adored her. And that's understandable. Even now—and she must be well into her seventies—she's got something. I mean something besides her millions. You know what I mean?"

"Oh, quite."

"She never got a divorce in her life. She seems—if I may state the case indelicately—to have simply worn out four devoted husbands in a row. They were all rich in their own right and each one left every cent he owned to Mrs. Riley. The problem was to persuade her to share all this money with us.

"But the problem was complicated by the fact that for the last two years Mrs. Riley has had as secretary a remarkable young woman named Amaryllis Allenby, known to her intimates as P'tite, because of her lack of height—or maybe her lack of weight before she wangled her way onto Mrs. Riley's pay roll! Without a green light from P'tite, Mrs. Riley will do nothing whatever. Though too stout for her height, or too short for her weight, according to how you look at her, P'tite is an extraordinarily beautiful young woman, gay, sharp-minded, and animated. But it is common knowledge that she is an insatiable nymphomaniac. I hope these details aren't boring you."

"Not at all. They enable me to gauge the kind of problems you face on behalf of the University."

"I thought you would understand. Well, it's clear I couldn't out of repect for Mrs. Pomton come to grips with this particular problem, even if at my age I could have caught P'tite's fancy, which I could scarcely hope to do. Although, of course, I might have. Sometimes an older man can exercise a compelling charm on a young girl—almost a perverse charm."

As, thought Schneider, I myself might on Dorothy Nast. I am a good deal younger than this old fraud, and Dorothy is at least as old as Amaryllis Allenby, secretary to Old Stockyards. But then, I judge Dorothy is not a nymphomaniac. Besides, she may disapprove of adultery. In any case, I disapprove, or tend to disapprove, or am supposed to disapprove. . . . Schneider shook off a momentary confusion.

"Anyhow," President Pomton was saying, "I could not envisage any leverage I could get on P'tite. That is one reason I took Bill on the trip. When he and I got to Chicago, we went to a moderate-priced hotel downtown. Frankly, I would have preferred the Drake. I like the Gold Coast. There it lies, a narrow strip of clear splendor on the shore of the lake, flanked by the most hideous squalor and crime to the west. It seems to me the perfect symbol of the success every American may achieve under free enterprise."

The heartless, muddleheaded old scoundrel, thought Schneider. No wonder they made a college president of him.

"Yes," said Pomton, meditatively blowing rings of cigar smoke and watching them drift, twist, break. "Imagine, Schneider, on every block of the Gold Coast, there are scores, perhaps hundreds, of legitimate prospects for an institution of learning."

Ah, thought Schneider, if he likes cannibals because they are edible, I confess I feel a twinge of sympathy for him. This charlatan serves a valid Keynesian function: he redistributes wealth; he funnels money from the very rich to the very poor. To the very poor, who—unless they happen to write a textbook—have otherwise no hope of meeting their bills. As for the towering wealth of the Gold Coast, flanked by misery, what is that but a bowdlerized version of the saints in heaven enjoying the misery of the damned down below, as a manifestation of God's justice? This old fraud merely wants to share briefly in that ecstasy. Surely he has done nothing worse than substitute free enterprise and Adam Smith's "invisible hand" for God. At the least he partially serves the function of Robin

Hood, redistributing wealth. Let him proceed. I am learning about universities from a man who has long experience of one. Faculties, like kept women, ought to know where their monthly allowances come from. Where have I heard that recently?

"Well, when Bill and I checked in, I contacted all three of my prospects, and Mrs. Riley asked me to bring Bill to dinner. And what a dinner! Mrs. Riley serves only the best prime beef; I have never seen a fish on her table. After all, why should she encourage the eating of fish?"

"Why, indeed?"

"P'tite was there. And, Schneider, although I admit she is a little plump, what a beautiful, eager young girl she is! Bill, of course, lost his head completely. Mrs. Riley ordered P'tite to devote the next few days to working out with Bill the details of the gift. She told me not to bother my head about them: she was sure they would get on like a house afire. And believe me, they did. She asked me what I was going to do the next evening and I said I had planned to take Bill to a performance of Shakespeare. He's never seen a Shakespeare, and I felt he ought to. Mrs. Riley said Nonsense, Bill would have his hands full with P'tite, and that I was going to take her to a night club to see 'the best strip tease in town.' "

That was too much for Schneider and he broke into loud, delighted laughter. "Oh, no! Oh, no!" he said. "And did you go?"

"Yes," said Pomton, a little shamefaced. "But I count on you not to mention it. I would naturally hate Mrs. Pomton to hear of it."

"Of course," said Schneider.

"The next day I borrowed Bill from P'tite long enough to call on Lanny MacDonald and Milton Marshall. Bill wanted to point out that if Lanny would give twenty-five thousand a year for three years, it wouldn't really cost him anything, what with tax deductibility and getting some fresh young ballplayers for his team; but I insisted on appealing to his love of education—which, of course, doesn't exist. I warned Bill that in operations of this sort one must always play up the higher motives of the prospective donor: the donor can be trusted to think of the low ones without assistance. He got the point: Bill's young, but he's quick.

"Within ten minutes Lanny had seen the low motives for himself, and clearly enough to write a check for the whole seventy-five right then and there. 'Seventy-five grand,' he called it. I deduce that seventy-five is still within his fifteen per cent of income subject to deductibility. I calculate he is netting a minimum of half a million a year—not just from his baseball club, surely. It is important that I draw these conclusions for possible future use.

"When we left, Lanny wouldn't let me thank him for his munificence. He said he had a deal on that day that, given any kind of luck, would net him his seventy-five again and more. 'Then,' I said, 'I'll pray for your success today,' and tried to shake his hand. He grabbed his hand back and said, 'Hey! Don't you put a hex on me! You pray for yourself. I'll take care of my own business affairs.' Lanny is a loathsome fellow; blasphemous; and, what is worse, vulgar. But I think we ought to give him an honorary degree, even if I have to hold my nose while I put the hood over his head. He's got lots more where that seventy-five grand came from, and we need to get hold of some of it."

"He sounds pretty bad," said Schneider.

"He is. But Milton Marshall is swell. He's gentle, courteous, and sort of wistful. He refused to look at the balance sheet. He said, 'I'm less interested in figures than I am in the kids. You see, I have some balance sheets of my own, but Mrs. Marshall and I never had children, Professor.' He always calls me Professor. I asked him to. When I'm off campus, I like to make it clear that I'm merely a wandering scholar; and that, if I'm President here, it's merely as *primus inter pares.*"

Poor fellow, thought Schneider. He's *primus* here all right, if only because he gets more salary than we do; but how many of his faculty would admit he was their scholarly peer? He's merely that vulgar, pompous man who gets the dough they are determined to have, by methods they scorn.

"You noticed, of course," Pomton was saying, "that Milton has no children; and I think a bequest is in order as soon as it can be tactfully proposed. Meanwhile, he has given us twenty thousand a year for four years, to enrich the library."

"That's wonderful. Eighty thousand can buy a lot of books, even at present prices."

"I'm not sure it should all go to books," said Pomton. "Fortunately, 'enrich' is a pretty flexible word. It would enrich the library a lot to put the building in proper repair. That would release funds that would otherwise have to be drawn from Buildings and Grounds, and we could spend those funds on something no donor shows interest in."

"This business of strings on gifts must be one of your chief worries," said Schneider.

"Oh, it is. I simply cannot see why donors won't hand over their money and leave it to the trustees to decide on its best use."

Maybe, thought Schneider, because they have seen the faces of some of our trustees. He thought of Joe Stanforth, who had put through a shady deal with a transit company, and shuddered.

"I have our attorney studying the possibility of diverting some of Lanny's money to making it possible for a couple of brilliant high-school tackles to get a decent education here and play football while doing it, too," said Pomton. "Even Bill remarked to me that Lanny's money had the feel of dirty money, but I told him every well-run university has a special washing machine for cleaning dirty money. If there's any legal way to do it, I'm going to see that Lanny's dirty money is put to educational use. Baseball, indeed! Our alumni don't care that—" and Pomton snapped his fingers—"for baseball. And sooner or later our alumni, if I meet them halfway on producing competent football teams, are going to want to help us with our more obviously educational work. Although I would insist, between you and me, that some of our students get more education from football than they do in certain classes I shall not name."

They could scarcely get less, thought Schneider. "Gossip has it," he said, "that even Mrs. Riley attached strings."

"P'tite claims she did. P'tite doubled the amount I had hoped for, from three million to six, with two provisos: one, that it be held in endowment, with all income going to increase the salaries of assistant professors, on the grounds that Mrs. Riley's primary interest was in the young; and, two, that the securities, which represent an equity in a stockyard, should not be sold."

"I can see," said Schneider, "how Mrs. Riley—or P'tite—might be more interested in young assistant professors than in middle-aged duffers like me, but why won't she let you sell the stock and diversify your portfolio? Wouldn't it be safer?"

"Of course it would be. I was thoroughly annoyed. But Bill explained that according to what he's picked up, this particular stockyard is involved in some pretty nasty labor troubles. Mrs. Riley probably figured that if she came down on the unions, it would look one way, while if a good share of the profits was going to support higher education, the union's case wouldn't look so good. After all, we need the money as much as the workers do and a lot more than Old Stockyards does."

"I get it," said Schneider, who felt he was rapidly learning a great deal about where his salary came from.

"Well, to make a long story short," said Pomton, "I'd done all I could do by Friday evening; but P'tite claimed she and Bill were not finished with the details and that it was easier for her to finalize things like this on weekends, when she was completely free of interruptions. To save time, she even invited Bill to move over from our hotel to her apartment for a week end of extra hard work. So I told them all good-by and came home. 'It's your service, Bill,' I said, 'if you will pardon the expression.' He looked pretty sheepish."

"But is it true, as local gossip has it, that poor Bill has trench mouth?" said Schneider.

"I'm afraid it is. In fact, he came to my office, made me look at his lips and mouth, and asked me if the University would foot the bill for treatment. I told him of course it wouldn't. Then he said he'd gotten the infection in line of duty. I told him it was merely an occupational disease of university treasurers. I thought his request impudent. I like Bill, but there's a side to financing education that simply cannot be allowed to reflect itself in the books. There has to be some reticence in every practical operation."

"But," said Schneider, "the faculty is all agog about the party the University gave in honor of P'tite—what they call the Party for Men Only. Was that stipulated too?"

"Not legally," said Pomton. "Not in writing. But P'tite told Bill that Mrs. Riley believed in following through personally on her gifts, that the gift without the giver was bare, and she directed P'tite to come out here and meet what she called 'the ultimate recipients.' There was nothing for it but to give P'tite her party. I thought the request was pretty cheeky; but, after all, it was six million. I warned Bill that the full professors and associate professors were going to be thoroughly angered by the terms of the gift. They ought, of course, to look on it as a matching operation: I can now go to prospects and say Mrs. Riley saw to it that the assistant professors were properly paid and ask them to help me bring the upper ranks into line."

"I suppose," said Schneider, "the upper ranks would say it's hard to get anybody to match a gift that's already been made rather than conditionally offered."

"I'm sure they've already said it." Pomton's voice was gloomy. "I knew the gift was academic dynamite when I accepted, but I have to think of the University as a whole, of the common good, as it were. And I'd accept six million with about any string on it that the most inconsiderate donor could dream up—and hope for the best next time. It makes for uneven educational development, but beggars can't be choosers."

"And," said Schneider, "those that pay the piper will call the tune." In essence, he thought, the educational policy of a whore.

"Exactly," said Pomton. "I'm glad you, at least, understand." Suddenly, he leaned forward. "Henry," he said, although he had never in his life before used Schneider's first name, and indeed until Schneider had started working for the government and sprucing up, he had heartily disliked the fellow, "Henry, I want to speak to you about something in strict confidence."

"You may trust me," said Schneider.

"I may shortly be called to other work, to a larger sphere of influence. I may have to resign the presidency of this university. If I do, the board will be looking for my successor. I've been assuming Nast was best fitted for the job. But now I'm wondering whether you wouldn't bring a quality of understanding to the job that Nast lacks. If the presidency were offered to you, would you consider it?"

Pomton's feeler was not serious. But one had to be imaginative about these things.

"I'm very honored, of course," said Schneider, "that you should think of me in this connection, but, frankly, I don't think I'm temperamentally fitted for it. I agree with you that Nast is."

Pomton looked surprised, then vaguely disappointed. After all, the fellow still lacks ambition. He glanced surreptitiously at his watch, then exclaimed inhospitably, "Good Lord, I must go over and sign my mail." He was obviously afraid of what Miss Stilton would say. They shook hands.

Schneider started strolling toward home. He suddenly felt quite sick at the stomach. But he remained grateful to this pretentious man for his candor, to this high-powered and eloquent administrator who had means of washing dirty money and could buy with it Schneider's own wretched salary, periodic revisions of departmental course offerings, faculty meetings of explosive vitality, trustees of the most dubious morality, powerful and uneducated alumni, fatuous cocktail parties, and Engel's Law.

~XI~

DOROTHY NAST sat next to the window of the plane silently staring down at the miniature farmland far below. Nast sat beside her, running over the notes he had surreptitiously taken on President Pomton's correspondence with Denby. The Nasts were often silent when together. Except where their separate ambitions overlapped, they had little enough in common. Nast was delighted that he had married Dorothy: first, because she ran his house well and forwarded his ambitions; and, second, because he found her physically attractive. Dorothy was glad, or certainly had until recently been glad, that she had married Nast. She had not been much drawn to him as a man, but she had believed in his star and she had hitched her wagon to it. She believed also that she would enjoy being the wife of the President and she believed the community would prefer her to old Mrs. Pomton.

Nast studied his notes and felt surer than ever that Pomton had fumbled. The Old Man's vanity was constantly betraying him. Nast, when he thought privately of Pomton, always thought of him as the Old Man—Old Man in the ancient tribal sense of The Man on the Way Out, the man whom younger men in their prime begin to eye narrowly. If Pomton failed to die, and if he also failed to get A. & M., he would have to resign before too many years. What would he be like, Nast pondered, as a president emeritus?

He suddenly remembered an outburst of Old Manley's a few days before at the Triangle Club. Speculating on Pomton's eventual retirement, Old Manley had expressed the hope that Pomton would not hang around the University, like some sort of Old Pretender capable of holding the loyalty of all the intellectual wild Highlanders and mavericks in the faculty. It would be better for him, suggested Old Manley, to wander off like the rogue elephants in Asia, those leaders emeriti of their respective herds who, driven out by younger and now stronger males and maddened by loneliness and lack of function, were ready to attack any passing stranger. Presidents emeriti, he had said, should all be put in a large academic stockade, since misery loves company, and since they would have incredible stories of their shady exploits to tell each other. They could hold oratorical contests with each other; grant each other honorary degrees; solicit donations in Confederate money; draft applications for foundation grants; draw up recommendations to their former boards, which somebody could manage to lose in the mails. Surely, Old Manley had said, the Ford Foundation could be interested in establishing such a place for rogue presidents, or rather for presidents emeriti. Old Manley's metaphors had bored Nast at the time, but now he wondered. Well, after all, the Old Man's future was his own funeral—maybe literally; it was not Nast's, and Nast began to analyze Denby.

Dorothy, miles away on the seat next him, was at that moment analyzing Denby too. Denby had insisted that Nast bring her along to New York and that her trip be put on Nast's expense account for the Winthrop Foundation to pay. He had told Nast he thought Dorothy had excellent judgment and could really help. To Dorothy he had stated the case a little differently. He had insisted she write him and tell him where she wanted to be taken while in New York. If he was busy with Nast, he would see that she had the most attractive escorts his staff yielded. But he hoped he wouldn't be too busy, and he reminded her that Nast himself had said he needed to see some people in New York about other matters, economists, editors of journals he wrote for, and even a television director who wanted to discuss with Nast his views on People's Capitalism. Denby promised that, even so, Dorothy would not feel neglected. Let her but tell them where to take her, and that is precisely where she would go. And if she decided in advance, she would have the advantage of knowing which clothes to bring.

Two months ago, thought Dorothy, staring down at the tiny distant farms, green in the May sunshine, and the occasional small town full of toy houses—even one month ago—she would have found this all natural enough. But recently Old Manley had taken to dropping by for an afternoon sherry or a cup of tea; and somehow those visits had reminded her of things her recent marriage had blurred in her mind. Dorothy was evidently as attractive to men as ever. To other men than just her husband. In fact, there was some evidence that she was more attractive to them than to him. To begin with, "Cousin" Freddie Landon, while he had behaved himself, obviously felt to himself, and even to her, like anything but a cousin. She depended on him for a kind of understanding that no woman would ever get from Nast, if only because Nast had clearly never fallen in love with anybody or anything but power. She and Nast cohabited, of course, but Nast's idea of cohabitation did not differ substantially from those of any other emotional adolescent. Nast was, in fact, or so she thought, a nice boy; or, let us say, a nice boy who could play rough when he was after something he wanted. But only a boy. He didn't want to love, or even be loved, really. Not that he was opposed to either: he had simply not found the time to consider what they might be like. He had been too busy succeeding. As a matter of fact, Old Manley, at his age even, would make a more satisfactory lover: he was whimsical, observant, malicious, tender, and he knew reams of French poetry. Dorothy's French was no better than that of most young women in Georgia, but she understood perfectly the poems Old Manley recited to her.

Denby, she told herself decisively, was trying to start an affair with her. He had clearly sized up Nast and knew she was lonely. Oh, he had said nothing improper, except, as the saying goes, by insinuendo. But Dorothy understood him without too much difficulty. For this visit, she had chosen a showing at a famous dress designer's atelier, a daring musical comedy, and a night club. She chose the designer by name and left the other two specifications to Denby to complete in the light of his metropolitan knowledge and his expense account. Meanwhile, she had given a good deal of thought to her wardrobe. She had even consulted Freddie and Old Manley, although she had not worried Nast with the problem. Nast had problems enough. Besides, she had come frankly to loathe the blank expression his face took on whenever she consulted him about her costumes. It was clear that he was willing to pay for them but not to think about them. Freddie and Old Manley did not pay for them, but they thought about them a great deal. Perhaps this was the division of labor to which economic historians apparently attached so much importance. Even with Freddie's and Old Manley's help, she could not at the last minute decide, and each occasion had called for a first choice and for an alternate in case she changed her mind. The least she could do to thank Denby was not to introduce a Corn Belt note at his parties for her. Besides, she liked Denby. He had been a good dinner guest, rendering direct and enthusiastic homage to her cooking; and he had been very much a male, rendering devious but no less enthusiastic homage to her femininity. Nast, of course, had not noticed.

Over their lunch trays, Dorothy and Nast talked amicably enough. The difficulty with Nast probably was that everything he said had only one meaning. She yawned slightly; and Nast attentively urged her to take a little nap. He even lowered the back of her seat for her. If only he had had sense enough to make a little love to her, right here in the plane! But he was not after Dorothy. He already had

Dorothy. First things first. Now he was after a grant from the Winthrop Foundation, and his lust for the grant left him barely enough psychic energy to lower her seat for her.

She pretended to sleep, while Nast made notes on his coming conversation with the television director. If only he collected stamps, she thought, she would buy some rare ones for him by way of thanks for his many kindnesses to her. Or a tropical fish, if he liked tropical fish. But how profoundly glad she was now that, guided by some deep instinct, she had insisted from the start on separate rooms. His visits to her room were like those of a cocksure high-school sophomore, and she always wondered whether he would rush out and write her name in chalk on a board fence. In a very real sense, she reflected, they had never really met. Yet she felt she had met "Cousin" Freddie—who had behaved with due circumspection; and Old Manley, who had never laid a hand on her except verbally by way of certain choice passages of Baudelaire. If she had indeed lost her virginity, and of this she now felt uncertain, it was not to Nast but to Old Manley. Or was it to Baudelaire?

She was surprised to find how much she looked forward to seeing Denby, to running around New York with him, to killing time, to playing, to flirting—if that was what he wanted. As to being unfaithful to Nast—even given the opportunity, she doubted if she would take it. The issue seemed somehow to lack importance, for her, and for Baudelaire. And yet . . . She remembered the two of them, Nast and Denby, lighting cigars after dinner. A cigar was wrong for Nast, somehow too big for him, clumsy and ostentatious, almost a small boy's defiance. For Denby the cigar had been natural, pleasurable; he had puffed at it with cheerful gusto, dominating it as thoroughly as he had his thick steak, his steaming yams, his two foaming, beaded glasses of beer. . . . She was suddenly thirsty.

Nast detected that she was not sleeping and murmured softly, "Honey!"

She thought, I am the only girl who ever came out of Georgia who really hates that word. Still, if he makes love to me here and now, no matter with how much restraint, I shall forget Denby; I shall forget Old Manley; and even Freddie. And I shall make him read Baudelaire, to teach him to love me worthily for the first time. She raised her long, dark lashes ever so little and gave Nast an adorable smile.

"Honey," said Nast more urgently than ever, "I want your advice. I've got a notion Denby has grave doubts about some of these social-science characters we have. Unless I miss my guess, he could be led by you, if not by me, to shift the whole project to a grant to the department of economics—and, boy, would that make my show hum! I think I could square it with Pomton. And unless I miss my guess, that would be the finishing touch: you'd be the President's wife before long. What d'you say?"

She smiled again, though with a difference he did not detect. She said to herself, The double-crossing bastard! I've got a good mind to tip off poor old Pomton. Why, the damned Yankee! He couldn't fall for Cleopatra: he'd mistake her for a useful contact. She wanted to cry, not because of his baseness toward Pomton. She and Nast had planned dirtier tricks than that, she reflected, for she was not lacking in candor with herself. But she did so want a lover and not merely a partner in petty crime. A lover, maybe, who would commit a crime, but a crime for her. Oh, she had heard about being the President's wife. But she didn't want a lover to commit a crime to get more power for her; if he must be a criminal, this lover she so sorely lacked, let it be just to see her once, just to meet her for the first time, even just to see which dress she had chosen and why. Was that too much to ask?

She smiled at him again, murmured, "Let me think about it a while," turned her head away from him as if to examine the landscape far below for inspiration, and silently, steadily wept. Then, because she was emotionally as well as physically tired, she really did fall asleep. Nast went on making notes.

When she awoke, twilight had enveloped the plane. Down below, great strings of colored jewels outlined the highways, and lavish clusters marked each little town. Diamonds, emeralds, sapphires, rubies—they were all there. But at the center of each town-cluster of gems was always a great burst of rubies, where the big red neon signs of the shopping center lay. They lay burning, burning, on the black velvet of the landscape below her. And she remembered some real rubies she had seen once, on a real piece of black velvet, in a full-page advertisement, and how avidly she had longed to seize them and fling them about her neck. These jewels far below her, too, she longed to snatch up and fling about her neck.

Finally, they circled over the harbor, and piles and piles of jewels were heaped up until they soared toward the sky. They took a cab straight to the St. Regis. Henrietta would have chosen the Algonquin, out of respect for all the intellectuals who had congregated there over the years, all the writers and actors. Arrived at the St. Regis, Dorothy and Nast were shown to their rooms; and in hers Dorothy found tall branches of dark, purple lilac that scented the whole room; and a corsage of orchids, both of course from Denby.

The four days that followed were an utter delight. Dorothy was radiantly happy. To her gratified surprise, and apparently to his own as well, Denby was able to be with her almost constantly. One of his underlings was concluding the business of the grant with Nast; and between conferences with the underling Nast darted about New York making contacts, contriving, negotiating, finalizing, briefing. Despite this dispersal of his enormous energies, Nast responded to Dorothy's radiance by trying to make love to her. Dorothy was now in love with the City of New York, not with Nast; and she put him off. She was in no mood to finalize.

Her love affair with Manhattan had been a case of love at first sight; and the affair was still young, beckoning, mysterious, and to-tal. She had never before in her life seen New York—in fact, her biggest city had been Atlanta—and she was drunk with excitement. Denby thought he knew this Babylon, but she quickly taught him better. Her appetite for adventure went far beyond theaters, night clubs, and *haute couture:* she dragged him to the Botanical Gardens, to the top of the Empire State, on a boat ride around the Island of Manhattan. Abandoning the limousine he had hired, they window-shopped Madison Avenue; they strolled up and down Fifth; and always they came back again to Rockefeller Plaza, to gaze at the rows of flowers among the towering buildings—those flowers which, like herself, were but fleeting visitors whose beauty beguiled every eye.

"Oh, I do like the people here!" she said to Denby. "They treat you so wonderfully."

And, indeed, she had abundant evidence: people who had not treated anybody even decently for months were warmed by her gladness into absolutely feting Dorothy. She talked freely to everybody: cabbies, news vendors, shopgirls, the attendants on the gay little pleasure boat that circles the island. The latter told her about the Staten Island ferry, and she insisted she must make the trip. She waved aside the limousine, dragged Denby into a subway, and was off to the ferry. They leaned on the deck rail in the cool May evening, while Dorothy turned her face to a stiff harbor breeze and laughed with pleasure as the lights twinkled in the tall skyscrapers clustered near the Battery, and the traffic of the harbor slipped almost noiselessly by.

Then they subwayed to Fifty-ninth Street, hired a Victoria, and ordered the coachman to drive slowly through Central Park. Dorothy sat blissfully by Denby's side, gazing at the tall lighted buildings that flanked the park; listening to the *clop-clop* of the horse's hooves; listening to Denby tell her how beautiful she was. She accepted his praise; she evaded his proffered kisses; but she put her hand in his and left it there.

That she should be stared at on the street by nearly every man she passed merely flattered and pleased her, but it no more astonished or dismayed her than it would have dismayed a reigning queen, stared after by her subjects. She accepted New York's admiration and loved it, for she had nothing but admiration for New York—for its seething traffic, its soaring buildings, and its people, people, people everywhere. Half the pleasure she found in it was so obviously the pleasure of an exhilarated child that even Denby, who had never in his life permitted himself to become unexhilarated, found himself looking at New York through new and joyful eyes.

But all play and no work might easily have made Dorothy a dull girl. On her third evening with Denby, sitting in a dimly lighted night club and listening intently while Denby discussed her favorite subject—herself—Dorothy tactfully stated the case for making the grant, not for social science in general but for Nast's department of economics. And, although she had drunk a good deal of champagne, she stated the case very clearly and convincingly. Denby teased her charmingly for being "a faithful and conniving wife" and promptly conceded the point. Dorothy adored winning points: she thanked him so provocatively that for the first time he kissed her. Considered merely technically, it was the most interesting kiss she had received since she had married Nast. Champagne or no champagne, she saw now with perfect clarity that faithful and conniving was just what she had been, and she had a feeling that she would go on conniving, although perhaps not exclusively with Nast. She felt a little puzzled, here in the night club this evening, that during all these months she had never once sent up the signal that Old Manley had patiently and hopefully awaited and that Freddie could certainly have read, promptly and correctly.

She was kissed next morning again. Nast was breakfasting with her in her room; and Dorothy was propped up in bed luxuriously. When Room Service had respectfully bowed itself out, Dorothy told Nast that the money was his, and he rushed to her bedside and kissed her, warmly and dully. Twenty-five thousand a year for five years, and all for his department, Nast considered worth a kiss, a very sincere kiss. Dorothy explained, a little coldly, that the proposal to shift from social science in general to economics alone would quite properly come from Denby. All Nast had to do was to protest vaguely that President Pomton would be disappointed, and he would be courteously overridden.

"Naturally," said Nast with great satisfaction. "I wouldn't want to be in the position of double-crossing the Old Man."

"Naturally," said Dorothy.

Next day, when Nast and Denby "finalized," Denby solemnly proposed the shift. Then, glancing at his watch, he muttered an excuse and rushed off to meet Dorothy while Nast went back to his television contact. It was Denby's fourth and last day of sight-seeing and it was both arduous and glorious. On the morning of the fifth day Dorothy and Nast flew from Idlewild, while Denby rested happily in his apartment, a cold compress on his head, his aching feet in a tub of hot water, and a dazed but happy smile upon his face.

~XII~

Twenty-four hours later he was fit to go to his office. And at the same hour, many hundreds of miles away, a triumphant Nast reported to Pomton that his mission was accomplished. He had entered Miss Stilton's office with a face so radiant that she asked no questions but clasped her hands above her head in a funny feminine imitation of a triumphant boxer she had seen on television. He smiled a kind of assent.

"Well?" said Pomton anxiously.

"It's good and it's bad," said Nast modestly.

"Go on, go on," cut in Pomton impatiently.

"Well, it's twenty-five thousand a year for five years all right," said Nast. "But Denby absolutely insisted that it all be earmarked for economic research. You can imagine what an embarrassing position that put me in. When he demanded of me whether my department wasn't the strongest in the social science division, I practically pleaded the Fifth. I definitely declined to say."

Pomton looked grave. Another golden apple of discord. Oh, well.

"But we know your department is the strongest, all the same," he said finally, remembering gratefully the numerous occasions when Nast had helped him dig money out of recalcitrant donors.

"It's kind of you to say so, sir."

"One hundred and twenty-five thousand dollars," said Pomton, speaking slowly and savoring the words, "is one hundred and twenty-five thousand dollars, even if they had given it for privies to be erected on the front campus."

"It really is," agreed Nast. And he reflected bitterly that a good many people in social science, if they had heard the news and the analogy, would loathe the one and love the other. But, he thought consolingly, power never stays unloved for long. Love may not create power, but power always creates love.

"If I should have to leave here," said Pomton, thinking joyfully of A. & M., "the trustees of this university are going to hear about your administrative capacity. Plenty."

"That's very generous of you, sir." Nast was elated by this evidence of the Old Man's loyalty to him.

"Milton will be disappointed," said Pomton reflectively.

"Mr. President," said Nast, "Milton was born for the special purpose of being repeatedly disappointed. He Who Gets Slapped."

"Well," sighed Pomton, "he can't blame me. You did your best to get the funds for the Institute for Research in the Social Sciences, and Denby wouldn't string along. Milton can't blame me for that."

"He won't," said Nast reassuringly.

He went over a few details with Pomton and submitted a draft of a press release about the rapid growth of the department of economics under Professor Nast's administration. Pomton felt the draft underplayed his own role in that development but said nothing. Miss Stilton could be trusted to fix that. And he was truly grateful to Nast for all that Nast had done to clinch the deal that he, Pomton, had worked on for so many weary months. He was a little bothered by the effect the new terms of the grant might have on those two business friends of his, who had been waiting shivering on the bank to let the Winthrop Foundation plunge first and test the temperature. Maybe, now, they would all insist on restricting their own gifts to economics, which would make one department stinking rich at the expense of the others. But, he reflected, there would be nothing more disproportionate about it than there was about the budget for football; and, despite malicious claims to the contrary, the University had stood up under the expansion of football pretty well. The chief trouble was that he and the Treasurer could scarcely hope to play any cigar-box tricks that would channel off some money to the other social sciences. Denby knew as much about cigar boxes as they did, maybe more. Anyhow, why worry? This was Nast's baby: let Nast worry about it. Pomton would have his own problems, bigger, more intricate, and more glamorous problems, at A. & M.

Nast hurried home, where he found Dorothy serving tea on the sunny terrace to Old Manley, and Freddie Landon arrived just then, without a cigar of course. Nast did his pretties, briefly and abstractedly, then hurried upstairs to his study to prepare an imminent radio speech and a book review. He had just noticed that Dorothy was looking even prettier than usual but made nothing of that. Old Manley and Freddie noticed it too and observed her as narrowly as a good doctor would observe a patient. For her part, Dorothy observed that at least two of the three men, perhaps the right two, were observing her. Externally, she preserved her calm, but despite her best efforts she could not conceal a certain new excitement.

⤚XIII⤙

I'D GO AHEAD and write it," said Old Manley. "Writing a textbook
is the least dishonest way open to a professor to make a decent
living. If I had a family to support, or even a full-time mistress, I'd
write one myself."

"You?"

Schneider was a little horrified that anybody so gay, so free, so
ironical as Old Manley should consent to write a textbook.

"Only for the pleasure of writing the preface."

"And what would you say in the preface?"

"I would say: 'Some persons may wonder why, with so many
texts already available dealing with the age of Louis Fourteenth, I
should have chosen to add one to their number. It is because all the
others are no good.'"

Emboldened by Schneider's chuckle, Old Manley continued. "I'd
rather like to do the dedication, too."

"Ah? I'm all ears."

" 'To the college students of America, the largest captive audience this side of the Iron Curtain.' Still, I'd also enjoy writing it 'To the wife I never met, whose perpetual and consoling absence gave me the peace of mind without which this book could not have been so quickly and easily composed.' Should I go on?"

"No," said Schneider with a light laugh. "I get the idea. And I warn you, I may steal a dedication from you. Jim Small says the thousand-dollar advance is waiting for me to say yes, and somehow this talk with you has decided me. Jim is the most literate of all the publishers' representatives I've talked with over the years, and his house does know how to sell textbooks. He swears he'll make my fortune."

"But what about your research for the government? Won't the textbook interfere with that?"

Did Schneider detect a shade of irony in the question? In any case, he didn't care. Old Manley had clearly got wind of Schneider's so-called security project and of the increasing deference his secret activities were winning him from the faculty. And Old Manley was a great doubter. But it would be utterly unlike him to accuse Schneider of a hoax. He would leave that to Nast, who was furiously jealous of Schneider's growing fame. The irony Schneider thought he sensed disturbed him chiefly because he himself disliked the ambiguous position he had without premeditation placed himself in by his playful remark to young Ripley about security. Faced now with Old Manley's question, he knocked out his pipe thoughtfully, placed it in the pocket of his shabby tweed coat, and lowered his voice.

"Dr. Manley, I'm going to ask a favor of you. I can manage the textbook; but others, less well disposed than you, will raise the same question. I'm going to ask you to say nothing about the textbook."

"I promise."

They entered the Triangle Club together. Schneider glanced around the lounge, at the gloomy plywood splendor of the wainscoting, at the leaded windowpanes of the Corn Belt Gothic, at the little groups of his colleagues clustered here and there. He caught fragments of the customary conversations drifting through the close air along with the blue pipe smoke. They were quoting to each other remarks they had made in recent lectures to their classes; exchanging professional gossip about colleagues at neighboring institutions; weighing the prospects of the political factions that were certain to collide at the next meeting of the college faculty, when Weed's committee on curricular reform would surely present its final report.

They were also busily piecing together the latest campus rumor. According to well-informed but unofficial sources, as the saying goes, President Pomton and his youthful, high-pressure, vulgar treasurer, Bill Sanders, had gone to Chicago several weeks before to enjoy their expense accounts and, if possible, to raise money. There Pomton had stupidly accepted seventy-five thousand dollars from a shady character named Lanny MacDonald, who owned a professional baseball club and intended to use the University as a sort of training ground for young talent. Then he had by sheer luck been given eighty thousand by a Polish immigrant who had made a fortune, who had aspirations toward culture, and whose gift was earmarked "to enrich the library." But there was an additional rumor that Pomton was maturing a slick plan for diverting this gift from its purpose. Finally, Pomton had by God knows what means persuaded an infamous but wealthy old character, who owned most of the Chicago stockyards, a Mrs. Riley, to shower down. It seemed that Mrs. Riley, who was probably senile by now, was the victim of a young and beautiful secretary, a nymphomaniac by the improbable name of Amaryllis Allenby, known as P'tite. While Pomton was dragging poor old Mrs. Riley off to a strip tease, of all things, the nymphomaniac went into conference with Bill Sanders and emerged with a gift of a cool six million from Mrs. Riley to the University, but with what might be called nymphomaniacal strings attached: it was to be an endowment, the interest on which was for the exclusive purpose of raising the salaries of assistant professors. This stipulation had left the upper ranks of the faculty thoroughly angry, and indignant that the Chicago stockyards should be dictating policy on one of the most vital educational problems the University faced: faculty salaries.

To rub it in, the administration had invited P'tite to visit the University and had given a reception for her to meet the assistant professors. Finally, there was a rumor that, as a result of his conference with P'tite, the Treasurer had developed a painful case of trench mouth.

This complicated story would have seemed to Schneider typical of the stories faculties circulate about university administrations: it was improbable, vulgar, and vindictive, although it indisputably contained some of the elements of low comedy. But Schneider happened, of course, to know that it was true. Besides, the problems of evidence and interpretation which the story involved could not fail to interest any professional historian; and Schneider, therefore, pricked up his ears. The remarks he could catch were urbane, to a certain degree witty, judicious, and disillusioned.

He thanked Old Manley for his advice and advanced curiously toward the groups, while a strange impression grew on him that he had entered a zoo. Some of his colleagues' faces actually took on the appearance of the faces of animals he had examined in zoos. Here was the harassed glance of the giraffe, and even its long neck; there, the immense and vacant face of the hippopotamus. An elephant stood in front of the fireplace rubbing his drooping buttocks and watching the other animals through discreet, beady eyes: by what happy chance was he disguised in daily life as the only McKinley Republican in the college faculty? A hyena's high laugh smote his ears, the shrill chatter of monkeys from a neighboring room, all the myriad noises of the academic jungle that only an academic ear can decipher. His swift daydream passed, and he noted with pleasure the cloud of affable deference that rose like incense and wafted toward him from every quarter of the large lounge. Since he had begun his imaginary government research, his stock on campus had steadily soared, in that meaningless way stock so often has, when the radio announcer says, "Rails up, wheat lower, cotton down, industrials off two points." Why in God's name should rails go up in the midst of such general disaster? He had always wondered. Assistant professors' salaries advanced sharply, presidentials up, treasurers up, diplomatic historians scored sensational rise.

"How's the project going?" asked one of his colleagues—the elephant, of all persons—respectfully.

Schneider instinctively thrust his hand in his pocket and caressed Jim Small's contract.

"Not too badly," he said.

The elephant found this modesty really charming in a man working under heavy security regulations, a man picked out by the State Department, not at Harvard, not at Yale, nor Columbia, but here in the remote Midwest. It reflected credit on them all.

A donkey suddenly brayed from the next room, amused by the phrase "The Reception for Men Only," deftly applied to the reception they had given P'tite, to meet the "ultimate recipients." Several of the ultimate recipients had since then visited P'tite in Chicago. That was the chief reason the donkey's bray had struck such a curiously lubricious note. What lascivious animals donkeys are, anyhow, Schneider said to himself. He stood, with one hand in his pocket, fingering Jim Small's contract. He smiled affably at the animals. The giraffe was craning his neck, looking at Schneider out of large, liquid, brown eyes, from his narrow, anxious face.

"You know," he was saying, "there's no use beating about the bush. For weeks now we've been piecing together chance remarks you've made. It's like a detective story. It obviously has to do with heavy water and hence with the Big Bang. My own suspicion is that, depending on what you find, our relations with the Kremlin will improve or else get decidedly worse. I wish we could depend on our Allies.

"If you could just let us have one scrap more of information, even by implication, this faculty would have something to talk about besides Pomton and his strip tease."

"Well," said one of the monkeys, who had now joined the conversation, "I'm sick of being held out on. Schneider is conducting his own strip tease—an intellectual strip tease. And I despair of ever seeing the naked facts. Now, Pomton's strip tease did conclude with something." And he wrinkled his malicious monkey face knowingly.

"How I wish," said the giraffe with mock earnestness, "how I wish I could have studied Pomton's face at that night club!"

How he wishes, thought Schneider without resentment, how he wishes he could have studied what Pomton was studying, sipping champagne, his eyes glued to the brilliantly lighted stage, while Mrs. Riley watched her man.

Freed from the necessity of conducting his own strip tease, yet still breathing the subtle smell of incense, Schneider half listened to the zoological yawping around him, while he daydreamed on. "I hear football is being de-emphasized at the precise moment—by pure coincidence, of course—that Mr. Lanny MacDonald, who owns a ball club, they say. . . ." "The Treasurer has contracted a severe case of trench mouth, which may become an epidemic among assistant professors. . . ." "I trust the Committee on Library Expenditure will check up on how much of Milton Marshall's gift actually goes into buying books. . . ."

What group except a faculty, Schneider asked himself, could reverse the whole long Darwinian process, go back through countless millennia, and recreate the animality of their remotest primeval ancestors? What other man than a professor, having once seen the divine light that shines from ideas, could choose to become a giraffe again, a donkey, an elephant, a hippopotamus? The treason of the intellectuals. Print or perish.

Schneider managed to drift off, undetected, from the zoo. He wanted to breathe fresher air. It was now full spring on the campus, and the May sun was boasting of what it might do in June. From far away came the staccato, concerted, Nazilike roar of a cheering section: a baseball game was in progress. There were in consequence few students about. Schneider loved the campus empty of students. It was green and quiet.

He wanted to reflect on his abrupt rise to local fame. How had he suddenly risen to royal rank, even in this Animal Kingdom? When

young Ripley had spoken to him in the library, the day Schneider discovered Engel's Law, he had merely placed his foot absent-mindedly
on the bottom step of a stairway, assuming subconsciously that it
would be better upstairs than down, and found himself on an escalator. Since then, he had moved forward and upward, gracefully,
with machinelike precision, smiling at those who greeted him, admitting coyly but discreetly that he was on his way upward to an
undisclosed level. Suppose the escalator ended, not on the second
floor, but on the sill of a high, open window? Suppose he was
plunged to his academic death? To this possibility, he remained
strangely indifferent. Yet how could he avoid sooner or later being
shown up as an impostor? He knew nothing, either of a secret or
public nature, of heavy water or atomic energy. Would he be asked
to resign from the American Historical Association or would he
merely be dropped from this zoo, where he had been so long and so
uncomfortably caged? He was barely curious. Certainly, he was doing no research for the State Department; but, beginning this very
evening, he would be doing research, if that was the word, for Jim
Small and for Jim's vast captive audience. That Jim's offer should
have come when it did was not surprising. Escalators operate that
way.

For twenty years he had been toiling up an endless stairway,
constantly shoved aside by those with stronger legs and stouter
hearts or merely more ruthless elbows. He had not even known
escalators existed, although, sitting at breakfast with Denby, crunch-
ing bacon or breathing the smoke from those heavenly Havanas, he
had divined something of the sort. What the devil, come to think of
it, made this escalator work? A button? Atomic energy? Heavy
water?

And then the plunge from the window into academic disgrace?
Who said there was a window? If he had not known of this escalator
he was on, from the first to the second floor, what was to prevent
them from having built another escalator from the second floor to
the third? At this moment he was willing to wager they had. Denby,
who had chucked the teaching profession as a bad joke and now

headed the Winthrop Foundation, had certainly found the second escalator. Why shouldn't Schneider? Neither he nor Denby knew what made them work. It was just that Denby got sick of climbing before Schneider did and decided to put his foot on the bottom step of any stairway that seemed to be moving upward in a methodical way. Now and then Denby doubtless passed some friend or other who had put his foot on the top step of one that was moving downward; and Denby would note his terrified expression as his friend went lower and lower. But there was no earthly way to rescue him and Denby would always wave cordially, feeling that some people perversely love basements, perhaps because that was where the advertisements claimed the best bargains were. Denby loathed basements, a fact he had made clear enough at breakfast that morning months before, although his job as philanthropoid inevitably took him back down on short trips. And in a basement he had found Schneider, discontented with the bargains. Denby had not used the term escalator but he had certainly hinted that one existed. Then Schneider, faced with the challenge of young Ripley's question and shaken out of his lethargy by Engel's Law, had almost inadvertently placed his foot on the bottom step of a stairway he had not really examined, and had been swept upward. He was still soaring. The sensation after all those long years in the basement was utterly delicious. He no longer reeled about the campus like a somnambulist: on the contrary, he was filled with an inner serenity and a quiet determination to avoid the sills of open windows.

He pulled out his billfold and remembered with relief that Henrietta had only yesterday given him his monthly allowance. He went into a chain grocery and bought a pound of the best Canadian bacon. Then he went home.

His three little daughters were out. They were supposed to be doing their homework at this hour, which meant that they must have sneaked next door to watch television on a set his neighbor had bought. Both he and Henrietta loathed television but he wondered now whether watching television wasn't as good a method as any for learning about the mysterious escalators operating throughout a highly technological society committed to People's Capitalism. He wondered if he would ever have married Henrietta if he had watched television first; whether he would ever have wasted four years on a doctorate. In any case, he was glad the kids were out: he wanted to talk with Henrietta.

He found her at her desk, busy with her household accounts. She had made herself an expert double-entry bookkeeper. Indeed, her double-entry bookkeeping had for several years been Schneider's chief grievance. He had felt that she was reducing her marriage, her motherhood, life itself, to a matter of bookkeeping. But this afternoon the sight of her ledgers and columns did not anger him; it tickled his imagination. Given his textbook assignment and his alleged top-secret government research, it struck him suddenly and agreeably that he was himself keeping two sets of books, which required more dexterity than even this black art of Henrietta's.

He smiled at her silently, laid his briefcase on a table, brazenly placed a brown paper package on it, walked over to her, and kissed her, thereby resuming a ritual that had fallen into some disuse. She registered the faint signs of embarrassment that she had always exhibited under a display of affection but flushed slightly and, he thought, pleasurably. Then she looked at the brown paper parcel.

"What have you bought?" she asked.

"A pound of the best Canadian bacon."

She frowned, the way any treasurer does when someone makes a purchase not authorized in the budget.

Schneider smiled, then pulled out Jim Small's contract and placed it on her desk.

"Take it out of that," he said.

She gazed silently at the contract.

"Henrietta," he said, "I need to talk with you, quietly, alone. Can you give me an hour?"

"In about ten minutes?"

"In our bedroom," he said.

He took the bacon to the kitchen and then carried his briefcase to his study—or, perhaps more precisely, to Henrietta's sewing room.

He washed up, and then rummaged in his dresser drawer for a handkerchief. Suddenly he smiled. He drew from the drawer a white Arab kaffiyah. Still smiling, he placed it carefully on his head and arranged it gracefully around his shoulders. Then he crowned it with the black braid circlet that went with it. He studied himself approvingly in the mirror. It was certainly not Lawrence of Arabia who stared back at him. It was not even Glubb Pasha. But neither was it the sick, debt-ridden, henpecked chairman of the history department who had started the second semester a defeated man. He wandered to the window and gazed out at the young leaves that screened the branches of the trees, and he remembered his long winter of defeat and despair. Henrietta entered. She glanced at the kaffiyah and raised her eyebrows ever so slightly.

"It's just," she said, "that I've never seen you put it on once since Tom sent it from Damascus a good two years ago."

"It was an unsuitable headdress for the most henpecked man on the campus."

"The agenda of our conference, no doubt."

"Without a doubt in the world," he said. "Sit down. You have been wearing the trousers in this household for several years."

"Somebody had to wear them," she said, and her voice was not angry but weary.

"I am not criticizing you for putting them on. I am merely ordering you to take them off. I intend to wear them again, from now on in."

"Till death do us part?"

"Till death do us part. Meanwhile, the budget has to be approved by me before becoming law, and I warn you that the sum assigned to Miscellaneous must be a reasonable one."

"That will be splendid. Where shall we get the sum from? From the column marked Rent?"

"You are forgetting that I propose to increase our income substantially. You are forgetting the textbook."

"And your salary from the government?"

She sat, as she always did, with her back very straight. In her carefree girlhood, when her father's Doughnuts were still Different, she had been an excellent horsewoman; and she still had, to use the horsey idiom, a good seat. She still held her head imperiously, although Henry's illnesses and frustrations and the three little girls' hatred of school and their love of singing commercials had streaked her dark hair here and there with gray. Not only had she been an excellent horsewoman, but those who insist that every human face reminds the discerning observer of some one animal more than of others would have seen in this face of hers the face of a racing filly. For she was wholly Anglo-Saxon.

She was not, thought Schneider in this split second, seductively beautiful like Dorothy Nast. Where Dorothy's eyes were violet, Henrietta's were light blue, candid, piercing, unambiguous. Where Dorothy's complexion was peaches and cream, Henrietta's was the healthy flush of a fall apple. Where Dorothy's hands were smooth and slightly dimpled, like a child's, Henrietta's were slender, strong, capable, and somewhat reddened by her years of house-proud labor.

She is intelligent, too, thought Schneider with a certain pride. She has a competent, analytical mind; and she cultivates it, as carefully and constantly as one would cultivate a garden. Dorothy would not recognize an abstract idea or a principle if she met one on the street; she has merely an infallible, almost animal, instinct for communicating with other persons, where Henrietta is baffled by the personal, both in others and in herself. Poems make Dorothy swoon with delight and incomprehension; they challenge Henrietta to literary criticism.

My wife has all the moral virtues, too, thought Schneider with some annoyance. She is prudent; just—except perhaps to Dorothy; as brave as a lion; and almost ascetic in her pleasures. Dorothy has a certain intuitive shrewdness, I judge—except when she picks a husband; but I think I detect lack of courage; she is not remotely interested in being just; and it is pretty certain that pleasure guides her life as it does the lives of kittens. Yet she has one kind of courage, too, that kittens have: she dares to love, and that is difficult for Henrietta.

"For certain reasons that I do not feel free to discuss even with you," Schneider heard himself saying, "we can for the present count on no salary from the government."

Henrietta shrugged. Her candid eyes expressed complete disbelief. She sees clear through me, thought Schneider. But does it matter? We are not engaged in rebuilding the relationship we had, or thought we had, before the children came. We are making diplomatic history. We are treating, as governments treat, and trying to build a viable peace based on mutual respect. We even like each other, which is more than many couples can say after fifteen years of the erosion of family life. Above all, neither of us is sufficiently irresponsible to break up a home that three little girls are busy growing up in. Or maybe the vital point is that neither of us is so much in love with the proverbial third party that we are willing even to rob our daughters of their home. There is no sign that Henrietta is interested in another man, although she feels a sort of perverse admiration for Nast. And I don't love another woman, not even Dorothy. If we use our heads, we'll keep this thing going. If we use our heads, and if this filly doesn't get the bit in her teeth again.

If they lived under Islamic law, and if Nast would just drop dead, he would buy Dorothy from her parents, as one would buy a Circassian slave girl, and make her his second wife. Henrietta's virtues would be easier to admire if he had a less virtuous woman near at hand to balance things a bit. There is something profoundly competitive about Henrietta's relation to me. There would be something co-operative about Dorothy's. But we do not live under Islamic law. Schneider unconsciously adjusted his kaffiyah, as if a Western wind had threatened to disarrange it. Henrietta smiled, and her smile disconcerted him.

"If we are to have a new dispensation," she said, "let's do a thorough job. Stipulate—if my sheik so wills, of course."

He ignored the gibe.

"Very well. Bacon for breakfast. Corn cakes sometimes, instead of always buckwheat. First deck on the morning paper. I know these things sound trivial, but they would make all the difference."

He paused, and thought. Then, "Less starch in my shirt collars. I know they look better with starch, but they feel like hell. And after all, it's my neck. And, above all, of course, a study to myself, which nobody is to enter but me and where nobody tidies my desk. If I think of other things later, I'll speak up."

"Good," she said. "How these little grievances mount up in marriage. And they're harder to mention in marriage, I find, than in any other relation.

"By tomorrow evening I shall have cleared the sewing things out of your study and given the study the last cleaning it will ever get—at least from me. Nobody but you shall ever enter it. In the closet of your study you will find a broom, a dustpan and hand broom, and some dust cloths. I daresay you won't use them, but they will be there just in case. I hope you won't mind if I call your study the piggery: it will make it easier for me to tolerate beneath the same roof I live under. Finally, as a boon to me, my sheik, I beg you when emptying your pipe to do it in the green faïence bowl on your desk and not into a waste-paper basket. I know you're absent-minded. I know the nineteenth century interests you more than the twentieth; but if you accidentally start a fire, it won't burn down some house in the nineteenth century: it will burn down ours now. I know that if you were really lost in thought, you wouldn't mind; but it happens that the children and I live here too.

"As a matter of fact, most of the things in you that madden me are merely aspects of your absent-mindedness. When you are worried, you absent-mindedly tug at your hair, or scratch the back of your hand. When you shave, you absent-mindedly all but cut your throat. On a hot Sunday last summer, when I had struggled in the kitchen to cook you an especially appetizing dinner, you ate heartily and were kind enough to commend my efforts. Yet, two hours later, lost in thought, you said you could plan the rest of your day better if I would tell you whether we had had dinner yet. Some people might have thought it funny. Fifteen years ago I probably would have. Now I find it merely loathsome. Wake up!

"It's the same with the children. I happen to know you love them

—when you remember they're alive. That hurts their feelings. And I hope you agree you have some responsibility toward these little girls: they were not born by parthenogenesis, so far as I can recall the circumstances. Wake up!

"On the rare occasions when we go out socially, don't ask me where your galoshes are. They are where you put them—either in the closet where all our galoshes belong or in the oven where you absent-mindedly placed them. When we get to a friend's house, with or without your galoshes, don't crowd off in a corner with the other great scholars and talk shop while we wives shift for ourselves. I would prefer a little adultery occasionally to this stupid armed truce between the sexes. We are not illiterate concubines, except perhaps Mrs. Nast. I can think of several of your colleagues whose students would gain if I took over their classes. So try hard to behave in a more civilized fashion when we go out.

"I am delighted you have apparently recovered your health. But you are forty-four and pretty sure to get sick again, at least for a day or two, before I am finally widowed. When you do, try not to act as if it were childbirth or something else serious. I cannot imagine why men exploit minor ailments to get attention."

She paused. If she had shrieked these things, if she had ranted, he would have remained the unperturbed sheik, secure in the knowledge that he belonged to the master sex, and that she belonged in purdah. But she had spoken quietly, cogently, rationally, occidentally. From a negotiator's point of view, he thought, she has put me far, far behind the eight ball. So he said cautiously, "I will do my best. May I suggest that each of us, if we think of other items, list them in writing?" This remark seemed to him rather telling. Her oral list was a lot longer than his, but she had no way of proving now that his written list wouldn't ultimately outweigh it. This consoled him, but not very much. His crimes, when dispassionately listed, seemed to him both appalling and chronic. In a moment of madness, and to compensate for his acute discomfort, he added, "I would add but one thing at present. You could aid me professionally a good deal by ending your feud with Mrs. Nast. What have you got against her anyhow?"

"Merely that she is a liar, a flatterer, and an ignoramus, and that she has therefore no place in a university community, certainly no place as the social leader of such a community."

Henrietta spoke with a new intensity. In the interest of successful negotiations, he chose to terminate the conversation. Besides, given Henrietta's premises, which he was unlikely to change now, her charges against Dorothy were all three technically true. Dorothy did have a lively and reckless imagination, a caressing tact, and not the slightest interest in ideas. That is why the phony intellectualism of this academic petty bureaucracy had surrendered so completely to her charm. That is why poor Henrietta, who had gone now to the kitchen to get dinner, had lost her Western empire. Henrietta, who had not been content merely to get meals and who had a moral need to foster culture, had dreamed of converting this vulgar, sprawling community into at least a recognizable outpost of Boston or of what Boston claimed to be. She had been operating in the great Anglo-Saxon tradition of uplifting the natives, of teaching, of civilizing, a tradition that had sent New England schoolmarms streaming westward after the prairie schooner and the plow. She has never loved ideas, he thought, but she has always recognized an obligation to spread them; and, before Dorothy appeared in all her glory, she was doing her best to elevate the community. She undoubtedly thought of herself as performing the functions of a professor's wife. If she lorded it a little, she lorded it not like a feckless tyrant but like a responsible representative of the Colonial Office who knew what the natives needed better than the natives did themselves. The natives were just beginning to believe her when Dorothy seduced them and they all took to gobbling down lotus. She has a real grievance, said Schneider to himself, given her premises.

~XIV~

SCHNEIDER glanced with a practiced eye at his class and judged there might be thirty students ranged in front of him waiting for him to begin his lecture on the last decades of the nineteenth century. Theoretically, there should have been fifty-three; but May had come around again; his students were beginning to cram for finals; the evenings were getting pleasantly warm; the fancy of the young men was lightly turning to thoughts of girl students, even to some girl students who had left them quite unmoved during the long and bitter winter. So they sat up late now; and lay abed till noon. In short, spring fever had combined with the pressures of memorization to disintegrate Schneider's class.

He supposed he should call the roll and report the absentees. But he had always hated rolls. They had seemed to him so eloquent of the fact that most students found most lectures truly not worth attending and would have been better off in their rooms or at the library, reading. Now and then a form card from the Dean's office reminded him that he was expected to report absences promptly; and he usually did so for several weeks immediately after receiving such a reminder. But he always stopped it again as soon as he dared.

He sat waiting for the bell to ring before beginning his lecture. One or two more students might straggle in. He glanced at his notes. But why repeat these so-called facts about the nineteenth century? Their textbook gave them. The Britannica gave them. Dozens of other books in the library gave them. Why should he make sure their lecture notes gave them too? Why on earth, as a matter of fact, should there be lecture notes? And why should these nice kids be asked to listen to fifteen so-called lectures a week on five different and apparently unrelated subjects?

Had they learned anything whatever from him since September? He wondered. They could scarcely be expected to learn much. He had ample evidence that they had never previously learned to read except in a very loose sense of the word; and, when they took quizzes, their writing was nothing short of terrifying. He already looked forward with horror to the examinations he must grade next month. They would be illegibly written, grossly ungrammatical, whimsically punctuated, and misspelled. As a professional historian who had worked in manuscript collections in several languages, he believed he could decipher nearly any handwriting, on condition that the writer was literate, could spell, could punctuate, and had some notions of grammar. He was confident also that he could read a manuscript with no punctuation whatever, if the words were recognizably spelled and the grammatical structure reasonably intact. But you had to have leverage somewhere.

These nice kids, here in front of him now, had never learned their own mother tongue. Brought up on comic strips, they had listened in infancy to soap operas, and in adolescence they had sat for hours before the television screen. These things had been their books. And, in terms of what he wanted to say in his lecture this morning, it would be interesting to know precisely why. How and why do civilizations collapse and crumble like Nineveh into dust, with or without benefit of guided missiles? He intended to talk this morning about the period of European history between 1870 and 1914, a period that slightly overlapped his own lifetime. He ached to take these students back in time, into that extraordinary nineteenth-century world, so confident of continuous progress, so sure of the imminent triumph of man, so innocent of the horrors just ahead, the massacres, the tortures, the exiles. But these kids could probably not even remember Hiroshima, much less Hitler's rape of Poland. The Second World War was now jumbled in with the other blurred memories of their early childhood.

Some of them just conceivably may have had an elder brother who fought, or even died, in Korea. But mostly, thought Schneider, they have lived their lives in a country steadily more and more stupefied by comfort, more and more hypnotized by the television screen, a country of "viewers." For viewers they are; spectators; waiting to be amused, and to be sold. They have lived their lives in a country where it pays not to say things that other people are not saying. They hope for jobs in business, and they expect their careers to be scrutinized by some monstrous I.B.M. machine in some automated, chrome-plated office. They do not propose to join anything or say anything that may cause an I.B.M. machine to retch, or snort, or even gasp. Although they are terribly bored from the eyebrows up, they have never known any other state. And since they are excited and amused from the eyebrows down, it is not accurate to say that they are depressed.

They live in a mild euphoria, enhanced now by the spring. Schneider noted that, as spring progressed, they tended to pair off heterosexually in their choice of seats in his lecture room. At times, he noted, they even held hands. Not ecstatically, not in the delicious agony of the romantic, but bucolically. It was clear that, although they were drawn to each other sexually, it was less as the great lovers of legend than as puppies who lick food off each other's mouths. They merely took pleasure in each other. If one of them found a third pup with a stickier mouth, he or she wandered off and formed a new symbiosis; and, although Schneider supposed that the deserted pup must feel some pang or other of rejection and pain, yet some fourth accommodating pup was likely to turn up all too soon. And so they all went their dreamlike, pleasant, unstrenuous, unexhilarated way through the merry month of May, promiscuous and tolerant, viewers and spectators, dynamic conservatives, their young hearts bursting with singing commercials.

But aren't these kids ultimately Europeans? he asked himself. It is true that the student body contained a small sprinkle of Negro Americans, of Chinese Americans, of Mexican Americans; but it happened that none of them was in his class. He glanced from the faces before him to his class roll. European names. Almost all of them North European. British, German, Scandinavian, Dutch, one or two Irish. Their grandparents in many cases, their parents perhaps in one or two cases, had been born in Europe. But they had swarmed across the sea to this new Europe of ours, shaking the dust of old Europe unregretfully from their shoes. They had swarmed across the Appalachians, and even across the broad Mississippi. Perhaps they were merely displaced persons, modern history's first vast consignment of D.P.s. Perhaps, thought Schneider, we are viewers primarily because we are the first wave of D.P.s, not yet recovered from the trauma of displacement, missing we know not what, half remembering the things we want to forget, resenting the efforts of Woodrow Wilson and Franklin Roosevelt to pull us back into Europe's orbit, drawn by our manifest destiny toward the Pacific and beyond, haunted by the old dream of Cathay and the newer dream of the Open Door in China, remembering with anger the white crosses of our soldiers killed in Europe's stupid wars, yet eager to shoot Japanese in the Pacific, to seize Pacific islands and to hold them, to follow the setting sun as we have followed it for generations. Would these D.P.s in front of him, dwelling now in their well-fed, hygienic euphoria, their amoral and unstrenuous promiscuity, want to hear about their Homeland of a hundred years ago? Should they want to? He noted their names on the roll, and for the first time his historian's eye was caught by the dullness of their names. Westward the course of dullness takes its way, bringing with it a faceless flotsam with names that remind one of nothing—names, he added to himself, like Schneider.

The class bell jangled shrilly, like a factory bell calling all men to the assembly line. Well, he thought, flotsam and jetsam that we are, here we go together. Let us now remember. He kept his seat at the little table and began to speak. He had thrust his notes from him.

"In the second half of the nineteenth century," he said, "we enter the Age of Progress. It is the age I was myself born into, although in 1914, when it came crashing to the ground, I was too young to know that my world had tottered. It is a world which, of course, you never lived in; but your grandfathers lived in it, and I should like to suggest this morning what sort of world they lived in and what gods they believed in. For clearly I do not mean that modern science and technology stopped progressing in 1914. Even if I told you it had, you wouldn't believe me. You know better.

"But when you and I started this course together, you may remember I pictured to you a Europe filled with petty wars, it is true, but united also by common memories of the crusades, worshiping in cathedrals dedicated to the same saints, tilling the fields for their daily bread, and living—at least, most Europeans—in similar huts and cottages. I tried to suggest that the El Dorado Columbus sought when he sailed west, a land of gold and gems, took the place in many men's imaginations of the Christian Paradise; and that the very painters of Europe in the Renaissance turned from the religious insights of Italian primitives to the brilliant, joyous portrayal of this world. I said that Luther and Calvin tried to call Europe back to her love of the invisible and unworldly, but that Shakespeare and Racine were calling European man to go forward to his tragic destiny. Galileo was calling him to the truth of his universe, in defiance of the Church's edicts. I told you about the great capitalists like Fugger of Augsburg; of the slave traders that ransacked the coasts of Africa for human labor to develop El Dorado and enrich their owners. I told you of the conquest of India, and eventually of much of Asia. Of the little children working under the lash in England's factories at the new machines; of the armies of Napoleon smashing the feudal structure of Western Europe.

"Now I want to speak of the middle-class paradise that the new machines built in Europe, with the help of millions of sweating, starving, dying coolies in Asia, and Negroes in the two Americas. Actually, we have been trying for eight months to understand a series of religions that Christendom has tried to substitute for the Christian doctrines of the Middle Ages. This morning I want to talk about the religion of progress, of the theology of science, of man's worship of the machine, and of his firm belief that by his own efforts he could bring Heaven to earth for you and me, his descendants.

"So-called pure science was as remote from the average man as God the Father had been, and maybe remoter. But it rapidly became applied science and entered the familiar daily world of Western man. Abstract scientific laws became incarnate in the machine, took on flesh, became modern man's mediator and redeemer. The machine mediated by becoming like man and dwelling among men: by pumping out mines as he had pumped out mines, by drawing his water, hewing his wood, spinning his thread and weaving his garments, by bearing his burdens faster than he could bear them, paddling his boats, plowing his fields, reaping his grain, and making his daily bread. The machine redeemed man from toil—or promised to. It entered into the hospital to heal him of sickness, or to protect him from pain. It transfigured itself into a telegraph and carried his messages by code; or into a telephone and put him in communion with all those who truly turn to the telephone; or into a radio and brought him knowledge and entertainment in his loneliness. It became a telescope and let him gaze at stars no man had seen. It became a submarine and took him to the depths that only the fish had known. It took on wings and lifted him toward the heavens themselves."

Schneider had started speaking quietly; but as he spoke, such an overpowering vision of Western man's dream of material progress seized him that the words poured uncontrollably from his mouth.

However, when he looked around, he saw that a good half of his class was not with him. Some were studying for a quiz that loomed ahead of them later in the day. One was covertly reading the comics. A couple of co-eds were busy with their make-up, studying their faces in the mirrors of their compacts. A singularly pretty girl, with a shapely body and empty, regular face, who never wore jeans but always dressed in charming skirts, had as usual managed to arrange her skirt and her legs so that Schneider and only Schneider could catch just a glimpse of one white thigh. She had often paid Schneider this personal compliment in the past: whether from sheer exhibitionism or to see whether she could put him out of countenance, or to soften him up when he came to grade her wretched examination paper, he could never guess. He had always in the past found her stimulating, but today he barely saw her in his excitement over a period into which he, though not she, had been born.

As a matter of fact, something else had caught his eye. A lad halfway back on the other side of the room had started to lean forward as Schneider spoke. He had a pale, oval face, quite unlike the acres of uncharted flesh that most of his students used for faces. His hair was slightly disordered. His eyes were fixed on Schneider and were burning with interest as Schneider evoked these lost and confident decades. Schneider forgot the others and hurried on, as if he were talking to him and to him alone. But as his own excitement grew, he rose from his chair and paced slowly in front of the blackboard while he spoke.

"The machine," he said, "would mediate between abstract science and the daily, concrete needs of man only if man imitated his new redeemer by achieving increased mechanical efficiency. And so man learned to imitate the machine, by living intimately with it, by serving it faithfully and promptly. It was a severe discipline, but it promised him redemption from all the evils of this life. It promised him his lost 'dominion over creation.' It promised him power and proud citizenship in a new city, the City of Nature, whose name is Industrialism, whose inexorable rulers are Matter and Force, and whose missionaries are commanded to spread ceaselessly the use of the machine. Like Augustine's City of God, this city too would be a pilgrim city, moving through the desert of agrarian peasant society with its primitive techniques, its poverty, its ignorance, and its military impotence."

He talked on, engrossed by the vision before him, and the young student with the burning eyes never glanced from his face. They were both unconscious of the co-eds who now manicured, of the students who jotted down for no genuine reason fragments of Schneider's tumultuous lecture, of one student who had fallen asleep. And Schneider spoke of the doubts that John Ruskin and William Morris had expressed; of the artists, like Van Gogh, who had gone insane, or, like Gauguin, to the South Seas; of the impressionists, the cubists. Of that new animal, the social scientist, who reported the facts of the social order and who more often than not failed to ask what a good life was. Of naturalism in literature. And of Baudelaire's bitter eloquence about the horrible burden of boredom.

He spoke, too, of the immigrants who crowded from Europe to America.

"What this river of immigrants," he said, "contributed to America besides their muscle, their energy, and their skill depends in part on what was in their hearts when they left Europe. There are no statistics on that, and there can of course be none. But all the evidence suggests that they sought primarily economic opportunity, the nineteenth-century form of personal salvation. They sought, too, freedom from the burden of military conscription, that burden which the democratic era had brought Europe's system of sovereign nation-states. And in America, where even second-rate skills fetched rewards that first-rate skills in Europe could not guarantee, they learned better even than Europe the optimism of the Age of Progress. They learned that land can be not only a peasant's family heritage but real estate, capable of bringing enormous unearned increment. They learned the joys of an anarchical economic system in an environment of apparently unlimited resources. They learned to reverse exactly the medieval hierarchy of economic pursuits; to respect, first the financier, whose backing would open a golden

West; next, the businessman, the industrialist, who supplied clothes and shelter; and last, the farmer, who produced only the food without which all would perish, but who was thrust aside in American esteem by the growing power of urban business."

But America was Cardwell's field, and Schneider guiltily skipped back to Europe, to Auguste Comte, to *Lockesley Hall,* to Victor Hugo, to Darwin, and to Herbert Spencer's vision of necessary progress.

"By the opening years of this century you were born in," he said, while the boy's eyes burned brightly in the sea of bored or neutral faces, "the citizens of Christendom proudly stood on a pinnacle of material power that exceeded every previous dream of man. Moreover, the pinnacle had been built by man's own efforts and hence invited an understandable pride. It had been built by human reason, by 'the scientific method,' by a rapidly growing technology. The rules were already known by which this mighty skyscraper city could be built even higher. To the critic who scoffed that it was a purely material achievement, modern man could reply that not only were he and his fellow citizens more comfortable physically than their fathers had been but that liberalism was everywhere triumphant or about to triumph, that political privilege had been sharply curtailed, that economic privilege was under attack, that, in short, social justice was a goal universally professed. If religion and art seemed often to be lagging, might not that be that they still lacked an adequate material base? Seek ye first a high standard of living, and all these things shall be added unto you. It was good to be alive in the years of man's unbelievable power and of man's increasing hope for the future. It was good to be alive in the opening years of the twentieth century, this century, your century and mine, for they were in all truth wonderful, glittering years."

He paused and looked about him as if in sudden pain. Some of his students stared curiously. Breathing harder, he began again.

"From this bourgeois, Baconian Eden modern man was ejected with a sudden violence unique in his experience. In a few days, millions of men were mobilized to kill and be killed. It was as if some terrible madness had seized on the citizens of the city that Matter and Force had so benignly ruled. Across the tranquil, smiling, midsummer countryside of Europe swept vast armies, bearing more deadly weapons than man had ever known. The earth rocked and the sky reeled. The great gray ships of the British Royal Navy hurried silently to their appointed posts. It was the summer of 1914."

Suddenly, such violent emotions arose in Schneider that he knew he could not go on. He glanced at his watch. There was lots of time left—but it was time he could not use. His throat became dry; his voice came to his own ears as if from a great distance. He felt slightly dizzy.

"I cannot discuss the First World War today. I am sorry."

He bowed slightly, rose clumsily to his feet, and left his classroom. What had he said, he wondered. Had any of it made sense? It seemed to him to have a certain rhythm. Had it had any genuine, logical structure? Whether it had or not, they were not interested, except for that one boy. They would remember nothing.

Two days later, at the next meeting of the class, instead of recounting the horrors of 1914-18, he invited questions, followed by a brief factual quiz. It was a glorious May morning. The sunlight poured into the windows, and sweet, cool air poured with it. A bird sang in a tree just outside. The girl with the lovely thighs obliged with her customary gleam of white. Some of the husky young men were sitting by their sweeties, holding them by the hands. Schneider remembered that, immediately before this period, came a class in sociology, on marriage, which was an enormously popular elective, and he smiled. The boy who had followed his last lecture sat silent, apparently reflecting. A few vanity cases were already in operation. A hand went up, and he recognized its owner by a glance and a slight nod.

One of the students asked a question about Bismarck's policy toward the Socialists. He was rather obviously trying to spot a question in the approaching quiz.

"Sir," said the pretty girl next to him, "I think Jim overlooks the fact that the Socialists were an in-group."

There, thought Schneider, is that infernal terminology again, that sociological jargon. He could not even remember what sociologists thought they meant by in-group.

"In-group?" he said.

"I mean to say, so far as the Socialists and their plans, and so far as they had systematicized their plans, weren't they a sort of we-group?"

"And if they were," said Schneider, "what do you think were Bismarck's motives?"

"I can't identify with Bismarck," she said, as if she had just cut Bismarck dead in a way the old chap would remember for a good while.

That's psychology, I guess, thought Schneider, though it could be sociology too. There's an overlap: illiteracy. And they are equally systematicized.

Another co-ed asked whether the Bavarians had any nationality feeling.

"If I understand you correctly," said Schneider in a grave voice, "they had."

An unusually plump co-ed opined that the East Prussian peasants could not have had much euphoria, although she supposed there was no euphorimeter that would tell.

"How do you mean?"

"Well, in what concerned the peasant," she said, "were they happy?"

"That is a difficult question," said Schneider. Then he smiled. "Are you?"

She didn't know for sure, and Schneider said the peasants were probably not too sure either. One thing was certain: by our stand-ards, they were dreadfully poor. She replied that she had thought she detected a "good deal of dead hand in modern German history," a guess that Schneider felt unable to appraise. The terms of dis-course were beginning to confuse him. Why did Milton and his staff fill these children's heads up with half-chewed ideas and flat-minded metaphors? It made him feel quite bitter.

Would Schneider say, asked a student eagerly, whether Bismarck wielded charismatic authority? Schneider replied that he apparently did.

Another said he gathered the situation process in Bismarck's Germany was not a social capillarity and that there was little socialarity, and Schneider cagily agreed that it was possible. For Schneider lacked the linguistic capability and semantic communications skill, as his students would have put it, to know what in God's name they were talking about.

The questions kept coming, and Schneider had to decide whether a bio-social change, like a first-class famine, might have shaken things up a bit in Bismarck's time—or, put in the actual language of the questioner, whether it wouldn't have induced catastrophic change. He thought so, but said the question was a bit iffy. The in-group girl said that, so far as reforms in the administration, she thought an affiliation of the peasant in-group to the Junker in-group would have helped, and Schneider imagined it would. She added that certainly telic change was needed. With this he agreed so deeply, though privately, that he put a quiz on the blackboard and re-treated to his near-by office. He felt like Alice at the end of her trip through Wonderland, when the playing cards suddenly fell confusedly on her head. He felt pelted by meaningless syllables. This terminology of the sociologists was a dreadful thing to try to speak. It was like a mouthful of feathers. You couldn't swallow them, and you couldn't spit them out. He remembered hearing that, in the course on marriage, a husband and wife formed, not too unexpectedly, a dyadic group; and also a direct-contact group. With something like despair in his heart, he gathered up his quiz papers. Feeling like a beast, he left them in young Ripley's office to correct—assuming he could find out what they said—and started home to lunch with his we-group—that is, with Henrietta and their three little daughters, whose school had been closed by catastrophic change: a case of diphtheria.

Out under the trees, now clothed in the shrill green of their young leaves, he saw, walking ahead of him in a dyadic group, a massive halfback and his sweetie. The girl was small and slender and, even in her dirty jeans, graceful. Her huge companion lumbered beside her, accentuating his physical clumsiness as if to suggest to passers-by that his bulk was too vast to be wholly co-ordinated, and he leaned one arm heavily on her slender shoulder while his hand grasped the back of her neck. Schneider, who had noted this type of symbiosis often in his daily rounds, had never been able to decipher it wholly. He knew, of course, that a male cat seizes his consort's neck in his teeth until she emits just the right feminine shriek; and the halfback's grip might be sexual in its symbolism. But he was unsure. And what was symbolized by his making this poor little creature partly carry him? Student customs, he said grimly to himself; I give up. But they have sense enough to know one thing: it's spring.

~XV~

Now tell me all the gossip," said Dorothy cozily, passing Old Manley his cup and proffering toasted English muffins.

"But, *ma chère*," protested Old Manley, "it is you who should tell me. You forget: last month you spent four whole days in New York. Things always happen to one in New York. What happened to you? I have never been able to persuade you to tell me."

To her annoyance, Dorothy blushed. Ah, thought Manley, then it's true. But who is he? Surely not that great animal of a Denby. But Dorothy had recovered her poise.

"I had a lovely time," she said with a great show of candor. "The people at the Foundation were simply charming to me. Even Mr. Denby, in spite of being terribly busy." I am sure, thought Old Manley, he was busy, the lucky swine. "But," continued Dorothy, "things must have happened here too. And things I know about must have been re-evaluated. I think that's the word I want." And she laughed lightly.

"But, *chère amie*," said Old Manley, munching his muffin with the greatest enjoyment and gazing at a magnificent clump of peonies, "you have already heard even the re-evaluations."

"Well, for instance," answered Dorothy, passing him some honey for his muffin, "I forgot to tell you, but I heard you attended the Reception for Men Only last month, and that P'tite, as they call her—" and she gave a little grimace—"clung only to you and ignored all the assistant professors the President had dished up for her."

"But," said Old Manley, "this is a ridiculous rumor. In the first place, as you well know, only assistant professors were invited."

"But you managed to get there all the same. No, don't bother to deny it. Young Ripley saw you there."

"So I was," he said shamelessly, in a vague tone as if just recollecting the event.

"And you were the hit of the party as far as P'tite was concerned."

"Now that," said Old Manley, "really is ridiculous. Miss Allenby never even glanced at me."

"How could she," asked Dorothy sweetly, "once you got your arms around her?"

"And, my dear, what was wrong about that? I saw that Miss Allenby wanted my arms to be around her, and I obliged. Could I do less?"

"How could you tell?"

"My dear girl," said Old Manley, "if a man can't tell when a woman is open to courtship, he should—he should enter a monastery."

"And, pray, am I open to courtship?" she asked playfully.

"Never before today," he said softly. "At least, not in my presence."

Dorothy busied herself with the tea. She said nothing.

"Never before today," he breathed. He took her hand, and she did not withdraw it. Then he lowered his face and kissed her hand.

He rose from his chair and paced a bit. He stood very erect. She had a sudden image in her mind of an old rooster, scraping his foot in the dust, turning his proud head, and flapping his wing, while his hen stands by, aware. Poor old man, she thought. But at least he is aware that I am a woman. That is something, in a faculty. No wonder P'tite spotted him, in the midst of those prematurely stooped and ambitious pedants.

Old Manley felt very young again, and very happy. The silly little academic town beyond Dorothy's split chestnut fence seemed thousands of miles away, much farther off than Paris, or even a provincial French town. Why is it, thought Old Manley, that only Woman can create a man, and only Woman can re-create him when his youth has fled? And he thought of old King David and the lovely Shunammite. In a room upstairs, a room whose windows did not give on this heavenly, quiet, sunlit terrace, he could hear the faint clicking of Nast's typewriter. What a blind, unaware, ambitious fool Nast was, anyhow. In his resentment, Old Manley wanted to put his arms around Nast's wife, but he knew that the moment for that had not arrived. He sat down again, and she smiled at him understandingly.

"Nast is always busy," he said, his irony too faint to be boorish but sufficient to be heard by a person who might be really listening.

"He works far too hard," she said, relapsing into a kind of automatic wifeliness.

"And now June has come. And so, day by day, his life passes away," he murmured, as if to himself.

And so, too, does mine, she thought to herself. An old rooster, but he knows I am on earth and values me. And instantly, as if in response to her thought, he began gravely to recite from his beloved Baudelaire, in a voice that was strong, vibrant, masculine, and miraculously young:

> "À la très-chère, à la très-belle
> Qui remplit mon cœur de clarté,
> À l'ange, à l'idole immortelle,
> Salut en immortalité!"

He recited all five stanzas, and she listened, comprehending with precision only a few words like *"très-belle,"* yet comprehending so well. He paused.

"Baudelaire?" she said softly.

"Yes," he said. "And he wrote this one for you, too:

"Mon enfant, ma sœur,
Songe à la douceur
D'aller là-bas vivre ensemble!"

All three stanzas of this one he recited, and by the time the refrain came round the third time, her voice joined his, in her soft, uncertain accent:

"Là, tout n'est qu'ordre et beauté,
Luxe, calme et volupté."

She understood every word of the refrain and knew that Old Manley meant to apply it to the garden she had made, and meant she had made it for him, and meant to thank her. And suddenly he chanted in a new strain altogether:

"Quand vous serez bien vieille, au soir, à la chandelle . . ."

He recited the whole of Ronsard's sonnet, the last two lines very slowly, very distinctly:

"Vivez, si m'en croyez, n'attendez à demain:
Cueillez dès aujourd'huy les roses de la vie."

She did not catch every single word; but she knew that this time she was being asked the oldest question a man can ask a woman. The color mounted to her cheeks, and instantly he sprang to her side and slipped one arm around her. She turned her face away, ever so little. The doorbell rang.

"Do you mind?" she asked.

He went to the door. It was Freddie Landon. Old Manley greeted him with a hearty voice and with such stricken eyes that Freddie wondered silently what had happened. Old Manley knew, as he knew so many things. He could reconstruct the coming days, without effort but in real agony of spirit. Whether it was Denby, or whether it was somebody else, Dorothy was accessible. Her fool of a husband was upstairs tapping out a book review. The peonies nodded their somnolent great heads in the sunlit private garden, and their delicate scent was a promise of poignant memories. He had recognized the moment and had seized it. Nothing was missing but his own youth, and now youth entered. But not his youth, not his.

"Hello, Cousin Freddie," she said, softly and with obvious pleasure.

"Hello, Cousin Dorothy," he replied, while Old Manley watched him narrowly.

"The tea is freshly made," she said. "Can you find a cup and saucer and teaspoon for yourself?"

"Let me go," said Old Manley. "I know where they are."

"Oh, Dr. Manley, how sweet of you," she said.

"I'm not going to budge," he said tartly, "unless you call me Horace."

"But—" she demurred.

"But I'm too old," he said savagely, finishing her sentence for her. "Is that it? Then what about calling me Cousin Horace?"

"But we are not cousins, are we?" she asked, in wide-eyed innocence.

"Didn't I hear you say once that your grandmother was a Meade of Virginia?"

"My grandmother was," she said, and Freddie noted that she was evidently lying.

"My mother was a Meade," said Old Manley. "Of Virginia." And it was evident to Freddie that he was lying too. "And now, Cousin Dorothy, with your permission, I will fetch a cup for Dr. Landon." And he started for the kitchen.

Freddie nodded his head toward the stooped, retreating figure. "What's up?"

Dorothy gazed abstractedly at her garden. Then she smiled, faintly but with obvious contentment.

"Cousin Horace thinks he is in love with me," she said.

"I can understand that."

Old Manley returned with the cup for Freddie, and Dorothy poured.

"I hear you're going back to Charleston after Commencement for a visit," said Dorothy to Freddie.

"Yes," he said. "And what shall you be doing?"

"If I can coax my sister-in-law into running her brother's house for him for a fortnight, I shall go to Georgia," she said.

"By air?" asked Freddie casually.

"Yes, by air."

"Perhaps we can fly together as far as Atlanta."

They will fly together, said Old Manley to himself. Because I am old, and for no better reason, while this fool upstairs types book reviews, or articles on People's Capitalism, they will fly together. But whether they ever get beyond Atlanta—ah, I would not vouch for that.

The fact that he himself was starting then for Paris seemed, just now, a dull and boring fact. He would gladly exchange destinations with Freddie. Freddie had a whole life before him. He was young and extremely personable. He could easily find another woman to fly with somewhere. But today, here in this garden, Old Manley felt he would either fly to Atlanta with Dorothy or he would never fly anywhere with any woman again.

"Another cup of tea, Cousin Horace," urged Dorothy teasingly.

Alas, it was another cup, one more cup, that Cousin Horace wanted. But not of tea. He would gain nothing whatever by staying now. So he thanked Dorothy, declined the tea, muttered something about an engagement, bowed to Freddie, bowed over Dorothy's hand and ceremoniously kissed it. Once more there were only two on the terrace.

The June sunlight had been clear gold all day, but now it showed just the barest tinge of copper. The shadows cast by the clumps of peonies began to lengthen. Unlike Old Manley, Freddie and Dorothy had no sense that time was fleeting. They knew the day would last forever. Both were wholly aware of Atlanta, but they deliberately chose an intricate, lingering path toward it. And since everything

Freddie said, regardless of the subject, felt to Dorothy as if it were directed toward her, she was glad to talk of many things. They spoke of Old Manley only once.

"Poor old goat," Freddie murmured, when Old Manley had closed the front door behind him.

"Oh, Freddie! You shouldn't. He's sweet. Really he is."

"Lots of old goats are sweet, contrary to vulgar opinion."

And that was all. But Dorothy was secretly grateful for the incense that had been offered her. Dorothy had always found that, without incense, the world had a pretty sordid smell. Still, Freddie burned incense too, perhaps in a less skillful fashion, but with no sense of panic or impending doom. Freddie attracted her and gave her just the slightest, pleasantest sense of giddiness.

"What's it been like, working here?" she asked, now that the session was nearing an end.

"It has meant knowing you."

She smiled with pleasure. "Yes, but the job itself?"

He shrugged.

"You don't like it."

"I'm a Southerner. You ought to understand. I like people. I like teaching because it means dealing with people. I even find it amusing to write books—and even about economics, too." He laughed. "Economics isn't dreary: it's just an unsafe subject at the moment. You see, I'm probably a creeping Socialist. Because, again, I like people."

"Aren't you teaching and writing books here?" she asked.

"I don't know whether teaching is any longer possible in universities. At least in American universities. I won't bore you with the reasons. I'm not even sure that they're good places to write books in. But I don't propose to talk shop, least of all to you. I'd rather talk about you."

So they talked about Dorothy, skirting the intimate but never leaving it clearly out of reach, while Nast's typewriter steadily clicked in the distant upstairs study. Before Freddie left, both of them knew that the trip to Atlanta would be different from any other trip;

but there were no plans. Finally, Freddie said good-by. Worse than that, he was to be out of town next day.

She sat on the terrace, alone now, musing. The telephone rang. It was Old Manley.

"I merely wanted to say I love you," he said. "But I don't want to wear out my welcome. So I let Henry Schneider persuade me to go fishing with him tomorrow. All day. We probably won't catch any fish, but we'll forget this ridiculous town, this Athens of the Mid-west."

"Persuade Professor Schneider to take me too," said Dorothy, on a sudden impulse.

"The first catch of the party! And not a catfish either, which was frankly all I expected. We've caught a mermaid instead! But I said Schneider, my dear. Schneider. The husband of your sworn enemy."

"Why, is she going?" asked Dorothy innocently.

"Oh, no. It was to have been a stag party—for two stags."

And what an old stag, thought Dorothy; but aloud she said, "But I love stags, and with two it would be so safe."

"Permit me to consult the other stag."

Schneider was, of course, delighted. Dorothy insisted on providing the picnic lunch. Then she composed for Nast a plausible account of her coming day's activities. Next morning, in glittering June sunshine, she drove buoyantly to Old Manley's; Schneider arrived in his jalopy; three home-made fishing rods with cork floats were loaded, a can of worms, and the picnic basket; and they were off. Schneider drove to a friend's farm, went through two gates, entered a pasture where a herd of Holsteins was contentedly munching grass; and found The Spot: the grassy bank above an old swimming hole, with a huge willow arching over it. The water in the swimming hole was brown with the silt from many cornfields, but it was cool looking and extremely smooth, until a huge bullfrog, annoyed by their intrusion, plopped suddenly to safety, while concentric rings spread slowly from the spot where he had disappeared. An antediluvian water terrapin, sunning on a log, chose to ignore them. They unloaded the car and spread a rug along the bank. Dorothy placed herself between the two stags. In the water she could see the reflection of her red print frock and her wide-brimmed leghorn hat, also a glorious red. Her face, she noticed, was flushed with excitement, and it, too, reflected the red of her hat. All in all, her image satisfied her quite as much as the original satisfied the two stags. But she removed her hat, now that the willow shaded them. To her surprise, Schneider carefully pulled out his kaffiyah, arranged it on his head, and placed the black circlet around the crown. She had heard about that kaffiyah. Now, here it was, and she liked it. She even liked Schneider's profile. Cousin Horace wore an old stiff-brimmed straw hat, which he did not remove.

"But it's a *fête champêtre* we have organized, not a mere fishing trip!" he said. "If I had paints and a palette I would beg you to pose for me, Cousin Dorothy."

"And I would refuse," said Dorothy. "I know the kind of paintings you mean. The ladies had nothing on."

"And what, my dear," asked Cousin Horace, "is so dreadful about that? I'm sure you have nothing to hide. And today we are not in the Corn Belt; we are in France. Would you care to hear me sing?"

"I would love it," said Dorothy, "but you must be quiet now so we can fish."

"Henry," asked Cousin Horace, "do catfish mind singing?"

"Yes," said Schneider firmly, "but you may whisper if you like."

A preposterous conversation ensued, conducted exclusively in whispers. Dorothy sat happily on the bank holding her fishing rod. Schneider sat next to her on her right and Old Manley on her left. Old Manley and Dorothy whispered to each other; Schneider and Dorothy whispered to each other. Out of respect for the fish they hoped to catch, or for whatever reason, Schneider and Old Manley did not try to converse. Nor could either of them hear what passed between the other and Dorothy.

Cousin Horace leaned slightly toward Dorothy and whispered, "You look utterly adorable in that dress. You are the most beautiful woman I have ever seen. I am sorry Schneider is along. I want to be alone with you. Could you ever care for me just a little?"

"I am glad you like my dress," she said. She glanced from under her lashes at Schneider, on her right. He sat, as impassive as an Arab, watching his cork float. A faint breeze stirred the fringe of his kaffiyah.

"I hope," she said to him, "you don't feel Cousin Horace and I are being rude. It was you who suggested whispering."

"I said it was permitted to whisper." She was surprised by the amount of firmness he could put into his own mere whisper.

"Let our Arab alone to fish," said Cousin Horace. "Come with me for a little stroll. I will pick wildflowers for you. I will make you a garland of flowers."

"It's cooler here," she said.

"Three's a crowd," he said, leaning much nearer her ear this time, to make sure she could hear him. But she merely smiled.

From under her lashes she glanced again at Schneider.

"You don't really like women," she said, turning toward the kaffiyah. "You are sorry I came."

"I am not sorry for anything," he said, his gaze still fixed on his cork float. "I enjoy women."

"Enjoy?" she said dubiously.

"Enjoy."

"You don't hold it against me that I was not nice to your wife?"

"I never mix in women's quarrels."

"But when I first came, you seemed unhappy at home."

"I was ill."

"And now you are well again?" Her whisper was still anxious.

"I think I could probably tear that willow tree up by the roots and thrash you with it."

"Why?" She glanced apprehensively at the huge willow.

"Because you are out of hand. Your husband—whom I don't care for, mind you—supports you handsomely. Old Manley adores you, in the French style, madly. I have reason to think Freddie Landon is in love with you. And you are profoundly discontented."

"I'm unhappy." She sighed.

{172}

"Then get out."

"Get out?"

"Come with me to Paris," said Old Manley, from her left. "I'm younger than you think."

"You are very sudden." She was smiling. "I shall have to reflect."

"Then reflect, but reflect in my favor," said Old Manley, in obvious excitement. "Now I shall leave my line and carve your initials on this willow." And he promptly got up and moved toward the tree.

"He is going to carve my initials on the willow," said Dorothy to Schneider. "He's sweet. You wouldn't do a thing like that, would you?"

"Not precisely that. But if it weren't for our absurd bigamy laws and if I had the money, I would buy you."

"Buy me? Why?" She was both horrified and pleased.

"Because you remind me of the Circassian slaves the Arabs sometimes bought as second or third wives. I should be delighted to possess you. But not to grovel before you or carve your initials."

He turned at last from his cork float, looked at her appraisingly from her head to her feet, and then whispered, "I should certainly buy you, and I would give at least six camels for you—white ones."

Dorothy sighed with content; glanced back toward the willow where Old Manley was carving her initials; then stretched full length on the rug and began to daydream. Schneider, she decided, knew a lot about her. But he did not know about Denby. And he certainly did not know that Denby had begged her to trump up a second trip to New York. There were several shows he wanted her to see: it was June and they ought not to waste it.

But I am not wasting June, she thought happily, while Schneider sat immobile at her side watching his cork float and thinking of Circassian slaves and Moslem marriage laws, and while Old Manley ecstatically carved her initials on the willow. I am having a lovely time. I wish this day would last forever. Her daydream was interrupted by a splash. Old Manley's pole had been dragged bodily into the swimming hole and was being pulled by some vast under-water monster toward the opposite bank. Deftly, Schneider maneu-vered his own pole in such a way as to rescue Manley's.

The fish was big and, being a catfish, utterly hideous. But Old Manley insisted on regarding it as a good omen. In the confusion, the whispering had given way to normal conversation and even to louder conversation than normal. To celebrate, Dorothy broke out a bottle of Scotch, Schneider got ice from the thermos, and they all had Scotch on the rocks, while the huge catfish lay gasping thirstily near by. Then they lunched, with never a word of love or anything else exciting. When they had stuffed themselves, Dorothy announced that she needed a nap; and Old Manley asked if he might share her rug, though he had not the slightest intention of sleeping. Schneider quietly set to fishing again. An hour passed pleasantly, and Old Manley declared that he was ready for a swim if the ladies present would withdraw. So Dorothy wandered down the bank of the stream, picking flowers and pondering Schneider's command to "get out"—but with whom?—while Schneider and Manley stripped and had a swim. Then they dried off, dressed, and hallooed her back.

"Was it fun?" she asked enviously.

"Delicious," said Old Manley. "Why don't you?"

"If I do, will you and Dr. Schneider watch?"

"There's nothing I'd like better," said Old Manley.

"No, no! I don't mean watch me, you *roué*. I mean, watch beyond the bushes there to give me the signal if anybody starts to come."

"Anything to oblige," said Old Manley, "but you'll admit it's a pretty dull assignment."

So the two men took their stations at key points, while Dorothy slipped her things off and slithered gingerly into the swimming hole. It looked awfully dirty, but it felt awfully good. Then Schneider noticed that Old Manley had deserted his post and had gone softly to a copse of hazelwood quite near the willow and was gazing ec-statically through it toward the swimming hole. Schneider ap-proached resolutely.

"Why, you rascally old *voyeur!*" whispered Schneider, really quite shocked. "You Peeping Tom!"

"Sh! Don't be a fool," whispered Old Manley. "Why, what I'm doing is the least a woman of her beauty can expect of us. Look at her! She's utterly exquisite."

Schneider obediently parted the branches of the hazelwood just enough and gazed.

"You're quite right," he whispered soberly. "Forgive me my rudeness. I don't know what I could have been thinking of. This kind of opportunity doesn't occur every day—certainly not in this community." And he made a mental note that he would raise his bid to ten camels. "Still, I don't know why, but I feel queerly sneaky, watching her this way when she doesn't know it."

"She would want you to," maintained Old Manley stoutly. "Any woman that beautiful would want you to. To watch her, and to feel queerly sneaky. So long as you didn't embarrass her by asking her permission. Anyhow, she would be less beautiful if she were self-conscious."

Old Manley was right, thought Schneider. In a complex civilization, so much depends on knowing what to do without shouting that you are doing it. As for this Circassian slave, every detail was artistically perfect. She had dried off with the third bath towel, which Old Manley had thoughtfully and hopefully brought. Then, standing naked and dainty on the rug they had all three sat on to fish, she examined her face carefully in her vanity-case mirror and retouched her lips slightly. Then she started to dress.

It was President Pomton's Chicago strip tease in reverse, and Old Manley found it unutterably melancholy. One vista of loveliness after another was closed off, as she put on her panties, then her bra, then her slip, and at last her print frock. Then she arranged her hair, which she had miraculously preserved dry. Then she hallooed.

They could not very well halloo back. They were so close they would have frightened her out of her lovely, sleek, rosy skin. So first they ran swiftly a few yards in the opposite direction, and then

Old Manley hallooed feebly, as if from a great distance. If she suspected chicanery, she gave no sign when they emerged after a decent interval from the copse.

"It was lovely," she said.

"It certainly was," they chorused with feeling.

She looked at them swiftly and her eyes narrowed.

"I mean the water."

"So do we," said Old Manley.

Again the narrowed eyes, and then a peal of laughter.

There were no more fish; and, bearing their single prize proudly with them, they drove the jalopy back through the herd of Holsteins, back through the two gates, out of Arcady, into a stupid world where professors lead circumspect lives, where the husbands of exquisitely beautiful women may nevertheless be wedded to their typewriters, and where bigamy is regretfully frowned upon.

Schneider went happily home. It had been a good day. In a phrase the great Gibbon loved, it had been both amusing and instructive. Dorothy attracted Schneider enormously, and he was pleasantly aware that he attracted her. If only the laws and customs of his country and his century had taken a little more cognizance of human nature, he would have brought her back with him and installed her in his home. Elsie, Charity, and little Jane would have loved her, and she would have loved them. Henrietta would of course have been nasty to her, but Henrietta no longer wore the pants in the Schneider household and he felt he could have brought her to heel. A fifth female in one house would have been in some ways oppressive, but he was confident Dorothy would have borne him a son.

In view of the short shrift America had given the Mormons, this solution of his domestic problem lacked viability. For much as he wanted Dorothy for a second wife—and he wanted her a great deal—it was not a point for which he was prepared to go to prison. Nevertheless, he felt quietly certain that, if he possessed Dorothy, his academic problems would quickly pale.

What our laws do permit, he reflected, is a plurality of wives successively but not synchronously arranged. More simply, he could get a divorce, or at the least ask Henrietta for one. But the fact is, he did not want Dorothy on a monogamous basis. He felt certain she would cloy. He deeply respected Henrietta. She had character, intelligence, and great loyalty. She was the mother of his children. Of course, she was a bully; but who had allowed her to become one in these latter years? And while he was eating his heart out and ruining his disposition over the petty problems of a university community, what had she been doing? Trying to bring up three children on his wretched salary: that is what she had been doing. If she had grown a little acid in the process, she had at least not wallowed in self-pity. And she commanded not just the respect but the love of the children she had borne him. She commanded his own respect and he would be hanged if he would walk out on her.

But did she command his love? Love is a big, big word. Certainly he no longer desired her as he now desired Dorothy Nast. In view of the ages and appearance of the three parties most deeply concerned, that was less remarkable than some men at his age, caught in a similar situation, were given to supposing.

Balked in his honest desire for bigamy, unwilling to ask his children's admirable mother for a divorce, and having an essentially well-ordered mind, he now focused his attention on a third possibility, the only one left so far as he could recall: adultery. Adultery presented, certainly, a pleasing prospect, and one from which in the long run even Henrietta might well stand to gain. Infidelity, remorse, reconciliation. The broken bone reset, stronger now at the point of fracture than at any other point. But there was not the slightest evidence . . .

~XVI~

Two DAYS after the fishing expedition, Commencement Day arrived. Few students from the lower classes remained on campus: they had scattered to take summer jobs, or to spend ten days at home before returning to summer school to sign up again for the courses they had just flunked. Even some of the faculty had manufactured successful excuses to leave before Commencement. Those who were left could talk of nothing but the sensational press given President Pomton for his Commencement Day oration at A. & M. and of the likelihood that his revised Cold War speech had cinched the new job for him there.

Commencement Day dawned unusually hot and sultry. The University, thought Schneider, has tried various dates in early June in an effort to rid itself of a kind of jinx in the matter of weather. In the memory of man it has been able to secure three types of weather for Commencement: either stiflingly hot, as it clearly would be this year, when strong men all but fainted beneath the weight of their academic gowns and hoods; or sudden squalls that caught the exercises half finished in the unprotected stadium and sent the robed scholars scurrying to Snodgrass Auditorium to finish their important ritual, in gowns that were soggy from rain and sweat; or once, in 1912, an actual tornado, which nearly blew some of the older and frailer faculty members off campus for good. But Schneider could not remember a comfortable Commencement Day.

From the Faculty Marshal's point of view, any of these three types of weather, undesirable in itself, was preferable to prolonged uncertainty as to which kind it was to be. Today it was any man's guess, and the Marshal reflected bitterly that he was likely to be blamed by his colleagues, whether he chose the football stadium, where the wooden stand was set up and the folding chairs for the faculty were already in place, or the appalling breathlessness of Snodgrass Auditorium, only to find in the end that neither snow, nor rain, nor heat, nor darkness would have interrupted the ritual out of doors where one could breathe, and that he himself would go down in local history as a knave and a coward. But, as on the night before great Caesar fell, the behavior of the elements was malicious and perverse, while the Marshal sweated out his agonizing reappraisals. At ten-thirty there was a short but violent shower, with some dangerously large hailstones. But a hideously hot sun soon dried out the stadium. An ominous wind arose at one-fifteen; and Schneider, for one, thought he detected a dust storm forming in the west. But nothing happened. At five, when it should have been growing cool, the thermometer stood near a hundred; the Volunteer Municipal Band waited on the front steps of the library; and the graduating classes stood in knots before the building, while relatives took individual photographs of them in their academic caps and gowns. The faculty was grumbling, inside the library, and the Marshal stood on a table and began to call their names in a loud voice. First, the assistant professors, two by two; then the associate professors; then the full professors. The longer one had seen service in his present rank, the farther back in the procession his honored place would be. At last, the deans took their places; then the trustees; then the candidates for honorary degrees; and finally the President of the University and the Chairman of the Board.

Although they had been requested not to, some of the faculty sneaked off their coats and used a safety pin to keep their gowns discreetly closed in front. And although they had been urged to wear dark suits, Schneider noted a good many seersucker trouser legs peering indiscreetly from below the hems of gowns. Their doctoral hoods, which were nearly every color of the rainbow, made a truly brave display. At present, those who flaunted them were fanning themselves with their mortarboard caps. One or two of the full professors, sensitive about the tardiness of their promotions to that august rank, had taken their places farther back in the procession than they should have. In fact, all down the line of the procession that was forming, a faint scuffling toward the rear reminded one of a halfhearted military advance.

Outside the library building the graduates were drawn up according to the degree about to be conferred; and, within each degree group, in alphabetical order. The latter requirement was a useless archaism, dating from the days when the institution was still small and when every graduate was called to the presidential platform by name to receive his imitation parchment, rolled and beribboned in the University's colors, and to have his hand shaken by the President. But although nowadays all but candidates for the doctorate merely stood as a group when any given degree was conferred, nobody had thought to abolish the alphabetical requirement, which may have been subconsciously venerated precisely because it had become vestigial.

The University bell now began to peal. Schneider noted that it pealed a little wearily, as if not even bells could survive the martyrdom of the usual Commencement weather; but he knew that this was because the janitor had always confused the order to peal on joyful occasions like this one with orders to toll when some professor dropped dead of old age or even from sheer frustration. Now the academic procession got under way for a kind of death march across the steaming campus and out to the stadium. First came the Volunteer Municipal Band, struggling with the University anthem, written by a loyal alumnus of the Class of Naughty-Nine; then the worried Faculty Marshal; then the long double column of alphabetized, hot, and greasy candidates for the various degrees; then the gaudily hooded faculty. They marched out of step and with that appalling inability of civilians to keep the distance between ranks, so that sudden clots formed dangerously in this line of learning, embarrassing gaps opened up, couples of gowned and hooded scholars raced suddenly forward as if afraid of losing their due meed of glory on this day of days for their profession, then came to a sudden and despairing dead halt when they struck another clot ahead.

Nevertheless, and making due allowance for the fact that not even a harassed Marshal can hope to regiment intellectuals, in whom the spirit bloweth where it listeth, they made a brave sight; and the wives who stood at a respectful distance from the line of march and pointed out to their children their unfamiliarly garbed fathers did so not without a twinge of pride and not without some mite of forgiveness for the domestic ineptitude of these remote and brilliant scholars they had married. Some of the older children took snapshots at the crucial moment and some of the little children emitted sudden shrieks of "Daddy!" The processing scholars, given these conditions, reacted according to temperament. Some looked straight ahead, aware of the importance of the tribal ritual they were engaged in. Others, more sophisticated, waved condescendingly to their all too numerous children as if to say, It is important that this be done, but it is old hat—or old mortarboard—to me personally. Others looked merely sullen, and a few looked frankly faint with the heat. Still, the total effect combined gaiety with dignity in a manner that left President Pomton feeling genuinely sentimental about this university of his, which, God willing, he would so soon leave for greener pastures. Pomton's emotions even included a kind of town-and-gown awareness of what he had done, not only for the institution he still headed but for the little municipality in which it stood. He had taken an active part in developing the real-estate values of that town, and it was not merely a love for learning that had led the local Chamber of Commerce to raise the money that had built the concrete stadium toward which even now the academic procession and groups of joyful townspeople slowly converged.

"Do you know," said Schneider to Weed, who marched, dripping with sweat, beside him, "I think this whole thing could be done better if more symbols were available—something to signify our purposes."

"But," said Weed, "we're wrapped in symbols now. Don't add to our burdens."

"Oh, these!" said Schneider with a snort of scorn. "These are the wrong symbols. Empty archaism. Very unimaginative."

"Well," said Weed, "for God's sake find us some alternative before next June. I can't survive many more Turkish baths of this type."

"Let me propose," said Schneider in a modest, conciliatory tone, "a square banner for the Marshal to carry in lieu of the mace he has recently pleaded for. Let there be inscribed on it symbols that describe the principal functions of these wandering scholars. At this point let us list these functions, in order of importance: research, committee work, and—last but also least—teaching."

"So far, so good," said Weed, panting beside him under the blistering sun. "But how in this weather can we hope to discover the three appropriate symbols?"

"For me," said Schneider, "it is easy. Protected from a cruel sun by this my mortarboard, I can think with ease. I give you, to symbolize research, a pair of scissors, opened to form a St. Andrew's cross—to symbolize the tortures we go through—and immediately and handily beneath the scissors, a pot of paste, to suggest the coherence of our thought."

"Now you're talking," said Weed. "Now you're being creative."

Schneider beamed with satisfaction and gazed benignly around him at the Commencement procession in which he too was playing a vital role.

"Allow me to propose," he said, "as a symbol for our second

function—committee work—something very simple, almost banal: a snarl of red tape."

"It's certainly banal," said Weed, "if that's the note you want to strike."

"But it would add a dash of color right in the middle of the banner, something to compete with our hoods."

"All right," said Weed, "but I want it recorded that your second symbol is very banal. Wipe your face. Your intellectual effort makes you sweat disgustingly."

Schneider, unperturbed by Weed's carping criticism, calmly wiped his face.

"I do this kind of thing without effort," he said. "It's just the weather."

"And your symbol for teaching?"

"I almost forgot. In these universities one so easily forgets teaching. Well, let me see. Could I interest you in some symbol with action in it? Let us suppose, simply to have something on the table to discuss, a professor rampant with three students dormant."

"I will not agree," said Weed, "unless you can produce a Latin motto that will—well, sort of tie the whole thing together. It needs —'packaging,' I believe, is the word now used."

"Permit me to package it," said Schneider. He pondered a moment, mopped his brow again, and then said, "How would this be? IN SNAFU LABORAMUS?"

"I don't want to be pedantic," said Weed. "But is it grammatical? My Latin's frightfully rusty. Can it be translated, 'We labor in utter confusion'?"

"That is a very passable translation. And it is entirely grammatical. SNAFU is the ablative case of SNAFUS, a noun of the fourth declension. Admittedly, it is dog Latin, but that is precisely the kind our profession has traditionally spoken and written."

"With your consent," said Weed, "and without retracting a word of my less favorable comments, I should like, in the event that you present this project at a faculty meeting, to have the honor of seconding the motion to adopt such a banner. I say, what's that?"

He cocked his ear and glanced up at the sky. For just then, Pomton's contented reflections on his achievements as President and Schneider's proposals for a faculty banner to render processions like this one more significant were interrupted by a long, low growl of thunder that drowned out a Sousa number the local band had just tackled. Far ahead, and leading the procession, the Faculty Marshal too heard the Jovian thunder; and his forehead, already beaded with sweat that could not evaporate in this cruelly saturated air, began to trickle, as he inwardly cast his official meteorological horoscope. Like the wretch in the local U.S. Weather Station, with whom he had recently kept in frequent communication, he knew that he would be held personally responsible by the numerous amateur weather prophets among his colleagues, wise in their hindsight, if it should now pour. But not a drop fell; and, since all the clouds were still massed in the west, as if for a sudden attack, and since the sun had not sunk far enough to take its place modestly behind them, only the people on the concrete tiers were protected from its fierce rays, together with the candidates for degrees, who now found seats below them and who also faced the east. Foiled of its purpose to torment the guests and candidates, the sun flared down pitilessly in the faces of the President, the trustees, the deans, and the candidates for honorary degrees, as they found seats on the platform; and in the faces of the rows of faculty members that flanked the central stand on each side. People fanned themselves with their printed programs.

President Pomton arose, advanced imperiously to the microphone, and declared, "By virtue of the authority vested in me by—" But the audience was amazed by the shrill, squeaky voice that the defective public-address system filtered through to their ears and was even more amazed when Pomton's lips went on moving and no sound came through for several tense seconds. Then the public-address system got its second wind, and Pomton's voice fairly roared, "—declare opened the Ninetieth Commencement Exercises of the—" the system caught its breath again and the silence was deafening; then in a normal and rich tone of voice: "—will be pronounced by the

Reverend Robert Tyler Westerfeld of the Second Congregational Church. The audience will please stand." Pomton then removed his mortarboard with a flourish and reverently bowed his head. The faculty stood and, except for its few female members, likewise uncovered. They, too, bowed, but with gradations. Traditionally, at this critical point the natural scientists and some of the more advanced social scientists, as a protest against medieval superstition, had indeed removed their mortarboards but had kept their heads fearlessly erect and their eyes wide open, as if to defy a nonexistent deity to do its worst; and at least in 1912 there was some evidence, in the shape of a really terrific tornado, that the deity had taken up their challenge, although they could still point out that no single unbeliever had on that occasion been injured, while several of the pious had been brutally mauled. But ever since the Cold War had got under way, and the American radio's taunts at Russian godlessness had increased, and more and more politicians had taken to signing off with the phrase "under God," most of the scientists had begun to bow their heads ever so slightly, enough to show that they were on Secretary Dulles's side, and yet not so much as to implicate them permanently if the Cold War should end and if God and American foreign policy should become once more disentangled. The death of Stalin, for example, and the rise of the New Look in Moscow kept several heads today as rigid as in the good old antifundamentalist days. And those who proudly held their heads erect, willing to defy a second tornado if one should come, and to depend on the well-known law of probabilities in the matter of possible injuries, knew that President Pomton's eyes were safely shut and that they were unlikely to be identified.

In a loud, clear voice, in the lachrymose tones of Gabriel Heatter, and with the elegance of diction appropriate to the occasion, the Reverend Robert Tyler Westerfeld began to pray. His prayer was strictly extempore and depended for its usefulness partly on direct inspiration, partly on some half-remembered shreds from Scripture and the Book of Common Prayer, and finally on a good deal of careful preparation. This was the very first opportunity that

Mr. Westerfeld had ever enjoyed to lead thousands of persons in prayer, not only the thousands who stood before him with bowed heads and sweating bodies, but the thousands who might well be listening in lolling comfort over the local radio. These latter, he explicitly commended to the Almighty, for it had long been his hope that he would be given a regular radio program over the local station, thereby increasing his power for service and even, conceivably, his wretchedly meager income. A lot hung, therefore, on this one prayer, and he was determined to make it one that God Himself could not forget. To Pomton it seemed that a regrettable number of phrases had been borrowed from his own triumphant oration at A. & M., where he too had sought a wider field of service. But, he reflected, many of these phrases were in the air these days, and not even in his private thoughts was he presuming to charge plagiarism. Still, it was strange that Mr. Westerfeld should cover the Cold War so thoroughly and it was extremely annoying that the time he took to do it was being purloined from the Commencement speaker who would follow. In his letter inviting Mr. Westerfeld to pronounce the invocation today, he had playfully but clearly suggested that such things on such occasions had to be brief. Mr. Westerfeld had not overlooked the suggestion, but he had calmly overruled it. He was convinced that he was only God's instrument, that it was really God who was speaking in an indirect sort of way, and that God was considerably better placed than Mr. Pomton to know how long the invocation to Him ought to be.

From the point of view of traditional theology, the prayer contained a fair amount of unintentional blasphemy; but Mr. Westerfeld prided himself on being neither a traditionalist nor a theologian, but a simple preacher. He therefore managed today to take God into his confidence as it were, and to report to Him on the progress the University was making intellectually and financially under the able leadership with which God had provided it. If anything could have placated Pomton's rising anger at Mr. Westerfeld's garrulity, this semi-divine endorsement would have done it. But when he recalled that Mr. Westerfeld would get the floor a second time, for the purpose of pronouncing the benediction, he was in no mood to forgive him now. When the prayer finally ended, an audible sigh of relief and exhaustion went up from the entire audience, as they half fell into their seats again. For Mr. Westerfeld, at least, it had been a great day. He modestly believed he had fulfilled his mission; and he began to turn over in his mind the phrases that might make his benediction also a memorable thing.

Inwardly angry but outwardly urbane, President Pomton arose and gave the Charge to the Graduates. He used several of the best phrases from his A. & M. speech, avoiding those that this ass of a minister had already stolen and murdered; he congratulated the graduates in a genial, fatherly way; he welcomed the members of their families; and he reminded the graduates that the free competition of ideas that had made their four years on the campus so exciting and stimulating had prepared their minds and hearts to participate in the outside world of free enterprise, whether in business or the professions. Then, simply and, he felt, movingly, he wished them Godspeed, and assured them their Alma Mater intended to keep in close touch with them and solicited already their loving support.

An Army officer now arose and ordered the student members of the ROTC to stand. He then gave President Pomton a sharp salute and reported to him that these young men had been reported to the War Department as fitted to receive reserve commissions as second lieutenants. President Pomton briefly but warmly commended them for preparing themselves to defend their country, its free traffic in ideas, and the American system of free enterprise. He spoke all the more feelingly because the Army Training Program was obviously the only form of instruction, except football, that paid its own freight. He only wished he had been able to secure similar units from the Navy and the Air Force. Universities today, like so many other businesses in our great country, maintained solvency largely by means of Federal government contracts. And it may have been partly this solvency, this constant (however minimal) solution of his fiscal problems, that made Pomton such a passionate proponent of the Cold War. But now it was time to award, not Army commissions, but academic degrees.

"Will the Dean of the College of Arts and Sciences present the candidates for the degree of Bachelor of Arts?" Pomton now demanded, in ceremonious tones.

The Dean rose from his seat, tipped his mortarboard to the President, and shrilled, "The candidates for the degree of Bachelor of Arts will please stand!"

Two or three hundred young men and women rose in a solid bloc.

"Mr. President," said the Dean in his high treble, "I have the honor to present these candidates for the degree of Bachelor of Arts and to report that in the judgment of the faculty they have satisfactorily fulfilled all the requirements for that degree."

"By virtue," announced President Pomton, gazing benignly at the bloc of standing students, "by virtue of the authority vested in me by the board of trustees, I hereby confer upon you the degree of Bachelor of Arts, and I welcome you to all the rights, privileges, obligations, and immunities appertaining thereto."

The candidates lumberingly sat down again, and there was prolonged applause from the audience. But Freddie Landon turned to a fellow economist next to him and murmured, "What immunities? Name one!"

"Immunity from listening any longer to lectures by this gang of bores who surround us," replied the economist without special bitterness.

"They should have been granted that at birth," said Landon.

Next, the Dean of the College presented his candidates for the B.S. Then the Dean of Engineering, the Dean of Agriculture, the Dean of Education, and the Dean of Law went through the formulary. In a remarkably few moments, considering the weather, a whole horde of new bachelors had been created. But the Dean of Graduate Studies, when he had disposed, politely but cursorily, of a fresh crop of M.A.s and M.S.s really got down to work. He now called up personally, by name, half a dozen candidates for the degree of Doctor of Philosophy, in as many subjects, reading out with relish the titles of the doctoral dissertations they had submitted.

The first candidate to receive his doctorate was one of Nast's section hands, and the spotlight of public interest fell on the advancing candidate and on Nast's department. Candidate Nast regretted the title of his protégé's dissertation when Pomton read out: "Prepackaging in chain groceries considered as customer stimulation toward slightly deteriorated fresh vegetables." The problem the thesis dealt with was real enough, but would these laymen know it?

"That young man," remarked Landon, this time to a botanist on his other side, "has discovered how greengrocers can cheat their customers better. He knows no more about economic theory than he does about astrology."

"You will admit that the two subjects are not unrelated."

"*Touché*," murmured Landon amiably.

Pomton was giving the new Ph.D. in cheating a hearty handshake and a kindly word of congratulation, along with the rights, privileges, obligations, and immunities he had already conferred upon all six Ph. D.s *en bloc*. Then he went down the line.

There was a Ph.D. in psychology for the thesis: "Possible reforms in high-school education suggested by the psychodynamics of white rats." Schneider smiled happily at that title and murmured to a neighbor, "Other white rats, he means."

The chemists had come up with: "An inquiry into flavor deterioration in peanut brittle." Poor old Weed's department of political science had grudgingly accepted: "An inquiry into the negative correlation between Democratic administrations and world peace." Milton's sociologists had blessed: "Mother-in-law behavior, role conception, and role discrepancy, in relation to anxiety motivation and criminal homicide," which Schneider felt deserved a Ph.D. if any jest ever did. Pomton, whose own Ph.D. had been earned in the field of "education," felt a pang of emotion as he watched advancing toward him a sallow-faced fellow with a hangdog expression, the last doctoral candidate he would ever congratulate from this platform; and his voice nearly broke when he realized that this young scholar too had done his doctorate in education. But he controlled himself enough to quaver in a semi-Gregorian fashion: "Motivational influences on academic underachievers among financially assisted athletes, with special reference to those with medium intelligence quotients and referral records as juvenile delinquents."

During Pomton's intoned recital of these dissertation titles, a titter had more than once arisen from an audience unaccustomed to the notion of disinterested inquiry and confused by the unfamiliar terminologies of modern scholarship. And more than once Pomton had muttered under his breath, "The louts!" while the doctoral candidates advanced to receive their final and personalized accolades for the dreary years they had put in, preparing themselves to teach the higher learning.

But now the time for the Bigwigs had come, the time for the VIPs or—put more brutally—for those who had paid hard cash for their honorary degrees. According to the printed program there were three of them, of whom one, being an old lady, could readily be identified on the wooden platform along with the President, the deans, and the trustees: Mrs. John O'Flaherty Riley. The other two were, expectedly enough, Mr. Milton Marshall and Mr. Lanny Mac-Donald. The two smaller benefactors were dealt with first; and Pomton had placed Lanny first of all, just to get rid of him as quickly as possible: he presented so many embarrassing problems. None of the degrees ordinarily bestowed on benefactors could be very well handed Lanny without causing public mirth. Pomton had therefore invented a degree and had pointed out to his trustees that, since the degree of Doctor of Fine Arts was not unusual, Lanny might well be allotted a degree as Doctor of Physical Arts. Milton Marshall was, of course, easy. Although he had never written anything, he was widely known as a booklover, and he was down for Doctor of Letters. Mrs. Riley, as a well-known philanthropist, was obviously interested in social welfare and could be squeezed neatly into a Doctorate of Laws.

A second problem was Lanny's first name. Pomton had written a tactful letter saying he assumed that his Christian name was Landon and might be so spelled on the Commencement program. Lanny wired back that his Christian name was Lanny and that he would be the laughingstock of the Chicago sports world if he were announced as Landon. So Lanny it had to be.

So today Pomton swallowed hard, approached the microphone, and intoned, "Mr. Richard Kurt Barlow of the Board of Trustees of the University will present for the degree of Doctor of Physical Arts Mr. Lanny MacDonald." Mr. Barlow and Lanny stepped forward, both of them in cap and gown. Pomton advanced with Lanny's new hood. The lining of the hood showed the University's own colors. The facing, which Pomton had himself designed, proudly flaunted the colors of Lanny's baseball club. Lanny removed his cap, and his bald head shone in the slanting sunlight. His face wore a broad grin. He was delighted by this new honor, and his delight had been compounded that week by the purchase at very moderate prices of two new ball players, both full-hitters, from another club, that had got itself into financial difficulties. Pomton now placed Lanny's new hood around Lanny's willingly extended neck.

"Lanny MacDonald," declared Pomton, slurring over the first name as much as he dared, "you have given the sports world an example of clean sportsmanship, of prudent business management, of assiduity in the search for new and youthful talent. You have ever interested yourself in the young collegiate player and helped him to perfect his art. You have reminded this nation of ours of its priceless heritage in possessing as its national sport a game that requires thought, skill, and daring. Therefore, by virtue of the authority vested in me by the Board of Trustees of this University, I hereby confer upon you the degree of Doctor of Physical Arts, and I welcome you to all the rights, privileges, obligations, and immunities appertaining thereto."

"Okay, thanks," said Lanny delightedly. He did not speak in a loud voice, but unhappily he was standing too close to the microphone, which in any case was enjoying one of its spells of explosive vitality, and his remark rang out across the stadium. There was spontaneous and grateful laughter, and then, to Pomton's relief, wild applause. Lanny clasped his hands together over his head and bowed in all directions, and both the applause and laughter grew. Then he modestly took his seat.

Pomton heaved a sigh of relief. It could have gone off a lot worse. True, Lanny had been coached to say nothing and to ignore all applause; but the sweating crowd in the stadium was obviously glad of this *divertissement,* and Pomton was always sensitive to good humor in a crowd. He turned again to the microphone and intoned the call for Milton Marshall.

"Mr. John Alden Cabot of the Board of Trustees of the University will present for the degree of Doctor of Letters Mr. Milton Marshall," he announced sonorously.

Milton Marshall stepped forward and was put through his paces. His citation mentioned both his love of books and his love of youth and held him up as an example to impoverished young men from a decaying Europe who come to this land of opportunity for all, amass a fortune in the service of others, and prove that economic growth produces culture.

Then came Mrs. Riley, looking very old in her cap and gown, her face pale and drawn from the hideous heat, her step faltering a little. Her escort aided her, discreetly. Then Pomton intoned.

"Bridget O'Flaherty Riley," he said to her in caressing tones, "you have for years made your private means the means of the Republic of Learning. You have especially interested yourself in the daily necessities of those who teach and have given them new heart as well as new means for the discharge of their important duties. With the help of your faithful lieutenant, Amaryllis Allenby, you have sought out and succored the teacher, and he will remember you. Now, therefore, by virtue—" But his words were drowned in the most thunderous applause, and nobody clapped more loudly than the assistant professors, who forgot all decorum. When the applause abated, Pomton quietly finished her citation and placed the hood around her bent old shoulders; and at that precise moment, Mrs. Riley, overcome by the heat, or by old age, or by the gratitude of the assistant professors, fainted dead away. There was a sudden commotion on the platform, a hush in the stadium. Several of the trustees carried her off the field of glory and to a standby ambulance—and the Volunteer Municipal Band struck up the University anthem.

This, except for the benediction, which everyone now dreaded and which Mrs. Riley had so fortunately escaped, was the last item on the printed program. The crowd stood solemnly, even the faculty going through the motions of at least moving their lips, and sang one fatuous phrase after another: "Alma Mater, we uphold thee," "Far her fame shall fare," "Back to thee we'll come," and other inanities. Pomton leaned toward the Reverend Robert Tyler Westerfeld and said in low but savage tones, "This has been most unfortunate. For God's sake, be brief." The minister smiled benignly, rose, went to the microphone, and raised his hand. The audience uncovered. Then, drawing a deep breath, he began precisely the long and thorough benediction he had been silently rehearsing throughout the ceremony. But this time Divine Providence sided with Pomton. With a roar of wind and heavy peals of thunder, such torrents of rain fell that the audience quickly took advantage in its own fashion of the discreet admonition at the bottom of the printed program: "In the event of rain, the exercises will be adjourned to Snodgrass Auditorium." In a sense, the Ninetieth Commencement Exercises never really adjourned. ("We were rained out in the bottom of the ninth," Lanny MacDonald reported later, displaying his hood to a utility infielder who had spent a year at Yale.)

Professor Henry Schneider went home, drenched but happy. On a score of previous Commencement days he had felt frustration and even shame. Today he had not cursed the cruel heat. His lip had not curled when the full professors surreptitiously slipped into rearward and more honored ranks. The wearily tolling bell had aroused neither his anger nor his derision. The clownish marching of himself and his colleagues had failed to mortify him. The pretentious platform formularies, full of false, inflated dignity, had left him unoutraged, as had Mr. Westerfeld's tête-à-tête with God. Pomton's charge to the graduates was certainly silly, but it was in keeping with the 1956 version of Federal aid to education, with the transparent rascality of Mr. Lanny MacDonald, with the absurd degree that Pomton had invented for him, and with Pomton's misuse of Milton Marshall's generosity to prove that dollar profit is the surest route to ideas. Old Mrs. Riley, backed by her "faithful lieutenant, Amaryllis Allenby," devourer of assistant professors, was at least as pathetic as she was reprehensible. Finally, it was nice that the whole obscene ceremony had been washed out at the end by God's cooling, cleansing rain.

Washed out and washed up, so far as Schneider was concerned. For though he could remember every detail of this Great Day, though his attention had never once wavered, nor his search for meanings in both acts and words, yet the scenes and leading figures of the day, even while before him, and certainly now in his memory, had seemed somehow pastel. Even the most brilliantly colored doctoral hoods had reached the retina of his eyes in merely pastel shades. The whole pageant had been soft and faint, like a mural by Puvis de Chavannes. Nor did he even once see himself inside the mural. It was a mural he rather liked, but only as a spectator.

Snug in her room at the University infirmary, Dr. Bridget O'Flaherty Riley sat up in bed contentedly sipping a glass of brandy and watching the downpour outside. Beside her sat her lieutenant, P'tite.

Dr. Riley examined her program again.

"P'tite," she asked, pointing to the printed caption above the names of the citations for honorary degrees, "what does that mean?"

"*Pro honoris causa,*" read P'tite. "Oh," she said, somewhat vaguely, "for the honor of the thing."

~XVII~

T HE STORM that washed out the Commencement exercises broke
the heat wave. The students had gone, and summer school
would not begin for another fortnight, so that many even of the
faculty had also left. A delicious quiet descended on the green campus. Granted that the University buildings were mostly architectural
abortions, hideous in the extreme, their brick walls were covered
now with young ivy leaves; and the elms would have done credit
to a New England village. Schneider found the place enchanting.
He walked beneath the elms these days with a youthful step and
reveled in his novel and abundant health. Over the four females in
his home, he reigned benignly. He sincerely regretted, of course, that
Dorothy could not be purchased and added to their number; but at
least Henrietta was deferential, loyal, and by no means disagreeable
to look at; and he loved his three fat, boisterous little daughters. He
hacked away happily at his secret research project for the government—or, rather, to be absolutely precise, at his textbook on Europe
since 1815. Never before in his life had he written so fast or so easily.

He had sent some early chapters to Jim Small; Jim was delighted; and Schneider had shaken him down for another thousand-dollar advance. As a result he was nearer solvent than he had been in twenty years. Even without a Circassian slave, life was pleasant, and he had a mysterious but overpowering premonition that it was about to become even more delightful.

He was strolling on the campus when he met Freddie Landon. To his surprise, Landon, usually so well poised, looked strained and vaguely restless.

"Well," said Schneider, "I hear you're off to Atlanta."

"Just to change planes. I'm visiting my parents in Charleston for a week or two."

"Ah," said Schneider. He knew from Old Manley that Dorothy Nast, the Circassian slave, would be on the same plane, at least as far as Atlanta.

"Why is it," he asked almost petulantly, "that campuses are so attractive when the students and most of the faculty are gone?"

"Ever see Tintern Abbey?" asked Landon.

"No. But I've seen pictures of the ruin. It must be lovely. Why do you ask?"

"I biked once for several days down the Valley of the Wye," said Landon. "Tintern Abbey interests me. But do you know why? The monks who once lived in it and quarreled in it and fattened in it on the donations of the poor must have been very like a faculty. They didn't believe in the efficacy of the Mass, I suspect—at least toward the end. But the poor did, so the Mass was worth celebrating. The more I see of faculties, the more sympathy I feel for Henry the Eighth's policy on monasteries. Ever hear or see anything hollower than the exercises at Commencement?"

"Oh," said Schneider, "I suppose we accomplish a little something. When I saw the faces of the graduates and then remembered what those faces looked like when they first appeared on the campus, I felt the effort had not been wholly wasted."

"Not even a faculty," said Landon, "can prevent eighteen-year-old kids from growing four years older. They can't even prevent them from learning a few things—from the radio, or television, or the newspapers, or from some chance conversation."

"I guess you've got something," said Schneider, laughing. "God knows the courses we made them take would have arrested the maturing process if anything could have."

Landon's bitterness over the futility of what was going on at the University fitted nicely the mood of a man who was riding an escalator to an unknown destination. "But when June comes like this, and they all clear out and leave the mere shell of a university behind them, like the skin a snake has shed, you can't help examining the skin wistfully and wondering how handsome it might be if something other than a snake lived in it. In theory, you know, a real faculty could teach real students in those buildings. The trees and grass are real enough, and rather nice. In theory, Tintern Abbey may be rebuilt someday for realer, leaner, monks."

They shook hands.

"Well, *au revoir*," said Schneider.

"Or even *adieu*," said Landon. Now why *adieu*, thought Schneider, as Landon strode away—for him, abruptly.

Two days later, Freddie Landon boarded a plane for Atlanta, but Dorothy Nast was not with him. She was sitting on her garden terrace, holding a letter in her hand, a letter which she already knew by heart.

"My dearest," it said, "When I heard your departure had been delayed, I suddenly realized that way down underneath I had counted on the plane tomorrow to take us up and out of all this. Out of your marriage, out of my job in this absurd university. Upward and out of it all. Forever? Forever is a long, long word.

"Maybe it was wrong of me, but I was not thinking of us in the future. I was far too absorbed by us in the present. I had no right to do that, I suppose. It's just that almost everybody I know but you is planning a future, planning so busily that they can't truly live today. It's become a nightmare to me.

"I've resigned my job. I didn't want to talk about it or to spoil our last few days. I've taken a job in Ethiopia, of all places, because it sounds a good deal less boring than postwar America. It's a job in economic development. For a moment I thought of telling you, of asking you to get rid of Nast somehow and follow me out. But I gather my job is in a place I couldn't ask you to share.

"I'm late now for the job. I shall see my parents for only a couple of days in Charleston, wind up a little business, and report for duty.

"The happiest hours of my life I spent alone with you, on the terrace in your garden. So happy that I could not face a parting—at least not out here. I would have told you in Atlanta. Never in my whole life shall I forget. If I had fully realized how much I love you, I would have never undertaken this new job. Now I am over-whelmed that I have never once kissed you, never once held you in my arms, even for a moment. I must have been mad! And yet, per-haps, considering everything, it's better now that I didn't. Better, anyhow, for you. . . ."

She sat, holding the letter and staring at the lawn. Why was she numb? She had never once guessed it would feel like this to learn suddenly that she might never see him again. She had never reflected on their relationship: it was not of the kind that invited reflection: it had been perfectly satisfying. Now he was gone, and he had not even left a forwarding address. Did it matter? Was there anything to say?

She rose from her chair. Stiffly, like an old woman. She wandered into her garden. Old Manley had gone to Paris, after a wildly flirtatious farewell. She was sorry: she needed to talk with some-body, somebody warmly human, somebody that loved her just a little. Denby? Yes, if he were here. Then she went to the phone and on a chance called Schneider's office. Schneider was there.

"When are you going to take me fishing again?" she asked.

"When can you go? Can you go day after tomorrow?"

She could indeed. Nast was leaving tomorrow night for a neigh-boring town, to discuss the presidency with his strongest backer on the board. Nast felt sure now that A. & M. would call Pomton. Dorothy would be free. It was a deal.

Through the sultry cornfields of a late June day she and Schneider drove to the fishing hole.

"I have a surprise for you," he said. They had reached the pasture land the creek ran through. Schneider cut suddenly right, around a hill, and pulled up beside a cabin.

"Welcome," he said, bowing, "to Roaring Creek Club. Old Manley and I are its only members. Old Manley pays the rent. We use it to spend week ends."

"Are women guests allowed?" She peered into a roughly paneled bunk room. There was a brick fireplace, before which lay a bearskin rug. The bear's face wore a most threatening grimace.

"Old Manley shot him," said Schneider proudly. "I mean, he paid for the rug. Have a look at the kitchen. We get our supplies from Tim Wright, who rents the cabin to Old Manley for a song. We had to repair it a bit. Women guests are theoretically not allowed, but I judge from certain objects I discover here and there that the other half of the membership breaks the rules behind my back. Well, he pays the rent; and, as you know, he is enormously drawn to women. So am I, so come in."

They got some fishing tackle. Dorothy had brought a picnic lunch.

"We'd better leave the car here," he said. "That storm left bad mud between here and the swimming hole. Mind walking?"

"Goodness, no," she said.

They sat fishing for hours and even caught a few fish. Schneider sensed she wanted to talk about something but decided to let her choose her time. And Dorothy kept postponing, until she began wondering whether she really had anything to say or whether she just wanted to feel Schneider near her.

After lunch the sky clouded up, and the fish bit even better. Black clouds formed in the west, as they had formed for Mr. Westerfeld on Commencement Day. They took no notice. Then a strong wind rose, and Schneider asked her if they should take shelter. She didn't want to. Then it rained.

They took refuge under the willow, which helped very little

Roaring Creek quickly earned, or re-earned, its name. Dorothy was fascinated by the speed with which it became a swirling brown torrent.

"We'll have to get out of here," said Schneider. "Remember the smaller creek we had to cross to get here? In a freak cloudburst like this, that'll be up too."

It was. And the current ran unexpectedly strong. It was only by hanging on tightly to Schneider that she kept her footing. At last, she slipped and fell. Without a word, he took her into his arms and carried her to the other side. There he set her down. He was breathing a little hard.

"I didn't know you were so strong," she said, laughing up at him, while her hair hung in thick strings down her face. "I wouldn't have thought you could carry me. You know, I weigh a hundred and twenty-seven."

"I guess," said Schneider, with dignity but breathing hard, "a man can carry more girl than any other sort of load."

When they got to the cabin, Schneider issued quick orders.

"Get those wet clothes off quick. Here are some fresh clothes of Old Manley's—not very pretty, but dry. Here's a bath towel. I'll change in the kitchen. And I'll make a pot of coffee."

Outside, the rain came down in sheets. Schneider turned on a battery radio and they began getting weather reports. Bridges were washing out. Road fills were collapsing. One road after another was declared impassable. Distress teams were out. "The worst flood to hit this section in seventeen years," declared a newscaster from his cozy, dry studio. He said it with ill-concealed satisfaction.

"Well," said Schneider, "apparently you are about to spend your first night at Roaring Creek Club. What'll the head of the economics department say? The road is closed. And the telephone lines are out."

"He's out of town—tonight and tomorrow night. He won't be back till Thursday afternoon. But what will your Henrietta say?"

"She's a sensible woman. She'll know I'm caught at the cabin."

"With me?" asked Dorothy, smiling.

"Oh, no. She thinks I came out alone."

They both laughed. The temperature had begun to drop precipitately and it felt horridly raw, even in the dry cabin. Schneider brought wood from the root cellar and built a fire. They sat, side by side, on the bearskin rug, fascinated by the flames, quite silent, sipping their hot coffee. Dorothy looked absurdly tiny in Old Manley's clothes. Then, as if another dam had burst, they began to talk, about themselves. What was happening elsewhere in space, even in Tim Wright's farmhouse nearby; what had happened in past time or would happen next week—all of this seemed completely unreal. There was a now and a here and a he and a she and nothing else anywhere in the world except perhaps fire, except perhaps water, lots of water, washing out bridges, flooding roads, inundating all other places on earth except this place, washing out all time except the present. So they talked. Now and then Schneider threw on another log.

Around five, Tim Wright knocked on the kitchen door. He stood in his oilskins, while rainwater ran off him in rivulets. He gulped a cup of the coffee Schneider had made.

"I saw the smoke from your chimney," said Tim. "I knowed you was trapped by the storm. So I brought over some provisions for you and your wife. I got milk and butter and eggs and some of Alice's bread and some new peas and a couple of broilers. That enough?"

"This is not my wife, Tim," said Schneider. "It's my niece, Miss Thompson."

Tim Wright touched his hat, and Dorothy exclaimed with delight over the provisions. Then he left, and they went back to the bearskin rug, and Dorothy began shelling the new peas while Schneider stared once more into the flames and they talked. Outside, the torrent continued.

She told him about her childhood, about meeting Nast, about her marriage, about her trip to New York, her realization that her relationship to Nast was empty, her happy evenings out with Denby.

"What a guy!" said Schneider, and another dam burst. He told her about his strange breakfast with Denby, about how the breakfast had freed him somehow of his worries and weaknesses. He pictured the absurd effort he had made weeks before the breakfast to shake down Pomton for a raise, of the harrowing but equally absurd effort to reorganize his department, of what he thought of faculty cocktail parties, of the meaningless bedlam of the faculty meeting that failed to reform the undergraduate curriculum. He told her of Engel's law and the gossip about his government research, of his growing prestige, of the textbook assignment. Of his revolt against Henrietta's tyranny, his donning the family trousers again, and a symbolic kaffiyah to boot. He pictured his negotiated peace as unconditional surrender.

At the story of the kaffiyah and of Henrietta's submission, she laughed until tears came. Then she looked very serious.

"I'm afraid," she said, "my squabble with Henrietta must have made things even more difficult for you."

"I'm grateful to you," he said. "It made things so damned difficult I finally found them intolerable. So I put my foot down. And since then, things have been most workable."

"I wish things were what you call workable for me," she said. "I can't go on. Denby freed me too. Then Dr. Manley helped. Then—"

"Then Freddie Landon helped?"

Unexpectedly for Schneider, she burst into tears. He put his arm around her and drew her head down on his shoulder. But he said nothing.

At last, still sobbing a little, she told him of her relation to Landon, of Landon's sudden departure, and of the note he had left.

"My poor dear," he said. "That's the way it so often is. We so often don't know until it's too late. And I had pictured you and Landon on the Atlanta plane, discovering each other."

"Oh, well," she said. "Who knows? He had already agreed to go to Ethiopia. If he had really wanted me, he would have told me he was leaving. He would have asked me to go with him, even, if he had really wanted me the way I wanted him."

"What did the great Nast say when Landon quit?"

"The day I got the letter he came home and said, 'What do you know? Landon has run out on me.'"

"And you said?"

"I snapped at him. I said, 'I understand he resigned to the President of the University. Are you President—yet?' And he said, 'I will be shortly,' and laughed."

"Why were you angry? Because you felt that maybe Landon really had run out, even a little on you?"

She reflected. "Perhaps I did."

They were silent a while. Then Schneider drew her face up toward his, looked down into her extraordinary violet-colored eyes, and spoke. "And all of it happened in another life. And in another life still, some other things, maybe worse things, will happen. But Now belongs to us. Now and Here."

He paused. This was a most depressing and pedagogical beginning. *Now* and *Here,* when taken in their full context, were interesting metaphysical concepts, but the girl in his arms was the most physically exquisite, metaphysically naïve girl he had yet met. She must think he was a fool. His body ached for hers, but his damned mind had intruded at just the wrong moment.

"Dorothy," he blurted out, "I adore you. I want you. I need you."

His head was spinning now, mindlessly, deliciously. She suddenly flung both arms around his neck, and his mouth found hers. Schneider entered a sort of Moslem paradise.

He sprang to his feet. Once again he lifted her in his arms, and this time it was in his bunk that he set her softly down.

Was it an hour later, was it two hours, that she lay sleeping in his arms, her young face faintly outlined by the dying fire? She breathed heavily and regularly, as children do. Outside, the storm had exhausted itself. The wind had fallen; the rain had stopped; and in this new silence Schneider could hear the rainwater dripping from the drenched cherry tree that overhung the cabin. It fell on the tin roof, loud, surprisingly regular, like the ticking of some huge old grandfather clock. The creek still roared in the distance, at the foot of the hill. But the soaked fields slept quietly now. The storm was over. Schneider, too, drifted off to sleep.

He was awakened by a flood of sunlight. He managed to slip out of the bunk without waking her, made his way to the kitchen, dressed, and got some breakfast ready. He slipped out behind the cabin to a bed of wild violets he knew; his bare feet felt cold in the lush, wet grass. Then he arranged his violets on her tray.

"Do I smell coffee?" she called from the bunkroom.

"No," he said, "you smell violets." And he bore in her tray triumphantly. "It's too wet to eat outdoors. It's too warm to make a fire and share our breakfast with Old Manley's bear. Why don't you have your breakfast right here?"

"I'll just wash my face and hands first."

Schneider pointed proudly to a wet washcloth that modestly occupied a corner of the tray and to the face towel on his arm.

"What a well-run club this is!"

"The management tries to please," said Schneider.

"And it succeeds. Why, Henry, you're blushing!"

"With pleasure, not with shame," he said.

"I suppose," she said, when they had finished breakfast and smoked, "I ought to be returning to the world." Her voice was gratifyingly regretful.

"There's no hurry. We can't possibly make it to hard surface before noon. I didn't bring chains. Time belongs to us; we don't belong to time. It's the rest of the world that belongs to time."

She lay back luxuriously in the bunk, but she evaded his attempt to kiss her.

"No," she said. "I want you to talk some more about me." Her egotism was unabashed, childlike, and charming. Or, anyhow, so Schneider found it.

"Well, then, let's begin at the beginning. What's the first thing you remember about the great world outside your little one?"

"That the Japs had bombed Pearl Harbor," she said.

"Really?" he said, his voice incredulous. "But how old were you?"

"Oh, seven or eight, I reckon."

"The first thing I remember about our world was the Armistice."

"The Armistice?" Her tone was vague.

"Yes, the Armistice. You know: the armistice that ended the fighting in World War One."

"World War One?" Dorothy sounded awe-struck, as if he had said the Spanish-American War. "But how old were you?"

Schneider winced visibly. He had never enjoyed being forty-four. Now he frankly hated it.

"I didn't mean it that way," she said.

"I was six," he said, with a good deal of masculine dignity.

Suddenly the memory of that tormented world flooded back upon him, the world of the Big Boom and the Big Bust and the early New Deal, the world this child had never lived in for a single day but that another girl, a girl named Henrietta, had.

"How old are you now?" he asked, feeling her somehow slipping away from him in time.

"Twenty-three."

Schneider was frankly startled: he had never dreamed she was that young.

"Good Lord!" he said. "My Elsie will be that in another ten years." Immediately, he could have bitten his wayward tongue.

"I'm sorry," she said, and her voice was taut. In fact, it was very much like Elsie's voice when her father got on her nerves. "I didn't mean to annoy you by being born so recently. You see, I didn't plan my own birth. Besides, I thought we decided to talk about me, not about history. I hate history. I hate the past."

Her voice had grown hysterical. She looked at him accusingly.

"You told Tim Wright I was your niece."

"Well, I had to tell him something."

"Maybe you were right. Maybe I am your niece. Maybe, professor, you've now committed incest. Or statutory rape. All I know is, you've ruined it all. Oh, take me home!"

"Dorothy!" he said, in a panic. He tried again to take her in his arms, but she pushed him away from her.

"Freddie," she said, sobbing, "was a senior in high school when the Japs bombed Pearl Harbor. He told me so. But I never want to see him again either."

In the end, she dressed, while Schneider morosely did the dishes and packed the car. We'll probably get stuck before we reach hard surface, but if she's determined to go, he thought, I'll damned well take her. He was so torn between desire for her woman's body and revulsion from her adolescent hysteria that he could hardly get on with his preparations for the trip back. When they had got into the car and had sat down side by side, with Time himself sitting between, he ventured, in a conciliatory tone, a single question.

"Dorothy," he said, "just what is it you want out of life?"

She pouted slightly, reflected, then said, "I want to live. I want to have fun."

They drove silently back to town, through the fields of young corn having fun in the hot sunshine. Some of the stalks were still bent from the high winds of last night. But the rain water they drank up from the soaked soil raced exhilaratingly through their veins and they praised the June sun joyously, confidently, innocently, greenly. The jalopy reached a neutral and now deserted street corner, at the end of a bus line; and she asked Schneider to let her out. She hesitated awkwardly a moment; then gave him a little peck on his cheek.

"I'm sorry," she said.

"Have fun," said Schneider.

It was more than Schneider himself had, during the days that followed. The more he reflected on the interlude in the cabin, the more humiliated he felt. Fate had lifted him and Dorothy out of the trivial round of a petty university community, had placed them alone together in a remote cabin, had sealed them off with an unprecedented storm, had literally thrown them into each other's arms. He had thereupon, promptly and pleasantly, lost his head. He had at last had his Circassian to himself. If this was adultery, then he was not surprised that not even the strictest laws seemed to prevent it. Then something reminiscent of a lover's quarrel, but even more reminiscent of a weekly quiz in an undergraduate history course, had hurled him down from this paradise to something pretty close to hell.

What on earth had Henrietta or Elsie or Freddie to do with it? What had generations to do with it? Historians are bemused by generations: granted. Certainly, he had possessed her; but almost as certainly, his clumsy lovemaking had lost her. Granted that she was young enough to be his daughter. So much the better. Even if she had been a mermaid, or a dryad, or an Olympic goddess for that matter, a more expert lover would have bridged the gap. In ancient Greece there were men who had lain with goddesses and even begotten distinguished offspring with them. Apparently, escalators play tricks on a man, and at the very moment when he least expects it. He tried to write her a note, but he could not find the right words. He was utterly wretched.

He tried to work, but it was no good. Her image got between him and whatever he tried to put his mind on. He doubted if St. Anthony had ever known torments like his. One gathered that St. Anthony saw more females in his visions than this one that Schneider saw, but did St. Anthony see his so vividly? In the end, it was she who wrote the note.

"Dear Uncle Henry," it said, in its large vertical handwriting, "I am gloriously happy and want you to know. Freddie has written again. He has delayed leaving for Ethiopia. You won't need to find me a husband. All you need to do is to help me get rid of the one I have, but you must, you must do that for me. Come at four o'clock Tuesday if you can. The subject of discussion will be absent."

What was it he had said to her so patronizingly in the cabin? "My poor dear," he had said. "That's the way it so often is. We so often don't know until it's too late." Don't know, or just don't act. He could swear now that he could have held her for at least these few, precious days, if he had acted like a normal human male, like a half-back, and not like a campus-bred underpaid pedagogue. Though, even then, this second note from Landon would doubtless have torn her from him. Yes, but that would have been better than his present stupid situation.

She was on the garden terrace when he called. She was more beautiful, more desirable, than ever, partly because she was more obviously, more radiantly, happy than he had ever known her.

"Hello, Uncle Henry," she said, and he flinched. She corrected herself instantly.

"Henry, dear, what's happened? You don't look well."

"After our—fishing trip," he said, "I discovered you were not my niece. I could think of nothing but you. Then I got your note."

"I'm sorry," she said.

And yet, thought Henry, your face brightened when I admitted I could think of nothing but you.

"I'm sorry," she said again. "But you already know that I adore Freddie and was brokenhearted when he left. He says he was a fool to leave without making me promise to marry him. So I've written him I would."

"Too bad you're married to Nast."

"Don't be ironical with me, Henry. I'm counting on you to persuade him to let me have a divorce."

"Nast is a fool; but he's not that big a fool. Do you think I'd let you go, if you were mine?"

She looked at him with swimming eyes. "You would if I asked you to, Henry," she said. "You're a good man."

"Oh, I'm not even a man. I'm just a gigolo they keep around the place to take young women on overnight fishing trips."

"Don't be bitter, Henry."

"I'm not bitter. It's just that for a few days you began to seem like some sort of Beatrice. I must have thought I was achieving a *vita nuova*, a new life, you know; but it was just change of life, I guess."

"Stop it! You say you love me: then help me get a divorce."

"Why on earth should Nast agree to divorce the most beautiful woman he's ever met? You might as well ask him to give a friend his Packard Executive."

"If you can't stop being horrid, you'd better go. I thought you'd want to help me. Henry, stop shaking your head! It can be done quite simply, I tell you. I'm leaving tomorrow night. I've told Richard my mother is ill and I must go to Georgia. I'm meeting Freddie in Atlanta, and we're making our plans. I don't want to talk to Richard. I want you to talk with him."

Henrietta, thought Schneider, would do her own talking.

"All you have to do," she said, "is to tell him I insist on divorce. If he balks, tell him I shall report the facts on the Winthrop grant. To President Pomton."

Schneider raised his eyebrows.

"Don't you remember the trip Richard made to New York at President Pomton's request, to finalize the social-science grant with Denby? Don't you remember I told you I went along? Well, Richard persuaded me to get Denby to shift the grant from social science in general to the department of economics."

"Well, well," said Schneider. "So that's why Denby shifted. I always wondered who did that dirty trick."

"I did," said Dorothy. She was clearly unashamed. As a matter of fact, thought Schneider, she is wholly without morals. That is what is so absurd about my night in the cabin.

"Pomton told the social-science people," he said, "that Denby wrote him it was economics or nothing."

Dorothy smiled. "He did," she said. "I explained to him that it would be improper for Nast to propose such a shift."

"Oh," said Schneider, "it would! And the social scientists have been pretty sore with Pomton for agreeing to the shift, too. If Pomton knew that it was Nast's idea and not Denby's, he'd be furious."

"He would hardly in the circumstances urge the board to elect Nast as his successor."

"Ah," said Schneider, "I see."

"At last." She smiled benignly.

"I'm only a diplomatic historian," he said. "Without the documents, I'm lost."

"You should always ask who wrote the document, and why."

"I think you have something," he said. Beatrice, he thought, was never like this. Then he frowned.

"Nast is going to be pretty angry," he said. "He may say the hell with it. He may feel he's got the board sewed up; that he can do without Pomton; that the trustees won't even believe Pomton's story."

"In that case," she said, "you'll have to get tough."

"With what?"

"You'll have to tell him that I shall sue for divorce immediately. I might not win, of course. But I think the fact of suit would block his election satisfactorily."

"Again," he said, "I think you have something." Really, he thought, she's a complete little blackmailing bitch. Still, blackmail is about right for Nast. As for her morals, is her blackmail any worse than my research hoax?

"My lawyer tells me," she said, "that if he signs these papers, we will have reached a friendly agreement. He promises not to contest my suit, and I promise not to sue until after his inauguration."

Then she said gently, "Since you say you love me, Henry, I ask you to get him to sign these papers."

"Can't your lawyer take care of it?" he asked. "To tell the truth, I'd rather keep out of it."

"You're always backing away from things, Henry." She had the good grace to blush. "You must stop it. I want you to do this. My lawyer doesn't know the local situation. You do. Richard may get nasty and we may have to shift tactics. I depend on your judgment. I depend on you to advise me until the divorce is safely through."

Her impudence stunned him; awe-stricken, he could only admire. "Very well," he said.

"You're a darling. Now tell me about your own future."

"I'm going to get out of here somehow. I can't stand this place. And now with what's happened between you and me, and with you leaving, I can't take it."

"Let me know if I can help," she said. "And now, good-by."

She stood and stretched out her arms. He took her and held her. Now she let him kiss her; now it was all right.

"My address is with the legal papers," she said. "Write to me."

He stumbled out into the street. For an aging womanizer, he said to himself bitterly, one of these little romances is approximately enough.

~XVIII~

WHEN DOROTHY reached Atlanta and Freddie, she went to considerable pains to avoid the appearance of disappearing. She telegraphed her mother to forward any letters or telegrams that might arrive from her husband to "care of Mrs. Frederick Landon," a very close friend of hers, at a certain Atlanta hotel. For her pains she received one letter from Nast, a strange adolescent mixture of news about his various projects and of clumsy, vulgar lovemaking. But Dorothy was grateful for the document: it so decisively confirmed her view of Nast as impossible.

Nast, who was one of the sharpest-eyed high-school boys on the faculty, might have suspected that Dorothy was bored with their marriage had he not been busier at this moment than he had ever been in his life. He was, in fact, passing through the crisis of his professional career.

In July, President Pomton finally resigned. While Freddie and Dorothy were wasting time in Atlanta planning their marriage,

President Pomton was announcing that he had accepted the presidency of A. & M. His Cold War speech had struck its intended mark, the A. & M. trustees. The trustees of the University accepted his resignation from that institution with the liveliest expressions of regret and gratitude, and secretly wondered if he would be able to carry his donors with him. They reflected hopefully that the State Agricultural and Mechanical College was supported by the taxpayers. But President Pomton's principal selling points with his donors had been, first, that intellectual freedom could flourish only when supported by, and responsive to, a system of free enterprise; and, second, that the politicians should keep out of it. The trustees of the University could reasonably hope that the donors Pomton had run to earth for them would write him off as a renegade, even a kind of New Dealer. But these thoughts they kept to themselves, just as Pomton kept to himself the new slogans he was already busy inventing about partnership with government in educational costs. Although the university over which he still technically presided would, like so many of its sister corporations in the business world, fold instantly if it lost its defense contracts, President Pomton was maturing the argument that it was only the Federal government, not the grass-roots state legislature, that threatened to dominate our intellectual life and dictate what we should teach our youth. Any institution that accepted money from Washington, he would say, might as well close its doors. Except for national defense, where the freedom of all our people was at stake, and the very existence of free enterprise itself was threatened by godless atheism.

The moment toward which Nast had been working for years had now arrived. Pomton had made it clear that he would do all in his power to pass the crown to him. Now the throne was vacant, and as so often happens even in wider fields than a college campus, with the throne vacant and the succession in doubt, parties were beginning to form among the faculty. Some vague atavistic feeling among them led to three assumptions. First, a company of scholars ought to be competent to choose who should preside over them. Second, in theory at least, the Republic of Learning can be presided over best by somebody who has participated in the actual teaching process—in short, by what the faculty liked to call "an academician," a word with overtones of extraordinary prestige. Third, again at least in theory, the best man might, just conceivably, be one of themselves. Most of the faculty would have frankly admitted that these principles were more often honored in the breach than in the observance, if only because the Republic of Learning, or at least its local chapter, was not a republic at all but a strict monarchy. True, it was a monarchy in which the subjects could effectually prevent the monarch from doing anything constructive, as for example in the case of Weed's curricular reform. Pomton had undoubtedly favored that reform, but it had now gone decisively down the drain. Similarly, the monarch could prevent the subjects from doing anything constructive simply by expressing regrets that it would cost too much, or even by plaintively announcing that the board of trustees would not go along.

It was the latter group of Homeric deities, the faculty knew, which really appointed and deposed presidents. Indeed, very few members of the faculty had ever met a member of the board in the flesh. But they knew that the board included no single academician. Except for one local politician and one lonely doctor, the members of the board were all solid businessmen, loyal Republicans, and to a man supporters of the late Senator Taft. The politician had been elected to the board during the McCarthy period. He was, indeed, chairman of the Committee on Un-American Activities of the State Legislature. It was clear that the only way to prevent him from defaming and perhaps destroying the institution was to get him in some sense inside it and to redirect his demagogic fury against its sister institutions. The formula had worked.

The doctor was a loyal member of the A.M.A., especially on the issue of socialized medicine, and exhibited no taint of that queer leftism that businessmen so often feel in their professional acquaintances. Dr. Bowers, the trustees felt, was genuinely one of themselves, just as anxious to make money as they were. That he did it by selling his professional skill to the highest bidders was no more calculated to give him crazy ideas than selling any other service. Indeed, he had first been proposed for election to the board by a wealthy mortician and a very successful pharmicist, both of whom, by the way, thought of themselves as being also professional men.

The faculty knew that a group of powerful men of this stamp was unlikely to select an egghead as president; but they still wistfully asserted that the board ought at least to invite consultation. Finally, although most of the faculty would have accepted even a general or admiral or retired banker rather than see Nast lording it over them, there was certainly nothing in the charter to keep lightning from striking one of them. This fact perhaps had no more practical political significance than the widely publicized fact that any native-born American may aspire to the White House, even the most intelligent. But it did tickle the professorial fancy, and it did give the faculty a fascinating sense of participating in the coming election.

It more than tickled the fancy of Milton, head of sociology and exponent of Engel's Law. Despite all Schneider's urgent if ironical advice, Milton had finally come up with conclusions that fully satisfied President Pomton and that might reasonably be expected to delight the board. He had proven beyond statistical doubt that university faculties in the Midwest actually receive a real wage as high as that paid in the East. It had taken some ingenuity to reach this conclusion, and the result had made Milton even less popular with his colleagues than he had been before. But Milton, like Nast, had long thought of himself as a candidate, and he was confident Pomton had thought of him that way too. Why else had Pomton planned to make him director of the Institute for Research in the Social Sciences? It is true that the Institute never got set up, but that was not Pomton's doing. For unaccountable reasons the Winthrop Foundation had suddenly decided to put the funds destined for such an institute at the sole disposal of the department of economics. Milton privately believed that, since that decision followed promptly on a visit Nast had made to New York, it was his present rival for the presidency who was responsible for that unhappy change in plans. But for many years he had seen signs that Pomton would back him when and if the present exciting moment ever arrived. Moreover, he had taken energetic steps of his own; various friends around the state were writing acquaintances of theirs on the board to point out Milton's particular qualifications.

Meanwhile, Milton's confidence steadily grew. So far as his colleagues were concerned, he felt he had an utterly clear field, because of their hatred of Nast. And it excited his imagination to buttonhole those of his colleagues whom he regarded as his most loyal friends and to seek their advice.

"Of course," he said to Schneider, "I may never have to face the problem. Elections are tricky things. There is no sign yet that the faculty is to be consulted. And I am quite aware that the board would prefer an admiral or a general to a scholar, even to a scholar in so practical a field as sociology. It's lucky I'm not in classics or philosophy or some other moonshine field. Still, I may be elected.

"But suppose I am? Ought I to take it? That's what bothers me. I am, after all, a scholar. The presidency would leave little or no time for research. Then, too, I owe some responsibilities to my students—particularly to my graduate students. Some of them are midway through doctoral theses and need me. What do you think?"

"Why worry about it?" said Schneider, fully aware that the board would sooner close the place than elect Milton. "Why cross that bridge until you come to it? If you are elected, which is by no means certain, surely the board will give you time to consider."

"Of course it's not certain," said Milton, a little impatiently. "But," he added mysteriously, "there are signs that it is highly likely. There are signs."

Milton talked this way to many of his friends.

"What an utter ape he is," his friends complained to each other. "I'm sick of being bored with it."

But as time went by, and no decision had been reached, Milton's consultations with his friends increased both in number and in urgency.

"It may well be," he would say, "that the board will not act decisively before Pomton leaves. In that event they will need an Acting President. If they ask me to serve, I don't see how I can refuse. I can't well plead that even a slight interruption of my scholarly research would be damaging. I could still lend a hand to my graduate students until the final invitation came."

The buttonholing steadily increased; and since none of Milton's friends was prepared to forbid him flatly to mention the moral crisis in which he found himself, they began to cast about for some defense against the boredom he was now daily inflicting on them. The device they spontaneously chose was to assume with him that the crown was all but his, to tell him in strictest confidence that the board's Committee on Selection was about to sit down with a committee from the faculty, and to urge him to build his fences politically among those faculty members most likely to serve on such a committee.

"But how?" Milton would ask, his fatuous, mole's face tense, his habitual mannerisms increased by his nervous tension.

Schneider had an answer: "You need a platform. And you need to make specific pledges. To use a striking metaphor, you need a pledged delegation."

"I am willing to pledge anything within reason," poor Milton said. "And of course I shall favor the development of those departments that show now that they feel better able to work with me than under the tyranny of Nast or some admiral. But there are some compromises I could not make and still retain my scholarly integrity. And as to pledged delegates, I do not wish to place my friends in a false position. You see, I still haven't decided definitely to accept when asked."

"Well," said Schneider, "I don't think you can afford to insist too much on scholarly integrity. Certainly no president insists on it after he is once elected; I think candor would suggest your not insisting on it before your election. Compromises have to be made in practical politics, and this is a practical political situation if I ever saw one. As to placing your friends in a false position, you can always release delegates to whichever of your opponents you deem best fitted to serve in your place."

"That's true," said Milton, with relief.

"But what's your platform?"

"What do you advise?"

"Higher pay for all hands," said Schneider.

The more Milton campaigned, the more convinced he became that this was the one important issue. "But suppose," he asked himself, "I simply can't find the money? Well, I can but do my best. The angels can do no more."

It was a remark his mother had often made when he was a kid on the farm. But something had slipped since Milton was a kid. These days the best you could do always turned out to be raising money. Milton was frankly baffled.

"Shouldn't I have an educational policy?" he demanded of Schneider.

"The very worst thing you could have," said Schneider. "The very quickest way to lose the support of the faculty. Faculties don't like presidents meddling with education. The president's job is to bring home the bacon, slice it, and pass it around. Then, after a square meal, the faculty will settle policy."

Milton recalled that the faculty hadn't done much settling when Weed had proposed his new curriculum, a curriculum that might stand some chance of educating the undergraduate. But then, he reasoned to himself, the faculty hadn't had any bacon for a long time. When children are hungry, they quarrel. The college faculty had been hungry. Was that maybe why they quarreled so horribly?

Milton canvassed insanely away. After weeks of this, he again went to Schneider, partly because he was confident Schneider despised Nast. He gave Schneider a quick review of his campaign to date.

"What do you think?" he asked.

"Why do you want to be President?" asked Schneider.

Milton was startled by the question. He had never before considered it. He had vaguely assumed that everybody in the faculty would like to be President if he could; and, indeed, he was not far wrong. He stared wonderingly at Schneider.

"Wouldn't you want to be?"

"I should like the President's salary. It's much higher than mine."

Milton looked shocked. "Oh, I'm not considering the post because of the salary!"

"Then why on earth consider it? Is there anything desirable about the presidency except the salary—and of course free use of the parsonage and an adequate expense account?"

Milton could think of several desirable features: fame, power, authority, and, above all, success. It would crown his academic career: that's all it would do! Schneider must be mad. But he shrank from stating these motives.

"It's a great opportunity for service," he said.

"You mean, to raise money?" asked Schneider.

There it was again—money, thought Milton. They always come back to it.

"Did the President always have to raise the money for this place?" asked Milton.

"I can answer that one. Once, for the hell of it, I studied the minutes of the board for the first fifty years.

"No, the President didn't. The trustees did. They raised it by prayer. You know, in those days most of them were Methodist ministers, and simple men. Whenever the University got in a jam for money, everybody at the board meeting fell on his knees, and then they prayed like mad. They just asked God to send them some money."

"And what did God do?" Milton's tone was less derisive than Khrushchev's might presumably have been. Still, Milton was a sociologist, and his tone was fairly derisive.

"The extraordinary thing is that God invariably sent the dough."

"They must not have asked for very large sums."

"Oh, they didn't. They only asked for what they had to have if the faculty was to go on teaching. If you're elected, why not invite the board to pray, Milton? They're all church members, I understand, as well as Republicans."

"They wouldn't do it," said Milton. "Except, of course, in church. They wouldn't suddenly interrupt a meeting and flop on their knees. They'd feel silly. And, besides, how would you report such a thing in the minutes?"

"Oh," said Schneider, "I suppose the Secretary would just write: 'They lifted up their voices.' Something of the sort."

"I think," said Milton, "they'd sooner go to the bank."

"Ah," said Schneider, "but then they'd have to pay it back, and with interest."

"Well, in the old days they may have got what they absolutely had to have, but they never got much more."

"Oh, if the Milton administration is determined to get more than it absolutely needs, that will involve trips to Chicago, and even trench mouth. But you must make your choice, mustn't you?"

Impaled on this shaft of logic, Milton looked utterly wretched.

"I ought to add," said Schneider, "that I think there is something deeply suitable about your presiding over this faculty."

"Thank you," said Milton. It was not, of course, a firm election pledge but it comforted the candidate. The irony was wholly lost on him.

It is not a pledge, thought Schneider, but a pledge would be meaningless, anyhow. It is quite clear that neither my opinion nor his nor that of any other faculty member will remotely interest the board. And it is the board that will shortly elect a new President. The odds remain in favor of Nast.

Candidate Milton departed, to consult with other colleagues.

If the board elects me, thought Milton, it will be because they believe I can raise money. The more money they believe I can raise, the more quickly they will elect me. The more the faculty believes I can raise, the more heartily they will welcome my election. If there is to be any praying, I shall have to do it in private. So Milton began to hint to his colleagues that he knew sources, hitherto untapped sources, which had only to be tapped. He still planned privately to involve God if he could, at least as adviser. Maybe the experience of the past had taught the University that God helps those presidents who help themselves. You could no longer count on the ravens. With the budget the University now operated under, the raven was too small a bird to be relevant. Maybe an eagle or a condor or a roc might be able to do a little.

In any case, Milton's chief immediate problem was, of course, not to find money but to beat Nast. Faculty betting heavily favored Nast. And it favored Nast's methods. For Nast wasted not an iota of his energies on courting faculty support, since he was pretty certain faculty support was as irrelevant to the problem as prayer or ravens. The board would do the electing, not the faculty, and Nast had cultivated the members of the board for several years during which Milton had merely nursed secret hopes and suffered *lapsus linguae*. From Nast's point of view, "all those who expected to be President" had better get next the board, and fast. He had done so.

It is true that he was less crudely discourteous to his colleagues than before. He exhibited a large geniality. But he invested no time in the enterprise. Metaphorically, he kissed babies when they were thrust at him, and no matter which end of the baby first confronted him; but he did it, again metaphorically, on the wing. His real attention was on smoke-filled rooms, rooms no faculty member ever entered. At the moment, his chief concern was a report from Pomton that one of the trustees had picked up a rumor most unfavorable to Nast, a rumor that Nast had undercut Pomton with the Winthrop Foundation. Nast was confident that Milton had started the rumor. According to report, Pomton had declared in full board meeting what was not strictly true: namely, that he had Denby's personal assurance that Nast had done his level best to hold the foundation to its original policy of setting up a research institute for all the social sciences, but that at a certain point Nast had had to accept the restriction of the gift to his own field of economics or perhaps see the University lose out completely. Pomton, now that he had clinched his new job at A. & M., lost nothing whatever by glorifying Nast's helpfulness to him over the past years, and he did a job of it. He declared that Nast had a genius for money-raising, was the darling of the business community for hundreds of miles around, and was incapable of double-crossing his superiors.

"I think I know the boy better than perhaps any other member of our board, and I assure you he's as clean as a hound's tooth."

This phrase struck a responsive chord in the hearts of the board, and the rumor was promptly laid to rest as the sort of malicious slander some left-winger in the faculty might easily have started. But Joe Stanforth, the leading banker of a near-by metropolis, was disturbed by the very phrase that had made Nast's fortune during the past months—People's Capitalism.

"It sounds New Deal to me, if not worse," he said sternly to Pomton. "It's all very well to call Nast 'your boy,' but are you sure he's not a member of the Democrat party?"

"I can only reply," answered Pomton with dignity, "that the Young Republicans have frequently urged him to run for Congress."

"Well," replied Joe Stanforth, "People's Capitalism sounds pretty communistic to me. The Reds are always talking about people's this and people's that."

"I happen," said President Pomton deferentially, for fear of antagonizing Joe Stanforth, "I happen to know that the phrase was invented by the Advertising Council, Incorporated, and is sponsored by the National Association of Manufacturers."

"It could be, those organizations could have been Communist-in-filtrated," said Stanforth stubbornly.

"I hold in my hand," replied Pomton courageously, "I hold in my hand—no, this isn't it either." He fumbled a moment in a folder. "Here it is. I hold in my hand a memorandum by the president of the Advertising Council, which was mailed to me at my request. When Nast first started using the phrase People's Capitalism, I thought he had invented it. And, while I never for a moment doubted his loyalty to the American way of life, I did feel that it is awfully easy for any professor to become a dupe. I thought that even

Dr. Nast, brilliant mind though he is, might have become—well, as you say, Joe, 'infiltrated.'

"Nast told me who invented the phrase and who was sponsoring it. Although reassured, I sent off for the statement, on the chance that somebody might in all good faith raise the objection that you have just so thoughtfully raised. Well, this thing says the phrase has already proven a powerful Cold War propaganda weapon. This thing says—just a moment, here it is, and I quote: 'At the Soviet Communist party's twentieth Congress, *Pravda* editor Shepilov said that People's Capitalism was as impossible as quote fried ice unquote.' So you see the Advertising Council has already drawn blood, Joe."

"As a mere banker," replied Stanforth, "I'm less interested in drawing blood than in drawing interest. This phrase, I tell you, is playing with fire. It could easily lead our people to conclude that capitalists ought to lend money at lower rates."

But Stanforth's opposition, according to Pomton, could be somehow overcome; and Pomton assured Nast that, as a candidate, he was 'way out in front.

"I suppose you know, sir," said Nast, "that the opening of the summer session, precisely because it has increased the number of faculty members on campus, has stirred up the animals, and that a group of them are meeting to elect a committee to work with the board."

"Who called the meeting?" asked Pomton sharply. "No dean has been given orders to call a meeting."

"They called it themselves," said Nast, his lip curling slightly.

"The fools!" cried Pomton angrily. "They know perfectly well they have nothing to do with the question of the presidency. I tell you, Nast, these interregnums are dangerous things. If I hadn't already resigned, they wouldn't have dared call a meeting about something exclusively within the jurisdiction of the board."

"They keep muttering something," said Nast dryly, "about the Republic of Learning."

"Nonsense!" said Pomton. "Bosh! They're hired to teach, not to run the University."

But the informal faculty meeting took place just the same. Nast's foe, the Professor of German, had called it and opened the meeting by demanding the election of a chairman. He was quickly chosen for the job, an eventuality he had partially foreseen. To accentuate their awareness that the meeting was entirely unofficial and therefore not open to just criticism, they had met at the Triangle Club. Schneider attended. If he was to persuade Nast not to contest Dorothy's suit for divorce, this election was important. He still could not recall the scene in the cabin without a pang; but he was determined that, if Dorothy was not to be his, she should at least admire his diplomatic finesse and be grateful for his help.

Schneider had decided that he must facilitate Nast's election. It was just conceivable that if he confronted Nast now with a demand that he let Dorothy go, Nast, cold fish though he was, might in anguish or in anger even risk losing the election for the pleasure of being vindictive. It was unlikely, but it was not inconceivable. But once he was chosen, he was highly vulnerable to Dorothy's blackmailing tactics. And he would not feel safe until after his inauguration. Once he was inaugurated, the board would scarcely dare to admit they had been made fools of and demand his resignation. Schneider was confident they would simply stomach their mistake. In any case, Schneider felt sure that the period between the election and the inauguration would be Nast's moment of greatest malleability. So he attended, and the meeting came to order.

"We are all quite aware," the Chairman began in his most brittle, bitter voice, "that the charter of the University places the election of presidents exclusively in the hands of the trustees. It nowhere, however, forbids the trustees to seek the advice of those who merely work here. It nowhere forbids the community of scholars which every university essentially is—it nowhere forbids those persons on the premises most likely to know what a university is—from humbly petitioning the institution's nominal and legal guardians to listen to competent advice. Despite the current mode for choosing generals, admirals, or bankers to guide the scholarly enterprise, the charter nowhere forbids the trustees to elect an academician to preside over other academicians. Even our outgoing president has written and published a book, although I cannot guarantee its worth. I am not aware that any other trustee has written anything whatsoever, but since none of them has been listed in *Who's Who,* it has not been easy to determine their scholarly accomplishments. In the circumstances, an offer of competent professional advice would appear to be not too extravagant a gesture."

There was a ripple of merriment in the group over this deft characterization of their legal employers. The Chairman was emboldened to extend his preliminary remarks.

"I can understand why no dean has done us the honor to attend; they are deans precisely because caution is an ingrained habit. I can also understand and wholly pardon those without permanent tenure for not coming. But—" and now he bared his teeth—"we here already have permanent tenure and we do not propose to be either bullied or ignored. It has been suggested that we elect a representative committee of five members, with full powers, to wait on the board and tender their professional advice. Before inviting nominations to such a committee, I hasten to remind those present that not only does the charter refrain from forbidding the trustees to elect an academician; it even leaves them quite free to elect a member of our own faculty."

There was an instantaneous tension in the club lounge where they met. There was a hush, during which almost every member of the group formed an image in his mind of himself as president. Those images once formed, they murmured their approbation of their chairman's felicitous reminder that in effect they were all candidates.

"The Chair, however," went on the bitter voice, "takes the liberty of suggesting that you may not wish to embarrass any persons known already to be candidates by asking them to serve on this committee."

There were covert glances in the direction of Nast and Milton.

Nast presented the perfect poker face; Milton's was wretched. Milton had counted on serving with this committee. It was the only way he had been able to think of to meet the trustees, or at least those trustees who were serving on the board's Committee on Selection, trustees whom his rival knew already. If he could but meet them, he would have a fighting chance of impressing them with his wisdom, his maturity, and his sense of institutional responsibility. But Nast was not in the least disappointed. He realized, of course, that the Professor of German had hated him ever since they had clashed at the faculty meeting held to consider curricular reforms; and that the Professor of German's last remarks were made for the sole purpose of preventing Nast from getting on the committee now being chosen and then perhaps sabotaging its operations. But Nast was quietly certain that the question of who served on this committee was purely academic. Finally, it was quite possible that they themselves would be unable to agree on any suggestions to make; although, if the Professor of German had done a decent job of stacking the present meeting, the committee now about to see the light of day would unquestionably hope to spike Nast's candidacy. Milton's was not worth spiking.

The meeting now acted swiftly and, with an admirable show of responsibility, chose a committee of five of their number, including Professor Henry Schneider, who was considered a famous research scholar, and safely anti-Nast. The committee of five was instructed to seek a meeting with the Committee on Selection of the board of trustees, and report back as soon as possible. They were given full powers to nominate and negotiate. Those present were deeply moved by their personal courage: every single man chosen agreed to this suicidal mission without objection. True, they were all full professors and therefore could not be fired, but pay rises within that rank were not automatic, and they all had wives and dependent children. They nevertheless agreed, presumably because they knew they were fighting for academic freedom. In fact, one of them declared, in accepting his assignment, "As for me, give me academic freedom or give me death."

Schneider had other reasons for accepting. Also his risks were few. He had just received a letter from President Camp of Barker University telling Schneider that he was more anxious than ever to get him at Barker. A wealthy Barker alumnus had become interested in founding a chair at Barker well enough endowed to attract even a man like Schneider. Schneider would after all find Washington more accessible from Buffalo and could more readily assist his government. And Camp begged Schneider to meet him in New York. He named a date only three days away and a hotel where Camp was reserving a room for him. Schneider had agreed he would meet him.

Meanwhile, so far as this meeting in the Triangle Club was concerned, he was a delighted spectator. He adored watching the faculty act in moments of crisis. He was visibly moved by "Give me academic freedom or give me death!" He considered the phrase a magnificent example of unconscious wit, since it was clear the trustees had things well under control and the only freedom this poor fellow could possibly hope for was a freedom that would prove purely academic.

Schneider's imagination was also stirred by a most instructive analogy he had only just grasped for the first time, the analogy between this manly struggle for academic freedom and the death march to the stadium on Commencement Day. At Commencement, these men had put on a costume that had been devised several centuries before for daily wear in a climate far different from that of the Corn Belt in June, and they had sweated it out. All that protected them from a heat stroke was the dim but proud memory of rights, privileges, and immunities that were no longer of the first urgency, since certain changes in the social structure which they willingly and perspiringly overlooked, had over the long centuries supervened. This afternoon, in the name of academic freedom, they had determined that for a few brief weeks they would go through the motions of having some effect on the election of a new president. Then the trustees would choose whomever they took a fancy to choose; the faculty would learn by reading their newspapers who would preside over their scholarly labors; and they would subside into their habitual docility, just as on Commencement Day they had taken off their rented gowns and taken on their routine duties again.

Schneider thought of the marionettes he had played with as a child. And he saw, more clearly than he ever had, the wires that moved these other marionettes here on the campus, that dragged them in steamy procession to sit on folding wooden chairs while Lanny MacDonald received a Doctorate of Physical Arts and while Mrs. Riley fainted from the heat and from the honor of the thing; that embroiled them in ringing debate whenever they held an official meeting; and that now led them to meet unofficially and almost conspiratorially to preserve a freedom they had never in their lives enjoyed. He found them infinitely pathetic, dangling at the ends of their wires, suspended not from ideas but from the vague emotions aroused by ideas that had once created a great culture and that had long since passed away. These ideas had left behind them a swirling mass of rhetorical tags, impressive postures, and flowing academic gowns.

The meeting had ended, and Schneider wandered contentedly under the majestic elms toward home. It was perfectly clear that the trustees would elect Nast. Did these colleagues of his deserve a better fate? These, he thought charitably, are not animals, nor is the Triangle Club a zoo. These are men like myself. No animal would give up his savage and dangerous freedom to dangle declaiming from a wire in order that freedom, even academic freedom, might not perish from the earth.

~XIX~

"GOOD MORNING, Miss Stilton," said Nast, giving Pomton's secretary his most ingratiating smile.

"Good morning, Dr. Nast," said Miss Stilton. "Did you wish to see the President?"

"Yes, but I'm in no hurry," said Nast, and he gave Miss Stilton a significant look.

"Did the 'unofficial' faculty meeting take place?" asked Miss Stilton, her voice stressing the word "unofficial" with fine irony.

"The fools!" muttered Nast presidentially. "They elected a so-called committee of five, who will request the board's Committee on Selection to discuss the problem with them. You should have heard the speeches; they were asinine."

"I would be happy to know who attended the meeting," murmured Miss Stilton softly, opening her stenographer's pad and poising her pencil. "And someday soon, you may find you are glad to have the names in the files."

Nast flushed with pleasure at this acknowedgment of his coming coronation.

"I shall know whom to ask for them when that day comes," he said, with a sort of lumbering gallantry.

It was Miss Stilton's turn to flush pleasurably. It was the nearest she had come to an assurance that Nast would keep her, if she did not follow Pomton to A. & M. Pomton still predicted he would need her at A. & M.; but his predecessor there had died, leaving in his office what might be termed a secretarial widow; and this secretarial widow was extremely anxious to remarry. Stated less metaphorically, the secretary to the president at A. & M. wanted to stay on when Pomton took over; and she was proving difficult to dislodge. Miss Stilton had also considered that Pomton was no longer a young man and that Mrs. Pomton, although badly battered by the hatred of innumerable faculty wives over several decades, bade fair to outlast him. Nast, it is true, was also married. But his wife was even younger than he, very beautiful, and, according to Miss Stilton's capably organized network of informers, definitely restless. Granted that informers notoriously exaggerate, either from avarice or from mere love of the art of informing, Miss Stilton was certain at least that Dorothy was seeing a good deal of several other men, while poor Nast wrestled alone with such problems of state as how to get elected, perhaps the number one problem of most statesmen.

Another way of formulating this administrative problem of Miss Stilton's was that, even if the secretarial widow at A. & M. could be persuaded to follow the ancient Hindu custom of suttee, a custom for which Miss Stilton felt at the moment considerable sympathy, Miss Stilton might still prefer to remain with Nast. In the first place, her woman's instinct told her that Nast needed her; and if Dorothy really had developed a wandering eye, he needed her even more than she had always supposed. In the second place, quite aside from her most recent information about the Nast marriage, that marriage was young and had clearly not yet made good any claims to durability. The Pomton marriage, on the other hand, no matter how detestable her present employer might secretly find it, wore a definite air of indestructibility. If there was basic incompatibility between Pomton and this wife on whose limbs so many faculty harpies had ecstatically fed, it was an incompatibility which she and her husband had learned to live with, if not like.

Miss Stilton realized that it would be fatal if anything like divorce should hit Nast before he was safely inaugurated as President of the University. Given its background of simple Methodist piety, this particular university would quickly drop a president-elect whose marital affairs had just been dragged, however discreetly, through a divorce court. The board of trustees, wherever the court assigned guilt, would view with alarm endorsing a broken marriage; they would prove as adamant as did the Archbishop of Canterbury when the King confronted him with a twice-divorced American for royal bride. Thirty or forty years ago, the board would have bridled at the divorce even of a monarch long established on the presidential throne. And it goes without saying that neither the old board nor the new would entertain a suggestion of some sort of *maîtresse en titre* to console a monarch whose queen had begun to pall upon him. But Miss Stilton was a patient young woman and was quite willing to wait. Miss Stilton was a permanent twenty-nine, which meant that she could ill afford to wait indefinitely. In short, what was wanted was a divorce decree dated only a decent interval after Nast's inauguration, although she did not know that this was precisely what Schneider was determined to have. Even if that happened, a grass-widower king would be in order for at least twelve months, by which time Miss Stilton would be at least in her third year as a woman of twenty-nine: on any count, she would be nearly as old as her prospective royal husband.

Nast was now calling the names of the conspirators from that flawless memory of his. Miss Stilton efficiently wrote them down, expecting to transfer them with equal efficiency to the individual dossiers which, in imitation of the latest government practice, she kept posted to date on every faculty member. Suddenly she became aware of two facts: first, that her trim skirt had ridden up a little; and, second, that Nast was covertly studying her legs in the way that high-school boys invariably will, whenever our national system of coeducation affords them the opportunity. While still listing names, she made the quick, instinctive gesture of any modest woman caught in this predicament. But, whereas a week ago, before her last batch of informers' reports had come in, the gesture would have been decisively completed, this time she arrested it halfway, patted out a wrinkle in her skirt, and put her mind on higher things. Miss Stilton had a good leg and knew it. In fact, in her own judgment her leg compared well with Dorothy's.

She realized in a flash that her deep compatibility with Nast had taken on new meaning. They had always shared a faultless memory, the power of quick decision, boundless energy, and a soaring ambition; and she had known for a long time that they shared these things. But in the drama that was now playing itself out—the choice of a president—she suddenly saw they shared one other thing. They were embattled on two fronts: each of them must solve both a public problem and a private one. The only difference was that Miss Stilton, being a woman, knew she was confronted with both problems and must therefore learn to operate in two gears. Poor Nast, she was convinced, had not become consciously aware of his private problem. His back to the wall, he was fending off Joe Stanforth's stop-Nast movement in the board and keeping a wary if scornful eye on the stop-Nast movement launched by Milton and the Professor of German. So intent was he on these attacks that he had failed to note that his home front was crumbling, and that Dorothy—or so Miss Stilton hopefully believed—had gone on the loose. Miss Stilton, on the other hand, whose efforts to ingratiate herself with Nast had always previously cast her in the exclusive role of super-efficient private secretary and political supporter, now had to play a less familiar role, the role of siren. It was a more difficult role for her, if only because, from about the time that she first became a permanent twenty-nine, she had found relatively few opportunities to play it.

It must be confessed that, since Miss Stilton was a woman, she had in some key or other always played her second role, if only with Pomton. He, too, had often noted Miss Stilton's legs, which were perhaps her best feature, and he was grateful to her for them. Both he and Miss Stilton had even had dreams about each other, although they were the kind of dreams that only a Sigmund Freud could have made much of. Their relationship tended to be purely Platonic, with all the confused connotations that this term has more and more acquired. But Miss Stilton was less of a ham than Pomton, so that, even though a woman and instinctively knowledgeable in such matters, she had found her second role continuously tending toward atrophy. Now, with news of Dorothy's restlessness uppermost in her mind, it was pleasant to mount once more these two horses, so to speak; to place one foot on each bare back, and to show that she could hold her own. It was pleasant to be a superefficient secretary, as always, and suddenly to be twenty-eight again and a woman. The trouble with being a permanent twenty-nine, she reflected, was that in some way it made time stand still, and that was boring. Now time fleeted, and life became breathless again.

All these things flew through her quick, sure mind with lightning rapidity. Meanwhile she automatically copied names for the dossiers and refrained from rearranging her wayward skirt.

"That's all of them," said Nast with finality.

"You'd better see the President now," she said. Her voice betrayed the most delicate shade of regret. "I know he wishes to tell you about the Committee on Selection."

"Okay," said Nast alertly, as if a bugle had blown. The interlude from politics had been both covert and brief, and could not without exaggeration have been called steamy. Still, a light vapor had risen in the air, no bigger than a man's hand, and Nast mechanically brushed it away from his eyes as Miss Stilton ceremoniously escorted him into Pomton's office and back to reality. Nast shared with his favorite hero, the Emperor Napoleon, a liking for, and a distinct disrespect for, the amatory arts. He had always admired Napoleon's habit of ordering a distinguished Parisian actress to go into his bedroom and undress while he finished the work on his desk. This admiration was not unconnected with his relative unsuccess as Dorothy's husband. In womanly fashion, Dorothy craved a little more ceremony—as did, indeed, the Parisian actress whose name, characteristically, Nast could never quite recall. Again like Napoleon, Nast had an orderly mind. He had courted Dorothy strenuously when he was persuading her to marry him; and there seemed to him a certain confusion in doing it all over again with a marriage certificate safely in his file among his other mortgages. As a husband, he had therefore tended to be merely punctilious in collecting the interest due him. For his part, he did his duty as he saw it in trying to prevent depreciation, as he did with any property on which he had taken out a mortgage.

But his masculine mind was not quick enough to review all these considerations now.

"Good morning, sir," he said.

"Good morning, my boy," said Pomton. "I trust Monmouth's Rebellion passed off pleasantly."

"Oh, I've already reported to Miss Stilton the little there was to report. They appointed a committee of five, all of them determined revolutionary leaders united by a single desire. They insist on conferring with the Committee on Selection."

"Is Henry Schneider by any chance on the committee?"

"Yes, sir. And I imagine he is delighted to serve on a committee that is stacked against my candidacy."

"I happen to know," said Pomton, "that he is for you. He told me so."

"For me?" Nast's voice was incredulous.

"My boy, Schneider is a changed man. And a valuable member of this faculty."

"I'm delighted to hear that he is changed," said Nast. "To return to the committee. Old Heidelberg took care not to let me get on it, even though that meant shutting Milton out too. Nothing really happened at the meeting. They just blew off steam. Old Heidelberg was pretty sneering about the board."

"The impudent oaf!" said Pomton feelingly. "Well, I won't take much of a candidate's valuable time. On Thursday the Committee on

Selection will meet here in my office, not in the board room. To play it safe, you'd better make a point of being in your office from ten to four. Things might take a turn that would justify my suggesting to the committee that they call you in and have a frank talk. I understand that Joe Stanforth, who is chairing the committee, is still upset about People's Capitalism, although God knows I did everything I could to reassure him. The fellow simply doesn't realize that Franklin Roosevelt opened Pandora's box and we've got to give at least lip service to a sort of populism. We've got to pretend to play along with the least substantial citizens in this republic of ours. It isn't what the founders intended. 'The people, sir, is a great beast.' You know—all that sort of thing. But if Stanforth wants to play King Canute, well, I'm not going to get my feet wet; and I agree with you that People's Capitalism is a very clever slogan. Still, I wanted you to know how Joe feels."

"Thanks very much, sir. But may I ask who the other members of the committee are? Yourself, obviously, for one."

"Obviously but not actually," said Pomton with some pique. "The board apparently thought it unnecessary to add to the committee the one person who knows most about the job they are trying to fill. The other two are Dr. Lyman and our friend from the state legislature."

"But that's indecent, sir!"

"So it seemed to me, my boy. But Joe Stanforth pointed out that I was only an ex officio member of the board, and that there would also be the charge of favoritism if I served. He's alluding, of course, to my backing of you. The Chairman finally forced him to agree that the President of the University should sit in with the committee unless otherwise requested. I tell you, Nast, my authority in this place is slipping fast. I'm on the way out, you see. They've squeezed me dry. I've raised more than nine million dollars for them, and they're through with me."

"I don't believe it, sir. It's just that hog, Stanforth. I'd like to ask your advice on one point. Has Stanforth ever said anything to indicate what I think of him, in connection with that consortium deal on the bus lines? He may feel I know he played a crooked role in that deal."

"But surely," said Pomton in horror, "you haven't said anything in public about that?"

"Only to intimates. Only to my colleagues. But he ought to be behind bars, you know."

"Of course he ought. And my administration would have been an easier burden if he had been. But you shouldn't have spoken frankly about it even to intimates. Least of all to colleagues. If you'll excuse my saying so, academicians are the biggest blabs in the world except women."

This remark frankly annoyed Miss Stilton, who had her ear against the panel of the door, while she covered her outside door with her eyes. She felt that, whatever her faults, she was not a blab. Yet for several minutes now she had been acutely aware that she was a woman. She was thankful that she had monitored the conversation, since she saw a means of helping, in an innocent sort of way, the two men who now occupied her life.

When Nast came out, she was seated demurely at her desk, apparently working on a memorandum which she was composing in shorthand.

"Dr. Nast, before you go, could you possibly help me? I'm bringing up to date the little who's-who sort of thing we keep on our board members for publicity purposes. Dr. Pomton tells me that Mr. Stanforth played a leading role in the banking consortium that expanded the bus lines. Could you brief me on the precise facts?"

"We were just talking about him," said Nast. And he skillfully briefed Miss Stilton, even supplying her with what he called "off-the-record background material" of an incredibly juicy nature. Surely, thought Miss Stilton, Dr. Nast is describing a penitentiary trusty rather than a university trustee. But these typographical errors occur in the make-up of many boards of directors where business success is for obvious reasons the criterion of membership. By a second typographical error, of a sort which even the most perfect freedom of the press seems to permit somehow, the trusty in question had managed to keep the story of his financial legerdemain out of the newspapers.

When Wednesday afternoon came, Miss Stilton got Nast on the phone for Pomton. Then she listened in on her own extension. This other manner of listening in Pomton had authorized, and even desired.

"King Canute is arriving by the four-fifteen plane," said Pomton, "and must be met. It's important to me to be here by my telephone for a long-distance call. Mike is sick; and besides, this job calls for more than a mere chauffeur. Maybe you ought to meet him. What do you think? You could of course use the presidential limousine."

"Gosh," came Nast's voice. "I've promised the five to sit with them at that hour. They're said to be not seriously considering Milton, which is understandable, and have come around to thinking I might be better than an admiral or general or anything else the board is likely to give them from outside. Oughtn't I to stick with them, just in case the board committee is soft enough to talk with them?"

"Of course you ought," said Pomton. "And I suggest a few discreet policy pledges, too. As for Canute, I'll find somebody else to roll out the red carpet."

They had no sooner rung off than Miss Stilton discreetly entered Pomton's office. "Would you permit me to meet King Canute, whoever he might be?" she asked charmingly.

Pomton laughed pleasantly. "I'd love to have you meet Canute," he said. "You know him well: he's Joe Stanforth." This, Miss Stilton already knew, given the thinness of the door panel, just as she already knew most of the things Pomton proudly passed on to her. But her rising eyebrows somehow acknowledged new information plus admiration for an ingenious and appropriate code name.

At the airport Joe Stanforth recognized her and addressed her most flatteringly by name. He had always felt an instinctive fear in her presence, like a schoolboy faced with an exceptionally strict schoolteacher. He had always felt she was somehow coiled to spring. This afternoon he chanced to be correct, which happened to him rather rarely in his numerous dealings with women.

Miss Stilton recognized Canute with a most cordial smile and handshake, but there seemed to him to be a glint in her eye. He watched her narrowly as they walked to the limousine and got in. The car had scarcely left the airport when she turned to him abruptly. Then she spoke.

"Mr. Stanforth, would you permit me to discuss something with great candor—something that may not appear to be my business but concerns the good of the University?"

"Certainly," he said, feeling vague alarm.

"It concerns you, too," she said, and her voice was a little hard.

He wondered which of his many deals she had gotten wind of. So, with a great show of calm confidence, he said, "Don't let that stop you, Miss Stilton. Whatever you say I shall keep in the strictest confidence."

"Good," said Miss Stilton, her glittering eyes still fastened on his, and her mouth shut a little tightly. "Mr. Stanforth, I am under the impression that you know Professor Nast."

"Yes, I do," he said. This was clearly no time to air his grievances against Nast as a candidate. Not until he knew what was on her mind.

"I am under the further impression that the board is considering Professor Nast among others for the presidency."

"Among many others," said Canute noncommittally.

"I happen to know," she said, "that Dr. Nast, whom I know only slightly, has written a book on transport finance, in which he analyzes the bond issue for Transprairie as a prime example of what People's Capitalism is not. I took the liberty of asking him where this information came from, and he replied somewhat coldly that he had gotten it from newspaper reporters who could not persuade their editors to print it."

Canute's face had gone ashen white, a fact that she took in by a rapid glance sideways. Then she turned the screw a little further.

"Because of my feeling for the University I asked him whether he felt a member of our faculty ought to publish such information. He said he owed it to the department he heads to publish whatever was both true and relevant. I pointed out that, since you are one of the trustees, his book would not be good for the University. He replied obstinately that what was good for the department of economics was good for the University."

But while she talked, Canute had been thinking rather fast. "Whatever the reporters thought they knew," he said, somewhat loftily, "our professor friend will be quite unable to prove in a court of law when I sue for libel, as I most assuredly shall do."

Miss Stilton's eyes remained neutral, expressionless, as if made of colored glass.

"Appendix One," she said in her icy voice, "will contain the documents of November second and the secret arrangement of November nineteenth, in photostat."

He deflated instantly and started to perspire. He felt weak in his legs, as little birds must feel when they look into the ancient wise eyes of a well-informed serpent and realize that everything they have ever done since they first broke through the shell is known to this antediluvian sleuth. So they flutter, and fall, and are devoured.

"What does Nast want?" asked Canute, in his directest professional manner.

"Isn't the real question: What must he have?" she asked, without emotion.

"What must he have to keep his mouth shut?" Canute barked out, expanding and rendering more explicit things of a kind Miss Stilton had put more delicately.

"He must have the presidency of the University first; and, after he is inaugurated, he must have your resignation from the board, due of course to the pressure of work. You see, I am prepared to state what he must have, because I asked him. I forced him to agree that if he were elected president, he would not feel free to publish the facts."

The color slowly returned to Canute's cheeks, and his respiration became normal. "I will do all in my power to see that Dr. Nast is elected," he said.

"I am sure," she said, "that his election will be best for all parties concerned. Well, well, here we are already at your hotel, Mr. Stanforth."

Back at her office, who should be waiting for her but Henry Schneider. She was puzzled.

"Might I get your advice on something?" he said.

She bowed slightly by way of consent.

"I have just come from a meeting of the faculty committee on the presidency. As you doubtless know by now, the committee is on the whole opposed to Dr. Nast's candidacy. That is, the other four members were. I happen to favor it." This much she had learned to her great surprise a few hours before by monitoring Nast's conversation with Pomton, via the usual panel in Pomton's office door. "Well," continued Schneider, "I think I have persuaded them that their distrust of Dr. Nast is irrelevant; that their scholarly ambitions depend on our getting a good deal more money than we now have and paying considerably higher salaries; and that Dr. Nast is more likely to raise that money than any other candidate they have a chance of getting elected. But now they're off on a new tangent: they keep getting rumors that the chairman of the Committee on Selection, set up by the board, is bitterly opposed to Dr. Nast, and they are anxious not to waste their influence by backing a loser. I don't want you, of course, to violate any confidences, but can you tell me whether Joseph Stanforth is against Nast?"

"In the strictest confidence, Dr. Schneider, I can assure you that Mr. Stanforth was. But he now strongly backs Dr. Nast, although I am not at liberty to say why he changed."

"Splendid!" said Schneider. "Then I think I can safely predict that our committee will wait on the board and urge Nast's election."

Miss Stilton thawed slightly at this news, but her puzzlement remained.

"Forgive me," she said, "but I was under the impression that you disliked Dr. Nast and would oppose him."

"I loathe the fellow," said Schneider, his voice perfectly cordial. "But then I am rarely attracted to college presidents, so my dislike is really in his favor. Besides, I don't agree with the popular assumption that elections are popularity contests. What we all desire is the right man for this particular job, and this job, Miss Stilton, fits Nast like a glove."

Miss Stilton was annoyed by Schenider's brazen personal scorn of her candidate, but she was far too cool an operator to show her annoyance. At least, until after the election. If Schneider could be useful, he must be dealt with.

"I heartily agree with you," she said, "that the problem should be dealt with impersonally and for the good of the institution. But I fear that all I can do to help you is to give you my solemn assurance that Dr. Nast is now Mr. Stanforth's choice."

The next morning Professor Henry Schneider reported to Miss Stilton that the committee of five was solidly for Nast. Whereupon, Miss Stilton, realizing how vitally important to the institution Professor Schneider had become, at least until after the election, filed for possible future use a letter she had written to the FBI. There would be ample time after the election to look into the matter of the hoax she was still convinced he was playing and to confront him with a cold statement that he was in fact not working for the government at all, that he had lied to his colleagues, and that his best course would be to resign quietly from President Nast's faculty rather than be exposed and disgraced. If, she thought to herself, Schneider is trying to purchase protection in the event of a Nast victory, then he has a surprise coming.

~XX~

Miss Stilton drove to her apartment, ate a light supper, and smoked a cigarette. But woman's work is never done, and Miss Stilton still had work to do. Fortunately, where there was constructive work to be done, she did not tire easily. She returned to the office and telephoned Nast.

Nast and his angular sister, who was keeping house for him in Dorothy's absence, were sitting on the garden terrace. Nast, too, was enjoying an after-dinner cigarette, since Miss Nast drew the line at cigars. The phone rang, and Nast leaped nervously from his chair.

"This is Thelma Stilton, Dr. Nast," said the voice over the phone, smooth, modulated, and efficient. "I regret disturbing you, but I have something I ought to report to you. Could you possibly drop by the office?"

The President's official residence was called the Parsonage, in memory of those prayerful years when the President had always been a parson and had indeed doubled at the local Methodist church. There President Pomton and Joe Stanforth were sitting down to cigars in Pomton's study. The dinner had been excellent, but Joe had been off his feed and had conspicuously failed to do it justice. Even the little he had eaten had not sat well on his stomach. Mrs. Pomton had proven a charming hostess. She was not the fool that a majority of faculty wives called her. She was merely a bruised and mangled woman, exhilarated this evening by her imminent escape from the local ladies and inwardly determined, once she reached A. & M., to plead doctor's orders and lie low. But his hostess's conversational charms were lost on Joe Stanforth, whom Pomton found curiously distrait and unlike his usual bluff, noisy self.

Nast and Miss Stilton conferred busily a few blocks off, in Miss Stilton's office. At Nast's home, Miss Nast cleared the supper dishes and allowed her imagination to play on her brother's brilliant future.

At the Parsonage, Joe Stanforth talked shop manfully with Pomton.

"You know," said Stanforth, "this thing has worried me a lot. We haven't a chance of getting any candidate in your class."

"That's very kind of you. Very generous."

"No, I mean it. Now, the more I've thought about it, the more I begin to share your view that Nast is our best bet. Now, you're a man of experience and Nast isn't. But we have your assurance that Nast knows the ropes."

"He knows them completely," replied President Pomton with eagerness. "As to his not being experienced, Nast is about to publish a book that will get him more publicity, I predict, than any book ever to be published by an academician in this section of the country. It will prove to the world at large that his grasp of public affairs is admirable."

He refrained from mentioning that the theme of the book was People's Capitalism: there was no good stirring Stanforth up again.

But at the word "publicity" Joe Stanforth emitted a thunderous belch. It was obvious that something had stirred him profoundly.

"Excuse me," he said apologetically. "I think something I ate on that damned plane thoroughly upset me."

"Have a crème de menthe," urged President Pomton. "And let me tell you about Nast's forthcoming book."

Stanforth's complexion had turned a queer greenish color.

"Thanks," he said, "but if you'll excuse me, I fear I'd better lie down. As for Nast, I'm convinced from what you've told me that our committee tomorrow ought to recommend him to the board."

Stanforth went to his hotel room, but not before he had sent a five-pound box of chocolates to Miss Stilton's apartment. Pomton, elated by Stanforth's last remark, seized the phone and rang Nast's home. Miss Nast stopped drying dishes long enough to express her regret that Nast was out, but she promised the President her brother would phone if he came in before eleven.

Her brother was still with Miss Stilton, who was briefing him on her conversation with King Canute.

"But," said Nast, "my book isn't about transport. I don't know a living thing about transportation. My book is about People's Capitalism."

"I took the liberty of reporting on your book a little inaccurately," said Miss Stilton in her overmodulated voice. "I believe I was wise in doing so."

"What'll he say when he finds out what my book is really about?" asked Nast dully, for he was confused and fatigued by the events of the week.

"He will be exceedingly relieved that you decided not to publish the other book, especially Appendix One, giving the texts of the November agreements on the Transprairie refinancing."

"How on earth did you convince him this other book, as you call it, would destroy him?"

"You are tired," said Miss Stilton softly. "You are forgetting that you briefed me at my request on the Transprairie deal, for my dossier on Canute as board member."

"So I did," said Nast weakly. He gazed admiringly at Miss Stilton. "What a girl!" he murmured.

Miss Stilton, who would have flushed with anger if any other faculty member had dared call her a girl, flushed with pleasure instead. She felt that her relation with Nast had passed the official stage, subtly but definitely, and the word "girl" sounded a good deal more like twenty-eight than it did like twenty-nine. She basked, but not for long. She must not let the candidate collapse, and she had never seen him so dulled by fatigue. She handed him a letter she had typed, a letter from Nast to Stanforth. Nast glanced through it and silently sighed. Then she spoke.

"May I suggest," she said—and her voice was very soft again, full of feminine solicitude, and yet faintly tinged with the respect due him from a woman who was about to become his secretary, and even more faintly tinged with the affection of a woman who might become even more than that—"may I suggest that you go home now and try to get some sleep? Tomorrow may be a difficult day for you. Above all, don't worry for an instant. Frankly, Canute is frightened to death of you. You will find him your most ardent supporter tomorrow."

"He's frightened all right. You've got him over a barrel."

Again the admiring tone. She inhaled the admiration for a moment and then rose from her desk. Nast seized her hand; and for one moment her judgment failed her and Miss Stilton thought that this was it. Her hand thrilled to his touch. Then her good sense returned and she noted that this was not a touch; it was merely a Nastian contact. Nast was not making love: he was thanking a political supporter. How could any man, she asked herself defensively, how could any man as tired as Nast be expected to make love? Tomorrow was another day, and it was obvious that victory was extremely close.

Nast stumbled home to bed, barely able to answer his sister's eager "Good news?" with a mumbled "Very good, I should say." A quarter of a mile away a spastic condition of the stomach forced a groan out of Joe Stanforth, who lay tossing on his hotel bed. In another direction, out at the Parsonage, Mrs. Pomton listened patiently to Pomton's exultant report on Stanforth's miraculous conversion.

Only Miss Stilton moved to and fro on the earth, like Satan. She drove to her apartment calmly, found the box of chocolates, and read the note inside: "From Joe Stanforth to his able colleague, Thelma Stilton, in confidence and admiration." Then he had added in his childish scrawl, "Nast for President!" Miss Stilton smiled a tight, constricted smile.

"Poor, frightened bastard!" she murmured contentedly in her chill, well-modulated voice.

Miss Stilton then bathed and placed a mudpack on her face to take out any wrinkles that her twenty-nine years might surreptitiously have strewn there. She dried her body; but, before putting on her nightgown, she examined her body critically in the full-length mirror. Her face, under its mudpack, stared grotesquely back at her, like a cross between the end-man's face in a minstrel show and the face of a human skull. She shuddered slightly, removed the pack, and gazed fixedly at her face in the mirror.

"I am not as beautiful as his wife is. But I am cleverer. And I am more patient. At this moment he needs a woman, in more ways than one. Why does the little fool stay in Georgia?"

She got into bed, turned out her bedlamp, and slept like a baby. At seven-thirty she rose, and by nine she was in her office looking as fresh and prim as ever. She arranged the round walnut table in the President's office for the meeting: the four chairs—no, five, in case they called in Nast; pads and pencils, cigarettes and ashtrays; and a neat file folder by each place containing the names of the remaining candidates. The names were arranged in alphabetical order, with a thumbnail biography beside each. She had compiled these biographies herself, on the basis of information supplied to her by Pomton. But she had done a subtle job of editing, replacing an adjective here, an adverb there, or tampering the tiniest bit with some title. She would have shown her biographies to Nast the night before, but he had been clearly too exhausted to examine them with a connoisseur's eye. They made the lives of all of Nast's rivals sound slightly dull and routine, but Nast's life was a saga of success. Even had Mr.

Stanforth been himself and in full possession of his independence, he would have found it difficult to stop Nast, without appearing either blind or spiteful. As for Dr. Lyman, although his fear of socialized medicine made him wary of phrases like People's Capitalism, he had already been convinced by Pomton that his patients were far less likely to vote for the Democratic party if they could feel that the existing economic system was in some subtle way stacked in their favor and if they could calculate that the richer Dr. Lyman grew, the lower their individual medical costs would undoubtedly get. The third member of the committee was the chairman of the state legislature's Committee on Un-American Activities. It had seemed safer to have him assume the fullest possible responsibility for the choice of a new president rather than run the risk of Red-baiting later on. Besides, these three formed a nicely representative group of leading citizens: business, the learned professions, and public service.

Joe Stanforth arrived a little earlier than the others, and Miss Stilton thanked him charmingly for the chocolates, insisting that they were her favorite brand. Stanforth, drawn and sallow under the bright light of an early July day, made bold to ask her whether she was absolutely sure that, in the event of Nast's election, Nast would refrain from publishing his book or any other account of the Transprairie deal.

"I felt an obligation to you," she said with charming candor, "to check back with Dr. Nast on just that point. He merely exclaimed in horror, 'How could I foul my own nest?' I then took the liberty of asking him for a letter to you, giving you unmistakable assurances. Here it is."

Stanforth hastily perused the letter, with growing relief. He looked so much relieved that Miss Stilton found it wise to remind him that he was not yet out of danger.

"I have again asked Dr. Nast whether, in the event he was not elected, he still intended publishing the book. He stated unequivocally that he would feel compelled to in the interests of scholarly truth. He even added that the new president, whoever he might be, would doubtless find means of persuading you to resign from the board before entering a prison."

King Canute shuddered visibly, while she watched him narrowly. "You can count on me," he murmured in low tones, for now Pomton was arriving.

The committee's deliberations turned out to be somewhat academic. The statesman and the doctor were now out-and-out Nastmen and wearily waited to defend him when the banker should strike. But Stanforth, although he insisted on wading through the seven biographies before them, in alphabetical order, gave not the slightest hint of striking. When they had listened to the last dreary biography, he courteously asked them what was their pleasure. The doctor said he still thought Nast the best man, chiefly because of President Pomton's informed judgment that he was. The politician agreed. He even hinted that a man like Nast, coming from the University faculty, was a good deal more likely to detect any subversive tendencies that might crop up, any Communistic notions that members of the Democrat party might wish to plant in young and growing and helpless minds, than a green outsider. Dr. Lyman quickly and forcibly supported this point.

"Well," said Joe Stanforth ponderously, "you fellows may be surprised to learn that I have surrendered. Your own arguments and those which President Pomton has already given me have made me see the light. I say Nast. And I imagine President Pomton will join me in saying the quicker the better. A. & M. wants Dr. Pomton the minute they can get him."

"I assume, then," said Pomton, glancing deferentially about him, "that your chairman, Mr. Stanforth, will recommend to the full board meeting week after next that they promptly elect Dr. Nast as the next president of this university."

Everybody agreed, particularly Miss Stilton, who once more had her ear glued to the door panel. If she had leaned her breast against it, the four men inside Pomton's office would undoubtedly have heard her heart pounding with excitement.

"Splendid!" cried Dr. Pomton. "You don't know what it means to me personally to see what I have tried for two decades to build here pass into safe and sure hands. I am sure Dr. Nast will have a brilliant administration. But before you gentlemen conclude your committee meeting I feel compelled to bring up one other matter, trivial as you may find it. I refer to an urgent request from the faculty that you consult with them before making your choice. Frankly, I regard the request as a case of impudent meddling, but I felt you ought to know that the faculty had so requested."

"I thought," said Joe Stanforth gruffly, "the faculty had all gone fishing for three months."

Pomton laughed appreciatively. "About a third of them are teaching here in the summer session. The others have left town, although they are expected, of course, to continue their research, or preparation of their lectures for the next regular academic session."

"Hmph," grunted Stanforth. "What decides a given faculty member to stay behind and teach when the others leave to fish—or do research? Just likes to teach?"

Pomton laughed again. "I guess," he said, "only those stay and teach who lack the money to get away."

"Why can't they live on their regular salaries?" the banker asked suspiciously.

"Well, we aren't able to pay them very much," said Pomton. "So those that are deepest in debt try to piece out by earning something in summer school."

"And this batch of debtors wants to advise us on who to get to run this college? How would they know?"

"Well," said Pomton, feeling an unaccustomed twinge of sympathy for his academic colleagues, "it's difficult to explain in terms of business practice. You see, they like to think I am one of them, merely designated to preside."

"Have any of them ever helped you raise the money to pay their salaries with?" asked Stanforth coldly.

"Only Dr. Nast," said Pomton.

"Well, I like their nerve!" Stanforth spoke with real feeling and with a certain admiration for this sort of boundless, moonstruck madness. "If these eggheads don't beat the Dutch! Any of 'em ever meet a pay roll?"

"I don't think so," said Pomton. "They would say they are busy doing other things."

"Well," said Stanforth, "if they ever tried to meet one, it wouldn't be long before they'd be on the sidewalk, and then they could get busy doing something else sure enough. Look, our board members are all businessmen, experienced businessmen, except for a leading doctor and a leading statesman, and I think both of them show evidence of knowing what responsibility is. Now, why on earth should they want the opinion of a pack of eggheads we hired to teach kids? Eggheads who never met a pay roll and who don't even dare meet their creditors on the street. Tell 'em to go put their caps and gowns and colored hoods on and hold a parade or burn a cross or something, Pomton. We're busy men. I've got a deal on right this minute involving a bond issue to expand a traction company—"

Suddenly and unaccountably Stanforth's voice trailed off. He cleared his throat loudly. "Well," he said, "no need to bore you with my own troubles. You've got yours, and I guess you'll have others pretty much like 'em at A. & M."

"Like 'em and worse," said the local statesman, "when he comes to the capital to get money from us. We're not a pack of Mrs. Rileys. This money is the people's money, and we have to be careful with it."

President Pomton's mind had begun to work extremely fast. This was the sort of crisis that stimulated him. For the first time he suspected he should be overwhelmed by the enormity of allowing a group of businessmen, between deals, to choose the head of a university. Yet, when he thought of his faculty, he shuddered. What an irresponsible choice they might easily make if they were given authority to choose! On the other hand, neither the students nor the janitors seemed up to the task. He suspected Miss Stilton would do the best job, but it scarcely seemed practicable to leave it to her. Who, he wondered miserably, ought to choose university presidents?

"Gentlemen," he said suddenly, and his tone was conciliatory, "permit me to make a suggestion. You have just chosen a new president. I realize, of course, that the board must act on your recommendation; but I realize also that they have the greatest confidence in the wisdom of this committee. So, in effect, Professor Nast is president-elect. What we do about the present request from the faculty may have a great effect on his relations with his faculty in the future and therefore on the good operation of the institution we all wish to serve. What about leaving the decision to Dr. Nast? I can fetch him here in five minutes. He can say whether he thinks it wise to consult the faculty's committee. Then he can withdraw, and you can decide in the light of his advice."

Joe Stanforth found the proposal unattractive. After all, Nast might be president next year, but he was a faculty member today, and it was the principle of having employees meddle in managerial decisions that alarmed Joe Stanforth. But the politician saw a chance to unload responsibility for a decision and was delighted; and Dr. Lyman could see no harm in getting Nast's slant on the problem. Canute once more yielded.

Pomton rang for Miss Stilton. After a decent interval, long enough for her to have walked from her desk to Pomton's door, had she not already been listening at that door, Miss Stilton entered and stood, respectful, attentive, expectant. She looked fresh, clear-eyed, efficient, and altogether charming. Pomton was secretly confirmed in his judgment that it was Miss Stilton who would best decide all these things if she were allowed to; and even Stanforth wondered why he had ever disliked her so.

"Miss Stilton," said Pomton, "we are adjourning to the board room, where we wish to confer with Dr. Nast in thirty minutes."

"Yes, sir," said Miss Stilton, and promptly withdrew. The four men made a leisurely start for the board room. Nine chairs had been already pulled up to the table, in case they should decide to invite the faculty committee to state their case. Three minutes later Miss Stilton arrived with their pads, pencils, biographies, and cigarettes.

These she distributed on the table. She was back in her office when Nast stopped by there for thirty seconds' briefing.

"The Committee on Selection has just chosen Dr. Nast as our next president," she said tranquilly. "They are confident the board will accept their recommendation. They now wish you to advise them whether to allow the committee of five to advise them. May I suggest that you advise them to do so, on the grounds that it is now quite clear that the committee of five merely wants to be heard and does not expect to be heeded."

From the expression in Miss Stilton's transfigured eyes, Nast knew he had been congratulated. He quickly took her hand in his and gave it a squeeze that was more than political and conceivably more than merely friendly. Then he went straight to the board room.

The president-elect, or at a minimum the president-select, entered. Tall, clean-looking, boyish, impeccably dressed, obviously full of the most driving energy, self-possessed, and modestly respectful toward the men who now rose from their chairs to greet him, Nast impressed even Stanforth, who was secretly exultant that Nast should be turning now from destructive muckraking to administrative tasks that would give his energies full and harmless scope. In the friendliest conceivable voice, Stanforth now addressed his candidate.

"Dr. Nast, as you perhaps know, the faculty—or at least those of them who have not gone fishing for three months—have chosen a committee of five, who wish to advise us. Ought we to hear them?"

"May I suggest, Mr. Chairman, that you have this committee in," said Nast in his directest, most engaging way, "since it is now clear that they merely want to be heard and do not expect to be heeded."

There was a spontaneous murmur of approval. All four conferees were immensely impressed, not only by the clarity of Nast's reasoning and by his ease of expression, but by the speed with which he reasoned.

It was that simple. Pomton asked if he might order Miss Stilton to tell the committee of five to report at the board room in an hour. He was promptly excused to do so. But Nast was not excused. Stanforth wanted to see more of his favorite candidate, who had deeply impressed him; and he questioned Nast for twenty minutes. Nast replied to every question promptly, incisively, infallibly, and with precisely the degree of deference required by his youth and his delicate political posture.

Pomton, who had quietly returned, had taken his seat and listened proudly to this oral examination. He beamed when the candidate was excused and watched him contentedly as he withdrew. Nast had scarcely closed the door after him when Stanforth sighed.

"What a man!" he said. "He ought to be in the banking business."

"I disagree with you," said Pomton archly. "He ought to be president of this university—although I may say he knows a good deal about banking." The Chairman shuddered imperceptibly.

They sat a while smoking, contentedly discussing their candidate, and waiting for the committee of five. Meanwhile, Nast had gone straight to his campaign manager.

"Have you any definite prediction of what the committee of five will say?" he asked her.

"The committee of five," said Miss Stilton, "has tried to think of some well-known scholar from another institution who might be persuaded to take the job. They can agree on nobody. They are desperately afraid they will get a banker or an admiral or a general. They have decided to advise the trustees' Committee on Selection to recommend the election of Dr. Nast."

Her eyes were soft again. This time he took her hand and held it.

"You're wonderful," he said. Then he said playfully, "I don't know what my administration would do without you."

Miss Stilton's heart beat faster. It would have fairly raced if he had left out the administration—if he had just said, "I don't know what I would do without you." But she was a patient woman, and she felt that time was fighting on her side and not on Dorothy's. She noted with pleasure that at the very crisis of his career he could do without Dorothy. He had had to. Dorothy was a little fool. Her place was clearly at Nast's side, not in Georgia. Thank God she didn't know it.

But men are creatures of habit, as Miss Stilton knew, and Nast, now back in his office, wanted to telephone Dorothy. Unhappily,

Dorothy had reminded him that her father's farm was not on a rural line and had merely given him directions for sending a telegram if that proved really important to do. But Nast reflected that Western Union offices in small college towns had some of the functional characteristics of a newspaper staffed by Pentagon cryptanalysts. He discarded the idea of telegraphing. He then decided to write her by air mail. He would tell her his election was now all but certain and would occur in a few days. This would bring her home quickly enough.

Meanwhile, the committee of five presented themselves at the board room. What a sorry-looking lot they are, thought Stanforth—shambling, shuffling, ill dressed, ill groomed. Why do intellectuals always need a haircut? The rising prices at barbershops? Or is it some kind of mysterious vanity, based on an equally mysterious masochism, the desire to look unattractive to their wives, to their students, and to the general public who must find the money for their salaries? Nast was just as much a scholar as they were, and Nast's hair was cut. It was beyond Stanforth.

Henry Schneider spoke first for the committee of five. He spoke simply, quietly, briefly, explaining why the committee preferred Nast. He stated that in his judgment the only problems the University faced and stood a reasonable chance of solving in the immediate future were financial, and that in this field Nast had proven himself. As to the intellectual needs of the institution, he assured the board that the faculty could be trusted to maintain its standards and even to increase its output of publications. If the board wanted the sort of assurance they had been accustomed to get from President Pomton that ample funds would be raised without throwing the burden of fund-raising on the backs of the trustees themselves, they could not do better than choose a man whom President Pomton himself had, as it were, trained for the post.

Schneider made a good impression. It was true that his worn tweed coat, with its leather elbows, scarcely struck the right note. It was also true that his gray flannel trousers were pretty baggy at the knees. But Pomton noticed that, for once, his hair was properly cut, and

Pomton felt thankful for small favors. Now, thought Pomton, if they will just excuse themselves promptly and get back to their dubious employments, this unwarranted intervention of theirs into something that is none of their damned business in the first place will at least have done no harm and may even prove useful.

But Schneider's fellow committeemen felt differently. One by one they insisted on saying "a few words." They yammered and mumbled and used those endless periphrases which seem to be the bread of life to their profession. It made Stanforth's head ache to listen. And when the thousands of words had all got spoken, when the dependent clauses had all had their meaning restricted away, when the little wittticisms had had their day in court, it turned out that all these second-rate jesters wanted to say was that the faculty thought Nast ought to be president. Stanforth was of course relieved; but he was furious at the five for taking so long to relieve him. He thanked them most urbanely, and they shambled out, leaving behind them an aroma of wandering minds and babbling tongues, of useless verbal distinctions, limitless pedantry, and a perverted sense of humor. Stanforth felt soiled from his brief encounter with learning in the flesh, depressed by their obvious poverty, by the notes in bank which undoubtedly worried them, by their constant scribbling and lecturing, their love of rank, and their half-concealed antagonism for men of affairs. Why a man like Nast should want to preside over this harem of eunuchs was beyond him. But he determined to cultivate Nast and to make him see that his true place was in banking. Dr. Lyman wondered how on earth they paid for the medical care of their families, given the salaries they received. And the local statesman was confirmed in his two suspicions: first, that they would bear watching on the score of Communistic thinking; and, second, that Nast was the man to watch them.

Pomton reflected for the hundreth time that presiding over an academic faculty was like being pecked to death by ducks. Mrs. Pomton would have agreed with him but would have added that to know their wives was to be pecked to death by hens, which, given the quite different conformation of beak, was a far worse fate.

Altogether, this joint meeting of the two committees had proven a most fruitful contact between board and faculty, if not in all respects a true meeting of minds. The members of both committees felt happy about it, and awaited with excitement the full meeting of the board, still twelve days off.

On his way home, Schneider met Milton. "Hullo," he said. Then, awkwardly, "I daresay you've heard what the faculty committee recommended. I'm sorry it had to be Nast. You would have made a wonderful president, and one fully worthy of this institution."

"Thank you," said Milton. His voice was hoarse; his face was solemn; but Schneider noted with relief that it bore no resentment toward himself.

"Of course," said Schneider, "it's only a committee of the board. The full board has yet to meet."

"I know," said Milton. "I am not ready to concede. I happen to know there are trustees who will fight for me. If I lose, it will be the power of money. It will mean the Winthrop Foundation has bought the presidency for their candidate."

This reading of current political history left Schneider too dazed to reply. Nobody on the campus except Milton had ever taken his candidacy seriously. And yet, the cause of all this madness was something more than mere vanity. It was only a manly ambition that had been fatally mixed with stupidity. What a magnificent fluke it would be if the board should go mad and choose him. Many boards of trustees had done even stranger things.

But Schneider was not alarmed: Nast, whom he and Dorothy needed to have the board select, was in no real danger of a fluke. There was a grain of truth in Milton's reading of events. The power of money really was the determining factor. And the smell of something akin to simony hung heavy in the hot July air.

~XXI~

SCHNEIDER was flying high. He glanced down at the floor of fluffy white clouds below him, glaring in the powerful sunshine of July. If only his sight were keen enough to pierce those clouds, thought Schneider, he could distinguish the thousands of tiny boxes that men below call homes, scattered on minute farmsteads, in clustered villages, in sprawling towns. Each home a little separately endowed hell, its denizens condemned to monogamy, bad cooking, and television. Or most of them, anyhow. This nation, under God—as the saying now goes—was sweating out a blazing summer day in its heavily mortgaged homes. If he could remove the roofs, if he could develop truly telescopic sight, he would see the ants who inhabited them. What curious ants they were, swiftly and blindly moving about their predestined tasks; driven by their little lusts, stinging each other, hunting for food, hunting for love; hunting for fame, raises, promotions, and even presidencies; flattering, cajoling, bullying, deceiving. If hydrogen bombs really should fall, would these insects be seriously missed? May God have mercy on us all, said Schneider to himself.

From his vantage point above the clouds, he looked through closed eyelids at the campus where he lived and worked, now hundreds of miles behind him, still tense and vibrant from the throes of choosing a president. Eisenhower and Stevenson were not the problem; the problem was, would Nast get it? Only yesterday Nast had come upon him in the Triangle Club, chuckling over a copy of *The Democratic Digest.*

"Scurrilous little sheet," Nast had said bitingly.

"Yes, it's wonderful," Schneider had said, still laughing. "Rough in spots. But politics is a rough game, isn't it?"

"I suppose so."

"You ought to know."

"I don't read *The Democratic Digest,*" said Nast with dignity.

"But you're a candidate!"

"Oh, that!" said Nast.

"I gather it's in the bag."

"Thanks for serving on the faculty committee of five," said Nast.

"Not at all. I nearly missed serving. I have to go to New York."

"Ah?" said Nast, with evident curiosity. Schneider, after all, was not in the habit of traveling.

"Barker University is after me."

"Take it," said Nast.

"Ah?" said Schneider.

That conversation had occurred only the day before. Now he was on his way to New York, flying high. President Camp of Barker had reserved a room for him at Camp's own hotel. The address was in Schneider's pocket. He had hardly reached the hotel when Camp phoned.

"I was wondering where you were," said Camp. "Well, you're here now. Can you dine with me and this alumnus I wrote you about? At seven. Name of Tommie Tomkins. Rich as Croesus, very loyal, keen about diplomatic history, and anxious to memorialize his father, who was a diplomat. He's heard of your government project and is thrilled that we may get you at Barker. I'll pick you up at six-thirty."

The dinner was a feast, and Schneider gorged himself. Given the salary scale of his profession, he reflected, stability breeds starvation. Only at those fleeting moments of hesitancy between two institutions can a scholar latch on to an expense account and eat, briefly, like other men. He determined to prolong this period of courtship.

As seasoning for the feast, he had a chance to witness at first hand a president operating on a potential donor. Tommie Tomkins reclined unaware on the operating table while Camp's deft surgery removed from his fiscal insides a handsomely endowed chair in diplomatic history. Schneider tried to calculate the salary it would yield, but he knew little about such matters and he did know at least enough to realize that the investment habits of boards varied enormously. Besides, there was sure to be skulduggery.

Tommie Tomkins, who seemed to regard his operation as a success and indeed was pleasurably impressed with his own generosity, graciously expressed the hope that Schneider would be the first of a long line of eminent scholars to occupy the chair, a chair which he had, so to speak, just pulled up to the table.

"I'd love to do it," said Schneider, remembering how briefly yesterday the President-Select had urged him to get out. "But I'd like to consult a friend in one of the big foundations here before making my next move. I'm sure you understand."

At the mention of friends in big foundations, Camp congratulated himself privately that he had offered Schneider a job. Not every candidate for a post of this sort has valuable contacts in the outside world. He assured Tommie that he would do his best to persuade Professor Schneider to be the first incumbent of his chair, a phrase that delighted Schneider, for etymological and other reasons. But Schneider was determined to consult Denby before he clinched. He did permit himself in the interests of a dignified courtship to accept a luncheon engagement with Camp, at the Colony, in order to pursue the subject further.

Next morning he saw Denby. It proved a delightful reunion. Denby insisted on hearing "all the dirt" about the University.

"Dirt," said Schneider, "is what we have most of." And he proceeded to give him a blow-by-blow account of the Nast campaign.

"Well," said Denby, "Nast is a frightful bore. But his wife will make the best-looking addition to a president's house that any board has provided this year."

"Confidentially," said Schneider, "his wife has left him."

"No!" said Denby. "But I would have thought your trustees would boggle at a candidate whose marriage had just blown up."

"They would," said Schneider. "But they don't know about it yet. Neither does Nast. To tell you the truth, I'm the only person at the University who does know. And I know because Dorothy Nast told me—and assigned me the job of making him promise not to contest her suit."

"Wonderful!" said Denby, roaring with laughter. "Wonderful! When are you breaking the news to the poor bastard?"

"As soon as the trustees act and before Nast can be inaugurated. I have decided that during that interval I stand the best chance of forcing his hand. Because he'll be furious, you know, at losing Dorothy."

"Who wouldn't be? By the way, how did she happen to deputize you to—force his hand, as you put it?"

"Well," said Henry, "to tell you the truth, I had been making love to her. Oh, all quite innocent. I'm not giving anything away."

Now why do I lie to Denby, he wondered. Atavistic chivalry? No; probably guilt. Most men doubtless suffered when they recalled an act of adultery. Schneider suffered acutely when he recalled the one he had spoiled. When would life offer him such a chance again? To murder, perhaps. To steal, certainly. But to commit adultery? Adultery is a curious sin: it always takes two to commit it. If so golden a night had gone sour through his stupidity, his hypersensitivity, think of the thousand and one stupid reasons people might fail to commit this interesting sin. Was his real reason for snarling, for reacting like a jealous adolescent, an ingrained Puritanism in whose tenets he no longer really believed? Or was it a secret fear that he had appeared to this goddess an inadequate and unsophisticated lover?

"Won't things be a bit tight for you," Denby was asking, "when Nast takes over?"

"I won't be there. Last night I all but promised President Camp of Barker University in Buffalo to join his faculty. For many reasons I couldn't bear to stay where I am. For very personal reasons."

He recounted to Denby the stages of his disillusionment: his telegram-waving act with Pomton, his effort to reorganize his dreadful department, the vicious brawl at the faculty meeting, Engel's Law. He told him about his fib to young Ripley, of the soaring deference paid him, of Pomton's question to him about the presidency, of the textbook he was writing. But he did not tell him of the peace he had negotiated with Henrietta or the pitiful figure he had cut as a lover at Roaring Creek Club. There are some things a man cannot even tell Denby. Denby roared with delight as Schneider recounted each stage in his odyssey. He especially liked the research hoax.

"But why Barker?" he said. "Won't that just be more of the same?"

"It pays more," said Schneider. "A good bit more, I have reason to suspect."

"But forgive me, my dear fellow. More than you are getting? So what? I can understand, though only just, a maniacal ambition to live in Buffalo, but not because of any salary a university is likely to pay. Look, I've got an idea. The guy I've had in charge of our Division of General Education has just announced he's quitting immediately to take a college presidency. His reason for quitting obviously shows he lacks intelligence and that I was a fool to appoint him in the first place. But let's skip that. We all make mistakes.

"I offer you his job. The pay is twenty thousand. You could pay your debts and get a change of occupation that would do you good. I know you want to teach, but you can go back to teaching after you get away from it a bit and get a sense of perspective. As for research, you should be able to scrounge a little time from your job to write. Our trustees rather like to have a staff member demonstrate his literacy. What about it?"

"I'll take it," said Schneider. "I'd like to work with you. You have a sense of humor. And since general education is precisely the missing wheel in our universities, maybe I could do something about it."

"Well, I'm delighted to have you join us," said Denby. "But I don't want you to expect too much in addition to the pay. There's not much a foundation can do. Broadly speaking, it has even more means at its disposal than a university has. But it has an equally ill-defined end. In short, it's a microcosm of our society: abundant means but no ends. You know: the American way of life, as they call it. But, if you keep your sense of humor, you may like it, at least for a while. If you get fed up, I'll understand."

"But is a foundation as much a racket as a university?" said Schneider. His voice registered incredulous horror.

"There's no real difference," said Denby. "Except in detail. Both have trustees, and the trustees have been entrusted with money. Nothing destroys your imagination quicker than being entrusted with money. Then there are minor ailments. Hungry, ambitious academics sit around, from coast to coast, cooking up 'projects' with an eye to pleasing the foundations. The projects all look as if they had been rewritten for style in some Federal bureau or other. They begin, 'It is believed that . . .' And sooner or later, some of them have to be 'finalized' or 'activated.' Administrators like to give you 'a breakdown of their setup' to show why it is believed that their institutions are strategically fitted, either by their geographical location, or by their clientele, or their architecture, to carry out the mission under discussion.

"If you give them the money—and you have to give some from time to time—that's what a philanthropoid is hired to do—they use it for some other ill-disguised purpose.

"Crackpots demand interviews and outline schemes for getting colleges to educate once more.

"Professors form research teams with small herds of secretaries, not to solve problems, but to study approaches to problems. More problems have been approached with foundation aid than you can imagine. It's an absolute miracle that one or two haven't been solved, if only by some untoward accident. But they're still being approached. From time to time a survey has to be made of fifty or sixty of these approaches; and eventually the surveys have to be correlated, so we can all see what the foundations are accomplishing. Oh, I assure you, it's pretty wearing work. But it's well paid."

"Are you sure nothing can be done?" said Schneider.

"Not absolutely," said Denby, "or I wouldn't be hiring you. I still believe that some day some fellow like you might get something started. God knows how. I'm merely listing the frustrations, so you won't join us under a misapprehension."

"I'll risk it," said Schneider. "I'll tell Camp tomorrow that I'm not available. When do I start being frustrated?"

"Is September first too early?"

"I'll report for duty September first."

He rose to leave, but Denby motioned him to take his seat again.

"Tell me," said Denby. "Where is Dorothy Nast? She must need her friends. And I must admit I found her excessively attractive."

"Ah?" said Schneider. "Did you make love to her too?"

"Oh, it was all quite innocent. But I'd like to help her if I can."

"Everybody wants to help," said Schneider. "Two days ago I got a letter from Paris, from Old Manley. I think you met him when you came out. Somebody had written Old Manley that Dorothy had apparently walked out on Nast. Old Manley asked me where she was. He said she should come to Paris, that she must need her friends, that he'd like to help her. If you knew Old Manley as well as I do, you'd warn her to keep away from Paris."

"What impudence," said Denby. "But where is she? Have you her address?"

Schneider evaded the question and became vague.

"Somewhere in Georgia," he said.

"Probably eating her heart out, too. Why, she's a mere girl. I tell you, she needs her friends. She needs to be taken out of herself. She needs New York, and diversion, and admiration. I'd like to help."

"So would I," said Schneider. "Terribly. But she claims that all she needs is a divorce. After that she knows who can help. She wants to get married."

"Who to?" asked Denby. His voice showed alarm.

"To a former colleague of Nast's who has resigned to take a job in Africa."

"I never heard of anything more despicable," said Denby. "She belongs in New York. Africa, indeed!"

"She would follow this gent to hell," said Schneider. "And I hardly blame her. He's young, tall, slender, handsome, urbane, witty, and highly intelligent. He's got everything—even Dorothy."

"And I say the hell with him. Look, I'm quite upset. Let's go on the town. What've you got to do?"

"Nothing," said Schneider, "until lunch with Camp tomorrow."

"Done. I can get hold of some evening clothes for you. We're off to The Arabian Nights. It's a club. There'll be lovely girls. They'll have veils on, of course. But not much else. We'll have champagne, and the food isn't bad."

"Swell," said Schneider, really excited by the word "Arabian." Instinctively, he put a hand to his head, as if to adjust his kaffiyah. "Let's go."

The girls at The Arabian Nights were indeed charming. They were the least bashful girls whom Schneider had ever met. For he did meet several. They seemed to know and like Denby.

But first there had been the Toast. The champagne was opened.

"To her happiness," said Denby, with a great effort. "And I hope I don't gag on this drink."

"To her happiness," said Schneider.

Next morning around eleven, when Schneider awoke, he quite naturally had a bad head. But he looked back without remorse on his evening with Denby. Although his memory of the details was blurred, he distinctly recalled that two of the girls had gone on to other places with Denby and himself and that nobody had been inhibited by differences in age, only exhilarated by differences in sex.

The night clubs they went to certainly lacked the innocence of the Roaring Creek Club, but they lacked its sorrows and frustrations, too.

He sent for black coffee, took a shower, and shaved. The face that stared back at him from the mirror looked a little puffed, but it also seemed relaxed and gay.

At luncheon with Camp, he ate sparingly but expensively. Then, in effect, he broke the news that the money for his luncheon had been wasted. But when Camp heard that Schneider would be running the Division of General Education for the Winthrop Foundation, he was not in the least discouraged. Camp began excitedly telling Schneider of his own ambitious plans for expanding general education, although he seemed to Schneider a little vague as to what the term might imply. And he explained in considerable detail why Barker was strategically placed to pioneer in the field. He volunteered to draw up a project.

Schneider saw Denby again briefly before he caught his plane home.

"Send me a chit for your expenses for the trip east," said Denby.

"But Camp is paying my expenses."

"The Winthrop Foundation feels no earthly interest in what President Camp pays or fails to pay. The foundation will have found a good man cheap if your expenses east are all it has to pay. Send a chit."

"All right," said Schneider. "But I already feel a fraud, taking twenty thousand a year, when you've rescued me from complete futility. What I really want isn't a large income but some function in life."

"In our kind of society," said Denby, "you'll have to lower your sights a bit. In our kind of society you aren't very likely to find a function. But we can manage nicely to pay you twenty thousand by way of—well, by way of compensation, as they say."

So Schneider lowered his sights, caught his plane, and flew high. By a technological miracle that always involved for Schneider the most disagreeable psychic consequences, he was whisked through space with what seemed to him the speed of light and plunged into a different human environment: this time a university community in the throes of choosing its president, or more precisely in the throes of having other people choose for it.

~XXII~

THE HOSPITAL LEAGUE met on Thursdays at ten and sewed for two hours. Its specialties were layettes for the frequent babies of the poor, hospital shirts for the wards, and of course University gossip. Henrietta Schneider was president, although Mrs. Pomton was naturally and permanently the honorary president. Henrietta had won the presidency on the eve of the Second Battle of Appomattox, when all was lost save honor. She had won it the way she had won everything else until Dorothy had appeared, by sheer force of character, tireless energy, and organizational skill. Under her leadership the league had increased its output of layettes almost as fast as the poor had increased their output of babies, had exceeded its target on hospital shirts, and had been stimulated by the Schneider-Nast conflict into an unprecedented outburst of gossip. For the last triumphant weeks of Henrietta's reign, the Hospital League had become almost a front organization for the hard core of Schneiderites who were fighting off Dorothy's guerrilla troops. When the Mayflower finally sank, to mix metaphors a bit, the quality of the gossip underwent a sort of postwar slump, and the members' attention had in some sense reverted to the original declared purposes of the league. But now, in mid-July and a bare week before the board of trustees was expected to take final action; with Dorothy Nast mysteriously detained in Georgia shortly after Professor Frederick Landon had, with mysterious suddenness, resigned to go to Ethiopia; with a persistent rumor that the trustees' Committee on Selection had decided to pass on to the full board meeting, with approval, the faculty committee of five's recommendation of Nast—now the dam broke, layettes were down two points, hospital shirts were mixed, and gossip was up sharply.

Early in her presidency Henrietta had looked upon the league as a powerful bastion, or as a salient that Dorothy could not hope to take and could not possibly outflank. But it was the old story, of course, of the surprise effect of new weapons. The chemical warfare of Southern flattery had so debilitated Henrietta's troops that layette production had sagged; the whole notion of good works had become subtly outmoded. Dorothy, who loathed sewing and had never felt more than an academic interest in the rapidly multiplying offspring of the poor, had thrown Henrietta off balance. She had personally visited the obstetrical wards and had cooed so charmingly over each hideous new arrival that its mother wept with joy, and remembered this beautiful angel of mercy long after the layette that Henrietta had grimly and efficiently delivered had seen its day and been metamorphosed into dishcloths.

But now, on this hot Thursday morning, the cooing had been stilled, the angel of mercy was mercifully absent in the Cracker State that had bred her, her chances of returning were being variously and heatedly estimated, and if she did return, she might well return as the Wife of the President. It was a confused military and political picture. If Dorothy was deserting her husband, then the members of the league would joyfully accept a grass widower and a money-getter as president. They had always liked him more than their husbands had; they had always admired him as a good provider and a model for their own husbands to imitate; and the possibility that this too good-looking hussy might have deserted him lent him a sudden glamour of a sort he had always lacked. If on the other hand she returned and the growing murmur that she was a fast woman could be plausibly confirmed, and if, even so, Nast was elected president, then the Schneiderites promised themselves they would make her life a living hell, such as not even the wives of other college presidents had ever experienced.

It was impossible to plan intelligently when one did not know what the board would do about Nast and when one also did not know what Dorothy would do about him, or perhaps had done while absent from him. Unhappily, some of the league's ablest scouts were on vacation with their husbands; and reconnaissance, so far as the trustees were concerned, had all but collapsed. Those of Dorothy's supporters who were present were spreading the word that Dorothy's mother was ill but that Dorothy hoped to be back by the day the board acted. Dorothy's supporters, however, were secretly demoralized by the fact that the letters they had written to their wandering chieftain went unanswered. They were absolutely without authentic information.

At luncheon, Henrietta could not question her husband because school vacation was of course now on, and the six curious ears of half that many young daughters seemed to stand out receptively. But in her bewilderment, Henrietta instinctively turned to the man she had so recently come to respect again, within limits.

"Henry," she said discreetly, "I should be grateful if you could spare me a few minutes this afternoon. There are some matters I would like to discuss."

"With pleasure, my dear."

How that remark of Henrietta's would have chilled my blood a year ago, thought Schneider to himself. Indeed, how it would have chilled his blood as late as the day before the Great Day, the day he had unwittingly launched his happy career by claiming he worked for the government. Now he was glad to discuss anything with his wife. But he was doubly glad today. He had received by the morning mail the letter from Denby that confirmed in writing his appointment to the staff of the Winthrop Foundation, and he wished to show it to Henrietta. For Schneider, though a deeply changed man, had retained his temperamental prudence: he had said nothing whatever to Henrietta about Denby's oral promise, even though confident this promise would take written form. So here the letter was. And any Arab wife, Schneider felt, whatever her former crimes of insubordination, had a right to advance notice when the family tent was about to be moved to a greener oasis.

Now, with the children gone, and without waiting for Henrietta's questions, the nature of which he felt quite competent to predict, he drew his letter of appointment from his pocket, passed it to Henrietta, and remarked quietly, "Perhaps you ought to read this letter before we discuss anything."

Then he leaned back, carefully loaded his pipe, and benignly watched Henrietta's face.

Henrietta's face was worth watching. Amazement slowly gave way to such bliss as it is rarely given to husbands to behold.

"Where will we live?" she asked in a hushed voice.

"Wherever my wife prefers to live," said Henry, indulgently and grandly, "provided it is within an hour of my office. My office, you will note, is near Grand Central." He knew what her reply would be, poor exiled New Englander that she was.

"Can we live in Connecticut?" she asked, almost in a whisper.

"If that is your choice," he answered softly, and his emphasis on the word "your" was a caress.

She sat back and dreamed a while. After all these years *in partibus infidelium!* After all these years of wrestling with an impossible budget! And how nasty she had been to him until that mysterious day when Henry, a strangely restored man, had put on his kaffiyah and firmly negotiated peace. And now, New England again. She sighed. An income multiplied by three, and a little more than that. Good schools for the children. The opera, perhaps, in New York. The Metropolitan Museum of Art. Theater. It was not heaven, perhaps. It was not even Boston. But it was certainly reminiscent of both.

"Can I tell the children? Can I tell my friends?" she asked.

"Not yet," replied Schneider. "But you had better speak confidentially to Storage and Van and get an estimate. Tell them, if they so much as mention our leaving, I will cancel the order and go to East-West Haulers."

She still sat; her strong and habitually busy hands lay idly in her lap, as if they too had been overcome by the news. Her mind went back to the meeting that forenoon of the Hospital League, and the questions she had wanted to put to Henry about Nast and Dorothy and the board and the committee of five. Why put them? What did it matter? It was doubtful now if she could get a mover in time to accompany Henry when he reported for work. But the University seemed to her now so ridiculous, so out-West, so crude and uncultured, that she could not care less who became president or even who became the president's wife. If Dorothy was in fact returning to share her husband's triumph, and to lay down the law to the Schneiderites, what a surprise now lay in store for her! She rose, went over to Henry, put her arms about his neck, and kissed him. Then, somewhat confused by this over-display of emotion, she hurried out to talk with Storage and Van. If they could not move her in time, so much the better. They could store the stuff here until she had actually found her permanent house—in New England.

But the moment she had talked with the movers her mind turned responsibly to her military duties. It was not fair, with her army in disarray, her scouts baffled, and her lieutenants bewildered, that she should secretly abdicate her command without, so to speak, signing off. Timidly and apologetically she tapped on Henry's study door and appealed to him again.

"Could I perhaps say we are to be away on a year's leave?"

"You may say I have applied for a year's leave."

That should answer her purposes. If Miss Stilton assured the enemy that he had not applied, it would be assumed that Henrietta had misunderstood his statement that he was about to. When the

Barker call had come up, he had taken the precaution of consulting his staff. With their full knowledge and consent, he had found a perfectly adequate replacement, willing to come for a year or for good, and available at short notice. That left Schneider with a free conscience and ample room to maneuver. Rumors of a year's leave would be construed to mean Washington and classified research. Even, perhaps, by Miss Stilton.

Henrietta's lieutenants came for a cup of tea that very afternoon and held a strategy meeting. The latest military intelligence came from Marjory Randall, a deserter who had reached the sorrowful conclusion that Dorothy had vanished for keeps; that her forces, even in their hour of triumph, were destined to disintegrate; and that the Schneiderites could rise from defeat, come out of their guerrilla fastnesses, and seize power, even if Nast should achieve the presidency. Marjory Randall was convinced that Dorothy's neo-Confederate movement would quickly crumble without her skilled leadership and would go down in campus history as an ugly piece of Kluxery, a meaningless resurgence of a way of life that America had once for all rejected. She could see no incompatibility between a Nast administration and the sort of social regime that the Schneiderites could rebuild, a regime in which moral rectitude, cultural activities, and good housekeeping would be the tests of female citizenship. Nast would have had enough Southern charm to last him the rest of his life. The deserter was but expressing the opinion of the guerrillas she had now joined when she declared that Nast had always been too good for Dorothy.

Henrietta's charge to her followers was a moving one and reminded more than one of her lieutenants of Washington's Farewell Address. And yet, when it was all over and her lieutenants had gone home, Henrietta heaved a great sigh of relief, as loud as the one Washington himself must have heaved when his own day of freedom had come. For Henrietta had merely, and characteristically, been doing her duty as she saw it. Her affections were not here but in a greener and less sprawling land, a land of tall trees and lush grass and trim colonial houses, the Connecticut shore of

Long Island Sound. And a budget of twenty thousand would itself be tall and lush and trim.

In the fullness of time, which here turned out to be three more days, the trustees met to make the Great Decision. Well-informed cynics made allusions to meetings of the Electoral College to confirm the People's Choice and to authorize the use of purple in January. But most people in the community were wiser than the cynics: they knew that something might slip. For example, where was Dorothy Nast? With that question unanswered, or too glibly answered, who could be sure? Milton had not conceded.

There was something deeply inhuman about the secrecy of that meeting of the board. The summer school faculty and their wives went about their daily routine duties, trying to keep their minds on their work; yet every one of those minds, even the most scholarly among them, was fixed on one room, where around a long, polished table their future ruler was being chosen. They were now resigned to seeing Nast chosen and they consoled themselves by telling each other that, after all, Nast would get the money. They could supply the ideas themselves. But there was always the chance of a dark horse, aside from Dorothy's mysterious absence. As a matter of fact, the older members of the community could remember only too well that Pomton himself had been a dark horse. Anything might happen. Not even an admiral or general or banker could be precluded.

The Chairman called the meeting to order; the reading of the minutes of the last meeting was quickly waived; and Mr. Joseph Stanforth was requested to report on behalf of the Committee on Selection of a President. Joe Stanforth began, with a great show of terseness, but with a surprisingly large number of very long and ill-chosen words, to recount the heroic efforts of his committee to find just the right man. He listed the qualities they had been determined to find in any man they would be willing to recommend for election by the full board. Across the table from him, Pomton listened intently. With some bitterness he reflected that probably no man now living possessed all those qualities. Probably, he reflected, the trouble with this presidency business was not the ignorance of boards of trustees on the very problems involved in such an election; or the equal, though essentially different, incapacity of faculties; but the picture American society had acquired of what abilities a college president should possess. He should be a great scholar, a skillful money-raiser, a brilliant orator, a clever administrator, a model of good morals. If he was married, his wife should be highly intelligent, socially knowledgeable, and unfailingly modest. After the election, thought Pomton to himself, both the successful candidate and his wife would be chained to a rock like Prometheus, while for years to come spiteful professors and their harpy wives would feed daily on their respective livers.

After this extraordinary build-up by Stanforth, any name would have been an anticlimax, except perhaps Nast's. Not that Nast clearly possessed all these qualities; but the fact that the stubborn Stanforth, after steadily opposing his candidacy, now announced that Nast's name led all the rest left the trustees feeling there must be a good deal more to Nast than appeared on the surface. All the board members had met Nast, although none of them knew what perfect coverage Nast had achieved during the long years of preparation for this meeting. All of them liked him. Now all of them felt the deepest gratification that the young man they had known and liked turned out to be one of the most unusual men of his century. There were a few cursory questions. Several trustees, on whom friends of Milton's had put unbearable pressure to push his candidacy, asked whether Milton had been seriously considered. Stanforth assured them that he had, but that in terms of both achievement to date and promise for the future he could not measure up to Nast. Then one of them raised the sixty-four-thousand-dollar question, as he had promised a friend of Milton's he would do.

"Has Mrs. Nast recently left her husband? And if so, why?"

Pomton who had been silently putting together a few extempore remarks congratulating the board on their wisdom in choosing

Nast, was for a moment stunned by the sudden blow. When he recovered, he mustered every ounce of his crumbling, lame-duck dignity for a reply.

"Mr. Chairman," he said suavely, "I suspect that the person best placed to answer that question may be myself. Mrs. Nast left several weeks ago for her parents' home in Georgia to be with her mother, who, I understand, is ill. She had hoped to be home by now, but her mother's condition has detained her. I am quite aware that there are wild rumors that she has left her husband. My very able secretary, Miss Stilton, has made the most careful inquiries and has satisfied herself that these rumors are wholly without foundation. I regret to say that Dr. Nast's enemies have seized on his wife's absence to assail her husband's home life.

"Mr. Chairman, I happen to have seen a great deal of both Dr. and Mrs. Nast. They are a devoted couple. Unfortunately for Mrs. Nast, the fact that she is easily the most beautiful woman on the campus has aroused violent jealousies."

But the author of the sixty-four-thousand-dollar question was head of a large firm of public accountants and was quite accustomed to glib explanations. He did not propose to be put off now.

"Is it true, Dr. Pomton, that Mrs. Nast's extraordinary beauty has cut the faculty of this institution squarely in two? And if so, do we want the wife of the President to be head of a bitter and triumphant faction?"

"Every university faculty," snapped Pomton, not even bothering to address the Chairman, "is cut sharply in two. And as long as professors have wives, it always will be. As a matter of fact, even without the wives it would be cut sharply in two. Old cleavages give way to new cleavages from time to time; but it is always cut in two. Nevertheless—" and Pomton's voice now rang with loyalty to his guild—"no matter how you slice it, it is still a faculty. The fact is, no other woman in this community would prove a more gracious hostess at the Parsonage than Mrs. Nast."

Pomton was now thoroughly aroused. If, he thought to himself bitterly, Dorothy Nast should enter this board room and give just one of her radiant smiles, this whole crowd of potbellied, cigar-smoking little businessmen would follow her like the Pied Piper of Hamelin to whatever death she might assign them. And here they were, hypocritically fumbling over her reputation with their dirty hands.

The Chairman of the board now gracefully stated that, unless he heard objections, the discussion concerning Mrs. Nast would be stricken from the minutes of the present meeting. There were no objections.

But the accountant had another trick in his bag.

"Mr. Chairman," he said. "I don't want to criticize the splendid report of the Committee on Selection, though I must say I still don't understand why our friend Joe Stanforth has suddenly reversed his position on Dr. Nast. Don't let's rush into this thing. Why does the faculty want Nast? That arouses my suspicions. I'm told they don't want Dr. Milton. Well, so far as them not wanting him, I say that's in his favor. But I'm told the Committee on Selection never even considered Lem Nordheim, and I happen to know we could get him. Lem's the biggest banker in this state. He could raise more money than Nast and Milton combined. He's led the drive against subversives in this state. He's a deacon in the Methodist church. Hell, what more do we want? If it's not out of order, Mr. Chairman, I place in nomination the name of Lemuel Nordheim; and, moreover, I move to recommit the whole question to the committee. I say, let 'em report back to us a week from today for final action."

The speaker was clearly not out of order, for there was now no longer any order for him to be out of. Several business cronies of Mr. Nordheim's were shouting, "Second the motion!" The Chairman of the board was pounding his gavel. The board, which had never been expert at deliberation, had through the years oscillated between tyranny and anarchy. It was now reveling in a sweet disorder, a disorder worthy of a faculty meeting. It was as if they had caught some contagion from the eggheads they so grudgingly hired. Some of the trustees were grumbling audibly at the thought of a second meeting. But others were by now glancing eagerly at their watches. The motion carried. Pomton swallowed his anger. And the meeting adjourned.

The news that the board had postponed the election hit the sweltering, worried community like a tornado. This tornado, unlike most twisters, did not shift the relative positions of material objects in space, but it did shift the psychic relations of persons. For the first time Nast's confidence failed him. Opposing that ass Milton was one thing; defeating Lem Nordheim was quite another. Moreover, while Dorothy's curious, silent absence had disturbed him, he had always believed that if she could return as First Lady, she would return all right, all right.

Nast's confidence was dampened but Joe Stanforth was terrified. If he could believe Miss Stilton—and he did—nothing but Nast's election stood between him and the publication of Nast's book, and nothing whatever stood between such publication and his own conviction for fraud. Stanforth must work fast to secure Lem Nordheim's withdrawal or defeat. Suppose he failed?

Pomton was furious. He had set his heart on the role of kingmaker. He had even, somewhat imprudently, implied to several of his trustees-to-be at A. & M. that his present trustees could be counted on to elect Professor Nast on the strength of his personal recommendation. It had never crossed his mind that the board would balk at rubber-stamping the choice of the Stanforth committee. Now he would look like a fool, and a vain fool at that. His prestige with his new board was at stake, and he fumed constantly to poor Mrs. Pomton.

Milton was elated. He told Schneider that the nomination of Lemuel Nordheim, who was a crooked banker, would in his judgment split "the corrupt money vote" in the board and throw the election to himself. Mrs. Milton sighed, and steeled herself for life in the Parsonage.

Schneider was deeply disturbed. His whole strategy to free his Beauty from her Beast was based on the assumption that the Beast, as President-Elect, would not risk the scandal of his dealings with

Denby on the social-science grant or even the scandal of his broken home. If Nast loses the election, thought Schneider, he will never consent to a divorce. He will turn vindictive, because his economist's eye will surely tell him that to indulge his vindictiveness will cost him nothing. Schneider decided not to tell Dorothy of this new barrier to her freedom. But the betting was certainly in favor of Nordheim, and Schneider began to cast around for a new strategy: the news next week would probably be bad.

The rest of the faculty—or, rather, those members of it in residence when the twister struck—prepared sadly to submit to a banker. They had somehow guessed all along they would have to. They had hoped that Nast, who was at least technically one of them, was enough like a banker to get by the trustees. And they admitted they needed a man corrupt enough to raise money, or their salaries never would be increased. So they had sorrowfully backed Nast. Now some of them remarked bitterly that, so far as the trustees were concerned, faculty support had proven to be the kiss of death—as everybody should have known it would. In short, wherever one looked, one saw the wreckage of hopes and aspirations, unless one deigned to look at Milton, who specialized in aspiration and hope.

Or unless one looked at Miss Stilton. Miss Stilton remained perfectly cool. She tried to comfort Nast. She again warned Joe Stanforth that he must either work fast or face a lengthy internment. Then, swiftly but calmly, she began her research on the dark horse, Lemuel Nordheim. Unhappily, he had not been involved in the Transprairie affair, but it seemed improbable to Miss Stilton that the leading banker in the state should have grown extremely rich merely by lending money. It took her three days of hard work to locate Mr. Nordheim's most dubious transaction and to get Stanforth to introduce her to her victim. In the conference that ensued it transpired that Dr. Nast was about to publish a book on banking which would inevitably make use of Mr. Nordheim's career. Mr. Nordheim was uncertain just which details Nast had got hold of and could document on a libel-proof basis;

but Mr. Nordheim was a banker who loved peace and hated explaining his acts. He therefore precipitately withdrew from the race when he had secured Nast's promise not to publish. It was only a repeat performance; but, then, Miss Stilton saw no real value in administrative experience unless successful techniques could be fruitfully repeated. And she lacked completely any exhibitionistic wish to use a different type of snare on each rabbit.

By the time the board assembled again, the dark horse had officially withdrawn. The public accountant knew better than to try to raise Milton's bedraggled standard again. And this time Joe Stanforth was nothing short of eloquent about Nast.

The Chairman then invited further nominations for the presidency of the University. None was forthcoming. Finally he stated that, unless he heard objections to the contrary, Dr. Richard Nast was the unanimous choice of the board of trustees, and his election would be so recorded in the minutes.

Word of his election was promptly sent to Dr. Nast and he was politely requested to appear at the meeting. He looked paler than usual, and his face, for so young a man, was a little drawn. But he accepted the presidency promptly and with dignity, declaring not wholly unexpectedly that "he was deeply sensible of the great honor the board had done him" and that "he would try to live up to the trust that they had imposed in him." He and the board then discussed the press release that must follow the board meeting and also the date of the presidential inauguration.

On the first point, Pomton distributed in mimeographed form a press release prepared by Miss Stilton, "in the event that the board chose to concur in the choice of the Committee on Selection." The release had said a little less about the achievements of Pomton's own administration than Pomton would have expected from Miss Stilton, but he of course said nothing. The President-Elect, however, insisted on inserting a line or two of encomium on that subject, and the board agreed.

On the second point, the date of the forthcoming inauguration, Pomton indicated that since inaugurations frequently followed the actual taking over of office by many weeks, and since it was already late July, the inauguration might well be held in late October, thus giving the President's office ample time to plan it properly. But the President-Elect seemed unaccountably eager to have the inauguration as early as possible after the coming academic session had opened. To this also the board agreed. As one of the trustees pointed out, the further ahead of the national election the inauguration was held, the less national politics would detract from the occasion.

Although Pomton remained unconvinced and puzzled by Nast's determination to be crowned early, Miss Stilton was not puzzled. Dorothy's failure to return in time for the election persuaded Miss Stilton that she would probably not return at all; and she was sure that Nast had drawn the same deduction. It was written all over his tense face; but she determined to have a conversation with him to make doubly sure. Obviously, she could not shape her own behavior appropriately unless she knew her new employer's marital status. But first she quietly issued the statement to the press.

Miss Stilton then awaited at her office the inevitable appearance of Joe Stanforth. Joe would be anxious to see "his able colleague."

After accepting gratefully Miss Stilton's congratulations on the board's endorsement of his choice, Stanforth thought he saw a change of expression in his colleague's face that made him distinctly uneasy. She spoke slowly and evenly.

"There now remains only the matter of your resignation from the board, Mr. Stanforth."

"I'd rather wait a week or so," said Stanforth pleadingly.

"I'm afraid," she said, her eyes growing beadier and beadier, "that Dr. Nast would prefer it now. I know he is deeply disturbed by the Transprairie affair and feels no member of his board should be open to charges in that connection."

"Okay, okay," Stanforth mumbled.

"I took the liberty of preparing your resignation, underscoring in my text that you chaired the committee that nominated the new president. This ought to make it clear to the public that you did not resign at his request—and, technically, you are not doing so. You are resigning at mine. You will note I give pressure of private business as your reason."

He studied the note, could think of no way to soften or improve it, and scrawled his signature at the bottom. A few minutes later she had submitted to the Chairman of the board Mr. Stanforth's resignation and a "suggested acceptance" ready for his signature if the Chairman approved her draft. The Chairman, who had an inkling of Stanforth's Transprairie problem and had always dreaded a possible exposé, gladly signed, expressing to Miss Stilton his deepest personal regret. This regret Miss Stilton heartily echoed. Miss Stilton had fortunately prepared a statement to the press announcing Stanforth's resignation, for release two days later, together with a brief encomium from Pomton as retiring president.

Miss Stilton went serenely home, tubbed, and supped in her dressing gown. She then dressed rather carefully, in the most feminine and least businesslike costume she owned. It seems likely that Miss Stilton was pyschic, for at eight the phone rang.

"Good evening, Miss Stilton." It was, of course, Nast's voice.

"Good evening, Mr. President."

The title was premature, but Nast liked it, as indeed Miss Stilton had known he would. Could he see her for a few moments, he wondered. She would come immediately to his home, she said, and she would bring her dictation pad. She had been careful not to propose a visit to his home a few nights before when she had had to explain her blackmail of Stanforth. She had been afraid of gossip, gossip that might affect his candidacy. Even now, she would have suggested the office if his presidency had been her only problem. But it was not. All her instincts told her that this evening was the evening. Nast probably thought he wanted to persuade her to stay on when Pomton left. Miss Stilton believed, however, that she understood Nast's motives somewhat better than Nast did. The triumph of the day's election had come, and there must necessarily have been a letdown. If Dorothy had kept her head, she would have been there for that moment. Nast would feel an intense loneliness, and certainly his sister's presence could not console him. Miss Stilton felt that gossip must be risked. She must see him at once, not after he had slept on his triumph and discovered that his loneliness had limits.

She stepped from her car, ostentatiously holding her dictation pad in her hand, since it was reasonable to suppose that the neighbors were watching Nast's house more narrowly than usual. Miss Nast admitted her and showed her to Dorothy's garden terrace, half lighted by a lamp in the adjacent sitting room. The July night was hot and breathless and brooding. From just beyond the terrace came the heady smell of some of Dorothy's beloved gardenias. From an iron terrace chair Nast rose and shook her hand. He was smoking a cigar, but Miss Stilton saw at a glance that it was not cigars he needed. Miss Nast, seeing the dictation pad and offended by the cigar anyhow, excused herself. A moment later she returned, asked Nast if she might borrow his car for an hour or two, and left for a friend's. They were alone.

"Just a moment," said Nast, as if he had suddenly remembered something. He returned in a couple of minutes with a bottle of champagne that Dorothy had purchased against this very day and filled two glasses.

"To our new president," said Miss Stilton, raising her glass.

"Will you stay and help me?"

"I've more or less promised to go to A. & M." Her voice nicely mingled regret and doubt.

"I need you more than Pomton does. Stay with me. Say you'll stay."

"Give me a little time to think," she begged.

"Pomton is no longer young. His administration at A. & M. can't last long. I need your judgment and your knowledge of this institution."

The dark, hot night, the heavy scent of the gardenias, and the first glass of champagne connived to give his pleadings an overtone he had not intended. Suddenly, a man was pleading with a woman, and what the man wanted of her became less clear in this garden than the fact that he wanted her. All this became unbearably evident to Miss Stilton, and half evident even to Nast. How enlighten him further?

"I will stay because you ask me to," she said suddenly, in a voice that was almost inaudible.

Then, either because of the suffocating heat, or the overpowering garden scents, or the stress of emotion, or even because Nast's knowledge of women did not merit a less familiar device, Miss Stilton fainted. Fortunately, the collapse came slowly enough for Nast to seize her in his arms before she fell to the stone terrace. She came around very slowly.

"Where am I?" she murmured.

"It's all right." But now his voice showed that he too was succumbing to the curious combination of sights and sounds and smells of which this singular evening seemed to be composed. Above all, he had become *troublé,* as the French put it, by a perfume that apparently emanated from just behind Miss Stilton's rather pretty ears. This is what the manufacturer of the perfume, and Miss Stilton in collaboration, had intended should happen. Her body proved much more yielding in his arms than the newly elected President was prepared for. As a matter of fact, Nast's angular nature had been, during the past few days, increasingly drawn to the angularity of Miss Stilton. He was in a sharp revulsion against curved flesh and slurred speech, and Miss Stilton's crispness and precision were what had drawn him. Yet, suddenly, on this magical night, she too turned out to be all curves.

Then the scales fell from Nast's eyes; and Miss Stilton, though she had hardly regained full consciousness, could see them clatter to the terrace and lie there, discarded, she hoped, forever. Nast now became surgingly aware that he held a woman in his arms for the first time in a considerable number of weeks—he who had been so accustomed to holding a very beautiful one in his arms whenever his boyish passion tore him momentarily, like Napoleon, from his desk. Moreover, he had become aware that this woman wanted to be in his arms far more than the other woman had. And before he had thought through the problem in any methodical fashion, he found himself passionately kissing her face, her throat, her parted lips. It was then, naturally, that the doorbell rang.

He leaped to the nearest electric switch and turned on a ceiling lamp, which poured a hot and blinding flood of light on the pastoral scene. He cursed softly. Then he went to the front door, flashing on lamps as he moved back toward his public life. It was Schneider.

Schneider wrung Nast's hand ostentatiously.

"Congratulations, my dear fellow," he said. "Just stopped by to exchange a word. I shan't be long." And he pushed past Nast toward the terrace, where Dorothy had kissed him good-by so few weeks before.

"Ah!" he cried. "Good evening, Miss Stilton. I'll wager our new President has been trying to corrupt you into staying on. Poor Pomton! He'd never think of champagne. A rather unimaginative administrator, I fear. But now things are brightening up. I'm thoroughly sorry I won't be here next session."

Miss Stilton was sitting, prim and erect, when the two men appeared on the terrace, her pad open and her pencil poised. She acknowledged Schneider's noisy greetings in her usual cool tone of voice. She had worked fast while Nast had stumbled to the front door, and her hair was in perfect order. Her cheeks were certainly flushed, and her eyes looked larger than usual, though that could have been the champagne. But poor Nast, partly because he was less dexterous than she and partly because he was trying to find the front door while she composed herself for the newcomer, was in less good shape. His hair was rumpled, his cheeks were strangely flushed, and to her horror she saw near his mouth a telltale smudge of lipstick. Schneider saw it too, and the sight rendered his voice heartier than ever.

Schneider accepted a glass of champagne, toasted the Nast administration, asked Nast if he could see him about an important personal matter next morning, preferably here at Nast's home, and excused himself on the grounds that if he delayed, his wife would think he was out hunting down pretty girls like Miss Stilton. Miss Stilton announced that, unless Nast had further dictation for her, she too must go. At the front door, they all three met Miss Nast, returning from her visit, a fact that obviously interested and pleased Schneider. Schneider urged Miss Nast to watch her brother more carefully and to keep him from working overtime. Then he was off.

In the confusion Miss Stilton had managed to wipe the lipstick off Nast's face before his sister could see it. Miss Nast urged her to stay; Miss Stilton explained that she really must go; and Nast insisted that in that case he would drive back with her to her apartment, and walk home. In fact, he added to Miss Nast, he would probably walk a bit after that before returning home. It was too hot to sleep. And he begged his sister not to wait up for him.

Miss Nast saw them out, tidied up, and reflected on what a nice girl Miss Stilton was. Miss Nast had always feared and hated Dorothy. She wished now that Nast had married a girl like Miss Stilton.

Schneider strolled meditatively on the campus before going to his house. Things were coming his way. It was both a pleasant and useful thing to know that Miss Stilton had been alone with Nast in Nast's house, sitting on Dorothy's terrace among the potted gardenias, drinking champagne and kissing the President-Elect. It would facilitate tomorrow's conference. And he felt certain that by now Miss Stilton had engineered more than the mere transfer of lipstick. It was, psychologically, a setup for tomorrow.

Not only was he going to a job in New York at twenty thousand. He even had a function, as Dorothy's envoy plenipotentiary, and by any likely estimate, he should shortly prove extremely effectual. He would hold all the cards. With a sudden pang, he remembered the old saying, "Lucky at cards, unlucky in love." He had always hitherto written it off as the effort of somebody who had just lost heavily at cards, to console himself. But now it seemed to fit him, Schneider, almost too cozily for comfort. Still, having lost Dorothy through his folly, he would feel a little less humiliated if he could at least play efficient knight errant and rescue her from this ambitious ass who held her now in legal chains. He reflected that with this newest card, all stained with lipstick and covered with telltale hearts, he could have insisted relentlessly on an early inauguration, early enough to impress Dorothy with his power and his finesse as a negotiator. But it had already been announced for a very early date indeed. He opened his front door and tiptoed to bed. Henrietta never even awoke. It was one o'clock.

Around the same hour Milton lay tossing in his bed. Only when he had received trustworthy news that the announcement of Nast's election had been released to the press had Milton conceded and punctiliously telephoned Nast his congratulations. It had been, he felt, a hot race. And, in a sense, he had never lost; the power of money had won. Still, he was too disappointed to sleep. Beside him lay his dumpy little wife. She had tried to share his manly grief; but, secretly, she had felt relieved that she would not have to face the social hazards of the Parsonage and the jealousy of the other faculty wives. Now, exhausted by wifely sympathy, she slept. Her sad, yellow face wore a faint smile. For she was dreaming of Dr. Manley, that connoisseur of Paris styles. She was listening to him praise a new hat she had concocted—this one, also, as brown as Roaring Creek in flood.

But no Paris touch softened her consort's ghastly disappointment. Although he was quite literally the only member of the faculty who had ever supposed he had a chance, yet this was one statistic which he, distinguished statistician that he was, had never guessed. Certainly, of the many influential colleagues he had earnestly canvassed, not one had urged him to withdraw from the race. Despite the wretched capitulation of the commitee of five, he told himself, the academicians had been with him at heart. It was the anti-academicians, the trustees, the money power, that had cut him down. And Nast, people said, had cultivated the trustees for years.

As the sleepless night wore on, his pain and humiliation gave way to anger. And the anger steadily mounted. It was not just Nast that had won. It was all the Nasts of this world who had won.

It was evil itself that had won. It was the anti-intellectualism that, in an America increasingly money-mad, always won. There was little he could do against that rising tide of anti-intellectualism. But there was something he could and would do, if it were not for the police. He would go now to Nast's house, enter it somehow, and kill Nast. He had never wanted to kill before. And he would never, he reflected, kill from personal spite. But he would gladly kill for the sake of academic freedom, for the sake of freeing himself and his fellow intellectuals from the rigged elections of the money power. But, frustrated by his knowledge that the police were on Nast's side and finally exhausted by his own anger, Milton fell asleep. He postponed his revenge—*some* revenge, some blinding and cataclysmic stroke for the honor of man—and twitched and quivered toward the crucial dawn.

Around the same witching hour, Nast, too, lay tossing on his bed. It was not because of the waves of hatred that came pouring through his window from the direction of Milton's bedroom, a good half-mile away. But much had happened to him since Schneider had insisted on seeing him the next day on an urgent, personal matter. In his drive to acquire the presidency of the University, he had won the presidency and had possibly lost an extremely beautiful wife. Had some other man acquired her? And if so, who was this other man? In Nast's precipitate drive to acquire, at Pomton's expense, the ablest secretary he had ever met, he had acquired a mistress as well. He began to feel that perhaps acquisition was a more complex phenomenon than the science of economics made it out to be.

~XXIII~

Next morning, Nast awoke exhausted and remembered that he faced two appointments here at his house. When Milton had telephoned his congratulations, Nast had asked him cordially if he could drop by after breakfast for a chat. For Nast had a plan. Milton, who was crushed but not yet angry, gladly promised to come. Then, last night, he had promised to receive Schneider "on an important personal matter." He only hoped that Schneider was resigning.

Milton arrived, his anger somewhat spent through exhaustion, and Nast greeted him cordially as "a good loser."

"Look," said Nast with flattering bluntness. "I face a tough job and I need your help. Frankly, I never approved of your candidacy. You're a scholar. A damned valuable scholar. You've got no business wasting your time on administrative work."

Milton beamed his pleasure. "You may be right," he said.

"All the same," said Nast, "I've got to requisition a little of your time, much as I hesitate to ask you to do administrative work."

"I would feel forced to accept, if you drafted me."

"Good," said Nast. "You're drafted. Well, I'm going to need a little expert statistical work from time to time. Not the sort of thing I.B.M. machines turn out. But when I want to take a stand with the trustees or the faculty or the alumni, I want that stand supported statistically. Get the idea?"

"If I can make statistics support it, I certainly will," said Milton.

"Oh," said Nast, "I shan't take any stand that an expert statistician can't support. Now, of course, there'll have to be some adjustment of your salary. Say, an additional five hundred a year."

"That's very thoughtful of you," said Milton.

"And some sort of title, too. What about 'Administrative Assistant to the President, in Charge of Statistics'?"

"As you like," said Milton, although he could not help contrasting the title, in his mind, with "Vice-President in Charge of Statistics." But the five hundred would help.

"Well," said Nast, "I'm grateful to you for accepting." He rose and shook hands. Milton took his cue. Nast escorted him to the door and stood watching Milton lumber down the street.

"He's not a bad egg," Nast murmured aloud, with a new presidential tolerance. "And he can even think in a sort of offbeat fashion. He may actually be useful. In any case he's neutralized."

On his way home Milton reflected that his campaign for the presidency had not been wholly in vain. The new President needed him. And, as Administrative Assistant, he would still be free to do the most important work of all: teaching and scholarly research. There would be no question of raising money in order to raise faculty salaries. The President would do that. He was already doing it. Hadn't Milton's own salary just been adjusted? A new era was dawning: an era of adjustment. And he, Milton, would play a vital role in ushering this era in. A friend passed. Milton bowed, with a new dignity, and gave the fellow a friendly smile.

Scarcely an hour later Nast's doorbell rang. It was Schneider. "Could we sit on the terrace?" asked Schneider. "It's such a marvelous day." It seemed right somehow that the ceremony of liberation should take place on this terrace that she had loved. Nast said nothing but led the way to the terrace. Then he lit a cigar. Schneider made a leisurely job of lighting his pipe.

"What is the personal matter?" Nast's voice was harsh and abrupt. "Did Camp offer you a job?"

"Yes," said Schneider, "but I turned it down."

"Why didn't you take it?"

Nast's voice was bellicose again. Schneider had been useful in connection with the committee of five. But how useful? The chances had always been overwhelming that the trustees would not listen to the committee of five; and Nast had now learned that the Committee on Selection had already made up its mind before they even deigned to receive the faculty representatives. So he owed the fellow nothing whatever. And if he had owed him something, he would by now have had no further need for him. He was a fraud, and Nast wanted to get rid of him. He thought he had made that clear enough.

"But you won't have me to bother with," Schneider was saying. "I've taken another job."

"Then what's the personal matter?" Nast was so much relieved that his voice was almost gracious.

"It concerns you, not me," said Schneider. "It concerns your marriage."

The impudent scoundrel, thought Nast. How dare he meddle with my private affairs?

"Your wife wants a divorce, Nast. She is ready to sue for one. She wants you not to contest it."

Nast's face did extraordinary things. It paled; then flushed; then grew hard and tense.

"And precisely what makes you think she wants a divorce?"

"She told me she did and asked me to arrange it with you. I have papers for you to sign."

"Well, by God," said Nast, "I shall most certainly not sign them."

"By God, Nast, I feel sure you will."

"And what are her grounds, may I ask? What have I done?"

"Oh," said Schneider, "she doesn't know about last night. At least not yet. From her point of view you haven't done anything. In fact, that's the problem. Another man has done things—to make her want to marry him."

Again Nast's face played tricks. The mention of last night made him thoroughly uncomfortable. He was deeply convinced that Schneider was a disreputable, sly fellow. He had caught Thelma and himself here on the terrace last night; and for all Nast knew, by some Oriental magic he had been under Thelma's bed by the time she and Nast had reached her apartment. Nast did not put it beneath him, or above him, according as one considered his motives or his skill. But the mention of another man aroused the competitive male in him.

"Who is the cur?" he asked.

"For our present purposes it doesn't matter," said Schneider. "Our first problem is to get the papers signed."

"Not a chance."

"I have the papers in question in my briefcase. But now I come to think of it, I have another paper at home. It's a letter from Dorothy to Pomton explaining how Denby happened to shift his grant from social science in general to economics in particular. I hope I shan't have to use that letter."

Nast flushed.

"She's lying," he said.

"Oh, no, she's not. I've discussed it with Denby. I forgot to tell you that my new job is running the Division of General Education for the Winthrop Foundation."

There was a painful pause. Then Nast struck back.

"I don't give a damn what Dorothy says or how much she gets Denby to agree to it. Pomton will believe me before he believes both of them combined. And from the trustees' point of view it's too late now. The public knows they elected me and they'd lose too much face if they backed down. Before October I'll be inaugurated. She'll have to think of another one."

"She has," said Schneider. "She's thinking very fast these days. She says if you don't sign, she'll sue anyhow. Immediately. She says she may not win her freedom, but neither will you be inaugurated. She believes the trustees will back down when she's through with you. I think she's right.

"She has generously consented to do nothing until after the inauguration, provided you sign these papers now. If you don't, she files —immediately. You'll be astonished, Nast, how quickly that gang on the board will find a way out. They'll never inaugurate you and you know it. On the other hand, if you play ball, she'll do everything in her power to square you with the board."

This time there was a very long silence, while Nast measured the dimensions of the trap he was in. Suddenly, he lashed out, "The hell with the presidency. Let her file. I won't sign a damned thing."

"Well, Nast, it means the end, not merely of the presidency, but of your career. If you want to play the retired scholar who had a wife but couldn't keep her, don't let me stop you. But her lawyer was handpicked because he knows how to make things messy. And she's desperate: she doesn't care. She's leaving the country in any case; preferably with her second husband; if necessary, with her lover. She's wild about this gent."

Suddenly, Nast's eyes narrowed.

"Are you by any chance the gent in question?"

"No. I wish I were."

It was Schneider's turn to blush slightly, not because he had made passes, but because she had eluded them. Here he was, perpetrating another hoax, like the government research. But he did not retract. It was half true; and it comforted him to think that, no matter how stupid he had been to permit her to elude him, they had shared an hour of love. No inadequacy of his could erase either the night in the cabin or the last kiss here on the terrace. To use Denby's terms, he may have muffed the functions of a lover, but he had received compensation. Now he had another function: he was her plenipotentiary; and he was convinced that he was doing well.

"If you tell me who he is, I'll consider signing," said Nast.

"You'll sign anyhow," said Schneider. "Take your time."

In the end he signed. Schneider congratulated him on his good judgment, swept the papers into his briefcase, and said, "It isn't as if you need be lonely, Nast. When Dorothy gets her freedom, you get yours. And there's another woman waiting for you."

Nast glowered at him. Schneider grinned happily, said good-by, and started for Western Union. Discreetly, he wired Freddie Landon:

MISSION COMPLETED STOP SENDING SIGNED PAPERS BY AIR MAIL TODAY STOP TELL D. I DID NOT FAIL HER THIS TIME STOP PLEASE ACCEPT MY JEALOUS CONGRATULATIONS STOP AFTER SEPTEMBER FIRST ADDRESS ME CARE WINTHROP FOUNDATION STOP NO FURTHER FUNCTION HERE STOP GOD BLESS YOU BOTH SCHNEIDER

Then he went to the post office. The lady was saved. He hoped he had not been pimping.

~XXIV~

PRESIDENTIAL INAUGURATIONS, like Commencement exercises, are similar to royal coronations: everything depends on the sensitive use of symbols and, to a certain extent, on the state of the weather. Today God and man had collaborated to render the ritual perfect. The weather, which could in late September have played almost any trick, was nothing short of superb—clear, golden, and by a miracle slightly crisp. The campus and indeed the little town were packed. There were, of course, the delegates from sister universities; and they had come in scores, equipped with their black gowns, their mortarboards, and their brilliantly varied hoods. But the parents of many of the students and the tradespeople of the town had converged on the campus too. Since the academic session had begun two weeks before, the entire student body was destined to play an active role. There was not only the exhilaration of a holiday; there was also the sense of impending tribal ritual. What was about to happen would be somehow of high significance.

The Republic of Learning was about to be glorified, as usual by complex monarchical rites.

The order of business and the line of march of the academic procession had been meticulously planned by the President's office—that is, by Miss Stilton. Miss Stilton, incidentally, although she remained, as always, efficiency itself, shone with a kind of radiance to a point where many of the faculty grudgingly admitted that she had become mysteriously easy to look at. All classes had, of course, been suspended, and the entire student body had been requisitioned to lead the procession in the usual column of twos, taking the place reserved to graduates on Commencement Day. Then, of course, came the assistant professors (some of whom had for the first time purchased their own academic regalia), arranged in strict order of seniority in service. Then the associate professors, who still lived on a pre-P'tite salary scale and therefore mostly wore rented costumes. Then came the full professors, bowed with learning and the financial worries of growing families. Next came the deans. Then, even more honored than these, at least for a day, came the delegates from other institutions, leading off with the youngest institution to be represented, whose ambassador looked sheepish with modernity, and ending with the much-pointed-at delegate from Hoary Harvard itself. The claims of the institutions represented concerning the dates of their founding had been Miss Stilton's chief headache for weeks, and at least two institutions had withdrawn their acceptances in high dudgeon when they found their delegates being pushed dangerously forward in the procession and dangerously far from Harvard. Following Harvard itself came the board of trustees, in gowns supplied by the business office free of charge. Good old Joe Stanforth's face was missing for the first time in many a year: he had loved marching at fall convocation, and today the inauguration had absorbed fall convocation without absorbing Joe. Last of the trustees was, of course, the Chairman. Then, cynosures of every eye, marched Pomton on the left and his young successor to his right, looking very tall, very young, and really imposing.

The Volunteer Municipal Band took its place even before the students, the bandmaster whirled his baton, and the brasses crashed into "Hail the Conquering Hero Comes." The faculty wives and faculty children had been successfully persuaded to seat themselves in the stadium in advance, instead of forming flying columns on the flanks of the advancing procession. Pomton secretly regretted the familiar shrieks of the little children as they recognized their fathers in their strange costumes, and the anxious faces of wives who wondered if their consorts would catch their trailing garments on the folding wooden chairs as they passed through them to find their proper seats. In the old days, academic processions had always been reasonably ostentatious but they had also exhibited a sweet disorder, like the disheveled hair of a professor buried in thought. Today there was an oppressive quality of precision and order, at least in Pomton's view; and he wondered if it originated in Miss Stilton's mind. He had always known how to use Miss Stilton without being used by her; would this young man on his right fall into her power?

Pomton was also worried by Dorothy Nast's absence. Miss Stilton had assured him blandly that it was common knowledge that Mrs. Nast's mother, whose illness had so long detained Mrs. Nast in Georgia, had sunk into what looked like a final coma on the eve of her daughter's proposed departure for this ceremony, and Mrs. Nast had been told by the doctor that her mother could not hope to outlive the day. But Pomton was unconvinced. He had assumed, when Nast was elected, that he and Miss Stilton would leave almost immediately for A. & M. His predecessor's secretary at A. & M. had offered to resign. And then Miss Stilton had unexpectedly declined to leave. Nast had then begged for two weeks in which to go to Georgia and be at his wife's side during this ordeal. And Pomton had not been released for A. & M. until mid-August.

The truth was that by the end of July Nast was at his rope's end and felt he faced a breakdown if he could not get two weeks in Colorado to fish and recover his forces. Blow after blow had fallen on him. He had invited Denby to his inauguration, and

Denby had written him that circumstances he could not now discuss would prevent his coming, but that he was sending Henry Schneider, who was joining his staff in a few days. Schneider had dropped by Nast's home one evening, just as Nast was preparing to dictate to Thelma on the terrace, to bid Nast one more last good-by. Thelma had gone to fetch Schneider a drink, into which she would have gladly thrown a teaspoonful of arsenic; and while Thelma was gone, Schneider had informed Nast that Dorothy's divorce would be announced two days after inauguration day. She was already at Reno, was well, and sent Nast her congratulations. Schneider had cheerfully promised to represent the Winthrop Foundation at the inauguration. Nast had assured him that he would quite understand his not dragging himself all the way back from New York, but Schneider had replied that he would not miss the inauguration for anything. It was then that Nast felt he must get away for a fortnight or he could not face the coming session.

He had returned, looking bronzed and fit, but Pomton thought he still seemed harried. Now, as Pomton and his young successor paced silently at the tail of the long procession, he remained thoroughly puzzled. For clearly Nast was alarmingly nervous.

The fact is, Nast felt trapped. The inauguration address that he and Miss Stilton had prepared was, he thought, a good address. But to pronounce it two days before the news of his divorce reached the press, and three days before the front-page stories reached the breakfast tables of the faculty and even the board, was to suffer a kind of torture that not even university presidents had ever been asked to endure. Yet this was precisely what was slated to happen.

The first draft of the speech Miss Stilton had offered him had convinced him that Thelma must be told frankly of the impending headlines if she was to help him find the correct rhetorical tone for the occasion. Thelma had long suspected and hoped that his marriage was on the rocks; but when her hopes and suspicions were finally confirmed, even poor Nast, whose knowledge of women had advanced only a little beyond the embryonic stage, saw with horror the orange blossoms in her eyes. Orange blossoms and a slight glitter, a glitter that was new to Nast but old hat to Joe Stanforth. In her eyes he read his fate. So far as public interpretation was concerned, he would have asked his utterly fascinating wife to divorce him in order to marry his secretarial paramour, or his paramourial secretary, according to the individual newspaper reader's preference. That his injured wife should meanwhile accept the consolation of another man's love would seem but too natural. Thelma had accepted the news of the divorce with secret exultation and outward sympathy; had agreed that it posed a delicate problem in inaugural rhetoric; and then had efficiently produced in record time an entirely new draft of his address, in which a dazzling self-confidence and implied promises of achievements to come were replaced by a young man's moving plea for indulgence for his defects and for the support of his colleagues when the going got rough. Whatever the defects of the second draft, such as the most obvious—that it was utterly out of character and would stun the audience who heard it—it had the great merit of not exhibiting pride three days before a colossal fall. Now, on inauguration day, it was this second and humbler version, typed in triple space, which Nast clutched in his shaking hand and was to have the honor of reading before his eager listeners.

The well-nigh endless procession of black-gowned figures moved slowly into the arena of the stadium and toward their appointed seats, their multicolored hoods flashing in the afternoon sun. Nast gazed with burning eyes toward the small section of the concrete tiers, marked off with ribbons in the University colors, reserved for those guests of honor not taking part in the academic procession. Sure enough, there in the middle of the front row he could see the representative of the Winthrop Foundation sitting where Dorothy might have sat had she not left Nast for an unknown rival, and certainly where Denby would have sat if circumstances he could not yet disclose had not prevented him from attending. Nast felt a surge of conviction that this Mephistopheles in professorial, or perhaps foundational, form was the only person in that vast multitude who could measure his present agony. He was convinced, as he stared at Schneider, that Schneider understood that agony in more of its implications than even Thelma could; than even he, the victim, could. For one thing, Schneider almost certainly knew the man whose wife Dorothy would shortly become— presumably Landon.

If Nast was thinking about Schneider, Schneider was certainly thinking about him. None of the marionettes whose words and actions Schneider had so recently learned to manipulate fascinated him so much as this tallest and strongest and stupidest marionette of them all. He wondered what Nast's other manipulator, so likely to become Mrs. Nast, had prepared in the way of a speech on such a ticklish occasion. He rather envied her the task of drafting it: it presented genuine and fascinating problems. He hoped he would see more of her before he left for New York tomorrow: she was clearly, as so many persons had observed, a schemer; but then, Schneider believed he had recently learned to scheme a bit himself. He would gladly have pitted his skill against hers. Perhaps he would see her at the inaugural ball. Less than twenty yards from where Schneider sat he saw her now, sitting and watching her victim approach the sacrificial platform.

"Poor swine," he said out loud, in a low voice, as the crowd rose and applauded. His sympathy was genuine. "Poor swine. To think of losing a Circassian slave and finding this creature wrapped around you. The man is a Laocoön. And what we are witnessing here is a tragedy of many dimensions."

Nast and Pomton had reached their seats. Behind them, the trustees obediently took their seats also. So did the distinguished delegates from other institutions of higher learning, the long rows of professors, the students, and the several thousand visitors. Schneider could not help feeling moved by the pageant before him, and its carefully planned detail made him all the more eager to see Miss Stilton again that evening. The long lines of black gowns down there in front and the little gleams of color from the now largely hidden hoods brought crowded memories back to him. For how many hours, counting through all the years of his service here, had Schneider too sat on one of those dangerous folding chairs, his backside aching with fatigue and boredom while some gentleman of the cloth windily exhibited to his bored audience his ancient and intimate relations with the Godhead, or while Old Pomton, God bless him, slowly and solemnly intoned the total amount of the donations the University had received for the past year, pronouncing the word "thousand" with unction, the word "hundred" with respect, and adding with some embarrassment a phrase like "and seventy-three cents." And how recently Pomton had been able to preface all these figures with the ringing phrase "six million," pronounced with a reverence that echoed the minister's invocation. If this ceremony had been frankly modeled on the Holy Eucharist, reflected Schneider, at that very moment a bell would have been rung. For at that moment People's Capitalism would have been recognized as incarnate in this spacious football field, with the score of the last game still posted high; in the dingy brick buildings, trailing their storied ivy like clouds of glory; and, above all, in the caps and gowns and hoods of the choristers. Schneider remembered the gasp of real awe which greeted the announcement of gifts—the announcement, so to speak, of the means of grace—and rose like incense from the academic community.

Undoubtedly this panoplied parody really was a sort of mass, a black mass, and a minor blasphemy against the truth and man's tragic and perpetual search for it. But at the moment Schneider felt no special shame for his guild. This band of gowned scholars that had stretched, not merely from Snodgrass Hall to the stadium entrance, but clear across the centuries too—had they blasphemed more than the others? Remembering the City of Man, could New York, so largely composed of glass houses, both metaphorically and literally, afford to throw a stone at Academe? Were the hypocrisies that Nast was doubtless about to utter any more hateful than the hypocrisies belched forth daily by the National Association of Manufacturers or the sanctimonious claims of the Cominform? Undoubtedly, the treason of the eggheads—not to their government, which they idolatrized, but to the truth, which exacts so much more loyalty than even the most hysterical government dares demand—undoubtedly this treason of the eggheads was more painful to an egghead like himself than the treason of the fatheads or the boneheads or the blockheads could ever be. Alas, betrayal, thought Schneider, was far more general than politicians would ever know.

His reverie was interrupted by Pomton's really graceful introduction of the new president. It seemed clear, at least to Schneider, that the old man had somehow sensed the futility of his years of office here; had sensed that something, the essential something, had been missing all along; that Weed was justified in taking refuge in drink; and that maybe under Nast's guidance some miracle might yet occur. But it was clear also that it was not Pomton's conscious intention to say these things. What presumably got through to the audience was gracefully dull and happily empty and worthy of the thunderous applause it earned.

Then Nast spoke. Out of his empty home, his empty heart, and his essentially empty head, what words would come? Would the thought of the third day, and the board's resentment, and the faculty's covert sniggers bring him some sort of tortured wisdom? And if so, had his paramour found the words to express it? Nast read on. And, inkling by inkling, Schneider glimpsed the miracle: Nast was being humble! It was too easy to say that Miss Stilton had merely managed to make him appear humble. Had her words found no echo in the caverns of his own emptiness, he could not have read them as he was now reading them. The audience was stunned; then, it was visibly moved. But this was eloquence, thought Schneider in open-mouthed amazement. But what a thing is the wingèd word. How it catches intellectual light. The Republic of Letters was being spoken for. A fire had been lighted on an altar. It was unbelievable.

They are right to dress up in medieval garments like this, said Schneider to himself. For the moment, I wish I were among them, sweating it out on my hard, wooden chair. They are right to march

in processions; their wives are right to look at them with temporarily respectful eyes; their children are right to shriek and dance
beside their ranks, as David danced before the ark. By dint of saying the right words, hypocritically; and wearing the right clothes,
hypocritically; and even by reading a few of the right books, and
spoiling them for their students with their pedantic historicism and
their lust for trivia—by dint of doing these things, they have blindly
placed an electrode near an electrode they have never seen, and only
for this moment, but quite certainly, a spark has flashed between
them.

Nast finished, and sat down. There was a moment of really
eloquent silence. Then the thunderous and banal applause destroyed
the vision and gave the signal that the words the crowd had heard
had now been harmlessly classified as a most stimulating speech, and
so appropriate, and could now be safely forgotten. A second minister, invited to give the benediction, was vying with his predecessor
as one of God's oldest friends. The inattentive crowd stood, with
bared heads, trying to remember where it had parked its cars.

The new president and the old slowly left the platform; the trustees fell in behind; the delegates of the sister institutions followed
them; then the full professors, the associate professors, the newly
rich assistant professors, followed by the whole student body.
The spell was broken. The faculty, a little ashamed of having
seen a vision and heard a voice, chatted with each other in
line; and some of them, to Miss Stilton's fury, even lighted
cigarettes and smoked while marching. The students, still obediently
marching, nevertheless changed their gait and swung their hips
more, while their chatter grew louder and louder. The crowd in
the stadium exchanged greetings and told each other shrilly that the
ceremony had been most impressive and that they had particularly
liked the numerous delegates from other universities. Now they prepared to drive home; and the distinguished guests, of whom
Schneider made one, went off to dine and dress for the inaugural
ball.

The ball was even more poisonous, Schneider thought, than such things have to be. The University community had managed to grasp, if only for a few moments, what they were doing when they had assembled at the stadium. The professional training the faculty had received, although much of it was irrelevant and some of it really damaging, furnished nevertheless some means for understanding the words and acts that had been spoken and performed. But if they had lacked the social grace to carry off a cocktail party, they proved even more helpless when faced with the social ritual known as a ball. Had Dorothy been present in the receiving line, beside the man with whom she would publicly break in two days now, she might have reassured them; she could have helped them to relax, to play. But Nast's secretarial mistress possessed neither the authority nor the ability to play gracious hostess at this purely social event. She was, in fact, discreetly absent. The inaugural ball, therefore, served chiefly to make the whole great day messier and to obscure further the brief significance that Miss Stilton, speaking through Nast's mouth, had unexpectedly and astonishingly set before them that afternoon.

President Nast now saw Schneider descending on him, wearing that irritating smile of his. By unhappy coincidence, not another guest stood within a good three yards of them.

He is coming to torture me some more, thought Nast.

Schneider held out his hand, and Nast grudgingly took it.

"Your address moved me deeply," said Schneider simply.

"Thelma wrote it," said Nast tartly. He was startled by his own reply. Why should he admit to his tormentor that his secretary had written the speech for his own Big Day? Why should he use her first name in front of Schneider?

"So I supposed," said Schneider in a friendly tone. "But it was you who chose your ghost writer, and it was you who read it—well."

"I don't think I quite understand the speech," said Nast coldly.

"I don't think any of us did," said Schneider. "I don't think Miss Stilton did. But it was written—or, maybe, cribbed. In any case, it was said. And for a moment I think all of us knew what it meant."

"I don't know what you mean," said Nast, still cold.

"No," said Schneider, without rancor, "I imagine not." And he drifted off.

He left next morning by the first plane for New York. But he got up an hour early, in order to walk about the campus in the cool of the morning. He loved the elms. He would always love the elms.

ABOUT THE AUTHOR

STRINGFELLOW BARR *was born in 1897, in Suffolk, Virginia. He claims to be the only living Virginian not descended from Pocahontas, although he speaks with a broad "a" that makes British speech sound Middle West.*

Mr. Barr completed his undergraduate education at the University of Virginia. There he took his B.A. in 1916, his M.A. in 1917, won a Rhodes scholarship from Virginia, and enlisted in the U.S. Army.

After World War I he studied modern history at Balliol College, Oxford, as a result of which he is a B.A. and M.A. (Oxon).

In 1924, Mr. Barr became Assistant Professor of History at the University of Virginia, Associate Professor in 1927, and Professor in 1930. Also in 1930 he accepted the editorship of The Virginia Quarterly Review.

In 1936, President Robert M. Hutchins of the University of Chicago set up a "Committee on the Liberal Arts" to devise reforms for undergraduate education, and persuaded Mr. Barr to accept a visiting professorship and serve on the committee. The next year Mr. Barr was elected president of St. John's College in Annapolis with a mandate from the Board of St. John's to set up a four-year, all-required curriculum that attracted nation-wide praise and blame as "the St. John's Program." It was based on the study of some hundred great books from Homer to living authors, but also required of every student four years of mathematics and four years of laboratory science. In addition to abolishing the elective system at St. John's, Mr. Barr abolished intercollegiate competition in athletics, stimulated intramural sports, and helped the local chapters of national fraternities to commit suicide. "Let's go out and walk on the grass," said one St. Johnnie of those halcyon days, "before they take it away." The grass is still at St. John's and so is the St. John's Program.

In 1948, Mr. Barr raised $1,000,000 and established the Foundation for World Government, which undertook to foster research on the problems involved in establishing a common government for mankind. Mr. Barr has served as president of this foundation since its establishment.

He is now Professor of Humanities at Newark College, Rutgers University. Purely Academic *is his seventh book and his first novel.*